The Mistake I Made

Paula Daly

BANTAM PRESS

LONDON · TORONTO · SYDNEY · AUCKLAND · JOHANNESBURG

TRANSWORLD PUBLISHERS
61–63 Uxbridge Road, London W5 5SA
www.transworldbooks.co.uk

Transworld is part of the Penguin Random House group of companies
whose addresses can be found at global.penguinrandomhouse.com

First published in Great Britain in 2015 by Bantam Press
an imprint of Transworld Publishers

A CIP catalogue record for this book
is available from the British Library.

ISBN 9780593074497 (cased)
9780593074503 (tpb)

Typeset in 11.75/15pt Minion by Falcon Oast Graphic Art Ltd.
Printed and bound by Clays Ltd, Bungay, Suffolk.

Penguin Random House is committed to a sustainable
future for our business, our readers and our planet. This book
is made from Forest Stewardship Council® certified paper.

1 3 5 7 9 10 8 6 4 2

THE MISTAKE I MADE

www.**transworldbooks**.co.uk

For Grace

July

1

BODIES WERE MY business. Living, not dead. And on a sweltering afternoon in early July the body lying face down in front of me was an ordinary specimen. He was my twelfth patient of the day, and my back was aching, my sunny disposition just about beginning to falter.

'How is it feeling?' he asked as I sank my thumbs into tough fascia running alongside his spine.

'Pretty good,' I replied. 'I've got rid of the scar tissue around L4 – the troublesome joint. You should notice a difference as soon as you stand up.'

He was a quarry worker. Often my toughest customers. They spoke very little, so I enjoyed the brief respite from the inter-action that most demanded, but physically, quarry workers were hard on my hands. They have a dense bulk to their musculature, a resistance to the tissues, which requires the full weight of my upper body, directed down through my overused thumbs.

My thumbs were my instruments. Essential for every facet of my work. They were my diagnostic tools, used to detect and assess the nuances in tissue structure; my means of offering relief to a person in pain.

I had contemplated having them insured. Like Betty Grable's legs. But I never quite did get around to it.

'When you've finished with my back,' he said, 'if you've got time, would you mind having a quick look at my shoulder?'

He lifted his head, smiling regretfully, as though he really did hate to be a nuisance.

'Not at all,' I said brightly, masking a sigh.

I used to be a self-employed physiotherapist, and I did my utmost to take care of the needs of every single patient. If I didn't get results, I didn't get paid. So I worked hard to build up a busy practice.

That thing we strive for? The work–life balance? For a while I had it.

Not any more.

When there was no money left, I found myself here. Working fifty hours a week for a chain of clinics, cooped up in an airless cubicle with a production line of patients. The fruits of my labours go straight into someone else's pocket.

I also found myself at the mercy of a practice manager named Wayne.

Wayne meant well, but his desire to get the job done correctly sometimes made him overbearing. And every so often he could also become flirtatious – though I should say that it was never to the point of harassment. But you had to be firm with him, or else his behaviour would escalate and he would begin suggesting dates. I think he was possibly a little lonely.

With the quarry worker now perched on the edge of the plinth, I knelt behind him and asked him to raise the affected arm out to his side. When he reached ninety degrees he sucked in his breath with the pain and jerked the shoulder involuntarily.

'Supraspinatus,' I told him.

'Is that bad?'

'Can be tricky. I can't treat it properly today, though, there's not enough time. But I'll pop in an acupuncture needle and see if I can give you at least some relief.'

I'd studied acupuncture as a postgraduate course and while I twisted the needle back and forth, back and forth, I could hear

Wayne outside in the reception area, cajoling a patient, trying to persuade her to make an appointment with one of the other clinicians.

'I want Roz Toovey,' she was saying to him.

'Roz is fully booked until the middle of next week. How about Gary Muir?' he pressed. 'Gary has one available slot left today. He could see you in ten minutes.'

No answer.

'Okay, what about Magdalena?' Wayne suggested.

This was the general order of things. First, Wayne tried to palm people off with Gary, who I was pretty sure didn't know his arse from his elbow, and, as far as I could tell, was accepted on to the degree course simply because there was a nationwide shortage of male physiotherapists at the time. Before his training, Gary had been a second-division footballer.

'Magdalena?' the patient asked. 'That the German woman?'

'Austrian,' said Wayne.

'She hurt me last time. I felt like I'd been hit by a bus. No, I want Roz.'

'But,' Wayne replied, losing patience, '*as I already said*, Roz is fully booked.'

I am Roz Toovey, by the way.

'Can't you just have a word with her?' she said. 'Tell her it's Sue Mitchinson and my back's out again? I used to be one of her regulars. I'm sure she'd fit me in, if she knew it was me. And I am in *incredible pain*. Roz is the only one who can—'

'Hang on,' Wayne said, irritated, and I heard footsteps heading my way.

Three sharp raps on the wood.

'Roz, there's a Sue Mitchinson here, wondering if you can see her.'

'Excuse me a moment,' I said to the patient.

I opened the door and stuck my head out.

Looking past Wayne, I cast my eyes directly over towards Sue, who upon seeing me marched across the reception area.

Before I had the chance to speak, she began to plead her case. 'Roz, I wouldn't ask if I wasn't desperate. You know I wouldn't. If you could just see me for five minutes, I'd be ever so grateful.'

Not only was I the only physiotherapist in South Lakeland apparently capable of fixing Sue, the two of us had a history.

I had a history with a lot of patients who frequented this practice, in that they all followed me from my own clinic when it folded. Most of them had been intrinsic in building up my clientele, so the reality was, I owed them.

In the beginning, I placed one small advertisement in the local press, and the second I offered people relief from their some-times chronic pain (something other practitioners in the area weren't always able to do), word spread. I became fully booked within a month. Of course, the trouble now was that those early patients, the ones who had been so kind in recommending me, suddenly couldn't get appointments. And so they would resort to the You-know-I-wouldn't-ask-unless-I-was-desperate plea.

'Sue, I can't,' I said firmly. 'I have to collect George from after-school club, and I've been late twice already this week.'

Without pausing to think, she shot back, 'What if I was to ring my mother and get *her* to pick up George?'

I didn't know Sue's mother. Never met the woman. Neither had George.

'We're over in Hawkshead now,' I said, as tactfully as I could. 'So that's not really doable.'

Sue screwed up her face as she tried frantically to come up with a solution that might work, just as Wayne looked on with the beginnings of agitation. It could irk him something terrible that patients insisted upon seeing me and wouldn't be palmed off with the likes of Gary. It made it impossible for Wayne to balance the appointment schedule. And what we ended up with was me working myself into a stupor, whilst Gary twiddled his thumbs in reception.

Generally, Gary spent this free time chatting to Wayne, discussing the Premier League and the merits of Puma King football boots. Both of them saying 'absolutely' a lot.

'How about you give me five minutes? Five minutes or less,' said Sue, in one last-ditch attempt.

'Okay, five minutes,' I said, beaten. 'But you'll have to wait. I have another patient in straight after this one and I'm running late.'

Sue wasn't listening. She was already hurrying away to take her seat in the waiting area before anyone had the chance to change their minds.

'Did you call that insurance guy?' Wayne asked.

'What? No, sorry. Slipped my mind again.'

Wayne sighed dramatically, rolled his eyes and spoke in the way one would when reprimanding a small child. 'Get it sorted, Roz. Everyone else has had their assessments.' He lowered his voice. 'Without that assessment, you're not fully protected. The clinic *is not fully protected*, unless—'

'I'll do it. Promise. As soon as I've got a free minute. Listen, Wayne,' I said, stepping out of the treatment room and closing the door behind me so the patient couldn't hear what I was about to ask, 'I don't suppose there's any chance of a small advance on my wage, is there? It's just things are really tight right at the minute, and I'm not sure I can make it till next Friday.'

He tilted his head to one side and looked at me with mild reproach. 'I told you this before, Roz,' he said gently. 'The company cannot make exceptions. Not even for you. I wish there was something I could do but, honestly, my hands are tied.' And with that he walked away.

As I finished off with the quarry worker I could hear Wayne informing Sue in reception, his voice now loud and dictatorial, that she must pay for the treatment session up front, and *in full*, regardless of the duration.

He was in the habit of doing this when he'd found himself overruled on a matter of limited importance, and today was no different.

When I started out on my own, years ago, I remember being terribly worried about whether I could make the business work or not. At the time, I voiced these concerns to one of my first patients, Keith Hollinghurst, and he had this to say: 'Those that have to make it work, do. Those that don't, don't.'

To this day, he has always remained scornful of people who play at running a business; not grasping what it actually takes to turn a profit year in, year out. 'Nine out of ten companies fail,' he would tell me. 'Make sure yours is the one that doesn't.'

Keith Hollinghurst was old school. He ran a scrap-metal firm. He was never without a wad of rolled-up twenties in his pocket, and was not backward at coming forward. Keith continued on as my patient and, while he lay face down now, his hairy back peppered with acupuncture needles, I listened to him rant about the general incompetence of South Lakeland district council. As he relayed conversations he'd had with various jobsworths – who, naturally, he'd put in their rightful places – I would chip in, oohing and ahhing, asking the odd question to give the impression of being attentive. Then I pulled the needles out of Keith's skin and asked him to turn over, face up, so I could manipulate his lower back – by levering his leg across the front of his body. He obliged, and as I propped a pillow beneath his head, I caught sight of the large, dried urine stain on his Y-fronts.

'I've got a proposition for you when you're done with my back,' he said, blinking rapidly.

'I'm not watching you masturbate, Keith.'

He'd suggested this more than once.

He kept silent as I levered his leg over, asking him to take a breath in, then a breath out, as I pushed down hard and listened for the tell-tale click.

Patients think this is the sound of an intervertebral disc being pushed back into place. It's not. It's either the sound of two joint surfaces distracting, coming apart – the gas coming out of its solution to give rise to a popping noise – or, more commonly, and in this instance, it's the sound of adhesions tearing around the joint.

But I go along with the disc idea because it's easier.

Other things I go along with are: one, the fact that anyone who has visited an osteopath will claim to have one leg longer than the other, two, the irritating assumption that blind physio-therapists have healing powers on a par with Jesus Christ himself and three, the false claim made by all middle-aged women to have a very high pain threshold.

'Look,' said Keith, 'I know you're short of cash. I know you're on your own with that kiddie. I'll give you an extra sixty quid in your hand *right now* if you do it. You don't even have to come anywhere near me. And I'll be fast.'

'Absolutely not.'

'Remember what I said to you when you first started out?'

'Remind me,' I said.

'That you have to go the extra mile if you're to survive. The ones who just do the necessary in business fail . . . the ones who don't give the extra customer satisfaction—'

'My business has already failed. It's too late for that.'

'Yes, but if you're going to get back on your feet, Roz, you can't just do the bare minimum. People expect more, they expect more today than ever before. What with the economy the way it is. Everyone is chasing the same money. Jobs are disappearing and—'

I looked at him.

'You're not seriously justifying what you're asking me to do by debating unemployment levels, are you, Keith?'

Shiftily, he looked sideways, before biting down on his lower lip.

'Eighty quid,' he said. 'Eighty quid, cash. Right now. You don't even have to pretend to like what you see.'

'I *don't* like what I see.'

'A hundred quid.'

'No, Keith,' I said firmly. 'Now get your trousers on.'

2

As the ferry groaned away from the shore, I got out of the car.

For tourists, it's a given they exit their vehicles the moment the ferry gates close – taking photographs of each other smiling, the lake as their backdrop, pointing to the pretty mansions dotted along the shoreline. But like most locals I took the beauty for granted. I forgot to look at the slate-topped fells, the ancient forests, the glistening water.

The sheer majesty of the place can become invisible when you're faced with daily worries, daily concerns.

The villages of Bowness and Hawkshead are separated by the largest natural lake in the country: Windermere. The ferry crosses it at its midpoint, the lake's widest point in fact, and there has been a service here at its current site for more than five hundred years. It's a fifteen-mile trip to go around the lake in either direction, and in the heavy summer traffic that journey can easily take more than an hour, so the ferry is essential. Early craft were rowed over, then later a steam boat ran. The current ferry, which carries eighteen cars and runs on cables, is powered by diesel.

On good days I would feel so fortunate. My heart would swell at the splendour of the commute home to Hawkshead, and I would feel glad to be alive. Blessed to live in one of the prettiest places on earth. The kind of place people dream of retiring to after working hard all their lives.

Today, I was late.

The *no excuses* kind of late.

Tall tales of temporary traffic lights, tractors with trailers loading sheep, or flat tyres would not wash. And no matter how late I was, the ferry couldn't go any faster.

Two weeks ago, my car sat alongside an ambulance carrying a casualty, and the ferry couldn't go any faster in that instance either. It was an arresting sight, the ambulance stationary, its blue lights on, as we crawled across the lake. The passengers were casting nervous glances at one another, wondering who was inside, who it was that required urgent medical attention. We never did find out.

I wasn't going to make it to after-school club until well past the deadline and by then George would be anxious, probably a little tearful. He was nine, and though generally a tough kid when he needed to be, since his father and I split, the past couple of years had been hard on him. I could see his easy-going nature gradually seeping away and being replaced by a sort of moody apprehension, a state more akin to that of a displaced teenager. More and more, he wore a guarded expression, as though he needed to be properly prepared for the obstacles thrown our way by the constant state of flux in which we found ourselves.

I took out my mobile and pressed redial.

The sun was still high in the sky and the heat beat down hard.

The diesel fumes from both the ferry and the couple of car engines still running gave the air a heavy, polluted feel, a contamination that was incongruous with the clean, clear lake water through which we cut. I stood against the rail, cradling the phone in my hand as I listened, once more, to the recorded message from the after-school club.

Then I dialled Dylis again in an attempt to locate my ex-husband. This time, she picked up.

'Dylis? It's Roz.'

'Who?'

'Roz,' I repeated. 'Where's Winston?'

'Oh, I don't know, dear,' she said vaguely, as if she'd just woken up. She was often like this, acting as if she were mildly drugged, not quite with it. 'He's at work, I think,' she said. 'Let me find a pen and paper and I'll write the message down, because I'm terrible at—'

'Dylis,' I interrupted, 'Winston doesn't have a job. He's out of work, remember? That's why I don't get any child-support payments. Are you saying that he's working at a job *right now*?'

'Oh – no,' she stammered, 'I'm not saying that. No, that's not it. I'm not exactly sure *where* he is. Perhaps he's out helping someone, you know, for free?'

'For free,' I mirrored flatly. 'That sounds just like Winston. Look, Dylis, if he gets back in the next five minutes, can you get him to run and pick up George for me? I'm late.'

'But it's not our turn to have him,' she said, confused, and I could hear her flicking through pages; must have been the pages of her diary.

'It's not your weekend to have him,' I explained, 'but I'm very late. And it would really help if you could locate Winston and—'

'Ticket, Roz,' came a voice from behind.

With the phone lodged against my ear, I turned, withdrawing a note from my wallet and handing it over. 'I need a new book, Terry,' I whispered to the aged attendant. 'I used my last ticket this morning.'

We made the exchange, Terry being a man of few words, and I went back to explaining the situation to Dylis. She couldn't drive, so I didn't suggest she should get George herself. She lived in Outgate, a hamlet a mile and a half or so from Hawkshead. But Winston Toovey, my ex, who was obviously doing work cash-in-hand – had been since Christmas, if my suspicions were correct – was probably breezing about nearby, passing the time of day with folk, in no real hurry to be anywhere whatsoever now that he was living with his mother and had absolved himself nicely of all major responsibilities. And since he didn't always carry a mobile phone, we couldn't locate him.

I ended the call with Dylis, not for the first time filled with the urge to slam my phone against something solid. She got me like that. It was like trying to get information out of a child. Often, she'd slip up, make some comment about Winston she wasn't supposed to – to *me*, in particular – and when I pressed her about it, she'd go mute and stare at her feet.

Pressed really hard, Dylis would lift her head and look at me, woefully, as though she knew she was in deep, deep trouble. She would look at me as if to say, *Please don't tell Winston.*

I wanted to shake the woman. I wanted to scream: *How can you let your son walk out and leave me with this mountain of debt?* But I didn't, because I was aware on some deeper level that Dylis's dreamy, scatterbrained manner was the best she could do.

By the time I reached the school it was 6.28.

Twenty-eight minutes late.

I pushed open the front door and was greeted by a silent corridor, naked coat hooks, the odd PE bag dangling.

I took a breath and went into the classroom. The after-school club used the Year 1 classroom and, whilst waiting as George gathered up his belongings, I liked to look around at their first attempts at writing, at portraits of parents – which were often surprisingly true in their likeness, highlighting qualities perhaps parents wished they'd not (jug ears, shuffled teeth).

Now George was seated on the floor, his legs stretched out in front of him, his eyes cast downwards as he played on a Nintendo DS. He didn't raise his head when I entered, even though he was aware of my presence. Instead he gave one quick flick of his head to shift his hair out of his eyes.

Iona, the young woman in command of the after-school club, glanced up from her desk and offered a wan smile. One to suggest that this really was going to be the last time.

It was Friday. The sun was out. She was ready for a bikini top, shorts, flip-flops and a cold, dripping bottle of Peroni in the village square.

'So sorry,' I said emphatically. 'I'm so, so sorry. George, quickly, get your things.'

'Roz?' said Iona.

'I know. This is unacceptable. How much extra do I owe you?'

'Ten pounds,' she said. 'We've had to start charging five pounds for every extra quarter of an hour, or parents don't seem to see the urgency.'

'Here,' I said, pulling out a note I could not afford to part with, 'take twenty. I know you can't keep on—'

'Roz,' she said sadly, 'it's not the money. It's my time. I've been here since seven thirty this morning, and I have a life, you know?' Iona didn't raise her voice as she spoke. She was too professional to get angry in front of George. It was almost worse in a way. She spoke as if I were letting myself down. Letting my son down.

'I'm sorry,' I repeated. 'It won't happen again, I assure you.'

'We're going to have to call an end to this arrangement. It's just not—'

'Don't,' I said quickly. 'Please don't do that. I can't manage without it.'

'It's not that I don't understand, Roz,' she said. 'I can see that you're struggling. But you're late practically every day, and it's not fair. It's not fair on us and it's not fair on . . .' She didn't finish her sentence, simply gestured towards George, who was pretending not to listen as he collected his lunchbox from the windowsill. Having run out of biscuits, I'd stuck a peach yoghurt in there this morning and was now regretting it. The school had a policy of sending the kids' rubbish home with them so you'd know if they'd eaten all of their lunch. That empty yoghurt pot would be supporting its own ecosystem.

Turning back to Iona, I saw she was waiting for me to speak.

'I don't know what to do,' I said honestly, as I thought through the logistics of the following week.

Iona didn't offer a solution. Unsurprising, really, since her patience had run out over a month ago. I'd had second chance after second chance.

I could ask my sister.

No. Today was her fortieth birthday. We were attending her party this evening and she was off to New York next week. My parents were too far away and I'd made a promise to my sister that I absolutely would not impose on them again. I'd let them down in the past, and I couldn't bear to ask for their help. At least not for a good while anyway.

Winston was unreliable. He had left George waiting at the school gates more than once when he'd become fascinated by extreme weather and had gone off storm chasing at the coast.

Iona cleared her throat. She was still waiting for me to speak.

But then, oddly, as she attempted to stand, she winced.

'Are you okay?' I asked as I watched her adjust her weight, moving from one foot to the other.

'Not really, no,' she answered, and she sighed. Twice.

'Oh, okay,' she said eventually, her expression beaten, jaded. 'Okay, Roz, one more chance.' And before I had time to express my gratitude, before I had a chance to tell her I would *absolutely not let it happen again*, she reached down and lifted her trouser leg.

'I don't suppose you've got ten minutes to have a look at my knee, have you?'

3

LOOKING BACK, I can see how everything was ultimately building towards this point, the point when life went off at a crazy tangent, but I think it was the note itself that was the trigger for the series of events that followed.

> DON'T GO INSIDE
> I SMELL GAS
> LOVE, CELIA

It was taped to my front door and had been put there by my neighbour. Celia had lived in the village for five years and was not a native; she was in fact a Scouser. But if you asked her where she hailed from, she'd say, 'Southport, Lancashire', in her best telephone voice. (Notice: Lancashire, not Merseyside. An important distinction, apparently.)

When I first moved into the cottage we had a few run-ins – Celia getting herself into a state of fractious agitation if I left the wheelie bin at the end of the garden path for more than two days running, or if my living-room curtains remained closed while I was at work or, heaven forbid, if I left my washing on the line when her book club was in attendance. Celia was a terrible snob. A working-class woman who liked to let you know that she was *just that little bit better* than everyone else. It was terribly amusing and, unexpectedly, I had grown to love her for it.

We reached an agreement early on whereby, because I didn't have time to give the cottage the kerb appeal Celia deemed necessary, and because she lived in mortal fear of falling property values, Celia had a key to my place. Anything that was going to fray her nerves, I told her to address herself. So her husband would bring my bin in the very second the waste wagon left. I would arrive home to find the fringe of grass edges neatly trimmed in the front garden, or small pink stains on the path where Celia had poured weed killer on my dandelions. Lately, I could feel her itching to affix a hanging basket or two, to match her four, but she hadn't yet broached the subject.

I pulled the note from the door. 'Come on,' I said to George, 'let's go to Celia's.' This was the last thing I needed, to be honest. We were supposed to be out of the house again by seven thirty for my sister's party. George needed feeding and we both needed smartening up. Glancing his way, I noticed some hair missing above his right ear. How I'd not realized it earlier, I had no idea, because there was quite a chunk gone.

'What's going on there?' I said, gesturing.

'I'm not sure.'

'George,' I said.

'I don't remember.'

A quick word about fibs. You've noticed, I'm certain, the inability of little boys to tell the truth. Don't hold it against them. They're simply afraid of making us cross. 'George, I'm not angry with you, I just want to know why you've cut away such a large piece of your hair.'

'I needed it for a creature I was making,' he said.

'Seems reasonable,' I replied.

We made our way down the path, out of the front gate and along the short stretch of road to Celia's. 'I'm really thirsty. I need a drink, Mum,' George said, and I said, 'You and me both.' The heat was fierce: thick, heavy air trapped in the basin formed by the surrounding fells. I pulled my tunic away from my midriff in a wafting motion, a lame attempt to get some ventilation. Sweat trickled down my skin, making me itch.

Celia's house was a detached cottage. Ours was a semi; the other side of my house was a holiday home. I never saw the owners. Instead there was a parade of similar kinds of people – folk who smiled if the sun was shining, were grim-faced and uncommunicative if it was not.

Remember the village of Greendale, from the children's television programme *Postman Pat*? Well, Greendale doesn't exist, but it was modelled on Longsleddale, a spot over on the other side of the lake, and it's close enough to form a fairly accurate picture of Hawkshead. Five hundred people live in the village and, aside from the holidaymakers, everyone really does know everyone. Set amongst farmland (mostly used for grazing sheep), the stone or white-rendered cottages are bordered by drystone walls. Those of us in the village centre benefit from gas and mains drainage, those on the outskirts heat their homes with electricity, or more commonly oil, and have septic tanks. Everyone within a mile of the village centre has a small notice next to the loo, requesting guests not to flush anything other than the necessaries, and the smallest amount of toilet tissue. It's something you're used to if you've grown up with it. Like pasteurized milk and half-day closing.

Celia must have been loitering by her window, looking out for us, as the second we opened her gate she was at the front door. 'Good Lord, George!' she declared loudly. 'What on earth have you done to your hair?' I suppose he *was* kind of scalped above his ear. 'He looks like that simple lad, Billy. You know, from *One Flew Over the Cuckoo's Nest*?' She was frowning, her chin retracted. 'Doesn't he, Roz?'

'What does she mean, Mum?' George whispered, worried, as we approached the house.

'Nothing. Just an old film. Billy was the kickass hero,' I lied.

'You saw the note?' Celia asked, and I nodded. 'Come in, come in,' she said and ushered us through. George removed his shoes automatically without being instructed to do so.

'Did you call Transco?' I asked her, and she didn't answer. Instead she became momentarily flustered, telling George to 'Go through to the back kitchen and find Dennis. He's out there messing about with his tomato plants. And Foxy's in the garden, too.'

Foxy was Celia's old dog. She was a spiteful, peevish little terrier who hated kids but for some reason allowed George access to her belly when she was in the right mood. She had recently started to refuse to walk on the lead. That is, unless she was heading back home. So now Celia and Dennis could be seen driving to the other side of the village, early each morning, whereupon Dennis would deposit Celia and Foxy, and they would walk back. Celia was delighted with this ruse, proclaiming Foxy to be 'almost sprightly', even pulling on the lead.

George traipsed off to find the dog, and Celia swallowed hard before speaking.

'A problem,' she began.

'A gas problem,' I said.

'Afraid not. I put that note there to stop you from going inside. I didn't want George to see.'

'To see what?'

'Prepare yourself, Roz, the bailiffs have been.'

'What did they take?'

'The lot. Well, all except the beds, because they belong to your landlord, apparently, who *has also* been slithering around, leaving his usual trail of slime, asking if I'd seen you. He left you a note demanding payment, I believe.'

'I'm late with the rent.'

'I did assume,' she said. 'Anyway, the three-piece suite has gone—'

'I was paying that off,' I interrupted.

'As well as the dining-room furniture, the cooker—'

'The cooker?'

'They said that was on finance as well.'

I sank down heavily on to Celia's sofa. 'It was.' I sighed, remembering now.

'I think they would have had your car away as well, if you were home. Good job I saw them, because they were about to break in through the front door. They said you'd be liable for the damage to that, too.' She paused. Then said, '*Bastards!*' emphatically, before continuing. 'So in the end I let them in with the key. Sorry, Roz, but they had all the right legal paperwork. I got Dennis to take a look at it before, and he said you didn't have a leg to stand on.'

Dennis used to work in a solicitor's. Doing what, I'm not entirely sure. Celia, naturally, liked to give the impression he *was* a solicitor, but I had noticed that Dennis had been quick to point out on more than one occasion that he was *not really qualified* to give advice.

Sitting with my head in my hands, I told Celia that it was okay to use the key. 'You did the right thing,' I said, because she was wringing her hands and I could tell she wasn't sure how I was going to react.

'I thought it best to stick that note on the door, and then you could prepare George. Not nice for the child to get home and have no furniture.'

'Did they take his PlayStation?'

Celia nodded.

'Bloody stupid thing to have anyway,' I said. 'Typical of his father. We can't afford to put fuel in the car and he goes and buys him that. And of course George loves him for it. Thinks I'm Cruella when I can't buy games for the thing.'

'That's men for you. No common sense.'

'Christ, Celia,' I said, the full weight of what had happened now dawning on me. 'What the hell am I going to do?'

I left George with Celia and went to inspect the house.

The place had been gutted. They'd taken stuff I didn't even know I owned until it was gone. Pictures I wasn't particularly fond of. Cookery books I never had time to read but were part of my history, that time when I revelled in domesticity for a few short, wonderful months when George was born.

It was like going back to the seventies when people owned nothing. When bare asphalt floors were the norm and orange crates doubled as bedside cabinets.

There was even an ugly, gaping gash in the fitted kitchen where the oven ought to be. That's when I made the decision not to face the problem tonight. George needed a quick bite to eat before we were to leave for Petra's party. '*Dress smart! Think cocktail dress!*' she'd inscribed on the invitation with a silver metallic gel pen. And so I headed back to Celia's with a change of clothes for us both, ready to collect George, with a hasty plan forming in my mind:

I would have one large glass of cold, white Torres Viña Sol in the King's Arms (low ceilings, horse brasses, welcoming smell of beer hanging heavily in the air) while George shovelled down Cumberland sausage and chips, and *then* I would tackle the furniture crisis, explaining to George the reality of our new situation.

The note from my landlord would just have to wait.

4

GEORGE SAT IN the front seat of the Jeep with a clip-on tie and
a worried expression.

'Will I have to go and live with Nanna Dylis?' he asked, after I'd
finished explaining what had happened to the furniture and
given him a quick lecture on that basic principle: don't spend
more money than you have.

'No,' I replied, hoping he wouldn't sense the uncertainty in my
voice.

We were just about to board the ferry to cross the lake to Petra's
house in Windermere, so George became silent. There's a tricky
bit that must be negotiated, where the ramp of the ferry meets
the dip in the shoreline. If you don't drive carefully you're liable
to take out the underside of your car. Not such a problem in a
Jeep, but hell if you're in a low-sitting sports car.

Once I'd cut the engine and was neatly positioned I told George
he could speak again if he wanted to.

'This is because of Dad, isn't it?' he said.

'Honestly?' I replied. 'Yes. But there's no point blaming him,
because it gets us nowhere. What we're going to do is put it out
of our heads until after Auntie Petra's party. Let's enjoy ourselves
tonight and worry about it tomorrow. We've got beds to sleep in,
we've got running water, and we've got each other. We'll be fine.'

The truth was, though, we weren't fine.

When Winston left I could no longer make the mortgage

payments on either our house or my business premises, and they were repossessed by the bank. Coupled with that, Winston had run up debts to the tune of twelve thousand on a credit card that was in our joint names, and now I was barely covering the minimum monthly payments.

Though I couldn't blame Winston totally.

Five years ago, life was good. We were earning plenty, we spent freely (more money than we had), and we thought it would continue like that for ever. But an event was to cause a change in our circumstances, and we didn't change along with them. Not nearly fast enough anyhow. Winston's building firm lost its major contract and his hours were cut, along with his hourly rate. Ultimately, we fell apart. Winston left and I found myself without a home, with my on tick furniture taken away, without a business, and with a small child to support.

I probably should have declared bankruptcy at that point, but a combination of pride and a fear of being refused credit in the future prevented me from doing so. I borrowed some money from my sister for a deposit, rented a house, purchased a few bits and pieces on finance to furnish the place, and now, thanks to Winston and the exorbitant monthly interest on the credit card, I carried a debt of close to eighteen thousand pounds.

After rent, the cost of my car, food, household bills, the ferry, after-school club, and the loan repayments, my wage from the clinic left me with around fifty pounds a month to spare – if things didn't go wrong. And things always went wrong.

I glanced at George to check if he was okay with what I'd just told him, and he seemed to be. His expression became wistful, as if he'd already moved on to other things. Kids. So resilient.

'Foxy bit me,' he said after a minute or two.

'Again?' I asked, and he nodded. 'Did it hurt?'

'No.'

'Show me,' I said.

He held out his hand and there was a small, raised nub of flesh on his knuckle, but no break to the skin.

'She didn't mean to do it,' he said. 'Sometimes she can't help it. I don't think she realized it was me. Is she blind? Celia says she is.'

'Getting that way,' I replied. 'Although Dennis reckons she can see next door's cat well enough.'

We had a dog. Once. A three-year-old shaggy lurcher which George named Cesar after his hero, the 'Dog Whisperer', Cesar Millan. George asked for a dog every Christmas and birthday from the time he was able to talk. When he was six, Winston and I finally acquiesced, and there never was a happier child than George Toovey.

Two years later and after Winston moved out, the dog had to leave, too. We tried to make it work. But the difficulty of finding a rental property which allowed dogs, and the hours I spent at my job, made it untenable. I'd like to say George bought the lie all parents tell their kids when they've taken their pet to the shelter – the one where the dog goes to live on a farm somewhere, running free, all happily ever after – but George insisted on my calling the Rescue Me animal shelter to check Cesar was okay and was told by a kind woman that he'd been adopted by a little boy around his own age who was enjoying his new companion immensely.

George still wasn't over it and was counting down the weeks until we could move from our current address into more permanent accommodation, where animals were allowed. I told him this wouldn't be any time soon, but he remained undeterred, keeping his dog-ownership skills up to date by continuing to watch Cesar Millan whenever he stayed over at Winston's mother's house. She was fortunate enough to have Sky TV.

I smiled at George and reached across, tousling his hair above his bald patch. 'I love you, you know,' I said to him.

'Love you more,' he said back.

31

We drove with the windows down because the AC was out of gas. Along the roadside there were mounds of cut grass and their desiccated hay scent filled the air. Couples walked arm in arm, making their way into Bowness for the evening. George rested his elbow out of the window, as he'd observed adult men do. But not having sufficient length in his arms, he was forced to lean awkwardly against the door.

My hair whipped around my face, strands sticking to my lipstick, some getting caught in the tiny hinge mechanism of my sunglasses.

When we arrived at Petra's I checked my face in the rear-view mirror and quickly applied some more lipstick and mascara. I'm not great with make-up. I mention this not as one of those statements you hear from irritating women – you know, when you're supposed to feel crap because you trowel it on and they're already naturally beautiful without it. No, I feel kind of silly wearing it, and only do so when forced. On occasions such as this.

At my sister's house I stood on the front step, rearranged my hair, adjusted the straps of my halterneck summer dress and whispered to George not to mention the situation at home. When he raised his eyebrows questioningly, I told him this was Petra's night and I didn't want her to worry about us. Which was mostly true.

Vince, my brother-in-law, swung the door open with his usual gusto, took one look at my painted face, and grinned, saying, 'What've you come as?'

'Not tonight, Vince,' I said, pushing past him. 'I'm not in the mood.'

'Hey, Georgie boy!' he said, slapping George's raised hand. 'How are you, my friend?'

'Very well, thank you . . . under the circumstances,' replied George a little stiffly, and Vince shot me a look.

'Are we very late?' I said, avoiding his eyes.

'No more than usual,' Vince shrugged before turning his attention back to George. 'C'mon, kiddo,' he said, 'let's get you armed with sugar and a ton of E numbers, ready to face the team of *petites dragonettes* upstairs.'

Vince was more at home in the company of kids. After a couple of beers you would find him wearing mascara (applied badly), and with one of Petra's underskirts on his head (long, princess hair), after he'd been attacked by his daughter and her bossy little friends.

He was good with the girls, but it was common knowledge that Vince craved a son. Petra had managed to quash that idea by selling the notion that her death was an absolute certainty if she became pregnant again. This was on account of the high blood pressure and gestational diabetes she had suffered when carrying Clara.

So Vince had to make do with George. Not ideal, since George had no interest in football, rugby and motor racing. But they had recently found some common ground when playing poker. And the occasional game of crib.

In the kitchen Vince poured me a glass of champagne with something bright and syrupy-sweet floating on the top. 'Can't I just have it on its own?' I asked him, frowning at the glass.

'Not an option.'

My sister went through these phases. Adding stuff to make things more exciting and ruining them in the process was one.

With his head cocked to one side and a quick sideways glance, Vince said, 'Nadine had these at her fiftieth,' mimicking his wife, 'and they went down very well with the crowd.'

'Oh, well, if *Nadine* had them,' I replied, playing along.

Nadine and her husband, Scott, were Petra's current fixation. Petra was prone to these obsessions – as I said, at the moment it was Nadine and Scott Elias, but it could just as easily have been slow-cooked shin of beef or National Trust lighthouse properties.

The women had become friends whilst watching the men play charity cricket, and at the moment Petra would slip Nadine's name into almost every sentence, though not in a boastful way; I think it was involuntary. Much like when you're in those early, exquisite stages of a relationship, and your lover's name trips off your tongue so readily that you couldn't stop it even if you tried.

Vince took a can of Fanta from the drinks fridge, pressing it into George's hand, saying, 'Good luck up there, my friend,' and George scooted off upstairs, but not before telling Vince that all our furniture had disappeared.

'What?' said Vince, turning to me, while I glared hard at George's back.

But I waved away Vince's concern, telling him it was a temporary blip, before striding out into the garden.

I had Petra's present (sparkly, hooped earrings) in one hand, a bottle of champagne in the other, and announced my presence by asking loudly, 'Where's the birthday girl?' with a lot more jubilance than I had cause for.

There is always a compromise to be made with property on this side of the lake. Planning restrictions in the National Park dictate that people are stuck with the houses they've got – unless you've got a spare three million to buy the 1950s bungalow on the lakeshore, and then you can bulldoze it and pop your McMansion in its place. The rest of the community buys what they can afford, and then make do. Usually, forfeiting internal space, and as often as not, a decent garden.

No one has a regular-shaped lawn in Windermere and Bowness – either the terrain is too steep or it's cut off at an angle by a brook or, commonly – and this was before the planning department became unwaveringly strict – residents built second homes on their plots to generate some extra cash.

The consequence of this was that Petra and Vince were the only people I knew to have a lovely, enclosed, rectangular piece of turf with great views of the Langdale Pikes. These pretty western fells – like the Rockies' Sawtooth Range in miniature – are pink when reflecting the early-morning sun and become bathed in a glorious orange light as the sun sets behind them. Which meant gatherings at Petra and Vince's often had a kind of bank-holiday feel.

There were picnic benches, wicker sofas, meticulously tended flower beds, and though Vince was laid-back about most things in life, his lawn was grade-one bowling-green turf, which he tended to continuously. He would snip away at stray edges with kitchen scissors, as one might do with award-winning topiary.

I made my way from the patio over to Petra, who was serving my parents with their usual – non-alcoholic lager for my dad, cranberry juice for my mum (cystitis sufferer). After I'd greeted everyone and apologized for my tardiness, my dad informed me that he and Mum would not be staying long, followed by, 'You know us, we don't like to be out late. What with the long drive we have to do now, and all,' and I said, 'No, no, of course,' both of us dropping our heads to avoid eye contact.

They had begun to look frail of late. Their natural vigour was starting to wane. My mother, particularly, moved carefully now, as though recovering from a bad fall, and it occurred to me that perhaps she had in fact sustained one, and had kept it to herself.

I told them I'd round George up in a moment, that he'd been eager to get upstairs to his cousin, which was not exactly true. The reason I didn't send George straight out to see his grandparents was because I was frightened he'd blab to them about the missing furniture. And they worried about my finances enough as it was.

'Roz! Roz, come and chat to Scott and Nadine,' Petra said now, dragging me away by the elbow. 'I'm dying for you to meet them. They're so lovely. I can't believe they came. And wait till I show you what Scott brought. See that wine over there?' She motioned to the benches on the patio, which were dressed with white table-cloths. 'He brought three cases!'

'It's good wine?' I asked, not really knowing what to say.

'What?' she said, frowning. 'Of course it's good wine. Scott doesn't drink crap. He has a guy who picks out the best for him and delivers. Anyway, don't mention it, or he gets a bit uncomfortable. He's very humble about his wealth.'

'I wasn't going to.'

'Scott, Nadine,' said Petra as we approached, 'this is my sister, Roz Toovey. She's the physiotherapist I was telling you about. Roz is super-talented. She can fix anyone. Even people who have been in pain for years.'

I coughed and stuck out my hand. 'I fear Petra might be over-selling me. Pleased to meet you, Nadine. What pretty hair you have.'

'She travels to Manchester for highlights, don't you, Nadine?' cut in Petra as Nadine rose, taking my hand, telling me how glad she was finally to meet me. She kissed me on both cheeks, and there was that awkward moment where one person (that would be me) pulls away after a single kiss, not expecting the second. It's such an easy way to wrong-foot a Northerner. 'We've heard *so* much about you,' she said, smiling genuinely.

'Likewise,' I replied, and then whispered in her ear, 'I think Petra's a little bit in love with you, actually.'

Nadine was gracious enough to take the compliment with a small raise of her eyebrows, then she ushered me towards her husband.

'Scott Elias,' he said and, again, two kisses. He was around six foot, stood very sure of himself and could have been a little imposing if it weren't for the way he smiled. He did it in a way that implied it was a real pleasure to meet me, as though he was genuinely interested in what I had to say.

'Perhaps you could take a look at my elbow when you have a moment?' he began, and Nadine gave him a swift nudge.

'He's joking,' she said flatly. 'Aren't you, darling?'

'Yes. Absolutely,' he replied, ducking as though expecting a swipe at his head, courtesy of Nadine. 'Wouldn't dream of asking something so inappropriate on a first meeting.'

But people do.

For some reason they don't equate my job as having the usual boundaries. I didn't know how Scott had made his money, or exactly what line of business he was in, but let's say for argument's sake he was a landscape gardener. Asking me to take a quick look at his elbow was akin to me asking him to pop over to my house and dig over the rough patch of land to the rear of the property. Or asking a chef if he wouldn't mind rustling up a few canapés because we were all feeling peckish.

Anyway, I didn't hold it against him as, like most, he said it without thinking. And people ask about their ailments because it's a conversation starter and they can't think of anything else to say.

Like throwing a punch at a black belt in Karate, and saying, 'And what would you do if I did *this*?'

We exchanged pleasantries for a while – the glorious stretch of weather we were experiencing – and, like many people I talked to, Scott was enjoying it all the more because the south of the country had rain. I asked Nadine about her children, and proudly she said her youngest was in Toulouse for the summer, before starting at Warwick in October, and their eldest was at the London Film School. At this she pulled a face to indicate she wasn't sure what would come of that. Scott and she not being artistic people, this had come quite out of the blue.

Well, this is unexpected, I thought.

They were nice.

I'd anticipated feeling fairly contemptuous towards them after the incessant commentary from Petra about how Scott Elias does this, Nadine Elias does that. Scott has a driver who is *part of the family*, Nadine likes fresh flowers in every room, every single day, the florist brings them specially, blah, blah, blah.

But they seemed normal. Quite down to earth, in fact.

Of course, Nadine was more polished than your average woman. Every small detail was refined, elevated to make the absolute most of her features. Think of an ordinary song after Giorgio Moroder has pimped it up, and you'll get the general idea. She, like Scott, was in her early fifties. She was a neat, trim woman, fine boned, with delicate wrists and ankles. She was dressed in white, wide-legged trousers with a scoop-necked top and wore a simple diamond on a chain at her throat.

'Are you on your own?' Nadine asked, casting her eyes around as she looked for a suitable match with whom she could place me.

'Yes,' I replied.

For a time I used to fill the void following this enquiry with explanations, with self-deprecating remarks about my single status, all the while being rather jolly so as not to make the other person feel bad in any way.

Now I couldn't be arsed.

'No man in your life?' asked Scott.

Before I had the chance to reply Petra butted in. 'What Roz needs,' she said, 'is a good, steady guy. You don't happen to have any nice single friends, do you, Scott?'

Scott made a show of thinking through his acquaintances, frowning as though weighing up each one carefully. Then he looked directly at me, holding my gaze for a few seconds too long, making sure I noticed. Making sure, in that way some men do, that you have been set firmly in their sights. 'I don't, I'm afraid,' he said. 'They're all taken.'

'Often the way,' I said quickly, embarrassed. 'Anyway, thanks for that, but as Petra knows, *good and well,* I'm off men for the time being.'

'They're not all like Winston,' said Petra, a little sharply. 'They're not all going to do what *he* did.'

I gave Petra a look as though to say, *Not now,* and replied, 'Yes, well, I'd rather not take the chance,' brushing it off with a laugh and a roll of my eyes.

Though our words were innocuous enough, I would say it was evident by Petra's tone that there was something else at play here, and the air became charged by our exchange.

Sensing this, Scott jumped to his feet. 'Let me get you another drink, Roz,' he said. 'Here, sit yourself—'

'Thank you, but no. I've had my quota. I've got to drive home, unfortunately.'

'That's a real shame,' he said and, again, the look.

At this Petra exhaled noisily. 'Oh, for goodness' sake, Roz, get yourself another drink. You're staying here.'

'No, I—'

But Scott was off. And within seconds he returned with what must have been half a pint of red wine.

I rolled it around the enormous glass a couple of times, transfixed as the liquid clung to the sides, leaving an oily amber hue.

I didn't ask what type it was. I didn't want to embarrass myself. Instead, I threw it back, told Scott it was absolutely exceptional and went off to get another.

Two hours later, and I was pretty sozzled. Petra was being loud and funny and enjoyable to watch. Her tongue became loose and gossipy when she'd had a drink and she was switching between anecdotes from work – she was a school secretary – and falling back into default mode, where she informed the listener of the pickle in which I'd found myself:

'And then Roz wakes up, and he's gone! Cleared off back to his mother's after running up huge debts in her name. And now she can't get a penny out of him. And she's in a huge financial mess. Isn't that right, Roz?'

'That's about the size of it,' I said sleepily.

Vince was lighting the gas heater. There were just a few of us left outside now and the night was still warm, though chilly on the skin if you were without a cardigan. The backs of my upper arms were goose pimpled and Scott handed me his sweater, asking if I needed it, but I told him I was okay, that I'd nip inside and get a couple of fleece throws from the sofa so we could all keep warm.

'Does this bother you?' he whispered, leaning in close, gesturing to Petra, who was now in the full throes of explaining to Nadine how men get around the Child Support Agency. Nadine's brow was knitted in concern as Petra told her of numerous fathers from school who'd fled and were out of work, meaning their wives and families received pretty much zilch in the way of support payments.

'Not really,' I told Scott. 'It's hardly a secret. I just don't think everyone wants to hear about it on a night out. That's why I try to shut her up. A losing battle, as you can see.'

Again, he held my gaze, and I felt something shift inside.

I looked away.

Alarm bells went off in my head. Married men were off limits, simple as that. I rose, asking if anyone wanted nibbles, as I was going inside. I told Petra I'd check on the kids while I was at it, but she was in the zone, lecturing poor Nadine on how the system was skewed against women, because, 'You can't up and leave your own kids like men, can you? Your biology won't let you.'

I went upstairs, paid a quick visit to the loo and listened outside Clara's bedroom for a moment. Vince had put the kids to bed earlier, telling them ghost stories (his speciality) about the Grey Lady and the Headless Horseman, old favourites he probably frightened little girls with back when he was a child himself.

I pushed the door open a fraction. The kids were still up – Clara, George and the two little girls from next door whose names escaped me. One was a dozy-looking child with a permanently wet lower lip who hung on Clara's every word. They were sitting in a circle, beneath a cotton sheet, with a torch.

I pushed open the door fully. 'Time to get to sleep, kids,' I said softly, and there was the silent movement of little bodies from beneath the sheet as they climbed inside their beds.

'Goodnight,' I whispered.

I headed downstairs, grabbed the throws and went outside with a family pack of salt-and-vinegar Chipsticks, taking my place by the gas heater. Petra was laughing at something, trying to stand, but she couldn't get out of her chair, so she sank down again, beaten.

'You okay there, Roz?' Scott asked.

'Long day,' I replied, trying to make my eyes match my smile. I'd been thinking about the bailiffs and my empty house.

Petra was now ranting about Winston's cheating, asking the small crowd why anyone would want to cheat on someone as lovely as her sister.

She tipped her glass my way, in case anyone had forgotten who I was, and I found myself saying, without really thinking, 'Do you know, a person once told me they wished Winston had visited a prostitute instead of having affairs.'

Someone coughed.

'What?' said Petra.

'A prostitute,' I repeated. 'I suppose it would have been a hell of lot less hassle in the long run,' I added absently.

There was a stunned silence. Everyone turned to me and stared.

Petra put her drink down. 'Jesus Christ, Roz,' she said.

I glanced around, and I could see by the look of confusion and awkwardness on each face that this was not a commonly held belief. The women seemed affronted, and the men didn't know where to look.

'It does go on,' I said, trying to justify what I'd just said.

At this Nadine leaned forward in her seat. Her expression changed to one of genuine inquiry, as though she was open-minded and wanted to know more. 'What makes you say that?' she said, blinking a little. 'Do you know people who frequent them?'

'Crikey, no,' I said. 'Of course not. It's just that after Winston's affairs were made public, one poor guy – Giles was his name – whose family had broken up on account of Winston carrying on with his wife, said to me, "Wouldn't it have just been easier if Winston had used a professional?"'

Petra began to panic. What was I doing talking like this in front of her nice guests?

'And, in that moment, I could sort of see his point,' I said. 'If Winston had taken himself off, instead of sleeping with half the women around here – women who were married, women who had families – then there wouldn't be all those broken homes as a result.'

Petra gasped. 'I can't believe you're seriously—'

'Oh, Petra,' I said, sighing. 'I'm not being serious.'

'You sound very serious.'

'I'm not. But, honestly, you don't know what it was like to have those poor bereft men glaring at you like it's *your* fault. Like, if I'd kept better tabs on Winston, then he wouldn't have jumped into bed with their wives. I'm only saying that if Winston had filled up whatever need he felt needed filling without wrecking everyone's lives in the process, I'd probably have more respect for him.'

'Good God,' said Petra standing up. 'Why did he need to do it *at all*, Roz? I can't believe you're justifying it.'

'I'm not justifying it.'

'Don't look at me,' Vince cut in. He was holding up his palms in innocence. 'I get all the excitement I need right here.'

Petra was dismayed. She raised her hands above her head as though to ward off a blow.

She looked from me to Scott, to Nadine, to Vince.

I had ruined the evening.

I had ruined *everything*.

Her eyes pricked with tears before she hurried off inside the house.

5

CLOTHING COVERS A multitude of sins.
You've probably already figured out that real people don't resemble the airbrushed, Photoshopped images you see in the media. I read a smashing quote from Cindy Crawford recently who, upon being asked how she felt about those images, replied, 'I wish *I* looked like Cindy Crawford.'

God love her for that. Because you wouldn't believe the number of people (men included) who apologize for the state of their bodies when removing their clothes.

Consider the following a public-service announcement.

I have treated a grand total of two skinny women in my twenty years of practice who have naturally big boobs. I have treated (at the last reckoning, anyway) zero patients over forty-five years of age who don't sag *somewhere*. Even the desperately thin ones. You get them to turn over and their skin falls away from their bodies in the most remarkable way.

Beautifully curved ladies are criss-crossed with Caesarean scars, with striations of stretch marks, with indentations as if they were still wearing an underwired bra. Bodybuilding men have purple, keloid-scarred, acned backs and give off a peculiar smell from steroid use. Elderly, wiry, super-fit fell runners often have bulging varicose veins like small bunches of grapes on their calves and have flaps of surplus skin around their upper arms and ribcages.

Voluptuous young women can be covered in black hair all the way from their navel to their knees, courtesy of the cruel polycystic-ovary syndrome.

There are botched tattoos, missing toes, missing slabs of muscle, missing breasts.

This is the human body.

It does not look like it does in the movies. But that doesn't make it any less wondrous, any less perfectly suited to doing everything you ask of it. Given the chance, the body will fix itself. Given rest and some TLC, it will recover, generate new tissue, even new nerve pathways. It is constantly aiming to return to a state of balance, a state of equilibrium. And if it can't? That's where I come in.

Physiotherapy is the treatment of the body through physical means. If the body is out of balance, I lay my hands on it to initiate the healing process. No drugs. I should point out, however, that this is not an exact science – no area of medicine is. You try one thing, and it either works or it doesn't.

There was a sign hanging in my treatment room that read: 'I AM NOT JESUS.' Though sometimes I wondered exactly what *his* hit rate was. I mean, did he cure everyone he came into contact with? I suspected not. I suspected he couldn't have done much to help my next patient of the day – one of my failures. I couldn't improve her symptoms, whatever I tried.

During the first consultation Rosemary Johns greeted me with the news that she had been to every single therapist in the area and no one could get her right. Now this sort of opening would usually lead one of two ways. Either I examined the patient and became quite giddy upon spotting the veiled symptom I knew the other clinicians had missed, or my heart sank because the patient was one of those people who just didn't *want* to get better.

With Rosemary it was the latter.

(Off topic, but patients such as this just won't die either. When I worked in the NHS I'd read the initials CTD in the margin of a patient's notes with a queasy kind of dread – Circling the Drain. They could be in hospital for *years*.)

Anyway, my state of mind was not what you'd call free and easy when I called out for Rosemary Johns on Monday morning. The weekend had been hellish. Petra was barely speaking to me after I had humiliated her beyond forgiveness on Friday night, she was so distressed about the impression I'd made on Scott and Nadine. Unbeknownst to her, however, Vince had dropped by my house on Saturday, slipping me a fifty and depositing two old armchairs, a nest of tables and a cooker with a decade's worth of grease on it.

His friend had pulled the unwanted furniture out of a house clearance over near Rydal Water, and Vince rightly thought I could make use of it until I got back on my feet. I spent most of Sunday applying for another batch of credit cards, hoping the over-inflated earnings I'd claimed to bring in would not be checked out too closely so that I could replace some of the furniture the bailiffs had removed. I'd have to wait a week to find out if I'd been approved.

So this morning it was hard to hide my surprise and, I suppose, my relief, when Rosemary Johns's mournful face did not appear at my treatment-room door, but rather, Scott Elias.

'I hope you don't mind,' he said. 'I called for an appointment earlier and they told me they had this cancellation. Were you hoping for a break?'

'A break?' I said, momentarily confused. 'Oh, no, I don't really get breaks. Wayne fills the cancellations with patients from the waiting list. I'm surprised to see *you* here, though. You must have jumped the queue.'

Scott went sheepish. 'I might have offered a little sweetener.'

I smiled. 'I won't ask. Anyway, come on in. What can I do for you?'

'My elbow? Remember?'

I nodded. 'Have a seat, and I'll get your details down. Then I'll take a look.'

I busied myself as he took out his phone and car keys and placed them on the desk. I didn't comment on the Ferrari fob, but I must admit it did stir my interest.

Here's something worth knowing about rich people, though, should you feel inclined to hang around them:

They don't give you any of their money.

They pay no more for your services than any other punter, and the likelihood of them leaving you anything in their will is next to zero. I gave up thinking they were anything other than another patient years ago, because, as a rule, they were generally more hassle to treat. They expected their wealth to guarantee they would be seen fast but lost no sleep over missing appointments once they were back on the mend.

I jotted down Scott Elias's details, his past medical history, the particulars of his injury, and asked him about his job – he owned a large electronics manufacturing firm near Preston. Then I told him to remove his shirt and asked him exactly where the pain was.

'Does this hurt?' I said, knowing full well it did, as I could feel some thickening on the point of attachment of the extensor tendon. I asked just to break the silence.

'Yes,' he replied, 'how did you know where to press?'

'Sixth sense.'

'Do you think you can do anything for it?'

'It's easy to treat,' I said casually. 'Shouldn't take long.'

'What will you do?'

'I'll use a complicated medical procedure,' I began, and he raised his eyebrows expectantly. 'First, I shall rub it like this. And then like that.'

'That's it?'

'That's it.'

'Okay,' he said, but he didn't seem convinced.

I spent the next few minutes breaking down the scar tissue that had formed around the tendon. As far as treatments go, this was a pretty mindless task, requiring negligible amounts of concentration. Over the years my thumbs had become attuned to the slightest changes, moving intuitively from healthy areas to damaged tissue without any real conscious thought on my part.

'I told your receptionist we could go for a drive in the Ferrari if he slotted me in today,' Scott admitted.

'Wayne?' I said, amused. 'Don't call him a receptionist. He won't thank you for it. On second thoughts,' I said, feeling mischievous, 'make sure you call him exactly that.'

'You don't like him?'

'I like him well enough, but let's just say he could make my life a little easier if he wanted to.'

Scott nodded. 'That stings quite a lot,' he said, gesturing towards his elbow, and I eased off the pressure through my right thumb.

'Wayne's really into cars,' I said, 'so you two should hit it off.'

'You're not?'

'No.' I laughed. 'As far as I'm concerned, they're all the same from the inside. Looking out through the windscreen you see the same as every other driver. Even when a car is bad, it's good. It still gets you to where you want to go.'

Scott Elias smiled mildly at my assessment.

Of course, nothing of what I told him was actually true. I'd love a flash car. Who wouldn't? But I wasn't about to start gushing over his wheels. I did have some dignity.

There was a lull in the conversation and I could hear the faint sound of Ken Bruce's *PopMaster* drifting through from the radio in the waiting area.

To be frank, Scott was in fairly good shape for fifty-four. He obviously took care of himself, did some resistance training, as he still had a bulk to his musculature, more typical of a guy in his thirties. His frame – and I refrain from using the term 'physicality' here, as it is currently so overused, and I'm not even sure it's a proper word – evoked vigour. Sure, he had slight inelasticity of the skin and the forward protrusion of the abdomen that comes from being fifty-four. But you would look twice if you were, say, poolside, pretending to read a paperback, and he was to walk past.

'I'll put some strapping on this,' I said, retrieving the five-inch Fixomull from the shelves. 'It shouldn't bother you. You can get it wet, but dab it dry afterwards. It's breathable, so it shouldn't affect the skin.'

As I laid the tape across his elbow, I sensed Scott surveying me closely. It was quite unnerving, as usually patients were so interested in what I was doing (everyone loves a bandage, after all) that I wasn't used to it.

'There's something about you,' he murmured softly.

I didn't look up.

'You're very attractive,' he said.

'You're a married man, Scott.'

'I'm not coming on to you.'

'Oh, well, that is a relief.'

'Okay, maybe I am, a bit,' he said. 'But not in the way you think.'

'There is more than one way?' I said, and I made one loud, final snip with the scissors.

'What is it about you?' he asked playfully.

I rolled my eyes and packed away the tape. 'Move your arm around and see if it feels okay. Check the bandage isn't nipping your skin at all.'

'It feels fine.'

'Put your shirt on then.'

He didn't move.

'Since Friday night,' he said, 'ever since I—'

I held up my palm. 'Please don't.'

'Hear me out.'

'No, Scott. This is my place of work. I have other people to see and, while you seem like a perfectly nice bloke, please don't compromise my position here. It makes things incredibly awkward when men start to—'

'You get this a lot?' he asked, and suddenly a shadow fell across his face. I could see instantly he was put out.

'It happens,' I said quietly.

Truth be told, it did happen quite regularly. And not because I'm some sort of goddess. Far from it. I have the sturdy physique of a lady golfer, straight dark hair and an unremarkable face. But it did happen.

Cast your mind back to that period when every single woman had a girl-crush on Sarah Jessica Parker. Her style, her general flamboyance, bewitched women the world over. At the time, though, men appeared thoroughly perplexed by this. They would scratch their chins, frowning, as if to say, *D'you know what? I just can't see it myself.*

Well, I have something akin to that.

I am not good-looking. My body is neither madly sexy, nor neatly packaged, but men do seem drawn to me, for reasons I can't fathom. Perhaps it's because I don't care any more. Perhaps, because of Winston, and all that happened, I exude an attitude of not caring and men are intrigued by that. Who knows?

'Your shirt, Scott,' I repeated. 'I have another patient waiting.'

He slipped off the bed. Pushed an arm through a sleeve and began clenching his fist repeatedly. 'The elbow feels really good,' he said. 'Remarkable, really, after just one session.'

I wiggled my fingers and said, 'Magic,' my tone deadpan.

He offered a rueful smile. 'I'm sorry,' he said, holding my gaze. 'I didn't mean to make you uncomfortable. It was silly of me, and I apologize.'

'It's forgotten,' I said.

I made a few short treatment notes: cross frictions, strapping applied, advised him to use an ice pack and rest his elbow, and while Scott was tidying himself up I straightened my desk. I returned the tape and scissors, moved the stool against the wall so I didn't trip over it. Then I got on with laying new couch roll along the bed before dragging out my hair band, rearranging my hair into another fast ponytail and fixing a smile upon my face, signalling it was time for Scott to leave.

'That husband of yours must have been a fool,' he said as I moved towards the door.

'That's one way of putting it.'

And then he reached out and touched my hand.

He did this in a manner to suggest I should be still for a moment. That he had something important he wanted to say.

My pulse quickened.

'Have a drink with me,' he said. 'Just one drink.'

6

I SHALL SPARE YOU the finer details of the demise of my marriage. There's nothing extraordinary about what occurred – just the usual disintegration of a relationship that comes about with broken promises, broken hearts, broken crockery.

Safe to say, we were *not* one of those ex-couples who had a very good co-parenting relationship. We did not do joint Christmases or have civilized get-togethers with our old friends.

No, we did our break-up t'Northern way.

Lots of old-fashioned screaming at each other in the street, plenty of backstabbing and irrationality. Once, we came across each other on a drunken night out, and ended up having sex in the toilets. It wasn't pretty. But then again, when is it ever?

I belonged to the brigade of women who referred to their ex as 'that wanker'. And everyone knew who I was talking about.

We split up two years ago and we were still married because we couldn't afford to get divorced – though I did think of him as my ex-husband. Winston was so feckless that trying to get him to sign anything – actually, scratch that; trying to get him to *do* anything – required such a surge of insurmountable energy on my part that I'd given up trying.

And yes, of course Petra was right when she said I should have severed all ties with the man. Got my name off everything associated with him, because I would never get credit, never get on with my life, while I had him hanging on from a distance, screwing things up. But with the hours I was working, and just with keeping my head above water, well, I couldn't seem to make it happen.

'Do the thing you least want to do *first*, Roz,' Petra had instructed on numerous occasions. 'You'll be far more productive when you've not got dread hanging over you all day.'

I imagined what would happen if I told Petra about Scott's invitation. Good grief! Her head would topple off.

Petra thought everyone had the same moral compass as her. She was genuinely astonished when people turned out not to be what she thought. She took it as a personal insult.

I had refused Scott, of course.

'I don't date married men,' I told him.

'I'm not asking for a date,' he said, 'just a drink. Surely there's no law against that? We could meet as friends.'

'Sorry, Scott, but no.'

'Can I ask you a question?' He was smiling now.

'Go ahead.'

'If I wasn't married, would you agree to it?'

'But you are married.'

'Say I wasn't.'

'But you are, Scott.'

He left, amused. As though my stubbornness was actually quite charming. I wondered if he made a habit of it, wondered if he was a serial adulterer and enjoyed the conquest. And I probably would have remained wondering about him for the duration of the morning if the call about George hadn't come in.

I was on my third sciatica sufferer of the day when I heard the phone ring at reception. I tried not to be distracted as this patient was in a bad way and needed my full attention.

True sciatica is rare. It occurs when the soft inner jelly of the intervertebral disc is squeezed out through a crack in the disc's hard outer coating. This jelly comes to rest on the sciatic nerve, sending crippling pain and often paralysis down the leg of the patient. Once the jelly is out, there's no going back. It's like trying to get toothpaste back into a tube. Surgery is the only cure. So, if you find yourself being told by a clinician that he's putting your discs back into place, you can be safe in the knowledge that he's an idiot.

But, as I said, true sciatica is rare. Much more common is for the patient to strain the fascia surrounding the lower vertebrae. I had a neat trick whereby I got the patient to bend over in front of me and then proceeded to administer a hard fingertip massage. Often, within a few minutes the patient was able to bend fully without me needing to manipulate the joints, which could be painful.

I was midway through this procedure when Wayne rapped loudly on the door, informing me there was a telephone call that I needed to take immediately. 'I'll have to call back,' I shouted, as the old braless hippy before me had flinched in response to Wayne's interruption and now her muscles were in spasm. She was stuck in forward flexion and couldn't move.

'It's George's teacher,' Wayne replied between his teeth.

There was no way I could leave the patient as she was: wrinkled breasts hanging low, like snooker balls in socks, stuck somewhere between a forty- and fifty-degree bend – the most precarious of positions. So I told Wayne I would return the call within two minutes.

I spent the next ninety seconds with my thoughts colliding, my brain Rolodex-ing through the possible injuries George could have sustained to warrant such a call. And being unsuccessful in alleviating the muscle spasm in my patient's back, I gave up temporarily, adjusted the treatment plinth to its lowest setting – around twelve inches from the floor – and supported her around the waist as she crawled piteously on to the plinth, collapsing into the foetal position, saying, 'Go on, go on. Find out about your son.'

I thanked her and darted to the shelves, grabbing a large towel and laying it over her to preserve her modesty (not that she cared). Then I dashed through to reception, where Wayne was wearing an expression that I was supposed to translate as 'No personal calls in work hours.'

The call connected and I said, 'Hello?' as Wayne pretended to busy himself, tearing open a new box of tissues, then dabbing dry his upper lip.

'Mrs Toovey, it's Hilary Slater.'

Hilary Slater was the headmistress. 'Everything okay?' I asked.

'Yes and no, to be honest,' and she sighed out heavily. 'There's an issue . . . an issue with George.'

'Is he ill?'

Around six months ago I began receiving phone calls from school on a fairly regular basis to say that George was unwell and needed to be collected. He had a range of symptoms: sickness, headaches, dizziness, the occasional limp. As you would expect, the school treated these symptoms seriously. As did I, initially.

Getting over to Hawkshead mid-afternoon, taking George home or else bringing him back to the clinic, did not go down well with either Wayne or myself by the third time. Particularly because on every single one of these occasions there was absolutely nothing wrong with him. Within twenty minutes of leaving school his pallor had vanished and he would be chatting away happily. I spoke to George's teacher. Explained that, for whatever reason, I thought George was trying it on, and I would try to get to the bottom of it but please could they make doubly sure in the future before assuming he was unwell.

A week later I got the same phone call, only this time George had been *witnessed* vomiting so I could hardly argue. Off I traipsed, leaving a patient with fibromyalgia mid-session in the less-than-capable hands of Gary. Gary, whose entire treatment repertoire consisted of ultrasound followed by whatever new electrical therapy the reps were pushing down our throats and ending with a nice chat about correct posture. Sod all use basically, if you were in constant pain.

George was fine, needless to say. His *witness* turned out to be one of his buddies, who I'm sure under interrogation would have cracked, switching his story to one of observing strings of saliva rather than vomit. And George had once again earned himself an afternoon away from Spanish. Or the War of the Roses. I forget which was his least favourite at the time.

'George is not ill, Mrs Toovey,' Hilary Slater said.

'He's not? Oh, that's a relief,' I replied, laughing nervously. Silence.

'Would it be possible for you to pop in around three thirty for a meeting?' she asked in a way that wasn't really a question.

I hesitated. 'George is in after-school club today. I'm afraid I work until five. What is this about exactly?'

Wayne was openly staring at me at this point and I tried to step away from the desk to prevent him from hearing. The phone cord, however, was too short and so I remained within earshot.

'I'd rather speak to you in person,' she said carefully.

'I understand that, but ...' I paused. How to word this without sounding rude and dismissive? Not possible. 'I don't want to reschedule patients, Mrs Slater, unless absolutely necessary.'

Wayne was making big swiping gestures. *Tell her no*, he mouthed. *No way.*

'I wouldn't ask you to come in unless it was absolutely necessary.'

'Then perhaps *you* could stay a little late?' I suggested hopefully. 'We could do the meeting at, say, five o'clock. I'm sure I could get away from here slightly early if—'

She cut me off. 'Not possible. Mrs Toovey, George has been stealing.'

'He's been what?'

'Stealing.'

'Stealing?' I repeated back, blindsided, and Wayne stopped what he was doing and stared at me, all interested.

'That's right,' she said.

'I . . . I . . . assume you have proof?' I stammered. 'I assume you wouldn't be throwing these allegations around unless you were absolutely sure, because if you were to—'

'There is no doubt, Mrs Toovey.'

'Shit,' I whispered, and then quickly apologized. 'Okay,' I told her. 'Okay, I'll be at the meeting.'

Unless you plan meetings to coincide with the ferry crossing times it's often hard to arrive at appointments bang on time. Unusually for me, in this instance, I was early. I stayed in the car outside school, electing to avoid the other mothers, since George would not be departing along with the rest of the children. In fact, he had not been allowed to rejoin any of the afternoon lessons with his classmates and had been working with a teaching assistant on his own in the school's IT lab.

I fiddled with the radio, trying to get a decent reception. Depending on your position, Hawkshead could receive sketchy transmission signals. Lightning, however, had no such trouble getting through and surge suppressors were essential if you wanted to protect your electrical items. I'd lost a freezer and two mobile phones since moving here.

Eventually, I gave up and chose to sit in silence. I observed the women in the playground in groups of three or four, making light conversation, the gist of which was likely to be: *No, I am undoubtedly the worst mother in the school because* . . . None of it said in earnest, of course. None of it truthful. The men were spared this litany of self-deprecating nonsense; they were allowed to stand alone, unspeaking, radiating ambivalence. You go in acting like that as a woman, and it's noted.

When the playground had cleared I made my way inside. I had decided not to defend George. I would listen to what Hilary Slater had to say. Tell her I would deal with it accordingly. Do whatever was necessary to stop him doing it, and as quickly as possible.

But when the secretary showed me into the head teacher's office and I saw George sitting on a too-tall chair, his thin legs dangling, his head downcast, I was overcome.

I rushed towards him. 'George,' I said, squatting beside his chair, 'are you all right?'

He nodded without looking up.

Seconds later we were joined by the headmistress Hilary Slater, George's Year Five class teacher, and the Year Six teacher, who wore a sickly, cloying scent which filled the room, making me queasy.

'Mrs Toovey,' began the headmistress, 'thanks for taking the trouble to come in.'

'It's no trouble,' I replied.

'Perhaps you'd like to sit there?' She motioned to an empty chair about two feet away from George. I looked at him before straightening up; tried to get him to meet my eye, but he wouldn't. I even went so far as to lift his chin with my finger, but he pulled against me, keeping his head low.

I sat, glanced at the three women in front of me, each wearing a sympathetic expression meant to infer *We do not judge here.*

'So,' began the head, 'I'm sure Mr Toovey brought you up to speed with last week's problem and, really, what we'd like to do now is get your thoughts and come up with a suitable plan of action for George. A plan that we can all work towards that will—'

I cut her off.

'Hang on,' I said. 'You've spoken with Winston about this?'

Hilary Slater frowned. 'Yes,' she replied. 'You haven't?'

'This is the first I've heard.'

'Oh,' she blustered, uneasily. 'Oh, that is . . . unfortunate. I just assumed that since . . .' Her words died off and she looked to the other teachers for inspiration.

George's class teacher cleared her throat. She was a kind, pleasant woman in her early fifties who was very approachable but who had the annoying habit of pretending not to recognize you if you should come across her outside school. 'We did *try* to contact Mr Toovey today to be part of this meeting but we were informed by the man who answered the call that Mr Toovey was out of the country on business.'

I cast a glance at George, who raised his head before quickly lowering it again. His knees were grass stained and the lace in his left trainer had rejigged itself so that one end was too long, and the other too short to tie.

'That's regrettable,' I said, all of us knowing it was Winston himself who had taken that call. 'But you say you've spoken to him already?'

'Yes,' said Hilary Slater. 'Twice. Last Friday, when Mr Toovey came to collect George from school. Things had been disappearing for some time—'

'What kind of things?' I asked.

'Stationery supplies and whatnot . . . nothing of any real value, but that isn't really the point. Stealing is stealing, Mrs Toovey.'

'And you told Winston about this?'

'Yes,' and she paused, biting down on her lip before continuing. 'Mr Toovey didn't seem to take it very seriously. He appeared to think that this was normal for little boys. In fact, he joked that his mother had to sew up his pockets when he was George's age. I apologize that you weren't informed, but I assumed that Mr Toovey would relay our conversation to you.'

I looked at George. 'Honey,' I said gently, 'you should have told me about this.'

'I'm afraid we can't get George to talk about it,' Hilary Slater said. 'He won't admit to his wrongdoing and we can't seem to find a reason *why* he's doing it. And, other than this, as you know, he performs very well in school. And it goes without saying that he is well liked. He is a kind and popular member of the school.'

'George?' I prompted, but he simply shrugged.

Turning my attention back to the head, I said, 'So, stationery supplies. Is that it?'

'I'm afraid not. The reason we were able to ascertain that George was the thief was because he was trying to sell these supplies to some of the other children.'

'Oh,' I said.

'One of the Year Two children was found with a staple gun in his backpack.'

I winced.

'And sadly, today,' she continued, 'we found George in the staffroom during lesson time going through the handbags. He had forty pounds in his pocket, and we're almost certain it's not the first time he's done it.'

I moved from my chair. 'Christ, George,' I said, crouching beside him, 'what on earth were you *thinking*?'

He started to cry.

'Mrs Toovey, we know things have been a little unsettled at home for George for a while now. Perhaps you could have a chat and see if there is anything worrying him,' said Hilary Slater.

'Are you going to punish him?' I asked.

She shook her head. 'We feel that is not the right way to tackle this. Obviously, if it happens again, then we would be forced to take action. But we're confident George now understands the seriousness of this and I'm sure there'll be no more incidents. Will there, George?'

He lifted his tear-stained face. 'No,' he whispered.

Moments later, when we were sitting in the corridor, I said, 'Look at me, George. What is going on?'

'Nothing.'

'George,' I repeated.

He wiped his eyes. 'I don't know.'

'Of course you know. Why did you take the money?'

And he started to sob. Big, wracking sobs, shuddering through his small frame.

'Because you haven't got any money,' he wept.

'I've got some money. I've got enough money,' I said.

He took a breath.

'And I wanted to buy Cesar,' he said. 'I wanted to buy our dog back.'

7

It was the day after Scott's first appointment. And he was back for another. I hadn't asked how he persuaded Wayne to reassign my third patient of the day, because I was fast becoming aware that Scott did not operate within the usual parameters. My mood was low after the meeting at school and the full weight of what my financial situation was doing to George was upon me. I didn't really feel like engaging in another dance with words, but Scott was insistent that I would want to hear what he had to say so, after the treatment session, I allowed him the courtesy.

'I know you're in financial trouble,' Scott began when I told him to go on. Yes, I would hear him out, because when you're eighteen thousand pounds in debt, and your son is stealing from school – because even George had realized how bad things had got – you're more willing to listen to business propositions (even though I'd had my fair share of pyramid sellers over the years. Patients have tried to get me involved in selling everything from algae food supplements to water purifiers).

'What I'm about to say might shock,' Scott said.

'I used to work in the NHS,' I said. 'I don't shock *that* easily.'

'I'd like to pay to spend the night with you,' he said.

I blinked. Then I laughed.

'I thought you had something serious to discuss,' I said. 'Is this to do with that thing I said about prostitution on Friday? I didn't really mean it. I'd had a lot to drink and it was just an observation—'

'I'm totally serious.'

'No you're not,' I replied, but I could see by his expression that he was.

'Shit,' I whispered.

I'd been asked some strange things over the years. Only last week one of my regulars – a diabetic drinker with gout in both feet – inquired if perineal massage could help him maintain an erection. To which I replied I couldn't say for sure that *it wouldn't*, but I didn't know of a person who provided such a service locally, stopping the exchange before it had a chance to go any further.

'Look,' Scott said, 'this would benefit both of us. You refused my offer of a drink—'

'Because you're married.'

'And I would like to spend some time with you – your humour, your candour, the natural way you have about you makes me want to . . . well, let's say it's refreshing.'

He paused, waiting for my reaction.

'And,' he went on, 'as I said earlier, I gather from what Petra said at the party that you could really do with the money. Though, obviously, Roz,' he said, his tone suddenly turning more serious, 'I am putting myself on the line here. So if you're really not interested, I'd rather you just said so straight away. I don't want to take the chance of this conversation becoming common knowledge.'

'I won't say anything about it,' I said quietly, and he nodded.

I said this *not* because I had any intention of going along with his outrageous suggestion but because of his wife, Nadine. From experience, I can say that the grief which settles around your heart after you've been cheated on never really leaves. Certainly, with time, the raw, ragged edges become smoothed, but it always remains, and I hoped to spare Nadine that.

'Will you think about it?' Scott asked.

'No need. The answer is no.'

'But you haven't even asked how much I was prepared to pay.'

'I don't need to ask. I'm not for sale, Scott.'

'Everyone's for sale.'

'Now you really are sounding like a dickhead,' I said.

He smiled in spite of himself and lifted both hands in a gesture to indicate he knew when he was beaten.

I probably should have been angrier than I actually was. I mean, *paying me?* For sex? Jesus.

Then I caught myself, because wasn't this exactly the kind of thing I had suggested on Friday night?

Petra's appalled face flashed into my mind.

'If you change your mind,' he said, 'the offer still stands.'

'I won't.'

The morning passed by quickly in a haze of sweating bodies, endless talk of the heat wave. Lots of *Well, if this is global warming, I'm all for it* type of conversations.

By lunchtime I'd all but put Scott's proposal from my mind. But I was left with a rather odd sensation – as if I were slightly soiled and in need of a shower.

I headed to the staff bathroom, where I filled the basin with cold water, removed my tunic and gave my upper body a good soaping. I was reluctant to dry off with the hand towel, as it was also used by both Wayne and Gary, but I decided the chances of them washing their hands after taking a leak were pretty slim, so I went ahead.

I smartened up my hair, securing it with some old kirby grips that were lying at the bottom of my handbag. Stuck to the lining was a Hall's cherry Soother that had managed to unwrap itself.

I examined my reflection and wondered if I had encouraged what had occurred earlier. Granted, my candidness on Friday evening had perhaps encouraged Scott's behaviour somewhat, but I couldn't remember actually suggesting that *I* should become a prostitute. My general idea was that for some men there is clearly a need – always was, always will be – so it might be a lot less fuss if they simply satisfied this need, without the call for affairs, and the subsequent break-up of marriages and families.

I could now see that what seemed a relatively straightforward, sensible idea to me could be perceived very differently. Petra had responded like she'd had a slap to the face. Her husband, Vince, as though it were a whistle he simply could not hear. And Scott – well, Scott had taken the idea and run with it to a whole other level.

Or perhaps not.

Perhaps Scott had been on the lookout for a while and decided I seemed reasonably game, so what did he have to lose?

The more I thought about it, the more I realized I had no idea what went through other people's heads.

I left the bathroom, planning to grab a coffee – to head off the afternoon slump – and to eat a banana in the sunshine. There was a wooden bench outside the front entrance to the clinic, which I avoided. This was because old people tended to arrive stupendously early for appointments and would take refuge on this bench. Before you knew it you'd find yourself ensconced in the kind of small talk you'd been having all morning: the heat, immigration, the frivolous spending habits of the daughter-in-law, the overcooked pork at the wedding reception they attended the previous weekend.

So I grabbed my rucksack with the idea of heading around the back of the clinic to eat lunch alone on a dusty step, very much out of sight.

Wayne, however, had other plans.

'A quick word, Roz,' he said as I passed reception. He did not lift his head. He had his eyes fixed on the monitor in front of him.

'I was just going to—'

'Won't take a minute,' and he met my eyes, giving me a sympathetic kind of smile. 'There's an issue with the takings,' he began.

Wayne Geddes was a colourless man. His skin, his hair, his eyelashes and even his gums were a peculiar shade of nothing. He was what I would describe as instantly forgettable.

Apart from, that is, his propensity to sweat.

If you've ever left a lump of Parmesan cheese out of the fridge for a time you'll notice a series of fatty droplets develop along the rind. That is Wayne's forehead. Doesn't matter what the weather's doing. You had to feel sorry for the guy.

'An issue?' I said.

He frowned at the computer screen as though trying to make sense of something. Then he looked at me. 'The takings don't always match the appointment schedule,' he said. 'There are a few inconsistencies.'

'And what has that got to do with me?'

He hesitated.

'Spit it out, Wayne.'

I glanced towards the open door. We have so few sunny days throughout the year the pull was irresistible. I stood regarding Wayne, twitching like a greyhound in the traps, primed and ready for release.

'Nothing you want to tell me?' he asked carefully.

'No.'

'You're quite sure? Because I could help you, Roz. You only need to confide in me and I promise I'll help you.'

I held his gaze intently. 'I really don't know what you're talking about. Now, I need to—'

'Okay,' he said. 'Okay.' And he regarded me sadly, as though I was letting him down. 'There is something else. You'll have to cut your lunch break short today,' Wayne said. 'I've booked Henry Peachey to come in at 1 p.m.'

'Who?' I asked.

'The insurance agent? The one you were supposed to call, and didn't?'

Oh. That guy.

'I couldn't let it run on any longer, Roz,' he said. 'You need this assessment. We're not fully insured without it.'

'So you keep saying. But did you have to organize it for today?' I asked, glancing at my watch. That only gave me fifteen minutes.

'Henry only works Tuesdays and Wednesdays.'

'That's nice for him.'

Wayne sighed heavily. 'Just do it, okay? Help me to help you. Besides, it won't take that long.'

8

'If I could begin by taking your date of birth,' the insurance agent said.

'Twenty-fifth of December, nineteen seventy-one.'

He raised his head. 'Christmas Day.'

I nodded.

Now people would generally say one of two things: 'Do you get twice the presents?' or 'I've always felt sorry for those whose birthday falls on that day.'

He actually said neither. 'I'm not really a big Christmas person,' he said, and smiled.

His smile was warm and sexy at the same time. And I was completely thrown off centre.

We were in the nutritionist's room. There wasn't enough work for a full-time nutritionist at the clinic, so Helen Miller split her time between four or five other set-ups around the North-west. This meant that her desk was always clear of the general detritus which accumulated on mine, as she moved her files and whatnot around with her. I had closed the blinds as the heat was fierce now on the west-facing windows, the sun having arced its way overhead, and the fan was on full blast.

My cheeks were hot and red.

Henry Peachey wore a polo shirt that was faded around the collar, along with olive-coloured canvas trousers that would be classed as jeans in certain establishments, therefore denying entry. I could smell his aftershave.

'Full name?' he asked.

'Rosalind Veronica Toovey.'

He typed fast. His face was relaxed, he was totally at ease, and I watched him unashamedly. The only men we ever got at the clinic (other than patients) were medical reps, and they were like androids. They would move amongst us, tricking us with their good skin, erect postures, spotless shirts and their keen, interested eyes. In the first moments of meeting them, you would rarely feel more engaged, more attuned, to another person. And then, suddenly, and without warning, their façade would fall.

The rep would reach into his briefcase, the spell would be broken and you would realize: *Ah, a salesman.*

The sharp banter of earlier cannot be continued as he is only able to sustain it for his opening pitch. At this point you might find yourself throwing in a joke to ease the discomfort. But you would be met with a dead, vacant stare. A stare that said: *Does not compute.*

Henry Peachey was not like that at all. And when he looked up and said, 'Place of birth?' his eyes locked on mine. It was as if he'd asked me to undress.

I was not imagining it, there was an immediate mutual attraction, and I stammered out, 'Kendal.' Following it with, 'How is it you don't like Christmas? Are you anti-religion?'

'I'm not against Christmas as such,' he replied, as he typed. 'It's more that we seem to have reached a point in society whereby we have to spend inordinate amounts of money just to show that we love each other. I suppose it's more that I don't like being told what to do by the advertising industry.' He looked up. 'Qualifications?'

'You want all of them?'

'The most recent is fine.'

'A BSc in Physiotherapy. I started an MSc but, you know how it is, life got in the way. Are you anti-birthdays then as well?'

There was mischief in his eyes, and he paused before speaking. I had to look away to catch my breath. 'I got a message from Apple a few weeks ago,' he said, 'saying I should treat my dad to an iPad for Father's Day. The sentiment being that if I really loved him, etc., etc., that I would fork out for one. Three hundred pounds on Father's Day? Crazy. Do you smoke?'

I hesitated. Then said, 'No,' firmly.

'Never?'

'Okay, sometimes when I'm drunk,' I admitted ashamedly. 'If I get a bit bored I do go off in search of a smoke. Not often, though.'

'That counts.'

'Really?'

He nodded grimly. 'We've had a couple of cases this year . . . the families of people who've been in car accidents have not been eligible for a payout upon their deaths. The policy holders claimed to be non-smokers, but because there was evidence of nicotine in the hair samples – well,' he said, and shrugged.

'That's a bit harsh.'

'The world we live in, I'm afraid. Occasional smoker,' he murmured, as he typed.

'What is this for exactly?' I asked. Wayne had told me, but I hadn't listened properly. Practice managers were always trying to get us to do irrelevant stuff; Magdalena the Austrian physio claimed it was simply to justify their existence. If I did half the things Wayne asked of me, I would see four less patients a day.

'It's to bring the public-liability insurance payments down.'

'But we're all insured up to a hundred million with the Chartered Society.'

'That's your individual insurance,' he explained. 'The company that owns this chain is also accountable if there's an accident with a patient. By doing these extra in-depth assessments of their staff, they are able to reduce their contributions. It's a bit like doing an advanced motoring course – you're considered a safer driver on completion, so your car insurance is reduced.'

I nodded.

'I forgot to ask, are you married, Miss Toovey?'

'Separated,' I answered too quickly. 'And it's Roz.'

He had such beautiful skin. And a mouth so soft that when I gazed at it I got a surge of longing all the way down to my—

'Okay, Roz,' he said, 'any operations, medical procedures?'

'I had a car crash four years ago and suffered a pneumothorax.'

'Pneumo—?'

'Apologies, I thought you were medical. A collapsed lung,' I said. 'I broke my arm, too, but I don't think that's relevant.'

'Any operations, any surgeries performed outside the UK?' he asked.

I paused.

He raised his head and looked at me with concern.

When I didn't continue he winced a little before saying, 'I'm sorry about this, but I need you to be fully transparent here. It's important.'

I exhaled. I didn't want him to know. Up until this point I'd been under a kind of lovely, hazy, dream-like spell where the real world was locked firmly behind the clinic door.

Now it was as if that spell was broken.

'I lost a baby whilst on holiday in Gran Canaria,' I said. 'I was twenty-six weeks pregnant – quite far along.'

He tilted his head and gave a sad smile. 'So sorry to hear that,' he said softly.

'It just wasn't meant to be,' I replied.

What I didn't say was that this was the beginning of the end for me and Winston. He had been screwing around. I was unaware of this at that point, but I knew we weren't what we once were. I failed to see what was right in front of my eyes and, somewhat delusionally, thought a new baby would bring us closer together again.

Silly, really, but in my defence I'm sure I was not the first woman to think a man would change his ways once he had a new baby in his arms. If women were to stop kidding themselves with that particular fantasy, I reckon the human race would die out pretty quickly.

Sadly for us, I started spotting blood when I boarded the plane at Manchester, and by the time we arrived in Gran Canaria it was clear something was wrong. We went straight to the hospital, whereupon I was hooked up to a saline drip, examined briefly and told I would be scanned first thing in the morning. They told Winston he could do nothing and, since I would be sharing a room with another woman, he was not welcome to stay.

At around ten that night there was a change of plan. A gruff obstetrician performed the scan, notifying me in her limited English, 'There is nothing.'

When I asked what she meant exactly, she said, 'No more baby,' and the assisting nurse informed me that I would be induced at seven in the morning, and would need to go through normal labour. I would have nothing to show at the end of it. Half consumed with grief, half terrified, I begged for a Caesarean. But I was denied.

I changed after that. I think I just gave up trying. I had neither the grit nor the energy and determination required to run our lives effectively and, ultimately, everything began to unravel. Winston slept around more. I didn't attend to our financial problems. And we lost it all.

'I'll need to take some blood from you,' Henry Peachey said now, apologetically.

'A blood test? Why?'

'Anything surgical performed outside the UK carries an increased AIDS risk. Did you have a D & C?'

I shook my head. 'Labour.'

'That's still classed as surgical, I'm afraid. The test is a thumb pinprick. I'll just need enough for . . .' His voice trailed off as he rummaged around in his briefcase, looking for, it transpired, two polythene envelopes, each containing a small plastic vial.

'Here we go,' he said.

He set about cleaning my thumb with an alcohol wipe. I was conscious of the drop in mood and Henry's careful way with me. The earlier playfulness between us was gone.

'Gives you quite a privileged insight into other people's lives, an assessment such as this,' I commented as he punctured my skin.

He squeezed my thumb and positioned the vial.

'As does your job,' he replied, screwing on the cap. 'You must see all sorts.'

He wasn't wrong. I carried more secrets from the folk around here than I cared to remember. It's an odd arrangement, the relationship between patient and therapist. Not really replicated anywhere else. I used to think it was the vulnerable condition of the patient – the fact that they were in pain, in a state of undress – which caused them, perhaps from a nervous response, to divulge. But I've since changed my mind. I don't think my patients ever really feel vulnerable. I work hard to put them at ease, to present myself as an affable, capable person who can be trusted to get on with the matter in hand with the minimum of fuss. So, no, it wasn't that. It was the closed door. The soundproof room. Something about knowing you wouldn't be overheard, about talking to a person who is bound by patient confidentiality, liberates people to unburden themselves in a way they can do in no other area of their life. Except, perhaps, with a priest. But who confides in clergy any more?

When Henry Peachey was finished he passed me a wad of cotton wool and told me to put pressure on the puncture hole. He was very efficient.

'Do you cover the whole of the north of England?' I asked, making small talk. 'Is that why you're only available around here on Tuesdays and Wednesdays?'

'No. I only work two days a week.'

I must have gaped at him then because he said, 'Is that odd?'

I raised my eyebrows. 'Lucky, more like. How on earth do you manage that? Do you have a trust fund or something?'

He laughed, the light returning to his eyes. 'No.'

'So how is that even possible?'

'It just requires a little self-control, and I suppose the determination not to buy into the common belief that hard work is a good thing in itself. That we should all be working our arses off just so we can spend more money on crap we don't need.'

'Ah,' I said, smirking, 'you're one of *those* people.'

He stopped and regarded me quizzically. 'One of what people?'

'You know – basket weavers, self-sufficiency. Do you have spider plants growing out of old work boots on your doorstep?'

'No.' He laughed.

'I used to go out with a guy like that. He spent so much time building wind turbines from bits of recycled tat, trying to live off the land, that he didn't have a penny to his name. It would have been far quicker and a lot less work just to go out and get a part-time job.'

He looked at me. Arched an eyebrow. Waited for it to dawn.

'Which is exactly what you have done,' I conceded. 'Oh, okay, good for you. Those of us with responsibilities have to earn a proper living.'

'Nice rant,' he said, passing me a plaster.

'Thanks.'

A moment passed.

'Did you go on to have children . . . I mean, after what happened to you abroad?' he asked gently.

'I already had one child. A son. But there were no more because we couldn't afford it.' And when he frowned, as though questioning my statement, I added, 'We didn't have travel insurance. My ex said he'd arranged it for the trip, but he hadn't. We had to pay for my stay in hospital by credit card, which I'm still paying off, along with a lot of other stuff. Anyway,' I said, more brightly, trying to change the tone again, 'in just a few short minutes you know everything there is to know about me.'

He held my gaze, and there it was again. The jolt of mutual attraction.

'Not everything, I hope,' Henry said.

9

THAT LATE-AFTERNOON George and I picnicked in the back garden. I grabbed a few bits and pieces from the village: a pot of reduced-priced hummus, some locally produced pastrami (with a same-day expiration date), a cucumber and a baguette that was down to ten pence because it had taken a bit of a bashing in transit.

From the outside looking in, you might think things were pretty much perfect. The heat of the day was on the wane. George was happy, pushing slices of peppered beef into his mouth, his school polo shirt covered with a combination of grass stains, spots of pollen and a formless yellow mark around the collar that I would later realize was sun cream.

I could hear Celia and Dennis over the fence pottering around in their garden, Dennis softly whistling the theme to *The Waltons*, Celia keeping up a low-level steady chatter, punctuating it occasionally with 'Dennis, start listening to me *now*,' when she needed to impart something crucial.

The holiday cottage on the other side was home for the week to a quiet, bookish, newly wedded couple from Billericay. They were the type of people who wore perpetual looks of apology simply for being there, which, I have to say, made a nice change from the boisterous, unrestrained groups of late. Last week, I had politely asked a gentleman in a Leeds United shirt if he wouldn't mind repositioning the barbecue a little further from the house so that the crosswind didn't carry the thick smoke right across our patio, and he'd responded by calling me a fucking lesbian.

I watched George chew, the straw-coloured light bouncing off his hair, the missing patch above his ear less apparent now. I really should neaten that up, I thought, though I knew I wouldn't. Petra said I was in the habit of holding on to George's babyish traits, which I thought of as endearing rather than babyish. She often chided me if I failed to correct George's speech, but I *liked* it when he said 'brang' instead of 'brought', when he told me he'd 'writted' me a letter, when he confused his Ps and Bs, asking me to pass the PBA glue. These things, I knew, would be gone all too soon, and I was in no hurry to see the back of them.

I pulled a daisy from the grass and passed it to George. He rolled his eyes. Too girly.

'What did you do at school today?'

'Science,' he said.

'Did you do an experiment?'

'We put white blocks into different bottles to see what would happen.'

'Different bottles of what?'

He shrugged. 'Milk and Coke and stuff.'

I remembered this experiment. It was used to demonstrate the rates of decay on teeth, the idea being kids would make wise choices when deciding what to drink. The thrust of it appeared to have been lost on George.

George finished chewing. He said, 'Finn Gibson-Morris says we would be rich, too, if we had a restaurant, like his parents.'

'Did he?' I replied flatly.

'He gets tons and tons of stuff, Mum. His parents have, like, so much money that they—'

'His parents don't own their own home. They rent.'

He frowned. 'Don't we rent?'

'Yes, but we're not going around making little kids feel shitty because they don't have much money.'

I'd heard a lot about Finn Gibson-Morris. Not just from George but from his little buddies at school. This line of conversation cropped up every week or so and, usually, I had the good grace to hold my tongue. Not today.

'You finished?' I asked George, motioning to his plate, and he nodded. 'Go and fetch yourself an apple then.'

I watched him go, his skinny, tanned legs, hyperextended at the back of the knee. He'd inherited his hypermobility from Winston. He could pull his thumb all the way back so that it touched his forearm – like Winston.

I've never known a man so agile, so flexible, as Winston Toovey. It was the reason we met. His left patella would frequently end up around the outside of his leg, and I would stabilize it so as to allow him to walk again. I managed two treatment sessions before I acquiesced and agreed to a date, disregarding the Chartered Society's directive advising against physio/patient relationships.

Turned out they were right about that, but not for the reasons they listed.

I watched George emerge from the back door, bite hard into the apple and wince. One of his milk teeth was stubbornly hanging on till the death and he would forget about it until it pained him. 'You okay?' I called out, and he took the fruit from his mouth, adjusted the tooth with his finger, pushing it back into the gum.

'Yep,' he said, as his attention was caught by a bold lamb that had strayed from the flock, closing in on the stone wall that bordered the back of the garden. Something about the way George gazed at it – kind of sad and reflective – made the breath catch in my throat. Perhaps he knew that the lamb would soon be removed, ready for slaughter, on account of being born the wrong gender. George made a flicking action, as if shaking the thought from his head, and asked if he could go next door to see Foxy.

'Don't get under Celia's feet,' I warned.

When he'd gone there was a knock at the front door and the postman stood there, holding out a letter. 'Special Delivery,' he said, 'I need a signature.'

I took the letter, thanked him, and went inside. Sitting on the back step, I opened it, knowing what it was.

An eviction notice. I had two weeks.

I was three months behind on the rent and I had absolutely no way of paying it.

In the end, all it had taken was one unexpected bill and my weekly budget had been blown. My car had needed two new tyres and a timing belt. The cost was close to eight hundred pounds. My dad had been nagging me for near to a year to change the timing belt, saying it was long overdue, that if I didn't have it done it would break and the car would be wrecked in the process. Eventually, I'd gone through with it, knowing I didn't have enough to pay the rent but, without the car, I couldn't get to work. Couple that with the winter heating bill that I'd been delayed in paying, and I was in a spiral of debt.

And now I was in real trouble.

And not the paltry kind of financial trouble that can be passed off with more credit cards, letters of regret and apology, with promises of minimum monthly payments.

I was about to lose the house.

I was about to lose everything.

10

'CAN WE TALK?'
'I hoped you'd call,' he said. 'I hoped . . .' Then Scott Elias paused, giving a small exhalation that sounded to me very much like relief. 'I really didn't expect to hear from you so soon,' he said.

'Listen,' I began. 'I'd rather not do this over the phone but, just so you know, my circumstances have changed. I would like to reconsider your offer, if it's still available.'

'Okay,' he said slowly. 'Perhaps we should meet. I mean, to discuss it further. I expect there are some things you'd like to clarify.'

I tried to keep my tone businesslike as I issued the instructions I'd decided upon earlier, but there was an unmistakable tremor in my voice. 'I've got a forty-five-minute lunch break,' I said. 'Come to the clinic. It'll be safer than meeting out in the open. We won't arouse suspicion if we act as though I've slotted you in as an extra patient.'

'That makes sense.'

'We'll be able to talk undisturbed.'

'What time should I be there?'

'One fifteen,' I said. 'Try not to be late.'

'I'm never late.'

When I cut the call I placed the phone down on the desk with a trembling hand. Then I waited a moment before calling in the next patient to observe myself in this act of treachery. I rose and faced the mirror. I had the hardened, pinched look of a woman who, at first, you would presume to be vexed but, on closer inspection, would realize was terrified.

Throughout the night I'd wrestled with the idea of Scott's proposal.

Would I? Wouldn't I?

Could I? How *could* I?

I came to no clear conclusions.

When I let my thoughts run free, it seemed almost easy. Sleep with a man and my monetary problems could be solved.

I kept trying to convince myself I'd had to do worse things – my physiotherapy training, for one.

Assisting stroke victims to the bathroom, some of them over six feet tall, heavy and with one side paralysed so it could feel like you were trying to lift a cadaver, required more in the way of acting, more joviality in the face of dismayed horror than would a night spent with Scott Elias.

When I thought about it in those terms, I had no doubt I could do it.

My doubts came when I thought about the risks involved: the risk of being found out; the risk of destroying Nadine – his wife, my sister's friend. Not to mention the fact that I had made a promise to myself that I would never, ever go near another woman's husband. Not after the devastation wreaked by Winston. When I thought about all that, I was absolutely certain I could *not* do it.

But now the call was made.

And the remainder of the morning was spent on autopilot. If you asked me to recall one conversation, one patient's viewpoint on the news of the day, I wouldn't be able to. I avoided Wayne. At one point he knocked on my door when I was between patients, bringing me a coffee. He placed the cup on my desk and asked if

I was okay. Asked if there was anything he could do to help, as I seemed unsettled about something this morning and he was always there for me. I knew that, right? It was sweet of him, but I told him I was fine, told him I appreciated his concern. Whether I duped him or not, I couldn't say, but he left without speaking, except to inform me that my next patient had nipped outside to make a phone call to his daughter's school, should I be wondering where he was.

By the time the clock edged close to one fifteen I was soaked with sweat and probably not in the best state to receive the man who was on his way over to discuss having sex with me for money.

He knocked on the door firmly, avoiding the reception area, and said, 'Thanks for fitting me in at the last minute,' as I opened the door.

I didn't reply. I should have, if only for Wayne's benefit, but my throat was so parched the most I could do was nod and swallow, ushering him in with a wave of the hand.

As he got himself seated I seemed to find my resolve and gathered myself. 'How are you?' I asked him. 'Are you well?'

He lifted his elbow a few inches, bending and straightening his arm repeatedly. 'It's so much better,' he said. 'You really do work miracles.'

I brushed it off. 'It's not a difficult thing to treat. I'm not so successful with frozen shoulders and gout; they take a lot longer. It just depends on the problem, really, because if you've got someone who is—'

I stopped.

'I'm babbling,' I said.

'You're nervous,' he replied. 'So am I. Doesn't really matter if we babble for a bit, does it?'

'I suppose not.'

'Frozen shoulders . . . you were saying?'

I shook my head. 'It's irrelevant.' Conscious of how much time we had available, and indeed, what we had to cover, I started again. 'Let's stick with what you came here to talk about, because I'm not certain of any of this yet. I've not decided that I definitely want to go through with it. It's just that I find myself in a bit of a mess financially, and so—' I looked up. Scott was watching me intently, but with an open face, no hint of judgement.

'Actually, it's more than a bit of a mess,' I admitted, dropping my gaze. 'I'm being evicted from my home. That's why I'm doing this, that's why I agreed to meet.'

'You don't have to explain,' he said.

'I think I *need* to explain. I don't want you to think—'

'I don't think anything. I know who you are. I *like* who you are. And I approached *you*, remember. I'm not concerned with what you think of my motivation, and you shouldn't be concerned with what I think of yours. This is a business transaction, that's all.'

'A business transaction,' I repeated.

'That's how you should think of it.'

I raised my eyebrows.

'It might make it easier if you think of it in those terms,' he said gently.

'Okay, but what *is* your motivation for doing this . . . with me?' I asked. 'Because it isn't exactly what you'd class as an ordinary business proposition.'

'I like you and I want to help. If you do decide you want to pursue this further, then perhaps we'll talk about that, but at another time. Just as I'm not asking you to account for your reasons, I would ask that you extend me the same courtesy.'

I nodded. 'Seems reasonable.'

'Perhaps, rather than the *whys*, we should think about discussing how you want to go about this. And there is of course the matter of your fee.'

I gave a nervous laugh. 'My fee,' I echoed back.

Naturally, I'd thought about this, thought about it over and over, totting up numbers in my head, apportioning out money to my landlord, the credit card company, the council tax arrears. But now, saying it out loud, it seemed almost comical, and all at once crass and ugly, to the extent that I began to lose my nerve.

'What would you expect me to do?' I asked quietly.

'Nothing weird, if that's what's worrying you.'

I let go of the air held inside my lungs.

'That's a relief.'

He spread his hands wide in a gesture that indicated he came in peace, he meant no harm. 'It's simple,' he said, 'there is nothing weird about me. All I want is a night with you.'

'The whole night?'

'Would that be a problem?'

'Er, no,' I stammered. 'No, I don't think so. Obviously, there's George to consider . . .'

'Would there be a way to arrange some cover, a sitter perhaps?'

'I think so.'

He nodded before moving on. 'The other thing to mention at this stage is that of course this arrangement would require complete discretion,' and he paused. With his eyes fixed on mine, gauging my reaction, he said, 'I have as much to lose as you, Roz, probably more, in fact. It's absolutely imperative that this remains between us. Only us.'

Affronted, I replied, 'Well, I certainly wasn't planning on telling anyone.'

He smiled. 'Sorry,' he said, 'sorry. I assumed it went without saying but, I don't know, I suppose I had to be sure. Apologies.'

'What exactly would you want me to do?' I asked again, my tone firmer this time. More sure of myself.

When I decided on this meeting earlier, this was the one thing

I had to be inflexible on, or else I couldn't go through with it. Any red flags at this stage and I would back out. I couldn't chance it. I expected a certain amount of kinkiness, otherwise why not just sleep with your wife? But I needed to know the boundaries, the clear boundaries, before entering into this business transaction – as Scott referred to it.

'Expect?' he said. 'Nothing that you're not comfortable with. I'm not expecting you to turn into something you're not, that's not what this is about.'

I raised my eyebrows and waited for him to go on.

'I certainly don't expect you to be some sort of dominatrix,' he said, shaking his head. 'I don't know what it is that blokes go in for nowadays, what fetishes they have. Whatever it is, that's not me. In straightforward terms, I would like a night with an attractive woman. A woman who could be herself and hopefully feel relaxed in my company. I really hope that woman can be you, Roz.'

He hesitated.

'I find you wildly attractive,' he said softly, 'the curve of your body, the way you laugh without pretence. I think about you when I shouldn't. I think about what it would be like to be next to you.'

Then he seemed to gather himself.

'And so if you do decide yes,' he said, once again more formal, 'then I don't see any reason why this can't work. We're both sensible adults, after all.'

'Just to be clear, though, Scott, this does involve sex, doesn't it?'

He smiled at my candour. 'Yes,' he said. 'Yes, Roz Toovey, this is very much about sex.'

'Right,' I said.

'And with regards to your fee . . . I thought four thousand pounds would be a reasonable amount. For the night.'

'Right,' I said again.

Then he stood.

'Okay,' he said, and held out his hand, giving mine a firm shake, 'if that's all in accordance with what you had in mind, might I suggest a date?'

I nodded.

'This is probably a little soon, but I was thinking, if it's possible, then tomorrow evening would work for me, I don't know if—'

I lifted my palm to silence him.

I said, 'I'll see what I can do.'

11

'JESUS CHRIST, WINSTON, when do I ever ask you for anything?'
We were in my ex-husband's mother's kitchen. It was around 6 p.m. and Winston had a can of WD-40 in his hand and was shaking it back and forth, back and forth, before applying it to the chain of his BMX, which was upturned on top of the kitchen table.

'I never ask you, and the one time, *the one bloody time,*' I said.

'What's so important that you need to stay away all night?'

'Do I quiz you on what you do?'

He shrugged. 'I'd tell you if you did. What about your sister, can't she do it?'

'She's in New York with Vince.'

Winston cast me a sideways glance. I probably don't need to mention that Winston and Petra never really saw eye to eye – and this was way before Winston's eye wandered off to look at lots of other women.

'What's she doing there?' he said.

'She's forty.'

'And?'

I sighed out heavily. 'It's what people do, Winston. What normal people do to celebrate the big milestones.'

'Oh,' he said, and nodded thoughtfully, as though learning this fact for the first time.

Winston didn't really get celebrations. For my thirtieth

birthday, he took me on a night out in Kendal. When I say 'night out', I mean a pub crawl – Winston never saw the attraction in spending a day's wage on a restaurant meal, not when it could be better spent on beer. At closing time we stumbled towards the taxi rank and, finding around thirty people in the queue, Winston kept on walking until he got to a kebab house.

He dialled the phone number displayed in the window and requested two large doners (extra chilli, no onion) for home delivery. When the clapped-out van drove up in front of the shop minutes later, Winston grabbed me by the hand and pulled me across the street, slipping the delivery guy a fiver. Riding home amongst pizza boxes and an odd assortment of gardening equipment (the driver's day job, it would appear), I fell in love with Winston Toovey.

Petra said Winston was a child trapped inside a man's body. She said he had no concept of the adult world and what it meant to put other people's needs before his own. Which I couldn't really argue with, given the state he'd left us in. But Winston's big problem – his real problem, in my mind – was that he had no understanding of delayed gratification. When Winston wanted something, he went and got it. Even if he was broke he would always find a way.

The BMX that was in front of me was a new toy. Winston was forty-three years old, living with his mother, no job to speak of, and what was he doing? Riding BMXs.

Winston thought Petra was a martyr. He said she liked to make life hard for herself, and therefore everyone else in the process. He glanced my way. 'New York, then,' he said.

'Yes.'

'Thought Petra would have preferred two weeks all inclusive on a crucifix.'

I ignored him.

'Is Vince all right?' he asked.

I nodded.

'I've not seen him around in a while.'

'Vince is fine, Winston,' I replied.

'Poor sod,' he said.

This was how Winston referred to Petra's husband: 'Vince, the Poor Sod'. Like he had some grave illness or had suffered a terrible tragedy. When Winston and I were a couple I would have to explain to people, if Vince, the Poor Sod, cropped up in conversation, that Vince was actually in good health, had nothing wrong with him, in fact, other than being the long-suffering husband of Petra.

'Winston,' I said to him now, sharply, 'will you look after your son or not?'

'I *am* looking after my son this coming weekend. As per our arrangement. But tomorrow night I have plans. I might come home, I might not. I don't know yet.'

'Who are you seeing? Some teenager?'

He put the can down. 'Who are *you* seeing, Roz?'

'No one. I'm not seeing anyone. You know I'm not. But if I were to see someone, don't think you could go and—'

'Roz,' he said, smiling, 'chill. You can see who you like as far as I'm concerned. In fact, it'd do you good to get a release. It might get you off my back for a bit.'

'Piss off, Winston.'

He laughed and began spinning the pedals of the bike backwards, leaning in to check the chain was running smoothly. 'I love it when you talk sexy, Roz. Swear at me again, it reminds me of when we used to have great sex after a big row. Do you remember that time when we were at Aira Force, the waterfall . . .'

His words trailed off as his expression turned wistful.

'Oh, for God's sake,' I said, grabbing my bag and shouting for George to come through from where he was watching television in the front room.

'Roz, Roz,' Winston said, reaching out, putting his hand on my shoulder. 'I'm just pulling your leg. ''Course I'll do it. Just wanted to see you sweat a bit.'

I slapped his hand away and looked at him. 'You're such a bloody child sometimes.'

'Don't be mad.'

'*You* make me mad. Christ,' I whispered, and closed my eyes.

Turning away from him, I placed both hands on the kitchen work surface and took a steadying breath. In front of me there was a neat row of vegetables. One large onion, two carrots, a stick of celery and six large scrubbed potatoes. Thursdays, I thought, picturing Winston's mother, Dylis, in her wipeable apron and Scholl sandals. Thursdays meant shepherd's pie, regardless of the weather, and Dylis had arranged her ingredients ready to cook for the following day. This was the simplicity of Dylis's life.

I turned around. 'I'm under a lot of pressure at the moment,' I told Winston finally.

'You put yourself under a lot of pressure. Anyway,' he said, just as George came in, 'are you going to tell me where you're going or not?'

I began busying myself, rummaging about in my bag, pretending to locate my car keys. 'Like I said, it's a work thing.'

I raised my head and Winston was regarding me sceptically.

'Oh yeah,' he said. 'A work thing.'

He took a pound coin from the pocket of his jeans, before passing it over to George.

'Be a good lad for your mum,' he told him.

A word of caution: should you ever find yourself in the same position as me, do not read up on the subject of escorts and escort agencies in preparation.

You will panic.

Granted, Belle de Jour's *The Intimate Adventures of a London*

Call Girl was probably not the best place to start, but it was the only book stocked by W. H. Smith in Windermere that was even vaguely connected with the subject. I had read only as far as chapter three before realizing what was 'normal' for me certainly didn't apply to large chunks of the population. I closed the book feeling pretty grubby, glad I didn't get a copy from the library, hoping that when Scott Elias said he wanted 'nothing weird' he actually meant it, and then I tried to get some sleep.

When I woke, it was with the deepest sense of dread.

Dread that I had to go through with this thing that I desperately did not want to do.

Petra got migraines when she found herself not looking forward to something. Not that dread had ever been openly acknowledged as the cause. She took a cocktail of medication to prevent attacks, which, according to her, came about from changes in atmospheric pressure, hormone fluctuations and, occasionally, preservatives in pork products. Invariably, though, they tended to coincide with trips to see Vince's mother at her nursing home in Wigan and school governors' meetings, where, as secretary, she was required to take down the minutes, and those things had a habit of running on and on.

I sat up and swung my legs out the bed. A layer of dust had collected along the skirting board.

Hanging down from beneath the radiator there were three cobwebbed clumps. The house badly needed attention.

From the open window I heard a door close and, a moment later, the soft whine of Celia's gate, followed by an engine turning over. Foxy's morning walk.

Like a lot of older folk, Dennis liked to reverse his car out ready for its outing, a half-hour or so before they actually planned to leave. As though the car itself needed a small preparatory run before being fully ready to be driven any real distance.

I got up and walked to the window. Watched as Dennis's Rover crept away quietly and disappeared out of sight. Such a gentle soul, Dennis. In contrast to Celia, who, when I'd gone around to collect George on Tuesday evening was blowing hard on a refereeing whistle straight into her mobile phone.

I'd noticed the whistle on a ribbon around her neck and assumed it was for retrieving Foxy if she strayed too far. Forgetting, of course, that Foxy was reluctant to walk, never mind stray. When I'd shot Celia a questioning look she informed me it was her way of dealing with nuisance telesales callers.

'Isn't that a little brutal?' I asked. 'I mean, they're wearing headsets, Celia.'

'Not at all. They are so insistent . . . not to mention *rude*. It's no less than they deserve,' she said. Then she went on to tell me how George had been walking Foxy and how Foxy *positively pranced* along for him. Hardly pulling on the lead at all, she said.

I walked away from the window and stood at the mirror.

The wrong side of forty. I lifted my right hand and gave a slow wave, watching as the flesh of the tricep swung methodically, as though unattached. This was a new development, the first deterioration I'd noticed as my body marched towards middle age. I was still strong. I had good upper body shape and a lean, hard musculature that came from the job, and yet . . .

And I'd started smiling at dogs recently. Which was definitely a sign of getting older.

We had arranged to meet north of Lancaster at a country inn not far from the motorway exit. It was an hour's journey from home, which I agreed with Scott Elias was ample, and it served the expensive gastro-pub-type fare at silly enough prices to put off the majority of people we might bump into. It was the kind of place that seemed purpose-built for clandestine couples; it offered a refined, elegant environment, with well-trained staff avoiding the usual interrogation a tourist would need to feel properly welcomed: *Where have you travelled from?*

Have you stayed with us before? Was the M6 truly awful today?

The difficulty came in knowing what to wear. I expected Scott wanted me to dress like a woman. But what *did* one wear for dinner at a country inn, midweek, in rural Lancashire?

Tricky.

This wasn't a date. And I found myself with the uneasy sensation of wanting to appear presentable for the job which I was employed to do, whilst at the same time feeling hugely self-conscious at the prospect of looking sexy for a man who, under normal circumstances, I wouldn't sleep with.

I opened my wardrobe and waited for inspiration. On the far right was a floaty, chiffon dress from Coast covered in tea roses that I wore for a wedding last year.

Too weddingy. And perhaps a tad virginal.

Next to it was my Christmas-party staple: a wraparound black dress that was cut too low in the front. I would pull it up high early in the evening, pull it lower nearer to midnight – depending on how much I'd had to drink and who was around.

Then there were three identical dresses, Petra's cast-offs and what I would describe as conservative. With the right underwear, though, they could be made to look a little sexy. Petra bought these dresses last year and she'd since lost weight, claiming they now buried her, and I was more than happy to give them a home, unoffended by her comment, because *Never look a gift horse,* and so on.

I decided on the vivid green version and slipped it on quickly to check there were no loose threads, no ugly creases across the tummy or stains I'd failed to notice when I'd last taken it off. I wouldn't have a great deal of time after work to prepare and so wanted to have this side of things well organized ahead of schedule.

It looked good.

Attractive, not slutty, and I could easily pass for a company

CEO, the type of woman who refused to dress like a man just because of her position.

Satisfied with the choice, I went to get George his Weetabix and sort out his packed lunch. We were down to the dregs again: slightly stale bread and an unbranded cream cheese that had the advantage of staying free from mould for around a month. I cut the crusts off to perk up the sandwich and examined a banana which, if I were a different kind of woman, with a different life, would declare was fit only to make banana bread with. I tossed the lot into a Bargain Booze plastic bag, along with George's water bottle, which was beginning to smell of damp dishcloth around the rim.

Poor kid.

Tying it up, I found myself murmuring that this would all change soon. This time next week, after my landlord was paid, there would be enough money in my account to afford a Tesco's home delivery, and George could have sushi for his lunch if he so wished.

This time next week things would be ticking over again and my evening with Scott would be on its way to becoming a memory.

12

'Good evening,' I said. 'I'm here to meet a resident, Scott Elias. Could you tell me if he's checked in yet?'

I hadn't spotted Scott's Ferrari in the car park, so expected he was running late.

'Mr Elias is waiting for you in the bar area. I'll show you through. Would you like to leave your overnight bag here, and I'll arrange to have it taken to your room?'

'Thank you, yes,' I replied.

I followed the young man into a pleasant, spacious hallway, dotted with antique occasional tables and freshly upholstered French dining chairs, before he stopped and gestured towards a doorway on the right.

He smiled. 'Just through here,' he said. 'Enjoy your evening.'

The furniture was cleverly arranged to give rise to a number of distinct spaces to afford privacy. There were no large sofas. Instead, highly polished maple coffee tables were encircled by armchairs of differing designs, all carefully chosen to blend with the muted sage and ivory decor.

As I entered the room further, I became aware of Scott rising from his seat at the far end and smiling my way. I passed a couple in their early sixties who were reading – she a copy of David Hockney's *A Bigger Picture* and he a biography of the jockey A. P. McCoy. She glanced up as I came their way and then immediately down towards my shoes, I assumed to see what I'd

paired with the green dress. Judging by her small smile of satisfaction, it appeared that the black patent pumps were entirely the
wrong choice.

'Roz,' said Scott, taking my hands and kissing me on both
cheeks, 'so good to see you.'

He smelled lemon fresh and had taken a little sun since I'd
seen him yesterday. It suited him: he looked younger, healthy.

There was an open briefcase on the coffee table and two stacks
of papers to the side.

'Nice ruse,' I said quietly, nodding to the briefcase. Scott had
skilfully arranged things to give the impression of a business
meeting.

'You look stunning,' he said. 'What can I get you to drink?'

'Oh – anything – anything,' I stammered. 'I'll have anything
wet.'

'I'm drinking red. But if you'd prefer some fizz, or how about
a cocktail?'

'Red's great.'

'It's really good to see you,' he said again, holding my gaze for
a moment too long before gesturing towards the bartender.

We settled into our seats. Nervous, I crossed my legs one way,
and then the other. Not in a Sharon Stone way, since I was wearing
underwear. Underwear that had a habit of misbehaving, forcing
me to wriggle in the chair.

'I didn't see your car,' I said.

'No, I'm in my other.' He dropped his voice. 'The Ferrari's not
great when my sciatica flares up, to be honest.'

I tried to smile. 'That's why the football players all switched to
Range Rovers.'

'Because of sciatica?' he said, surprised. 'They're too young,
surely?'

'If you drive with your knees higher than your hips, it irritates
the nerve root, sending the hamstring muscles into spasm. Which

means they're more liable to tear when suddenly stretched.'

'Ah,' he said as my glass arrived. 'Anyway, you don't want to talk shop, I'm sure. How was your day?'

'Hot. Tedious. Yours?'

'The same.' He poured, passed me the glass and raised his own. 'To you,' he said, and waited as I lifted the glass to my lips.

We were presented with the menus and guided through the chef's recommendations of the day by the maître d', an affable chap who made an impression on account of his immense bulk. It occurred to me as he and Scott went on to talk of vintages and regions, the *terroir* of some obscure valley in the Languedoc region of France, that it was a position usually held by a very thin person.

I declined the option of a starter and went for John Dory with clams for the main course. Under normal circumstances, I would choose something slow cooked and indulgent – roasted pork belly with a port wine jus – something I would never cook for myself at home. But this was work. And I was nervous. And, as I mentioned earlier, Scott was in good shape. The night could turn athletic on a sixpence, and I would be sure to regret a heavy stomach.

This was what was going through my head when Scott leaned in and whispered, 'You're frowning. Relax.'

'I've never done this before.'

'It doesn't mean we can't enjoy the evening. I asked you here because I want you to have a good time, I don't want you to be on edge.'

I dropped my head.

'Do you regret coming?' he asked.

And I hesitated.

Reaching out, he touched the skin of my throat with his middle finger. His manner was lazy, as though he'd done this action a thousand times before, and I found myself casting around the room, furtively, as though he'd performed something terribly illicit. 'I don't regret it for a second,' he said, and then our table was ready.

Though the British countryside was enjoying another hot summer evening, the light inside the dining room was subdued and dim. Dark, heavy curtains lined the windows and the walls were covered in a chocolate, hessian-type of wallpaper, which gave the room an elegant, sultry feel.

For no reason other than I was programmed to do so (every twenty minutes), my thoughts turned to George. Instinctively, I opened my handbag to check for the red warning flash of my mobile.

'All okay?' Scott asked as we were seated, and I nodded.

'No disasters to report.'

I went to speak again and thought better of it, closing my mouth.

'You were going to say something?' he said.

'It's not important.'

'You were going to tell me about your son.'

It was true. I was.

'Go ahead, please,' he urged.

So I rambled on for a while about nothing in particular, all the while Scott regarding me with a keen interest, as if what I had to say was both enlightening and humorous, neither of which was accurate. I'd been around enough people to know that divorced parents of an only child can talk about the kid until hell freezes over if allowed to. Parents of three or four children barely mention them. I made a concerted effort not to bore people about George and had decided before the start of this evening that the whole point of it was to let Scott talk about himself. He wasn't paying to hear about me.

Except now it seemed as though he was.

He poured more wine and, when I'd got to the end of my anecdote, I leaned forward, rested my chin on top of my hands.

'Tell me why we're here,' I said bluntly.

He laughed, replying with, 'I thought I'd made that clear.'

I shook my head. 'I want to know why. Why me? Why like this?'

And he shrugged.

'Scott,' I said in a forced whisper, 'there are plenty of options available for a man in your position. I mean, if we're going to get real about it, I'm quite sure there are women – plenty of women – you come across in your everyday life, who would be willing to become your mistress for free.'

'For free?' he answered, his tone cynical. Meaning nothing was for free, as far as he was concerned.

'Okay, maybe not for free,' I said. 'But you get my drift. You could throw in the odd mini break, and a nice necklace now and again, and you would get what you needed out of it.'

I raised my glass to my lips, studying his face. His expression was neutral, but there was a playful quality in his eyes and I was unable to hold his gaze. It was the first time I would sense that there was more to Scott, more going on beneath the surface than he was ready to reveal.

'Mistresses don't quite work out like that,' he said.

'No?'

'They want more. They always want the whole package. Sure, they start off saying what it is that you want to hear. They don't want a relationship, casual meet-ups suit them fine, and so on and so forth. But these women want romancing, they want two or three dinners before they'll even entertain the idea of . . .'

He paused. Tilted his head to one side to let me work out the rest for myself.

'I can see that could take some time,' I said.

He leaned in. 'Basically, it becomes hard work. And once the initial sex is out of the way, they want more. They're not happy with being on the sidelines, even though they protest it's not like that. They sulk because they want to take Nadine's place. And I can understand it, I really can. But I just don't need the earache, frankly.'

'Well, what about the more straightforward approach?' I suggested.

'You mean an escort?'

'Yes. Why go to all this trouble, all this expense,' I said, making a sweeping motion with my hand, 'for a normal person like me? Christ, I'm no expert in this stuff, Scott. I might not be able to give you what you're expecting.'

A smile played across his lips as he weighed his response. The room was now filling with diners, couples pausing as they entered the room directly from the garden, their eyes adjusting to the reduced light. Men in pressed short-sleeved shirts, their foreheads shiny from the sun, waited for their partners before proceeding. The women tottered in on platform heels, carrying champagne flutes, each with a rosy blush developing at the top of their cleavage.

Scott placed both palms flat on the tablecloth on either side of the cutlery, and tapped his fingers twice.

Unusually, he seemed reluctant to talk. After a minute, he said, 'I have explored the other options available in the past and without going into too much detail, I can tell you they were not for me. Each has its own drawbacks.'

'What about Nadine?' I asked softly.

'What about her?'

'Do you still love her?'

His eyes widened. 'Of course,' he said. 'Of course I love her.'

'But . . . ?' And then a thought occurred. 'Scott,' I said quickly, panicked, 'she doesn't know about this, does she?'

He shook his head in bafflement, as if to say, *Why would you ask such a thing?*

'Nadine doesn't know,' he said. 'Nadine will never know. This is not some game, Roz.'

'Then what is it?'

He reached for his wine and downed the remainder from his glass. 'Okay,' he said, 'I'll do my best to explain. I love Nadine. I will always love her. We have a good life together. It's just—'

'She doesn't understand you?'

'No,' he said. 'It's not that.'

'She doesn't enjoy the physical side of the relationship any more?'

He gave an awkward laugh. 'Not so much, no. But that's not it either.'

I sat back in my chair. 'Oh,' I said quietly.

The food arrived and the waiter made a big show of listing all the ingredients in each dish. I felt impatient, wanting to interrupt him and say, 'Yes, *I remember what I ordered*, thank you.' He was doing that thing they do on *MasterChef*, trying to make the food sound more upmarket, saying he was serving me *a* fillet of John Dory on *a* potato rosti, with *a* artichoke and clam . . .

A artichoke.

When did people lose the ability to speak?

I rolled my eyes at Scott as the waiter rattled off his list of ingredients, and Scott smiled. With the mood lightened, I said, 'You don't need to explain further. I didn't mean to pry. I suppose I just needed clarification.'

'That I'm not a lunatic?'

I nodded. 'I think I assumed that the men who pay for this kind of thing are looking for a different experience. Something they cannot get from their wives.'

'You mean paying entitles them to do whatever they like to a woman?'

'Yes.'

'I'm not looking to dominate or demean,' he said. 'Nadine and I have lost our connection, that's all. We still have a sex life, but there's no intimacy, no real feeling there. And I miss it. Just as it's necessary for some men to see an escort as a means of release, a means of getting rid of their stress, for me it's the opposite. I need physical love to function and, for a variety of reasons, I cannot get it from Nadine any longer.'

'But why me? Why all night?'

'You mean as opposed to a professional?'

'Yes.'

'Simple. You're exactly what I think a woman should be. You're sexy without trying, you exude a kind of warmth that's missing from most women. And with regards to a professional, I don't want to be where another man has been.'

I coughed, inhaling a small amount of wine. 'I'm no virgin, Scott.'

'No,' he said, smiling, 'you're not. But I don't want to be where another man has been just *hours* beforehand. It feels unclean. It really is a conveyor belt. That's not for me. And I don't mean to sound boastful when I say this, but I've reached a stage in my life when I can afford to do it my way. I can afford to have the experience as I want it. Real intimacy with a real woman.'

The full weight of his gaze upon me, he leaned back in his chair. 'In short,' he said, 'I can afford to have you, Roz.'

13

THERE IS A memory I have of watching the film *Indecent Proposal*. A gaggle of us who were home from university for the spring bank holiday went to the Royalty Cinema in Bowness. It's one of those quaint old cinemas that are becoming obsolete. Back in 1993 it had just a single screen and the girl who issued the tickets also showed you to your seat, as well as appearing with a tray of ice creams (hung by a strap around her neck) as the film was about to start. She would stand at the front, self-consciously waiting for people to approach, valiantly ignoring the sweet wrappers aimed at her from the balcony above.

Indecent Proposal was the one film that we came out really talking about. As a group, we were split right down the middle on the would you?/wouldn't you? issue.

Would you spend one night with Robert Redford in exchange for a million dollars?

Those of us who were naive and highly principled at that age exited saying, 'Definitely not. You can't *buy* love.' (But then we all quickly agreed that Demi Moore's black strappy dress was *amazing*. To die for, in fact. And who knew what you'd do if someone presented you with such an item? Sure, Robert Redford was getting on in years by then, but that dress was *so* nice.

How uncomplicated our lives were. Silly girls, each of us certain we were going to set the world on fire and that, if we didn't manage it for some reason, there was still a chance a good-looking guy would come to our rescue, because that's what happened in the movies.

Before leaving for my assignation with Scott, I'd stood in my underwear, examining my reflection, wondering if it was really possible for a man to pay to have sex with a normal woman like me. I had big doubts. Physically, I was no horrorbag but I was a long way from the images on the front of the lads' mags, a long way from the quintessential male fantasy. Now, though, from what Scott had just said, and the fervour with which his small speech was delivered, it appeared that I was wrong. Scott was more than willing to pay for a normal woman like me. Normal was exactly what he craved and couldn't find.

But could *I* actually do it?

Could I lie next to a man, let him inside me? For money?

I thought about the past couple of years since Winston and I had parted. There had been drunken sex, sex with a couple of sad fellows whom I went to bed with because I felt sorry for them. There'd been that sex with Winston that I pretended didn't happen but Winston liked to bring up every time I asked him for money. And there'd been sex with a guy I didn't really like, but it did my ego some good on account of him being younger and attractive and the school football coach. Every woman over thirty would flick her hair excessively in his presence. All this to say that I had enjoyed sex with each of these men, despite none of it being perfect, or hearts and flowers, so yes, I thought, I could go through with it.

Except now I was nervous.

Facing Scott Elias, I realized that this wasn't drunken, no-strings sex. This was an intelligent, articulate man who expected *an experience*. As we pushed our chairs away from the table, and he took my arm, gently, guiding me away from the other diners, I just hoped to hell I could give it to him. Because the spark of attraction I would normally feel before going to bed with a man had just diminished. Sure, I was flattered by his words, because, who wouldn't be? It was nice to be talked about in that way. And I have to admit when I first met Scott there was a real magnetism between us. But the way he was so sure of himself just now, the way he assumed that money could buy whatever he liked, whatever he wanted, had the effect on me of making him somewhat *un*desirable. He'd crossed a line few people would ever think of crossing and his remarks about buying me had left a sour taste in my mouth.

Even though he was just being honest. Even though I was here for that very reason – to be bought.

So I hoped I could go through with what I'd signed up for. Because in less than two weeks I would be evicted if I didn't do *something*. And, up to now, praying for a miracle hadn't helped at all, so the way I saw it, this was the only chance I had.

'Would you like another drink at the bar?' Scott asked, and though I didn't, I accepted, deciding that another drink would take the edge off my nerves and also delay things a little. I ordered a gin and tonic. I did have to go to work the following day, after all, and I was always better in the morning after a long drink rather than wine. It was only as we were well into a conversation about Scott's electronics business and how he was forever faced with losing clerical staff for weeks at a time due to repetitive strain injury and other such work-related illnesses that I noticed I was beginning to drift a little, not really concentrating on his words. So I excused myself and headed to the Ladies to splash some water on my face.

Passing the cloakroom, my attention was caught by a man sitting at the small second bar just a short distance from the reception area.

It was the insurance agent who'd taken blood from me. He wore a white shirt, a tie was loosened at his throat and he'd rolled up his sleeves on account of the heat. He sat side on, next to a heavy-set man whose bulk appeared too much for the stool and they were both drinking pints of bitter.

My heart stuttered.

On realizing who he was I must have blanched, or else my expression froze, because he smiled at me before tilting the rim of his glass my way. It was an almost imperceptible gesture – his companion didn't turn around to look – and then he continued talking happily, taking a handful of whatever snack had been placed on the bar.

My pulse thumped in my throat as I hurried to the Ladies. I hadn't expected to bump into anyone I knew, least of all him, and the riskiness of what I was doing suddenly hit home.

When I returned, Scott asked, 'Are you okay? You've gone a little pale.'

'What? Oh, no, I'm fine. I was thinking I could probably do with freshening up a little before . . . What I mean is,' I stammered, because hadn't I just done exactly that? 'What I mean is, I didn't get a chance to unpack my things on arriving.'

'No problem,' he said, realizing it was probably nerves making me so jumpy, 'I'm happy to remain down here. Whatever you need to feel comfortable.'

He reached out and stroked his thumb along the back of my hand.

I stared at it, fixated. The urge to check over my shoulder was overwhelming, but I kept my eyes downcast.

'Roz?' Scott asked. 'You're sure you're okay? Your hand is shaking.'

'Is it?' I pulled it away. I smiled at Scott and started to stand. 'Give me fifteen minutes?'

Walking towards the staircase, I stole a look across to the second bar. The insurance agent was standing now, ready to leave, laughing as his drinking partner made big expansive gestures with his hands, as though waving in aircraft. I got the impression it was forced laughter. Perhaps he, like me, was here on business.

He glanced over and, when he saw I was watching, he winked.

Embarrassed, I hurried away.

Cards on the table: the night was not what I expected.

Money changes everything, that much I know for sure. If you were to speak to a random selection of my patients they would report that Roz Toovey physiotherapist was kind, attentive, a remarkably good listener, non-judgemental and always happy to listen if someone needed a good moan or to give out advice if asked.

Of course, I wasn't always those things. I was being *paid* to be those things. Think about it, when was the last time you said exactly what you were thinking to your boss? Or to anyone at work, for that matter?

When you're self-employed, the customers are your bosses. If you don't give them what they want, you don't get paid. Simple as that. And even though I was no longer self-employed, I was very much aware that if I didn't perform well as a clinician, if I didn't give the patients exactly what they expected, I would be replaced. And so I gave my best physical self: performing back-breaking lifting and manoeuvring, bending over for extended periods, my thumbs losing their feeling from the unremitting pressure put through them. I gave my best empathetic self: listening to patients' worries, concerns about their lives, their children's lives, their money worries, their health issues. I gave my best educational self: repeating facts about healing, posture, about the links between stress and myofascial pain, facts that I'd been reciting all day, every day, year in, year out. And I gave my best in merriment and entertainment, acting as though the patients were the funniest, wittiest, most enjoyable people in the world to spend time with. I listened, smiling accordingly, as old men recited tedious jokes, as old women discussed how funny Alan Carr was. At the end of each day I would have so little left for George – so little left for me, in fact – that the most I could do was sit mute and expressionless, until it was time to go to bed.

As I prepared myself, and the room, for the knock on the door, I believe I lost the feeling of shame about what I was going to do. I had been scared up until that point, scared of being found out, scared of being judged by society at large. *What kind of women sells her body for money?* When I realized that I'd been selling myself for close to twenty years, albeit in a way that was deemed acceptable but, to be honest, was ultimately just as damaging and, perhaps on some level, even more soul destroying, I became filled with the kind of strength I'd not felt in the longest time.

There is a moment just before a woman gives birth, a moment when terror turns to might, a kind of *take no shit* attitude, when she realizes it is up to her to take control and get this baby out safely. If she doesn't do it, no one will.

It was this feeling, this strength of purpose, this capacity to prevail, that filled me in those moments alone in the hotel room. No one was going to come and rescue me from the financial situation in which I found myself. I either lay down and surrendered, conceded defeat, or I found a way to keep going.

So I was no longer scared. I was defiant. If Scott Elias wanted a warm, attentive woman to satisfy his sexual needs, then here she was. Right here.

The suite had a New England theme going on: white furniture, pale duck-egg fabrics, pictures of Nantucket lighthouses, a bleached wooden floor with a large, downy white rug at its centre. The bed was a four-poster, which I'd been kind of dreading. Images of me, tethered and spread-eagled, a sock stuffed in my mouth, had plagued my dreams the night before. But I got the feeling Scott had chosen this suite *on account* of its simplicity, its non-boudoir feel. As though he was above all that sex-inducing claptrap.

I adjusted the slatted wooden blinds to allow just a small amount of twilight and unpacked my overnight bag. In the bathroom, I stepped out of my dress and arranged my cosmetics, taking a moment to swipe a dampened cotton-wool ball beneath my lashes. I performed a perfunctory toilet before applying a fresh coat of lipstick and gloss. Finally, I arranged my hair into a loose chignon which could be easily unclipped should that be required.

I stepped back into my dress and checked my appearance from all angles.

I *had* toyed with the idea of a negligee. But then answering the door in heels, full make-up and a babydoll seemed bordering on sleazy. Rightly or wrongly, I'd decided that Scott was the type of man who enjoyed undressing a woman, or enjoyed watching the ritual of her undressing and, besides, a negligee was not something I was in possession of.

I pulled back the bedclothes and switched on one of the bedside lamps and then another over by the TV. Then I cut the harsh overhead light before surveying the room. Almost ready.

In the drinks cabinet, which housed the fridge, there was a selection of miniatures. I took two single malt whiskeys and poured them into tumblers.

A knock at the door.

I took one final look in the mirror. My general appearance I was happy with, but I had the hardened, steely expression of an Olympic sprinter before a race. One set on unnerving his opponents before getting in the blocks.

I took a deep breath and shook out my arms, rolled my shoulders to loosen the tension.

Ready.

I opened the door and regarded Scott. 'The room's great,' I said.

'Glad you like it.'

I moved aside to allow him past.

One thing I will say about Scott, his confidence was magnetic. Here he was, doing something considered *just not cricket* in polite society, and there was no hint of apology. No dip in his posture or uncertainty in his eyes. He held himself with utter assurance. It was hard not to be affected by it.

I wondered in that moment if women were programmed, in an evolutionary way, to be turned on by such self-belief as a means of self-preservation. Breed with such a man and he will protect you to the death. Or maybe that was nonsense and it was simply down to money. Women were turned on at the sight of money because it meant security, and perhaps the only reason Scott Elias was so confident was because he had plenty of it.

Scott sat down at the table. 'What are we drinking?' he said.

'Single malt.'

With the glass in hand, he examined me slowly, from my head to my toes, and then up again, with a steady air of appreciation. The way one might do when looking over a classic E type, or well-proportioned, prize-winning livestock. In a matter of seconds he'd become serious. 'I like your hair like that,' he said.

Instinctively, I lifted my hand to my face, never entirely comfortable with a compliment.

I moved towards him so we were almost touching. I stayed standing, and the air between Scott's thigh and the bare skin of my leg became charged. In that space I could feel the rapid exchange of heat.

'So how does this go?' I whispered.

'You give yourself in whatever way you feel you ...' He paused. And then, 'I'm simply here to—'

But he broke off again. I sensed he wanted to say more, wanted to reveal more of himself, but for some reason wouldn't, or else couldn't. He began tracing his fingers up the outside of my thigh. I watched him admire the curve of my hips. Watched him carefully as he exhaled, his fingers now resting beneath the cheek of my rear.

I took the drink from him and placed it on the table.

Leaning over, I put both hands on the back of his chair, and with my face inches from his, murmured, 'It's your party, Scott. Tell me what it is that you want.'

He pressed his mouth against mine and I was surprised by the small, heady thrill that came over me.

The kiss. Sweeter than anticipated.

I pulled back and looked into his eyes.

'Take off your dress,' he said.

14

I SAT ON THE bench waiting, arranging crisps inside a sandwich.
Petra had returned home from New York the previous
evening and she seemed to have forgotten about the humiliation
of her birthday as she was straight on the phone telling me we
absolutely had to have lunch, because she was bursting to tell me
all about the trip. She then proceeded to tell me *all about the trip,*
but I was looking forward to seeing her nonetheless. I tended to
miss her when she was away. Sometimes to the extent of experiencing a real visceral ache, a kind of homesick feeling, which
perplexed me because, when she was around, she drove me
crazy.

Families. I'm not sure we ever fully make sense of our
connections.

The bench was one of the few scattered along Cockshot Point,
an area of lakeshore owned by the National Trust. There's a wide
shingle path, free from cars, which at first winds its way through
a pretty wooded area, before opening up to give expansive views
both up and down the lake.

It's popular with tourists and locals alike, dog walkers, and
young mums with prams. I would often head down here if I
needed to clear my head. There's something about gazing at the
water, it lapping gently at the shore, which would unclutter my
thoughts. Enable me to see a way through whatever problem was
plaguing me.

I'd suggested to Petra we should meet here because it wasn't far from the clinic, or her school, and Bowness itself would be teeming with tourists on a day like today.

Four swans landed on the water in succession and a delighted teen in a wheelchair clapped his hands together at the spectacle, just as I saw Petra approach.

Emerging from the trees, she looked city-chic in a pink, fitted dress and matching pumps. She carried with her a new handbag and wore oversized sunglasses, and I wondered what the denim skirts and cheesecloth smocks at school must have made of her appearance that morning in the staff room. Petra gave a small, excited wave to signal she'd spotted me and headed my way. Her pace was fast but her stride length restricted on account of the close-fitting dress, which all went to give the impression of a woman on a mission, a woman who was on her way to give a person a piece of her mind.

Perhaps she was, I thought idly, as she left the path, cutting an angle across the grass. Perhaps, in between speaking with me this morning and this moment, she had come to discover just what I'd been doing with Scott Elias in a country hotel. I was scheduled to meet Scott once more at a different venue later and, apart from the general feeling of anxiety that comes with conducting oneself as a secret prostitute, unlike before, this time I wasn't totally dreading it.

Here's what I had learned about Scott Elias: his pleasure was derived directly from the pleasure he gave to the woman he was with.

I'd say he wasn't unusual in this respect. Most men I'd known were not selfish in bed. Scratch that, *none* of the men I'd known were selfish in bed. They wanted their woman to come. They wanted to be the one to *make* their woman come. They needed to feel her muscles contracting hard around them to reach orgasm themselves.

Scott was no different. Except that I'd mistakenly assumed that, since he was paying for it, my enjoyment wouldn't be part of the deal.

I was wrong. Scott was tender, lustful, giving and, as I lay there at three in the morning, when we finally decided to call it a night, I was thinking, *Did that really just happen?* It was not the most mind-blowing sex of my life, but I'll say this, it certainly wasn't the worst sex I'd ever had. The electrifying joy of true desire was absent, but I was more than a little into it. And compared with some of the shoddy experiences I'd had in the past, there was the additional turn-on to be had just from the sheer decadence of the whole thing.

I made up my mind there and then that if Scott wanted to repeat the evening, I would do it.

Four thousand pounds for one night?

I didn't have the luxury of refusing.

In a few weeks I could be back on my feet. I could pay off my landlord, clear the credit-card balance and reimburse people I never thought I'd be able to pay back in this lifetime.

It would be a chance to start over. To finally put the mistakes of my past behind me. I had to do it again.

'Crisp sandwiches?' said Petra disdainfully after we'd embraced, tutting and shaking her head as she dusted down the bench before sitting next to me.

'Do you want a bite?'

'Go on then,' she said, and opened her mouth wide. Still chewing, she held up her left index finger. 'Does that look swollen to you?'

'Maybe.'

'What do you think I've done?'

'No idea.'

She rolled her eyes. 'Roz, at least pretend to be a little interested. I know you have to deal with this all day, but I'm worried. Could it be arthritis?'

'You've probably strained it picking up a suitcase.'

'So you don't think I should go for blood tests?'

'No.'

'But what if it *is* arthritis?'

'It won't be. But if it'll make you feel better, go for the tests. I wouldn't bother, though. If it still hurts in a week,' I said wearily, 'I'll look at it.'

Pacified, Petra let her full weight fall against the bench, tilting her face towards the sun, before exhaling long and hard. 'God, I feel like I've been cooped up for ever in that office. It's so nice to be out.'

'You've only been back a day.'

'Yes, but you want to see all the crap they've left for me. They do nothing when I'm not there. Honestly, they just throw everything on to my desk with no thought as to how I'm going to get through it.'

Petra worked three mornings and one full day a week as the school secretary. The size of the place didn't warrant a full-time position. To listen to her, you'd be under the impression that the place would fall down around them without her there to run it properly.

'Did Clara have a nice time with Liz?' I asked.

Liz was Vince's sister. She was single, again. Relationship after relationship seemed to fizzle out, leaving the poor woman wounded and bewildered, with no clear idea what she was doing wrong.

Keeping her face angled towards the sun, Petra shifted in her seat. 'I wanted to talk to you about that,' she said, her words taking on a sharp tone. 'Clara says that Liz has been bullying her.'

'Bullying?'

'Well, perhaps bullying's too strong a word,' she conceded, 'but she *has* been picking on her. How do you think I should broach the subject with Liz?'

'Perhaps Clara's exaggerating?' I suggested, thinking of Vince's gentle sister, who doted on her niece and who I'd never once witnessed being unkind to anyone.

Called to mind also was the brooding nature of Clara, who protested if she felt outshone or excluded, even in a minor way. Petra would feel her daughter's hurt, often launching a direct attack on the perpetrator as a result.

This mindset made Petra unwaveringly fair when dealing with groups of children. Which I admired – everyone was included, everyone invited. But if her own child was shunned? Woe betide. She'd be out gunning for whoever was responsible.

'I'm sure *you'd* have something to say if George was being bullied,' Petra said.

'You know I would. But I think you should check again with Clara first before you risk offending Liz. She's a sweet woman, Petra, I can't imagine she would even dream of—'

'Okay, okay, let's drop it,' she said abruptly, when it was clear I wasn't going to give her the outraged response she was hoping for.

Oh dear. Liz was in for a roasting.

'So what have you been up to since I've been away?' she asked, now brightly.

'Not a lot.'

'Seen anyone?'

'Not really. Work and more work.'

She turned to face me, lifting her sunglasses and giving a small, sympathetic smile. 'Vince let it slip that money was tight again,' she said carefully.

'Money's always tight.'

'How bad is it this time?'

'I'll manage.'

Silence.

'It's just—' Petra said, and stopped. She blinked hard a couple of times and I thought for a moment she wouldn't actually go where I knew she was going with this.

Ultimately, she was unable to restrain what she had to say. 'It's just that I really don't want a repeat of last time, Roz.'

'Don't worry, there won't be.'

'That's the thing,' she replied. 'I *am* worried.'

'You needn't be.'

'You've said that before.'

'Leave it, Petra.'

She dropped her glasses to cover her eyes and fell silent as we watched a young bearded guy throw sticks into the lake for his retriever. He wore an olive-green T-shirt, which hung loose around his lanky frame, and a pair of matching olive trousers. The uniform of a tree surgeon. At one point the dripping dog hurtled out of the water straight towards a pug being led along the path a few feet in front of us. Petra flinched, gripping the seat of the bench with both hands. One fast shake from the retriever and we'd be soaked.

'So you've not asked them then?' Petra said, her words casual, said in a way that belied just how much weight they carried.

'No.'

I could feel the static in the air. A quick sideways glance towards Petra revealed she was rigid with tension, and it was clear what this meeting was really about.

'Because I'd rather you asked *me* for money than it come to that again,' she said.

'It won't come to that.'

And she nodded.

'Okay,' she said finally. 'If you say so. I suppose I'll have to take your word for it.'

When I first began hunting for premises from which to run my physiotherapy practice, it was evident pretty quickly that it was going to be slim pickings. There were no short-term leases or what I would consider fair rental agreements. Property was in high demand and so was at a premium. Landlords around Windermere and Bowness were tying tenants up in ten-year leases, the majority of the buildings needed extensive external and internal maintenance; some were even without heating. I needed a place with two treatment rooms, a waiting area, a toilet (all preferably at ground level, for patients who had difficulty walking) and within easy reach of somewhere to park.

Such a place did not exist, and it was at this point, when I was considering giving up on the dream and either staying with the NHS or renting cheaper premises in Kendal, that my dad advised me to buy. Naturally, the prices were extortionate, the business rates cruel, but my main problem was that I wasn't eligible for a commercial-property mortgage unless I had a forty per cent deposit. Which I didn't.

Not wanting to see me walk away from my vision, my parents came to me one evening, with the intent of withdrawing money from their savings to invest in the practice. Property prices were still rising, interest rates on savings were low, and they decided that their money was safer in bricks and mortar rather than the bank and they could even see a greater return on it.

They loaned me a hundred and ten thousand pounds. Money they'd accrued from downsizing to a two-bedroom bungalow, money that was to supplement their pensions when the time came. And I borrowed the remaining two hundred and forty thousand from the bank.

After Winston's wage cut, his womanizing, the loss of the baby, the credit cards and his subsequent departure from our home, my mind wasn't exactly on the job. I couldn't make the payments on both the mortgage on the business and the one on our house, and I lost it all.

The properties were repossessed by the bank. And because I

was too ashamed, I didn't tell anyone about the extent of the mess until it was too late and there was no time for a quick sale at a much-reduced price – meaning my parents ended up with nothing, when they could have perhaps salvaged at least some of their money.

What I should have done at that point was declare bankruptcy – wipe out Winston's credit-card debt. But a combination of pride and worry about being turned down for a mortgage in the future meant I couldn't bring myself to do it.

Just before retirement, and after much soul searching, my parents put their bungalow on the market and moved to Silloth – over an hour's drive away, in a cheaper part of the county – to ensure they could live out their years with adequate money.

Our family became fractured.

Sick with shame, *I* became the culpable person everyone now knew me to be: not to be trusted with money, not to be given any real responsibility, looked upon with a mixture of disdain and pity.

And Petra lost her babysitters. Which was what today's dig at Liz was really about. *If you didn't lose all that money, I wouldn't have to make do with Vince's sister . . .*

And so it went on. We danced around the issue with normal sisterly chitchat, Petra covering her annoyance and disappointment in the best way she knew how, but, ultimately, all roads led back to this: how could you have sabotaged our parents' lives in that way?

I wish I had the answer.

Petra gave a small shudder as though to rid herself of the negative energy that threatened to take hold. 'Lecture over,' she said, and placed her hand on top of mine. 'Listen, we're going out to dinner with Scott and Nadine on Saturday – nothing flash – why don't you come? My treat.'

'No, I . . . I have to—'

Petra turned to face me and frowned. 'What do you have to do? It's not your weekend to have George, is it?'

'No, but I . . .'

I couldn't think fast enough. Words escaped me. Lies escaped me. There was no way I could sit through a dinner with Scott and Nadine after spending the whole of Friday night with Scott.

'Roz?' she prompted. 'What's going on? Are you seeing someone?'

'No,' I said quickly, and immediately realized I should have said yes. A pretend relationship would be the perfect foil in this instance.

Petra, bewildered, shook her head, before giving my hand a squeeze. 'I know what this is about,' she said. 'And it's high time you got over this inferiority thing, Roz. You can't keep thinking of yourself as worthless like this. Just because Scott and Nadine are wealthy doesn't mean they won't want to spend time with you. They're not like that. They don't judge the way other people do.'

I stared down at our clasped hands, unable to bear looking at my sister.

'Please come,' she pressed. 'I know you'll enjoy it. I'd love you to be there, and you never get out for a nice meal. Go on.'

I was about to speak when she cut me off.

'Roz,' she said seriously, 'I will take it as a personal insult if you don't.'

15

L IKE A LOT of criminals, it wasn't the crime itself that was problematic, rather, it was what to do with the cash.

In an age when everything is digitized, from earnings to dental appointments, clearing debts with freshly minted twenty-pound notes was not as straightforward as I first thought. In fact, it wasn't straightforward at all.

I had assumed I could deposit the four thousand Scott paid me directly into my bank account and, from there, I could pay my rent arrears.

But no.

Shortly after making the deposit I received a phone call from my bank, apologetic, but firm nonetheless, requiring verification of the origin of the cash deposited. They were now obligated to check on large cash withdrawals and deposits in the fight against fraud. Thinking on my feet, I explained that the money was a loan from my parents to help me out of a financial fix, but it was quickly apparent that I would not be able to use this excuse on a regular basis. If ever again. Apart from anything else, Her Majesty's Revenue and Customs would also want to know the source of any further deposits.

What I thought was a fail-safe way to earn my way out of debt suddenly wasn't. And it got me wondering, just exactly how did those escorts operating from their spare bedrooms in their semi-detached houses 'show' the money they earned? You can't run a home on nothing. Either they were claiming benefits and the cash supplemented their income or else they listed their occupations as something other than 'prostitute' on their tax returns. 'Masseuse', perhaps.

I had an appointment with Scott that evening, as George was to be picked up directly from after-school club by Winston (the international man of business was now back in the country, it appeared), so I had the rest of the afternoon to come up with a way of accepting payment for my services that didn't arouse suspicion. It seemed almost unfair. I was doing my utmost to pay off my debts, but the law said I wasn't allowed to do it in this way. I thought about the drug dealers that commonly featured on *Traffic Cops*, their pimped-up Range Rovers with the blacked-out windows, and wondered how they got away with it (assuming drugs, like escorting, was a mostly cash business).

As it turned out, Scott was experiencing similar difficulties. And to make sure I didn't turn on my heel and leave mid-date when I discovered he was without a satchel full of cash, he made an impromptu call at the clinic to discuss our arrangement, our options and to put a new proposal to me.

It would be this decision, within the list of bad decisions, that would send our lives on the roller-coaster trajectory that was to change everything.

Earlier, I had dropped George at school with a small rucksack containing the essential toys and bits and pieces for his stay with his dad. Winston, though incompetent in paying me child support, was fairly good at providing enough clothes, pyjamas and games consoles. And because Dylis supplied three square meals a day and a constant offering of clean laundry, I never worried George was going without when he stayed over there. George and Winston would rollick around, following their noses into adventures, with none of the ties or responsibilities that anchored most parents to their homes at the weekends. I imagined it was like staying with your favourite carefree bohemian uncle, and a weekend of this was probably just what George needed, after the upheaval following the bailiff's visit and the meeting with the head teacher.

After speaking to Winston at length about George's stealing, Winston finally admitted that George had stolen from his mother a few times as well. When I'd blown my top at him for keeping it from me, his response was, 'He just wanted a dog, Roz. Don't be so hard on him.'

'Well, he can't have a dog, can he? He *knows* he can't have a dog while we're in rented accommodation.'

I didn't stick the knife in as I might. Didn't drag up that it was Winston's fault that the dog had gone in the first place. Because it was pointless. Not because we were past tit for tat but because it would be lost on Winston. He would no more make the connection between his infidelity and George's dogless state than he would between it and my moonlighting for extra cash. As far as Winston was concerned, his behaviour didn't have repercussions.

Winston told me he'd found over fifty pounds stuffed inside George's pillowcase – which meant he'd been at it for far longer than any of us suspected. And probably meant he'd thieved from Petra and Vincent on a number of occasions as well. I decided to keep that piece of information to myself for now, confident that my warning to George of *No dogs ever again* was enough of a deterrent against his stealing in the future.

It was around 11 a.m. when I heard the telltale roar of the Ferrari outside in the car park. Peculiar, isn't it, how an elderly woman over-revving her Fiat Panda's 900cc engine is mocked heartily by people but doing the exact same thing in a performance car commands general respect?

I could hear Wayne tripping over his feet, scrambling to get to the front door to greet Scott, in expectation of another ride through the Lyth Valley. Scott had tolerated Wayne, he told me, to get to me. He'd given him a loop of countryside, riding through Winster, taking a right to Strawberry Bank, over Gummer's Howe and finally speeding north along the eastern shore of Windermere before depositing Wayne back at the clinic. Somewhere during the twenty-minute journey Scott reported that Wayne began to speak differently, changing the cadence and rhythm of his words to match that of Jeremy Clarkson. When I'd scoffed at this, ridiculed Wayne, Scott told me it happened with every man who rode with him. It was an unconscious thing, and they really didn't know they were doing it.

Rather than wait for Wayne's knock on the door, I popped my head out. The patient I was with was prone, stippled with acupuncture needles, and could be left alone for a few minutes. Patients were often reluctant to continue any conversation with needles stuck in their head. I suppose they worried that any movement at all might result in their brain being skewered. Not possible, but I wouldn't disclose this information readily, as I enjoyed the brief snatches of silence it afforded.

The clinic door was wide open, with Wayne standing on the threshold, his back towards me. We'd had a monsoon-like downpour that morning, the rain rhythmically thrumming on the roof, like a marching military band. The delicate, desiccated scents of summer that for the past few weeks had been carried on the breeze were now in vapour form. And all at once the air had become dense, sickly sweet and overbearing.

Scott must have dawdled inside the car, as it was only now that I heard the car door slam, followed by Wayne clapping his hands together, greeting Scott in a way that was meant to be blokey but sounded sycophantic.

Seeing me peer out of the treatment room, Scott said he needed to speak to me as a matter of great urgency and, where Wayne would no doubt usually ignore a request such as this from a patient – telling them I could not be disturbed, they must make an appointment – he watched helplessly as I gestured across the reception area to the nutritionist's room, which I knew to be empty.

It would be the first time I would witness Scott without his usual charming demeanour, with this rebuff of someone he had no further use for. I was surprised by the ease with which he moved past Wayne, briefly acknowledging his presence but giving him no further attention, as though they had never had even a conversation in their lives. Wayne looked taken aback. He was perplexed by Scott's snub and didn't know what to make of it.

The nutritionist's room had been used that day as a dumping ground for a large delivery of couch rolls, boxes of tissues and toilet paper, ready for Wayne to sort out.

'We have a problem,' began Scott.

'How's the elbow doing?' I asked in an over-loud voice, pushing the door closed. But I neglected to close it completely, my thinking being that if I were to shut myself away with Scott it might arouse suspicion that there was something between us. Best to appear relaxed. Best to appear as though we were discussing his elbow, so there was no need for total privacy.

I turned, and Scott shot me a look as though to say, *Fuck the elbow*. Then he strode across the room, took my face in his hands and kissed me.

'Don't,' I said, aghast. 'Not here.'

He didn't apologize.

'What sort of problem?' I asked, instantly feeling that queasy dread that comes from the threat of discovery. 'Is it Nadine?'

He shook his head.

He seemed agitated and edgy, not the Scott I was used to, and I wondered what it had taken to unsettle him so.

'It's money,' he said. 'I can't raise the money.'

I took a step back. 'You can't raise four thousand pounds?'

That seemed unlikely.

'I can't raise four thousand pounds in *cash*. Not right now, anyway.'

'Ah,' I said, 'I thought . . .'

He smiled. 'No, I'm not quite that strapped.'

'Okay, so what happens now?'

'I have an idea, but I'm not sure how you'll feel about it.'

'Try me,' I said.

'Well, if I continue to draw cash from the business, it won't go unnoticed. The accountant's going to want to know what it's for and, though I think I can trust the guy, I don't really want him poking around. Plus, his wife and Nadine are friends. And as much as he likes to promise total confidentiality, we all know everyone confides in their wives.'

'Is tonight still going ahead?' I asked.

'That depends on you. I would very much like it to, in fact,' and he paused, reaching out and running a finger along my jaw-line. 'I think I may have a solution. But it means you'll have to wait a short while for your money.'

'How long?'

'A few days.'

'Oh.'

'I realize you need it fast, I'm aware of that. But think about it: you can't hide that cash from the Revenue. They'll catch up with you eventually and want to know how you came by it. And when they do that, depending on how you handle yourself, they'll come sticking their nose into my business, Roz, and I just can't take that chance.'

'Okay,' I conceded, 'so what do you suggest?'

'You call yourself a consultant.'

'A consultant in what?'

'Anything you like. Really doesn't matter. What's important is that you come up with something credible, something you can invoice my company for, and we'll credit your account within twenty-four hours. I was thinking something along the lines of ergonomics, but if you can come up with anything better, I'm all ears.'

'Ergonomics would work.'

'The sooner you provide an invoice, the sooner you'll be paid,' he said. 'You could say you advise us on desk height, back support, that kind of thing, yes?'

'I could do that.'

'And you're okay about tonight?' he asked tentatively.

'You mean about not being paid?'

He nodded.

'It's unexpected, so I can't say I'm totally okay with it, but I do have a little breathing space after your last payment. I don't want to compromise our arrangement though, so . . . Do you still want the whole night?'

'Of course,' he said. 'We'll meet at seven?'

'Seven.'

'I'll go then,' he said. 'Let you get back to it.' He moved towards the door, pulled it open and turned back around to face me. 'Thank you,' he said, 'thanks for understanding.'

I lifted my hand to bid Scott goodbye and instantly froze. Beyond him, Wayne was at the water cooler.

Again, Scott didn't acknowledge him as he passed.

Only this time there was no sign of hurt or rejection in Wayne's eyes. Rather, he began to whistle.

He filled his cup, whistling a jaunty, made-up tune, before flashing me a knowing smile.

16

A<small>REN'T PEOPLE SURPRISING?</small>
I have always had a particular fascination with the concept of pecking order. For each person in any given situation there is a hierarchy – whether they are aware of it or not.

Often it's an invisible dance we do around each other. *Where do I fit with you? How important am I in your life?*

Generally, though, we know where we fit. We know where we are on the importance scale, and we behave accordingly. We tend to sit in our allotted spaces, uncomplaining, not daring to move out, not daring to ask for more for fear of a rebuttal.

So when, in the late afternoon, Wayne hit me with the news that he wanted in on the arrangement, well, understandably, I laughed in his face at the preposterousness of it.

When I saw that he was actually serious, I said, 'What arrangement?' and he said, 'Don't insult me, Roz.'

Here's what I thought he was proposing: a cut of my earnings to keep quiet. A thousand pounds or so to hold his tongue, not to reveal the true nature of my business with Scott, to his wife, my employers, the wider community.

But it wasn't that.

'I want a night with you,' Wayne said earnestly, and my mouth dropped open.

'Wayne,' I began, 'there is a difference . . . a very big difference with what goes on between—'

'There's no difference,' he said simply.

A pause.

'From what I could make out from that conversation you had earlier,' he said, gesturing to the nutritionist's room, 'Scott Elias is paying you. He's paying you a substantial amount of money for your services. Or have I misunderstood?'

I didn't deny it. I wanted to see where he was going with this.

'I would like the same,' he said.

I regarded him, trying not to show my outrage. 'Wayne,' I said carefully, 'I don't want to do that.'

'Roz,' he replied, 'I don't think you have a choice,' and he motioned towards the computer. 'Remember the anomaly I pointed out to you,' he said, gesturing to the screen.

Evidently, I was not allowed to look as, when I craned my neck to see, he minimized the page.

'An anomaly with?'

'The accounts,' he said.

'Yes. And you're telling me this now because . . . ?'

'It's been brought to my attention by the accountants at HQ,' he said, 'that this particular clinic has been the victim of – shall we say? – the misappropriation of funds.'

HQ, I was thinking, trying not to scoff at the silly officiousness of his tone, when it hit me what he was really saying.

'Stealing?' I asked.

'It certainly looks that way.'

'But there's nothing to steal,' I protested. 'We don't stock any-thing . . . Nothing of any use anyhow.'

I was thinking about the teabags and toilet rolls I'd taken recently, wondering if he could be referring to those. But then I put that out of my head because *surely* nobody was spending their hours quantifying normal usage?

'How does this affect me?' I said eventually.

'Across the ten clinics – and that includes more than fifty clinicians – you have the highest patient cancellation rate.'

'But I have the highest number of patients,' I reasoned. 'The number of cancellations is bound to be higher. It's proportional.'

'Apparently not. The accountants at HQ have done an audit, and your rate of missed appointments is five times higher than anyone else's. What's more, now that I've had a chance to look at the data more closely, those missed appointments all tended to coincide with when I was absent from the clinic myself.'

I swallowed.

'And they are all patients who usually pay in cash,' he added.

'Careful what you're suggesting there, Wayne.'

I stared at him hard.

He stared back.

'Of course, HQ might be willing to overlook any misdemeanour that may have taken place,' he said carefully. 'Perhaps I could *persuade* them to overlook it, if you catch my drift.'

'You have no evidence. No evidence at all, Wayne, that this has anything to do with me.'

And he then proceeded to show me the 'evidence' he'd been collecting over the last week or so.

The series of thefts from the clinic, and my part in them, was irrefutable, he explained. He'd gone so far as to contact the patients I'd marked down as absent, asking if they could confirm or deny their presence at the clinic at the allotted times. Most were only too happy to oblige, flicking back through their diaries, their wall calendars, as he didn't inform them why he wanted to know, just that there had been a problem with the computerized diary system and he needed to re-enter the information.

'What if I refuse what you're proposing?' I said to Wayne.

'Then I go to the police.'

'You would do that?'

'Tell me why I shouldn't? You've been ripping the company off. And not only that, you now have this sideline going, that for all we know could be going on behind the closed door of the treatment room—'

'That has *never* happened.'

'We don't know that, though, do we? Think how it would look, Roz. Think how it would look if it came out that you were charging people for sex, as well as purloining the takings? Patients wouldn't come here any more. It would be an unviable business. And with a purpose-designed clinic such as this, the owners sinking in hundreds of thousands in investment, you can be sure they would pursue you with everything they've got. Their reputation as a healthcare provider is on the line.'

'Please don't go to the police.'

'I won't,' he said. 'Do as I ask, and I give you my word I won't go to the police. I'll tell no one. You know I've always been fond of you, Roz. I'll keep it to myself, I promise.'

I exhaled, closed my eyes. Tried to think.

He had me, and I couldn't come up with a way out. I'd pocketed that cash when I was desperate. Truly desperate. It wasn't much. Thirty-five pounds here and there. But it was theft, nonetheless.

There were no good options; just one bad option slightly worse than the other. And you know what you should do. Your gut is screaming at you to back up. Reverse. Come clean now and take the hit before things get really out of control. But you don't, because you are weak. And your habit of taking the less bad option is what got you here in the first place.

'How will you explain the loss of takings?' I asked eventually. 'I assume the Accounts department will still want to know where that money has gone.'

Wayne made a dismissive gesture. 'I'll blame the cleaner who left a fortnight ago. I'll tell them I have no direct evidence, but I trust the staff I've got implicitly, and can't see who else it could have been. Of course, now that the thieving has stopped, that will all make sense.'

He waited for my reaction. Wetted his lips.

'Please,' I said, appealing to him with one last-ditch attempt, 'don't do this. It's ludicrous.'

'Is it?'

'You know it is. Please, Wayne, don't make me beg.'

And he laid both palms flat on the desk before letting out a long, exasperated breath.

'Am I that repulsive?' he asked.

'No.' (*Yes.*)

'Is it *so* absurd that I should ask this of you?'

I didn't answer. My eyes pricked with tears as the scene of what he was advocating played out in my mind.

There was no way.

There was absolutely no way I could go through with this.

'You appreciate it's game over for you now,' he whispered as a patient exited Magdalena's room. 'You will never work again. You'll never be *allowed* near patients again.'

He handed me a tissue.

'I'd think long and hard about this before rejecting my offer, Roz.'

17

I HAD JUST STEPPED out of the shower, wrapped my head in a towel and slipped on my bathrobe, when I heard knocking on the front door.

Opening it, I saw my visitor had a bottle of champagne in one hand and a large punnet of ripe strawberries in the other.

'You'd better come in, Celia,' I told her.

She stepped inside and began casting around the naked room.

Taking in the bare walls, the bare floor, she said, 'I don't know how you live like this,' her Liverpool accent sounding more pronounced than usual. 'I really don't.' Then she asked, 'Is George with his dad?' And I told her he was, told her he was staying with Winston until Sunday evening, and she trotted off to find a couple of glasses.

Oddly, the champagne flutes were one of the few things the bailiffs hadn't seized. I leaned against the doorframe, watching as Celia bustled about the kitchen, unable to suppress a smile when she put the tea towel to her nose to check that it was clean, before using it to gain some purchase on the lodged cork.

'What's the occasion?' I said as she poured first into one glass and then the other.

'Occasion?' she asked. 'Do we need one?' She handed me a glass. 'Cheers,' she said. Then she admitted that she had watched me from her bedroom window earlier on my way in from the car, and it seemed as though I could do with some cheering up. 'You look like you've got the weight of the world on your shoulders.'

'Just a few problems at work.'

'Ooh, that reminds me,' she said, slipping off one of her sandals, 'Dennis has developed a pain, right here.' She pointed to the fleshy part on the underside of her heel.

'Does it hurt him in the morning when he gets out of bed?' I asked.

'Like a knife!' she exclaimed. 'He can hardly walk.'

'Plantar fasciitis.' I scribbled the name of the orthopaedic insoles I recommend on a scrap of paper. 'Pick him up a pair of those from Boots,' I said. 'I'll take a look at it over the weekend.'

Celia frowned as she read the note. She thought the insoles would be a waste of time.

'They work,' I told her firmly.

She folded the note, put it in her pocket and reached for her glass. 'Why don't you come for dinner?' she said. 'I've got some lovely halibut and I've done what I always do and bought enough for six. You can do Dennis's foot, and I'll—'

'I can't.'

She put her drink down. 'Why can't you?'

'I'm meeting someone.'

'Who?' she said, her eyes suddenly bright with interest.

Since we'd become neighbours, Celia had tried, on numerous occasions and without success, to set me up with a selection of eligible men. A couple of them were the sons of her reading-group friends. Another was the brother of her picture framer. Another, the nephew of the guy who came to clean her oven once a month. They all looked good on paper. But as I tried to impress on Celia, when someone said they couldn't understand why their son/brother/nephew had been single for as long as they had, there was still usually a good reason.

'The good ones are snapped up quickly,' I told her.

'Then why have you not been snapped up?'

'I make bad choices.'

'Maybe you're too picky.'

'Maybe,' I said. And I left it at that.

But, honestly, you should have seen these men. I don't want to be cruel, but you had to wonder how they managed to tie their own shoelaces and get out of the house each morning.

'Don't get excited,' I told Celia now as she waited for me to elaborate. 'This is just somebody I know through work. It's not serious.'

Celia made a face. 'Your generation.' She tutted contemptuously. 'How can romance *not* be serious? And what does that even mean? You see these silly men on the television saying they don't want to settle down, saying they want no-strings relationships, and I say to Dennis, "What fool of a woman would put up with something like that?" Good Lord, for all they get out of it, they may as well go on the game.' She paused, musing on this fact as she finished her drink.

Shaking her head, she added, 'Oldest job in the world.'

'That so,' I replied.

An hour later I was in the car, heading north.

During the trip, all I could think of was Wayne. I was so bloody angry. Angry with him. Angry with myself. If I'd swallowed my pride and asked Petra for a little cash when I needed it, I wouldn't find myself in this position. I negotiated the slippery curves along Rydal Water and my stomach began to cramp at the thought of him. Wayne had cornered me at the end of the day when the clinic was emptied of patients and there was only Gary left, catching up on notes, as he did each day. Wayne asked if I'd reached a decision.

As he waited for me to speak he held his mouth open slightly, something he often did when concentrating, and I became transfixed by his large tongue. It was swollen and covered in a thick, furred white coating – indicative of a chronic yeast infection, I suspected.

'Since you're giving me no way out of this, I'll do it tomorrow evening,' I snapped at him. By then I was livid that he'd put me in the situation, and I didn't try to hide it.

'Oh,' he replied brightly. 'As soon as that?' The stupid bastard was flattered.

Staring at his tongue, I refrained from saying that I had no choice but to get it over and done with. That if I allowed myself time to stew on the idea I was sure to back out and, well, the repercussions of not doing it at all, he'd made very clear earlier.

'George is with his dad for the weekend,' I told him. 'So it's either tomorrow or in a fortnight's time.'

'Tomorrow,' he replied quickly. 'Yes, tomorrow would suit me perfectly, actually, because I have a couple of busy weekends planned later in the month, in fact . . .'

He then proceeded to give me a list of activities that constituted his tedious little life.

When he had finished I'd stared at him for a moment, still totally shocked that he was capable of this blackmail. Wayne and I had always got along pretty well. Sure, he had his annoying traits: his jokes were mostly crap, and he could take his role in the clinic a little too seriously. But he'd been consistently kind to me. We'd been kind to each other. I couldn't believe this volte-face. I felt betrayed.

I tried to put Wayne out of my head for now, as I didn't want to arrive for Scott in a state of fractious agitation. For someone who had known me for such a brief time, Scott had an uncanny ability to intuit what I was feeling, and I knew it would be a disastrous error to inform him of Wayne's demands.

To Scott, Wayne was a pointless individual who didn't even warrant a courteous nod. That much was evident from his behaviour that afternoon, so I didn't need to ruminate for long over whether to tell Scott about Wayne's intention.

Firstly, even though Scott had not aired this view, I knew that, while he was paying me, I was his. And his alone. The way he'd described the ugliness of conveyor-belt sex was less to do with the girls themselves and more to do with his imagining the series of revolting lowlifes that had been there before him.

So there was that.

But also, in neglecting to inform Scott, I was considering that vainglorious state you find yourself in after the person you have slept with sleeps with someone else. A person you deem to be below you. And although you may have liked the person you first had sex with perfectly well, you couldn't now repeat it, on account of feeling insulted by them putting you in the same category as the subsequent partner. It was humiliating. Anyway, all this to say it would not be wise to inform Scott of tomorrow's agenda with Wayne. I couldn't risk him ending our arrangement.

And of course I still needed the money to pay off the credit cards.

I would deal with the Wayne issue tomorrow. For now, I had to prepare myself for the night ahead. So I switched on the radio, fiddled about until I found a station playing a mindless track with a heavy bass, and when the opportunity came I overtook a pair of cyclists on a blind corner, which gave me a jolt of adrenalin, the kick that comes from a moment of recklessness, something I needed to summon Roz the Sexy Plaything and banish Roz the Total Shambles.

Scott was waiting for me on the hotel balcony. He'd instructed Housekeeping to dry off the floor and furniture, now that the rain had cleared, so we could dine alone outside, overlooking Grasmere. I had gone directly to the room upon arrival. Scott had texted the number earlier and given me directions so I wouldn't have to stop by reception. He had taken pre-dinner drinks with his accountant and the firm's solicitor, explaining to Nadine that he would be away for the night, as the meeting would run on into the early hours. Then he'd left the two men in the bar with a twelve-hundred-pound bottle of cognac, telling them he was sorry, but he would be bowing out early on account of a full session's drinking scheduled for Carlisle Races the following day.

'Sorry I'm a bit late,' I said. 'Traffic.'

Scott brushed it off and said not to worry. He held the door wide and I walked in, dropping my bag by the armchair. This room was traditional. The type of room an older couple might find pleasing should they spend Christmas in Grasmere. The decor was busy: gold wallpaper covered with lilies and heavy crimson curtains. The fixtures were either brass or gold and the furniture was solid oak.

Scott and I regarded each other, not speaking.

He gave a faint half-smile and, though I knew he wanted to be here – knew he probably *needed* to be here – it was plain by his expression he had other things on his mind.

This didn't fall into the category of Second Date in a traditional way, but it did bear some of the hallmarks. While Scott was freshly showered and clean-shaven, while he had that jittery tension that came from being alone with a new woman, the bright glint of inquisitiveness was missing from his eyes. We'd already had sex. The mystique was gone. Work, real life, would now crowd his thoughts. And I guessed that, should we engage in polite conversation over dinner, his mind would be elsewhere.

I glanced through the open door of the balcony. The table was set, complete with candles, a bottle of something on ice. 'Would you prefer we went straight to bed?' I asked him.

A little taken aback, he gave a small cough and widened his eyes. Then he said, 'Would you mind?'

'Not at all. We can dine later.'

So we did. This time, he stayed fully dressed and took me from behind in the bathroom. I saw by his expression that he wanted fast, slutty sex, so I remained in my heels, facing the mirror, while he pulled my knickers to one side and fucked me like I imagined he used to fuck Nadine – back when she was still into it.

Afterwards, we sat outside beneath the gas heater, as the air had chilled (it was now after nine), and he thanked me with what seemed to be a sense of wonder for anticipating his needs.

'It's not rocket science,' I replied, but to be honest I'd done it for myself as much as Scott. Wayne was still looming heavily at the forefront of my thoughts, and it was as good a way as any to get rid of him.

Scott remained dressed in his navy suit but he'd asked that I wear just my underwear, with a hotel robe around me, while we ate.

'You look beautiful,' he told me. 'How's the crab?'

'Good.'

'I wish I'd ordered it now.'

'Have some,' I said, and he told me to help myself to a razor clam. 'Thanks,' I replied, 'but I'm not keen.' The truth was, I'd never tried one. But on first viewing I couldn't shake the image of a tapeworm, pickled in formaldehyde, which had rested on a dusty shelf in the biology lab at school year upon year. Petra had been raving about razor clams recently, and I realized she'd more than likely tried them when out with Scott.

The last of the daylight dwindled as we heard a succession of car doors slam. Non-residents perhaps, who had dined at the hotel and were on their way home, or else were on the lookout for a little more excitement from their Friday evening than this sedate hotel had to offer. Tomorrow the place would play host to another wedding. Come to the Lakes, stay in a country hotel like this and find yourself outnumbered by noisy wedding guests each Saturday night, along with brides who are worse for wear, false eyelashes falling off, watching the prerequisite firework display, their children pulling at their dresses, each sporting their brand-new double-barrelled name.

'What are you thinking about?' Scott asked.

'This and that. Mostly that.'

'Does it ever bother you to be alone?'

'Yes,' I said truthfully.

'You don't relish the solitude? I always fancied my own private—'

'Idaho?'

'Campervan,' he said.

'Oh, like a shed on wheels to hide in. I can see how that could be nice. I have George, remember, so there isn't a lot of solitude to be had. But I do miss a man.' I finished eating and laid my knife and fork neatly on the side of my plate. 'I miss someone to share in the responsibility – not the romantic stuff so much, I can live without that. Or maybe I learned to live without that, so I don't notice it. But I miss the presence of a man. Someone to say, "I'll check your oil and water for you," someone to get the pilot light going. Saying all this, I sound like I just miss my dad. Winston was crap at looking after me.'

'Is that what you want, someone to lean on, someone to take care of you?'

'I think so, yes.'

'You can always ask me.'

'No, I can't, Scott,' I said. 'I wouldn't ask you because it's not part of the arrangement. Isn't that exactly what you wanted to avoid?'

He frowned. Threw me a look to say, *I don't follow.*

'You wanted it this way *precisely because* you don't want to take care of another woman. Paying for sex frees you of that. Your words, Scott. I have no problem with it. It works well for me, too.'

He reached for his glass and looked at me seriously. 'I really hate the thought of you struggling by on your own,' he said.

And it was as though his words caught on the hairs of my inner ear. I shivered in response.

I wasn't sure why. Perhaps it was the way he spoke, his words loaded with a meaning I couldn't quite comprehend.

'Next time you have a crisis, Roz,' Scott said darkly, 'you make sure you call me.'

18

THE FOLLOWING MORNING I rose early, leaving Scott in bed, deeply asleep. I'd told him last night I would slip away first thing. He was planning to eat breakfast at the hotel before driving north for the races. Then he and Nadine were dining with Petra and Vince at the no-frills Italian to which I'd agreed to go but would back out of later with a migraine.

I never got migraines. But since Petra used the excuse so frequently, she could hardly question it. I was quite pleased with my ploy and planned to give Petra a quick text at around two, tell her I was feeling a bit off, to foreshadow the last-minute cancellation I would deliver later at around six.

What did we do before texts?

Remember the nauseating dread on the build-up to calling in sick with a hangover? Hearing your disbelieving boss question you as you spoke in a thin whimper: *Yes, I think it's something I ate . . . No, you're totally right, you can't be too careful with fish.*

Wouldn't it be great if I could get rid of Wayne by text?

I slipped on jeans, flip-flops and a pink T-shirt. I thought about leaving Scott a note, but decided against it. Evidence has a way of finding itself in the wrong hands. I ate two slices of Scottish shortbread and a couple of figs from the complimentary bits and pieces on the desk, and drank a quick cup of lapsang souchong. Then I headed off.

With my bag slung over my shoulder and another lump of

money on its way to my bank account – as soon as I invoiced Scott – I had the puritanical sense of accomplishment that comes from striving towards a goal.

But who was I kidding? Look at what I was doing.

I drove beneath a thick, lush canopy of trees. It was still early enough to spot the occasional deer, tearing at saplings in the fields beyond the road; still early enough to catch a convoy of Fleetwood fish vans on their way towards Grasmere to make their first deliveries of the day. The morning stretched out in front of me, full of possibilities, with only one huge blemish on the horizon. Wayne. After paying off my immediate debts, I had eighteen hundred pounds in my bank account. I planned to get to Kendal for just after 8 a.m. and spend most of the morning there. I would stock the house full of food and basic essentials, before heading over to B&Q to buy a new sofa, new crockery, new linen and a few scatter cushions and whatnot to brighten the place up. If I kept myself busy, maybe I could put tonight's meeting with Wayne from my mind until the last moment.

I would not be spending the entire night with him. I had flat out refused to do that. But I did acquiesce to sex. One time, and one time only.

Turning into Morrisons' car park, I made a mental note to pick up a couple of miniature bottles of Jack Daniel's that I could knock back in the car outside Wayne's immediately before entering. There would be no payment for this service. Only the freedom to continue earning in the way I do, and of course the promise that no action would be taken regarding the theft. Which Wayne had now tallied up to total around seventeen hundred pounds.

As far as I could tell, there were two things that could go wrong. One, Wayne had lied and would hold me to ransom for ever (quite possible but, again, I had little choice). Two, I became so sick to my stomach I couldn't go through with it (see above re: Jack Daniel's).

I checked my watch: 8.53 a.m. Twelve hours from now and this would all be over.

The shop was almost empty, so I was able to peruse the aisles without the nuisance of too many other shoppers. I filled the base of the trolley with various fruits and vegetables before heading straight to the medicines and cosmetics. There, I was able to examine the display of condoms without fear of interruption, before hiding the packages safely beneath a bunch of bananas, away from prying eyes.

I had told Wayne I expected him to wear two Extra-safe condoms and I would be making a full inspection prior to intercourse to check for any ulcerated lesions or breaks in the skin. This was all very routine, I told him, and he had nodded seriously, saying, 'Couldn't agree more. Absolutely.'

I dropped some antibacterial bodywash into the trolley, some antibacterial mouthwash, a bottle of Femfresh (yes, I know the vagina is a self-cleaning oven, but this was *Wayne* we were talking about) along with two bottles of Night Nurse to knock me out afterwards and hopefully send me to oblivion.

I was all set.

The house itself was a pleasing little cottage located on the edge of Ambleside, just off the road that leads up to the Kirkstone Pass. If Kirkstone Pass sounds familiar, you've most likely heard it mentioned on the national travel reports. It's often the first of the mountain passes to close after heavy snowfall, and lays claim to having the third highest pub in England.

Wayne took the house over from his parents. His father was a postal worker, dead ten years, and his mother lived in sheltered accommodation.

Because Wayne was savvy, and had persuaded his mum to

transfer the house into his name upon his father's death, the state paid for his mother's care, leaving Wayne mortgage- and dependant-free, with plenty of money in his pocket to spend on – would you believe it? – fish.

'I didn't know you had an aquarium,' I said, before taking in the room fully – lots of chrome. Clean lines. Two leather sofas in ivory.

A large rectangular glass coffee table took up most of the floor space and the decor was very much stylish bachelor pad. I was surprised by the standard of cleanliness. He was obviously very house proud.

He began pointing out the most prized fish in the tank, which covered one entire wall of the living room.

The house itself was pretty isolated. It was accessed from a single-track road. Back in the sixties, it had been a working farm but, upon the farmer's death, the house was sold to Wayne's parents, and the surrounding land divided up and sold off separately. It was now rented to two farmers in Troutbeck who used it to graze their sheep. I'd agreed to come here because I knew no one would see my car, and because I was not about to meet Wayne at a hotel and set myself back eighty pounds. And I'm sure it goes without saying, but the thought of Wayne at my house was totally out of the question. Even without the prying eyes of Celia.

Two seahorses bobbed about in the corner of the tank and, without really meaning to, I reached out my hand, touching the glass. Such endearing, vulnerable little creatures. They are terrible swimmers, apparently, flapping about in the same spot. And was I correct in thinking it was the male of the species who became pregnant? Now there's a thought.

'Do you have a generator?' I asked Wayne.

'Naturally,' he replied.

'What happens when you go on holiday? Who feeds the fish then?'

'My cousin in Glenridding. He keeps reptiles.'

Of course he does.

'We look after each other's menageries,' he explained, 'when we're away.'

I found myself thinking it strange that I knew none of this. I had worked with Wayne for some considerable time, during which he'd told me about the farmhouse, but I couldn't recall him talking about the fish. Odd, as this was clearly his life. I could only imagine that I switched off when he spoke, absorbing just the bare essentials. Petra said I did the same with her. She said my hard drive was full and I needed to defragment to clear up some disk space.

'So,' I said after a moment, 'this is a bit awkward.'

'It is?' He seemed surprised.

I felt like I was in a bad porn film, the actors exchanging a series of stilted lines before suddenly having sex.

Or perhaps an arty French film. A grotesque, loose-fleshed man and a woman without make-up (*'Brave!'* the tabloids would declare her) have a huge, vicious row . . . before suddenly having sex.

It was kind of tragic the way Wayne had prepared himself for tonight. He'd had his hair cut – somewhere different to his usual barber; perhaps he'd paid a bit more on this occasion. The result was that his blond, almost colourless hair had been left longer on top and cut razor-short at the sides. With his thin lips, sweating brow and dark shirt buttoned right up to the collar, he favoured an SS officer.

I smiled wanly his way and suggested we might as well get on with it. I almost said, 'Get it over with,' but managed to reel myself in at the last second. After downing the Jack Daniel's in the car before entering Wayne's cottage, I had that heady impertinence that comes from teetering on the border of being drunk, when your confidence is at its highest and everything seems a lot funnier than it is. Now was the time to do it. Any longer and my blood alcohol level would drop fast, leaving me melancholy and, most likely, ashamed. And if I remained true to form, this shame would manifest itself as mild aggression.

I removed my shirt.

Wayne's eyes grew wide. 'What, here?' he said.

'You really didn't think we'd be rolling around on your bed, did you?'

'No,' he said quietly, but it was apparent by his crestfallen look that was exactly what he'd had in mind.

'Wayne,' I said, wrinkling my nose in disgust. 'Sorry, but no.'

'Should I get undressed?' he asked.

I shrugged. 'It's your call.'

I was hoping he would remain fully clothed, but no. First, he unbuttoned his shirt, exposing the fishbelly skin of his chest. He glanced my way, uncertain, nervous I may flee, I think, so I gave my best encouraging look. The longer he dawdled, the longer I was stuck here.

I drew the curtains, stepped out of my flip-flops and slipped off my jeans. My movements were fast and mechanical. I had the businesslike air one adopts when undressing for a medic and, when I caught Wayne watching, for a second I almost felt sorry for him.

At work, both his position of authority and the fact he was a stickler for detail combined to make him unappealing on occasion. He was the boss everyone liked to dislike because he had power over his staff, who were both better educated and earned more money than him. It was an odd situation, but a necessary one. You go removing the hated figure from any workplace and the staff turn on each other. It's far more effective to have one person who everyone can complain about. I'm sure the owners of the company were well aware of this. On the days that Wayne was absent from the clinic, we bickered. And I would find myself wondering just how far we'd go with our snipes if he wasn't there at all. Perhaps we'd turn on each other, just as those inhabitants of Easter Island are purported to have done. Though I should say I couldn't imagine actually eating Gary. No matter how much he got on my nerves.

All this to say that the Wayne standing in front of me was a sorry-looking specimen in his underpants and socks. And even though he was holding me under duress, and even though I beyond despised him for making me come here, I now saw the reason for that was pure desperation.

I removed my underwear and Wayne flinched. I thought he might come right then and there, but he managed to hold it together.

'When did you last see a woman naked?' I asked, and he shook his head. He wasn't willing to say. 'Okay,' I said. 'I just need a couple of things from my bag.'

I walked the few steps across the room and, out of the corner of my eye, I was aware of Wayne removing his socks and underpants.

With the two condoms in my hand, I made my way towards him.

Ripping open the packets, I held his gaze.

'One time and one time only, Wayne. That's the deal. Are we clear?'

He nodded repeatedly.

'I want to hear you say it.'

'I promise,' he said breathlessly. 'Hurry up, can you?'

'No. Not until you tell me you won't bother me again. That you won't *speak* of this again. And you absolutely will not inform anyone of my arrangement with Scott, nor the thing with the missing money.'

He screwed up his face. 'I won't. You have my word. Hurry, Roz, for Christ's sake.'

'Are we clear, Wayne? I mean it.'

'Yes. Yes. Absolutely.'

'Okay then.'

With Wayne suited up and ready, I turned around, put my hands on the windowsill and told him to go ahead. I didn't want to face him. Certainly didn't want his tongue near my mouth. I expected doing it this way would be such a turn-on for him that he wouldn't last long.

I expected it would be over within seconds.

Except nothing happened.

I waited. Twenty seconds passed, and there was nothing.

'Wayne?' I whispered.

He didn't answer. I went to turn around, but he reached out, preventing me from doing so. 'Don't,' he said. 'Don't look at me,' he repeated, his voice catching.

'Wayne, what is it?'

'I can't do it,' he whimpered. 'I can't go through with it.'

Then he was rambling, something about his body betraying him. I wasn't sure if he'd had some sort of moral epiphany or he was simply unable to sustain his erection.

'Wayne, it's okay,' I said, trying to pacify him. Then I told him I wouldn't look at him. Told him I would keep my eyes away, but I would get dressed, and then maybe we could talk.

A moment later, I was reaching for my flip-flops, almost dressed.

After that, I have no idea what he was doing, because the fucker hit me on the back of the head, knocking me out cold.

19

I HAD NEVER BEEN knocked unconscious. I've fainted, but that's hardly the same thing. In fact, I'm just going to take a moment to explain the difference between the two.

Fainting occurs when there is a lack of blood flow to the brain. It's the body's righting mechanism. You faint, fall over, the blood doesn't have to fight gravity to travel up through the carotid arteries in your neck and the brain instantly receives the oxygen it's been lacking. This is why soldiers faint when standing for extended periods on parade. Their blood is literally in their boots.

Unconsciousness following a blow to the head is quite different; it's a serious affair. It is not like, say, in the movies, where the villain is put out of action for a few moments, allowing our hero to escape, and then he comes to, fully functioning, only a bit more cross.

No one really knows what causes a concussion, but most are agreed on this: the brain has become damaged, resulting in a temporary and sometimes permanent loss of function. Long-standing problems can occur, the extent of which are under continual investigation. After sustaining a blow to the head, patients may have permanently slurred speech, facial expressions may alter and, in some cases, personality traits change. I knew of one guy, a tradesman, who fell off a ladder, and, where he'd always been morose, the kind of unhappy, scheming type who was highly critical of other builders' work, suddenly he became happy. It must have felt strange for him to be babbling away to folk, his face animated and joyful, while they viewed him suspiciously through narrowed eyes, none of them quite ready to believe the miracle that stood before them.

And then of course there was Mama Cass. She reportedly increased her singing range after being hit on the head with a piece of copper pipe whilst on a building site – although this story has been challenged over the years by friends of Cass Elliot, who said it was used as a way to explain why John Phillips left her out of The Mamas and the Papas for so long (his real reason being she was too overweight).

But I'm getting off my point.

I lay there on Wayne's carpet, more or less in the foetal position but with my head extended backwards, swallowing repeatedly, as I appeared to have a surfeit of saliva. I wasn't afraid at this point, and I was curious as to whether I was unconscious or not. Not many concussions result in a loss of consciousness, and I couldn't say for sure exactly what had happened. All I knew was something was not as it should be.

I could hear Wayne's voice as though through water. He was panicked and calling out my name and, in my head, I was answering. I was answering loudly, shouting as you do when your ears are submerged in the bath and you're asked a question.

But Wayne couldn't hear me. And I couldn't see Wayne. And I couldn't move my head to see where he might be located.

My auditory system was all off kilter. Wayne's calling was diminishing, just as the hum from the aquarium, the sound of the bubbles rising up every few seconds, became insufferably loud. I tried to cover my ears with my hands. But movement wasn't possible. And then, naturally, I thought of George.

Oddly, up until that moment, it hadn't even occurred to me that I might be in danger. Silly, really, but I was so focused on trying to wade through my thoughts, on trying to understand my immediate environment, knowing that on some intuitive level my senses were compromised, that I actually felt safe.

More saliva flooded my mouth. That's when I was able to open my eyes and realize I had been sick earlier. The blow to the head had caused me to vomit.

I began searching the room, and my eyes came to rest on Wayne.

He was rocking to and fro on a dining-room chair, his hands clasped in front of him.

Was this how it would end?

Had the laughable risks I'd taken to try to right past wrongs led me to this?

It seemed as though they had.

It was the cruellest of ironies. In trying to free myself from a life enslaved by debt, I'd become a prisoner.

'Wayne,' I said, but it didn't come out right. The word was blurred and formless. The sound was shocking for me to hear. And for Wayne, too, because he snatched his head up and stared at me.

'Fuck,' he whispered. Then he resumed his rocking action.

I turned over on to my back away from the vomit, with my legs straight out. After lying with my knees flexed for I wasn't sure how long, it was a relief to stretch my hamstrings. I pulled my toes towards me, felt the stretch run right through my calf muscles and into each Achilles. Then I tried to raise my hands to test if I'd suffered a stroke. Both arms lifted evenly, so I turned my head towards Wayne.

I smiled at him.

'Why the hell are you smiling?' he asked, appalled.

And I thought: *Good.* Facial muscles were still functioning properly. Stroke was now an unlikely event. With any luck, my speech would come back when the inflammation in my brain began to subside.

So I did nothing.

In fact, I felt an overriding tiredness, so I slept a little.

When I woke, the room was in semi-darkness.

I could sense Wayne nearby before opening my eyes. I stayed still and listened. At first I thought he was experiencing difficulty with his breathing; it sounded laboured and uneasy. But after listening for a minute or so I realized he was trying to calm himself.

I watched him for a moment and then readied myself for speaking, fearful of the sound I was about to make.

'Help.'

To my ears it sounded normal. So I said it again, only louder. 'Help me.'

Wayne went stock-still. Then he put his hands to his face and his body quaked irregularly as he tried to hold back his crying.

My head was throbbing. He must have got me right slap bang on the occipital protuberance. I had to keep my face angled to the side to avoid the back of my skull connecting with the floor. My tongue was thick in my mouth like cotton wool. And my thoughts were woozy and disconnected.

'I wanted you to stay,' he whimpered. 'That's all. I panicked. I just wanted you to stay longer.'

'My head really hurts, Wayne. What did you hit me with?'

He motioned towards the desk. On it stood a small, chrome, hand-held fire extinguisher. The type you might see inside a boat's cabin, or a caravan. It was smeared with blood. I felt around the back of my skull. My hair was matted with blood and the skin was raised around the wound.

I looked at Wayne. He was uncertain of what to do with me, which was not good. And he was sweating a lot.

I went to sit up but, at the smallest movement, pain crashed through my head, keeping me glued to the floor.

'I'm not angry with you, Wayne,' I lied, placating him. I kept my voice warm, steady. 'But you really need to help me up. I need the bathroom, and I'm not steady.'

'I won't *hurt* you, you know.'

He said this in a way that suggested he found the thought unsavoury. Like it was beneath him. Like he wouldn't stoop *that* low.

'I know you wouldn't,' I said, going along with the insanity of the situation. 'I'm not scared, Wayne, but I am uncomfortable.'

He stayed exactly where he was; it was as if I'd not spoken. His leaky eyes became empty as he looked past me towards the window. He must have opened the curtains after he'd hit me. 'I won't be able to face you at work on Monday,' he said absently.

'You panicked. You just got out of control for a second. It's understandable. I totally understand.'

He blinked. 'You do?'

'Yes,' I said gently.

'I shouldn't have made you do this,' he said. 'It's unforgivable. It's not the way I wanted it to be between us. Not like this. Never like this.'

'Neither of us is who we want to be right now, Wayne. I'm pretty sure of that. But you felt helpless. It's partly my fault. I made you feel bad about yourself by saying I would only do this one time, by saying I wouldn't stay. But you have to understand, Wayne, I'm only doing this thing with Scott because I'm desperate, too. Like I said, it's not who I want to be either.'

I tried to move again, but pain shot through my skull.

'The only way I get to keep anything is if I trap it,' Wayne said, his voice trembling.

'That's not true . . . and, Wayne? Spare me the melodrama.'

He turned on a lamp to the side of him. It was dim, thirty

watts maybe, the kind you leave on through the night when you're breastfeeding. When you need to locate the baby without tripping over your slippers.

'Will you go to the police?' he asked.

'And say what? I came here for sex because you're blackmailing me, but you decided to knock me unconscious instead? Not sure they'd really believe that.'

'You could say I raped you.'

'But you didn't.'

He rose and came close, kneeling beside me.

Oddly, even though inside I was still livid, livid with Wayne, livid with myself for getting into this situation, I wasn't scared. I watched Wayne's sad, apologetic face and could feel only pity.

Gently, he put one hand beneath my neck, and the other under my shoulders, preparing to lift me into a sitting position. 'I'm so, so sorry,' he said.

'Wayne,' I replied softly, 'it will be okay, you know. I promise, this will all be okay. On Monday we'll pretend it never happened and we'll never speak of it again. No one needs to know but us.'

And he closed his eyes and shook his head solemnly, as though grappling with a deep thought. As though he knew without a doubt that it *wouldn't* be okay. This was not the end of the matter, whatever I said.

Because how on earth could it be?

20

I COULD BARELY REMEMBER the trip home. After Wayne got me sitting up, the pain in my head was too intense for me to remain vertical for more than a few seconds and I found I needed to rest some more. I must have either lost consciousness or slept – I wasn't sure which – for I awoke covered with a blanket, no sign of Wayne, and then I got in the car and headed home to Hawkshead. It was a wonder I arrived there in one piece.

Now it was the following day, and I was in Petra's kitchen, her grilling me about flaking out of the dinner the previous evening with Scott and Nadine.

'Did you get the aura?' she asked.

'Aura?' I replied, having no idea what Petra was referring to.

'Yes, the *aura*,' she said snippily. 'The blurred vision, the numbness in the face, the pins and needles?'

I gave a small shrug. Took a sip of orange juice. 'I don't think so.'

'Well, you've not had a proper migraine then. You had a headache. There's a world of difference. Headaches are inconvenient. Migraines are incapacitating. If you'd had one, you would know. Did you take Ibuprofen?'

'Of course.'

'And no change?'

'Nope. No change at all.'

'Did you try lying down in a darkened room?' she asked.

I almost laughed. Kind of, I wanted to say.

'No, I didn't try that,' I said. 'I will next time.'

She looked at me suspiciously, as though she didn't believe I'd had a migraine in the first place. She knew I'd cried off from her dinner last night without good reason, and this, coupled with her knowledge that I was playing my cards close to my chest regarding my financial situation, had got her all jumpy.

Petra couldn't stand not to know.

She separated rashers of streaky bacon before laying them on the grill. A loud wail came from the garden, the kind of wail that would normally merit Petra running wildly through the house to find its source, breathlessly checking if her child was lying bent and crooked at the foot of the stairs.

She looked up, cast a sidelong glance to the garden, tutting dismissively. Then she went back to the bacon, rejigging it, moving each slice along a fraction, to allow her to cram a little more on to the grill.

'Do you want me to go and check on Clara?' I asked.

'Vince is out there.'

'Yes, but she's still crying pretty hard.'

'She'll live.'

Rinsing her hands beneath the hot tap, she told me that last night hadn't exactly been a success. Their dinner with Scott and Nadine had come to a close rather early, *rather abruptly, actually,* after Scott made an excuse about a work problem that needed dealing with, and the brittleness to her tone told me she felt snubbed.

Before I could respond in a suitably soothing manner, as was my way when Petra was pissed off with someone, suggesting they probably didn't mean to be thoughtless, probably had a lot on, she changed the subject, telling me that even though I'd not *technically* suffered a true migraine attack, I did look very tired, and not at all well.

'Is something worrying you?' she asked.

I feigned surprise. 'No,' I said. 'Nothing that I can think of, anyway.' I didn't sound at all convincing, but then who does when asked such a question? 'Do I really look that bad?' I asked. 'I thought I was looking rather perky today. That's a lot of bacon.'

'There are six of us. Mind you, Clara will only pick at it. She raided the cupboards before we were up and found the doughnuts Liz left last night.'

'Six?' I asked. 'Who are the six?'

Petra frowned. 'The four of us . . . and Scott and Nadine. I told you they were coming for brunch.'

My forehead prickled with heat. 'You didn't.'

Petra cracked eggs into a bowl, pausing to count up on her fingers. 'Two for Vince,' she said out loud. 'Two for Scott . . . will you have one egg or two?'

Without really realizing what I was doing, I slid off the stool and went to reach for my bag.

'Where are you going?' Petra said. 'You're not leaving, surely?'

Of course I'm leaving, I wanted to say. *You don't actually expect me to stay.*

'Just clearing a space,' I replied weakly. 'I wish you'd told me they were coming, Petra. I'm not really up to making polite conversation this morning. My head hurts, and—'

'I *did* tell you.'

She hadn't. If she had, I wouldn't have come. I couldn't say that, though, obviously, so I had to let it rest.

'I look like shit,' I said after a moment.

Petra stopped what she was doing and turned to face me. A smile played at the corners of her mouth. 'You just said you were looking quite perky. You're not bothered about what Scott thinks of you, are you? Because I can tell you right now he won't even look at you. He's that kind of guy. Doesn't notice women. You could be naked in front of him and he'd be more bothered about—'

'I was meaning Nadine,' I replied quickly. 'She's always so well groomed.'

'Go and wash your face and put on some of my lipstick, if it makes you feel better. They'll be here in five minutes. Though I don't know why you're fussing, I keep telling you, they're not what you think. They're really not as . . .'

Petra rambled on, but I'd stopped listening. Inside, I was flapping. I was looking around for an escape, an excuse, so I failed to notice right away that she had also taken on a high colour. Her neck, the tops of her arms, had gone a deep, blotchy red. Angry red, like patches of psoriasis.

At first I thought it was because her crush on the couple had waned. Petra threw herself into these new friendships with such energy, such gusto, that when the time came for the other party to cool things a little, perhaps by accepting another invitation rather than her own, she would behave like a jilted bride. Well, maybe that's a little harsh, but she did feel the hurt extraordinarily deeply.

I watched Petra move about the kitchen. Watched her staccato actions, her breath catching in her throat, and knew right then that there was something more at play.

Dread poured through me.

Petra was attracted to Scott.

Then Vince appeared at the French windows. 'Morning, Roz,' he said brightly.

'Morning.'

'How long till brunch?' he asked.

Petra regarded him, and her jaw tightened. 'Fifteen minutes. And you'll need to change those shorts.'

'Right-o,' he said, and shot me a quick smile. 'George okay?'

'Great.'

'Think he'll be up for a spot of fishing Thursday evening?'

'He'd love it.'

'Six thirty, then,' he said. 'I'll pick him up after his tea.'

Vince disappeared upstairs. Petra watched him go, giving the impression of being unreasonably irritated by him. There was nothing unusual in her bossing him around. That was how they functioned. But the look in her eyes – the scorn – as he shuffled past in his shorts and flip-flops, that was something entirely new. The shorts, incidentally, were pretty bad. They were fawn in colour and a shade too short for a rotund figure like Vince. The type worn by out-of-shape American spectators at golf tournaments.

'Have you two had a row?' I asked Petra, hopeful her behaviour was caused by something other than Scott.

'A row?' she said, distracted. 'We never row. I ignore him when I'm angry, you know that.'

'Are you angry then?'

Her shoulders heaved visibly as she exhaled. 'No,' she said. 'It's just . . . it's just sometimes he can be so' – she paused before saying – 'disappointing.' Then she looked at me guiltily, like she knew she was out of line but she couldn't help it.

The doorbell rang.

'Christ,' she said, peering at the bacon. 'I need to turn these over now. Would you mind getting that?'

Long story short, Scott was able to disguise his look of shock upon seeing me answer the door. And what could have been a period of supreme awkwardness turned out not to be when everyone's attention was taken by Clara, who threw the most splendid tantrum. I love watching a good tantrum. It brings out such odd behaviour in the surrounding adults, none more so than Petra, who had a torrent of excuses as to why Clara was conducting herself in this manner. And also from Nadine, who did her best to reassure Petra (on some subliminal level, anyway) that *she was not a bad parent, and in no way at fault.*

In the midst of all this, Scott shot me a look across the kitchen that said, *Shit! This is unexpected!* but then followed it quickly with a shrug and warm smile as though to convey: *It is what it is. Let's not fuck up.*

So we didn't.

We each stuck to the harmless conversation about one's own offspring. Listening to Nadine and Petra cluck away was dull but safe, and I was about to make my excuses and leave when Nadine threw a spanner in the works.

'You know, Roz, I've been thinking. I'm sure you would get along with my brother.'

'Oh?' I said.

'Yes, he's been single for a long time. I've no idea why. He's got such a lot going for him.'

'Wonder why I've not come across him,' I said vaguely, and glanced at Petra, who was absolutely beaming. You would think by her expression that Nadine had mentioned royalty. She gazed towards Nadine, eager for her to go on.

But Scott said, rather bluntly, 'Your brother's no use to Roz.' And Nadine turned to him, her expression calm but masking deep offence.

'Why?' she said. 'Why is he no use?'

Scott shrugged. 'He's' – he paused, choosing his words care-fully – 'he's not what you'd call properly employed, is he?'

I glanced at Petra, and her smile fell. She looked as though all the air had been sucked out of her. Reluctant to upset Nadine, but feeling as though she must say something, she uttered, 'Roz is looking for someone stable. Financial stability is the key, more than anything else, really.'

This might have come across as pompous if you didn't know the history. But Petra was protecting herself here as much as me.

As it was, Nadine didn't appear concerned with what Petra had to say, she was clearly fuming about Scott's assessment of her brother, and the rest of us looked at one another, helpless, waiting for her to blow.

'My brother,' she said through her teeth, 'is a perfectly decent human being, who has no financial burdens. He is kind to women, incredibly loyal and, just because he doesn't have *your ambition, Scott*, it does not make him a loser.'

Scott sat back in his chair. 'I didn't call him a loser. I just don't think he's right for Roz, that's all.'

Nadine did a double take. 'And you would know this how?'

'Because' – and he looked at me as he said this – 'Roz seems like she would want a guy with something about them. Your brother's a drifter. He's a nice guy, but he's not going anywhere. He'll still be living week to week when he's sixty.'

Nadine shook her head. 'I can't believe you come out with this stuff.'

'To be honest,' I interrupted weakly, 'it would be impossible at the moment, anyway. George isn't staying with his dad for another couple of weeks, so I'm stuck at home. Not that I mind, it's just—'

'You could go on Thursday,' Vince piped up, the first words he'd uttered since we'd sat down. 'You could go out with him on Thursday.' He'd fashioned himself a bacon-and-egg sandwich, and as he bit down a little of the yolk spurted. Petra looked away. 'I'm taking him fishing. He could spend the night here, or I don't mind dropping him back late, give you a chance to have a couple of drinks with this guy. If that's what you want.'

Nadine turned back to me, her head angled to one side. She was waiting for a response.

'Okay' came out of my mouth without my realizing I'd actually spoken.

And it was only when I glanced at Scott that I saw what I had done.

He was angry.

He didn't want me to meet Nadine's brother at all.

Winston dropped George back at home just after seven.

'You need to have a talk with him,' he said, as George walked past me, glum and silent, and went straight upstairs to his bedroom.

Celia was in her front garden watering the hanging baskets with a pump-action watering can specifically designed for the task. She appeared fully focused, even frowning slightly as she adjusted the spout, but she was clearly eavesdropping.

I tilted my head in Celia's direction and asked Winston if he wanted to come in, indicating that I'd rather not discuss George on the front step. But he declined.

'Got a hot date,' he said.

'Oh yes?'

'Mickey Tallis. We're kite surfing on Morecambe Sands.'

'Try not to kill yourself.'

Winston had known Mickey Tallis for years and knocked about with him when he couldn't find anyone better. He was the last of the unmarrieds. I tended to avoid Mickey (particularly when he'd had a drink) as he always managed to bring the conversation back around to Ultravox. And what an absolute travesty it was that 'Vienna' was denied the number-one spot on account of Joe Dolce's ridiculous novelty record, 'Shaddap You Face'.

None of which was relevant now, but it popped into my head.

Winston remained with his weight against the doorframe, not quite ready to leave. He glanced towards Celia, nodded hello, and then turned back to me. 'He's still pretty cut up about the incident at school.'

'George is? What did you say to him?'

'I told him he couldn't take money and other people's stuff, because they make a massive deal out of it. But it didn't mean he was a bad person or anything.'

Silently, I mouthed, *Shhhhh*, to get him to lower his voice. 'What did he say?'

'Says he wants to go back to his old school. He reckons he hasn't got any friends here and he wants to go back to Windermere.'

'I'll talk to him,' I said.

'Okey-doke.'

Then a pause.

'Roz?'

'What is it, Winston?'

'You look tired.'

I shrugged. 'It's been a rough weekend.'

'Are you okay?' he asked tenderly. 'I mean, are you managing okay?'

'I'm fine, Winston. Go fly your kite.'

Upstairs, George sat on the new beanbag I'd picked up for him from Poundstretcher. It was cheap. It would probably last about five minutes. George had his back to the door and was wriggling his small body, trying to envelop as much of himself in the thing as possible, as though trying to disappear.

'Hey,' I said softly.

'Hey,' he replied.

'Do you like the beanbag?'

'Yeah.'

I sat down on his bed. Gesturing to his duvet cover, I said, 'I gave this a wash for you. It'll smell nice and clean when you climb in later.'

'Thanks,' he replied, and I felt silly. What did he care?

For a time that afternoon, while making up his bed with fresh linen, smoothing out the creases, fluffing his pillows, rearranging his Pokémon figures on the windowsill, I'd had the short-lived sensation of feeling like a good mother.

'Your dad says you're worried about school.'

'I want to *move* schools.'

'Okay,' I said carefully, 'but where would you go? There's only one school in Hawkshead. That makes things kind of difficult.'

He turned to face me. 'We could move back.'

'We can't, honey. Not straight away, anyhow. And, besides, you'd still have to go to school tomorrow, whether we move house again or not.'

'I could go to my old school and you could take me there on your way to work. Ollie Mundine goes to Windermere each day because his mum works at the post office.'

So he'd really put some thought into this.

'Okay, I see where you're going, and yes, it would be doable. You could move schools, and yes, I could drop you there on my way to and from work, but I'm not going to do that.'

'Why not?'

'Because the only reason you want to leave is because you're ashamed of what you've done. And you can't run away from things, George. What happens if you get into trouble at your next school? Then what? We move again? And again? Every time you don't like something, you can't just pack it in or run away.'

'Why not?'

'Because you run out of options, honey. And sooner or later you have to face up to stuff.'

21

AT WORK THE following morning there was no sign of Wayne. It was now ten fifteen, I was on my third patient of the day and the other clinicians were speculating as to the reason for his absence.

Absence with no explanatory call was not like Wayne.

Gary took it upon himself to phone him but could get no answer on either the mobile or landline, so after asking each of us whether we thought he should inform head office, and each of us saying no, inform them the following day if he still hadn't turned up, he went ahead and did it.

After the events of Saturday, I wasn't completely surprised Wayne had gone AWOL, but it was a little worrying, as it was so out of character. Wayne never missed work unless he was incapacitated by illness, and he would always call. He would leave lists of instructions for us, as though he were truly indispensable.

Where the hell was he? If I could turn up for work after what had happened, so could he.

Perhaps Wayne was thoroughly ashamed of his behaviour on Saturday and had gone on a drinking bender. Perhaps he'd be back tomorrow, looking worse for wear, full of apology.

As I said, after my bang on the head on Saturday night, my memory of leaving Wayne's was a little hazy. I could recall him babbling, telling me repeatedly he was sorry for his actions, that he might not make it into work on Monday. He said he might need a few days to clear his head. Or at least I think he did. Now I wasn't sure what I remembered.

I'd gone home and crashed. I didn't need the bottle of Night Nurse, the trauma to my head inducing a solid ten hours of dreamless sleep, the like of which I couldn't remember having since I was a teenager. I'd woken disorientated and dizzy, with little memory of the drive home, feeling relieved nonetheless that my body had taken charge, falling into such a depth of sleep that I was spared the ordeal of reliving the night at Wayne's over and over in my head.

After a long soak in the bath, by ten o'clock the following morning my body seemed intact. My senses were functioning again and with only minimal swelling to the head and a scalp wound hidden by my hair, brunch at Petra's hadn't seemed such a disastrous way to finish off the weekend – all things considered.

Except now I had a date.

I had a date with the brother-in-law of the guy I was screwing for money.

I had tried, repeatedly, after agreeing to it, to worm my way out of it. But Nadine was smarting after her exchange with Scott, and the whole situation became a stand-off between the two of them. She was convinced that Scott was unfairly pigeonholing her brother, as was typical when people chose to live differently to him, and the more he tried to talk her round, the more she dug her heels in.

Also, where at first Petra had sided with Scott, in so much as she believed Nadine's brother would be an unsuitable choice *at this stage in Roz's life*, as she phrased it, she ended up doing a complete about-face, declaring, 'Who are we to decide who's right for her?'

Petrified of saying the wrong thing, of tripping myself up, I watched the situation unfold with increasing horror, as Scott dragged up instances of Nadine's brother's fecklessness.

Needless to say, with all that swimming around in my head this Monday morning, and a full patient list, I couldn't ruminate for long on Wayne's absence, so I left it to Gary to try to track him down.

Keith Hollinghurst groaned now as I sprung the joints of his thoracic spine. There was a spinous process – T8 – that had become perpetually lodged and proved stubborn to get moving. I climbed on to the treatment couch, straddling Keith from behind to get my full weight perpendicularly over the top of him, and pressed down through my thumbs.

After twenty pushes, Keith begged for mercy, and some air – it's pretty impossible to take a breath when having this performed – and told me, craning his neck and puffing hard, that he had a proposition for me.

'Not another one,' I said, remembering the last time.

'Hear me out. Not . . .' and he nodded his head where the word 'wanking' should be, not able to bring himself to say it in the presence of a lady. 'No more of that nonsense,' he said guiltily.

I climbed down and washed my hands as Keith struggled with the task of turning himself over – imagine a woodlouse trying to right itself. It occurred to me that it wouldn't be long before Keith, like the humble woodlouse, would become marooned in one position and couldn't turn over without assistance.

Once sitting, and with his breathing near normal, he told me he'd bought a small bed and breakfast at auction. 'Daft, really,' he said. 'The money was burning a hole in me pocket and I bought the thing without thinking.'

I had no idea where he was going with this, and knowing Keith and his previous requests, it really could be anything. So I remained quiet.

'Anyway,' he went on, 'when I looked at it, I realized it's going to be hell to staff. You gotta live on site with those things, or else they don't make money . . .'

He started to cough at this point. Big, hacking coughs.

I handed him a wad of tissues and waited as he hawked up the phlegm. This took three growls and another long spate of coughing. Without comment, or even a flicker of disdain, I passed him the bin to drop in his deposit of soiled tissue.

On first qualifying as a physiotherapist, each clinician rotates between departments to accrue a wide base of knowledge and to give them some idea of the area in which they would like to specialize. It was on one such placement, respiratory care, that I developed my poker face, used for dealing with such stomach-turning situations as the removal of Keith's phlegm.

The woman was a tiny bird-like thing, as most chronic bronchitis patients are – the sheer amount of energy needed for breathing, to get the air into their compromised lungs, tends to use up calories faster than they can ingest them. Her chest rattled like an old Ewbank as she spooned tomato soup into her mouth. Beside her was her sputum pot. Each respiratory-care patient had one to spit their secretions into, and it was my job to check the colour of them every few hours for signs of infection, blood and other nasties. With her glazed eyes fixed on the TV hanging from a bracket high in the corner of the room, I watched as she dipped her bread into the sputum pot, twice, before chewing on it thoughtfully.

Anyway, all this to say, I was not totally grossed out, as most would be by Keith in this instance, and was genuinely interested in what he had to say next.

He dabbed at his eyes. 'I've got builders in there at the moment, tearing the place apart.'

'What are you planning to do with it?'

'Offices,' he said. 'I thought you might want one.'

I waited.

'Not on a lease,' he said. 'Just month-to-month rent. All bills included except phone. There'll be a downstairs toilet and space for your punters to wait in the hallway.'

'How much?'

'Seven hundred a month. But I'll waive the first two months' rent, let you get on your feet, if you treat me for free when I need it.'

'You would do that?'

'You've always seen me right, Roz. And I know you don't like it how Laughing Boy out there's always got his eye on you, controlling your every move.'

'You mean Wayne?'

'You could work for yourself again, love,' he went on. 'Be your own boss. What do you say?'

I did a quick sum in my head. With what Keith was offering, overheads deducted, I could increase my weekly wage by around thirty per cent. That was as long as I didn't screw up again.

'I'd say thank you, Keith,' my voice catching as I spoke his name. 'Thank you, thank you, thank you.'

And he smiled broadly.

'Grand,' he said. He touched my shoulder affectionately, as he could see I was tearing up. Then he gave me a firm pat, the way you would a Welsh Cob you were particularly fond of. 'That's my girl,' he said. 'That's my girl. It'll be yours to move into in a month.'

22

THE PHONE CALL came on my mobile at around mid-morning, during my tea break. I was outside watching with interest as a song thrush tried to smash open a snail shell using a piece of broken roof tile as an anvil. The repetitive tap-tapping had caught my attention, reminding me of the pieces of grit Winston used to launch against my bedroom window, back when he was on his way home from the pub after I'd thrown him out for good.

'Roz Toovey?'

'Yes,' I replied. 'Can you speak up? The traffic from the road is quite noisy.'

'I was told to ring you,' the caller said. 'By my sister. Nadine?'

'Oh, yes.' I found myself screwing up my face. Wanting to cut the call without further conversation.

'So then,' he said, 'this is me calling you. Bit awkward, really.'

I took a breath. 'Did Nadine mention why she wanted you to get in touch?'

A small laugh. 'Yes. You are a nice person whom she thinks I might find interesting.'

'She said that?'

'Of course not. You want the truth?'

'Why not?'

'She said she was friends with your sister, who was desperate to get you together with someone who wasn't a total fuck-up. And I immediately sprang to mind. Frankly, I think she's probably sick of hearing about your single status.'

'What else did she tell you about me?' I asked, amused now.

'Nice figure, bit scruffy – which she thinks I am, too, so I took that with a pinch of salt. She said you're a could-be-kind-of-fun-for-a-while type of person. What did she say about me?'

'She said you were definitely *not* a loser.'

'I'm not,' he said.

'Well, that's good then.'

'I believe we have to go out on Thursday. Is that correct?' he said.

'That's correct.'

'Do you have anywhere in mind?'

'Surprise me,' I said.

'All right, Roz Toovey,' he said. 'I will.'

When I finished the call I was smiling. And it was only later, when treating Scott's elbow, that I realized I'd forgotten to ask him his name.

'His name is Henry,' Scott said, regarding me steadily.

I had hold of his forearm in one hand, and with the other I was pushing down on his wrist to stretch out the extensor muscles. His elbow was almost better, and this would be the last treatment session. 'So you *are* going to go out with him?' he asked.

I stopped what I was doing and took a step back.

'You'd rather I didn't,' I said. A statement.

'No, you can see who you like,' he said. 'It has absolutely nothing to do with what I think. It's just, like I said yesterday, Henry's limited.'

'Limited? He sounded nice.'

'Nice,' he repeated. Spitting the word from his mouth.

'Look, Scott,' I said, losing patience with whatever game he was playing, 'what do you suggest I do? It was your wife who orchestrated this, your wife who basically bullied me into doing it. I tried to say no. In fact I did say no. Perhaps if you hadn't been so vehement in your attack on your brother-in-law yesterday, then we wouldn't find ourselves in this pickle.'

'You think she did it because she suspects something between us?'

'I think she suspects nothing. She forced the issue because you were so against it. Because you were so fault-finding about her brother. It was puzzling to watch. I could see Petra didn't know what to make of it, she—'

'Fuck Petra!' he snapped, out of nowhere. 'Petra hasn't got an original thought inside her head.'

Again, I pulled away.

Quietly, firmly, I said, 'Stop it, Scott. That's enough.'

I was taken aback. I'd not seen him like this before.

'Stop what?' he demanded.

Keeping my voice low and without provocation, I said, 'I don't understand why you acted like that. It was like you *wanted* to be found out. Do you want them to know what's been going on between us?'

'Of course not. Don't be fucking ridiculous.'

'Then what? What?'

And it was as if he had stalled. I stopped speaking because, all of a sudden, his expression collapsed and he lifted his hands to his face.

He bowed his head before exhaling deeply.

Then he reached out his hand, gesturing as though to say, *Give me a minute. I really need a moment to regroup here.*

With his eyes soft, remorseful now, he whispered, 'This is so hard for me. When can I see you again? I *need* to see you.'

*

True to his word, as soon as my invoice was sent to his offices, an hour later the four thousand from Scott landed in my account and I began to dream about the future. Not the fantastical dreams of the desperate that had occupied my thoughts in recent months. Instantly, I stopped dreaming about lottery wins and surprise windfalls and got back to planning the upcoming months. I couldn't repay my parents overnight, that much was clear, but I could, if things worked out with Keith Hollinghurst's benefaction, begin to earn a decent living, putting away some money each month that would go towards making up for their loss.

At this point, I didn't know how long the thing with Scott would continue. Not for ever, I knew that, and his recent behaviour – going from nasty to oddly clingy in the space of a second – had unsettled me somewhat. But when you see that money start to mount up, when you've lived each day frightened of what else is coming through your letterbox, it can be hard to give up on something so lucrative. Two more nights with him and the credit-card balance would be zero.

And, if kept secret, no one was going to get hurt by our actions. I wasn't ripping anyone off to make money, trampling over the little people. There were no harmful environmental effects. I was even going to pay tax on my earnings. The socialist in me almost approved.

And yet I couldn't persuade myself that what I was doing was okay. No matter how many ways I looked at it.

Also, I now had a sense of growing unease that what had started out as a business arrangement – what for me was *very much still* a business arrangement – was perhaps taking on another significance for Scott. And of course I felt sick with guilt when my thoughts turned to Nadine.

It would be our third meeting when I would get a sense of things to come.

This time we did not need the whole night. Scott wanted to meet badly and I told him an entire night was impossible. I explained that George was fragile. He understood, and we negotiated a one-thousand-five-hundred-pound fee for an afternoon of fun and pleasure to be undertaken the following day.

So now, on Tuesday morning, without Wayne's prying eyes, I was able to do something I would not ordinarily do, and that was to cancel the afternoon patients. I moved them around and slotted them in elsewhere, giving the vague excuse of a 'hospital appointment'. Patients tended to be too worried you might have something sinister wrong with you to pry, so they rescheduled without complaint. And should the worst happen, should Wayne return while I was out, my excuse would be that I was at the hospital for 'a head X-ray', which ought to keep him quiet.

Scott had rented a cottage on the north-eastern shore of Coniston Water for the next three weeks – paid for in cash so no one could track it. His plan had been to take it for the whole of the summer, but he was told by the letting agent that a family from Bristol had booked for mid-August.

Coniston lies due west of Windermere, the lake itself is a lot quieter, and the cottage was accessed either directly from the water or from a private lane. I suspected the owners had run a little short of money after fixing the place up for renting, as the lane needed attention. Presently, it was just two gravel tracks, with rough grass in between, which caught on the undercarriage of the car. I could just about make it through in the Jeep and Scott was able to negotiate it well enough in the Range Rover, but a standard saloon would have to park in the lay-by off the road and its passengers would have to arrive on foot.

I assumed this was one of the reasons Scott chose it.

We could stay there undisturbed, invisible to the occasional car which came along this side of the lake. Of course, the main attraction was that we could come and go as we pleased. It was a

175

hideaway. In fact, once he'd organized the booking, Scott chided himself for not thinking of it earlier. Why waste time in hotels, where there was the risk of discovery, when he could simply take a place like this?

The advantage for me was it was only five miles and a twelve-minute drive from my house. I could slip out of work, get the car ferry across Windermere, have sex with Scott for the afternoon, be there to pick George up *and* have tea on the table, all before five thirty.

And be fifteen hundred pounds better off.

At 1.50 p.m. I made my way along the track. It was bordered not by the usual drystone wall but by thick hedgerow. From my elevated driving position, I could see over the tops to the flat floor of the distinctive U-shaped valley beyond, carved out by a glacier in the last ice age. At the end of the track, Scott's Range Rover was reverse parked neatly to the side of the wood store. With the sun reflecting off his windscreen, I didn't realize he was in the front seat, and he startled me by climbing out of the car unexpectedly.

'Sorry,' he said. 'I wanted to wait out here for you.'

'You needn't have.'

'I thought we could go in together. I thought it might be nice.'

'What, and pretend like we're a real couple, on our holidays?'

He seemed hurt. 'Something like that,' he said quietly.

Inside, the cottage was pretty, but had been finished in a rush. The light switches were spotted with emulsion and parts of the skirting boards didn't quite run together correctly. There was a note on the table to say an electrician would be in the following morning to fix the shower in the main bathroom. Sorry for the inconvenience, it said.

'Quaint,' I said to Scott, as I wandered from room to room.

'It's shoddy,' he replied. 'I'm glad I didn't take it for the whole summer. I'll look for something better.'

We stood looking out of the French doors. Beyond was the lake, flat and calm as glass and reflecting the trees on the opposite bank. Along with the other stretches of water that make up the Lake District, Coniston has a speed limit of 10 miles per hour. For a long time Windermere had no such limit, and the shoreline had a perpetual oily iridescence from spilled diesel. Early-morning walks would be spoiled by tossers in wetsuits revving their jet-skis loudly. I wasn't sorry about the introduction of the speed ban, though many were. Including Scott. He'd had to sell his powerboat.

Aware of the time, I turned to Scott and began to kiss him.

Pushing my hips forward into his, I slipped the tip of my tongue inside his mouth.

I could feel resistance.

Unsure how to play it, I started to unbutton my tunic, but he reached out. 'Don't,' he said flatly, 'you're behaving like a prostitute.'

I let my arms fall to my sides and looked at him. 'What exactly do you want me to do, Scott?' I asked. 'We haven't got much time. I assumed you'd want to—'

'Get cracking?'

His voice was laced with sarcasm. His expression hard.

I pulled away. Fastened up my buttons.

'Would you rather we didn't do this today?' I asked.

'I just don't want to fuck as soon as we walk through the door,' he said.

'Apologies,' I said, irritated, 'but last time you did. Last time that's exactly what you wanted us to do.'

He swallowed, and we stood in silence. Neither of us knew quite how to act.

'Hey,' he said after a moment, touching my cheek with his finger-tips. 'Don't get upset. I don't know what I want. I know I want you, but I don't want it to feel like you're only here for the money.'

What to say to that?

'I couldn't do this with just anyone,' I began, intending to smooth things over. Massage his ego a little.

'I know, I know. And I'm sorry,' he said. 'I shouldn't have made you feel that way. Let's go upstairs.'

I managed a weak smile. As we climbed the stairs he told me he wanted to watch me undress slowly while he waited naked on the bed.

With reference to my physio uniform, he said, 'You can be a nurse.'

I undressed as he requested and he asked me to lie down. 'Close your eyes,' he whispered, then proceeded to kiss me tenderly, starting at my ankles. When I went to respond, he said, 'No, don't.'

He made love to me that afternoon with such affection, such devotion, that I really should have realized the extent of his feelings.

But I didn't. I was a fool.

Or maybe I just simply chose to ignore it.

23

'WHERE *ARE* YOU?' asked Petra crossly. 'I'm outside your treatment room, holding a cheese-and-tomato quiche, and that guy Gary says you've gone to the hospital. What are you doing at the hospital?'

'Can Gary hear you?' I replied, sitting up quickly and sliding to the edge of the bed away from Scott.

'No.' She lowered her voice. 'I don't think so. He's back in his room.'

I exhaled. 'I'm skiving,' I said.

'Oh, that's a relief . . . I thought you were ill—'

'Petra!' I warned, before she blurted out anything more.

'Yes, yes, sorry.' She stopped speaking, and I heard her heels move across the floor. 'I'm outside now,' she said a moment later. 'He can't hear me. Why are you skiving?'

'Because I can. Wayne's not there to watch my every move, so I thought I'd give myself the afternoon off.'

'Lucky you.'

'Coming from someone who hasn't worked full time in over fifteen years.'

'You're counting, I see. Anyway,' she said, 'what am I supposed to do with this quiche?'

'Will it keep until tomorrow?'

'Should do.'

'Okay, pop it in the fridge.'

'What fridge?'

'In the kitchen, at the back of the clinic. You'll have to close your eyes when you open it, 'cause it's pretty grubby. No one cleans it. Stick a note on the top saying "Hands off" or Gary will help himself. I'll take it home tomorrow instead.'

'All right. Where are you now? You're not at home.'

'I am.'

'So you've gone and got carpets all of a sudden, have you? Speaking to you, it usually sounds like you're inside a shipping container. All tinny from the lack of soft furnishings.'

'I'm in bed.'

'In the afternoon?'

'Yes, Petra. In the afternoon. People do that, you know.'

'Oh,' she said, genuinely surprised.

Petra often had a puritanical view of resting. She was suspicious of anyone who rested without a valid medical reason and thought people who slept late were wasting the day.

'So, thanks for the quiche,' I said lamely, trying to bring her back on track.

'Not a problem,' she replied, and she rushed me off the phone at that point, because she had a text and couldn't access it while continuing to speak to me.

I turned around. Scott had his arm thrown across his face.

'You lie so easily,' he said, his voice heavy with post-coital sleepiness.

The following morning, Wednesday, I arrived at work early. As I'd rearranged a patient from the previous afternoon to come in at eight, I dropped George at breakfast club – unlike after-school club, you don't need to book in advance. I was twenty minutes into the session when I heard voices in reception. I popped my head out to investigate, expecting to see a patient wanting to make an appointment, or else buy some of Wayne's pointless health-food supplements.

But it was a couple. And an ill-matched couple at that.

Seeing me at the door, she stood first. She was around forty, medium build, wearing a grey, smart, two-buttoned suit, with black piping around the lapel. Beneath, she wore a round-necked T-shirt which had the white-white newness of a first wear. Her hair was pulled into a neat ponytail at the nape of her neck and she wore little make-up.

There was something immediately familiar about her – an old patient perhaps? I decided not, because though her expression was pleasant, eager almost, she didn't regard me in a way that expected recognition.

The man was older and bordered on scruffy. He was short, rounding and wore yesterday's shirt, which was heavily creased. He had a moustache that needed trimming.

'Hello. Sorry to bother you,' the woman said. 'I'm DS Joanne Aspinall and this is my colleague DS Ron Quigley. We were hoping to speak to a Mr Geddes.'

'Wayne Geddes is not here.'

'Any idea where he is?'

'I've not, I'm afraid.'

'When did you last see him?'

This caught me unawares.

'I . . . I'm so sorry,' I stammered, 'but I'm actually in the middle of a treatment session right now. Would we be able to do this later?'

'Sure,' said DS Aspinall.

'I may be some time.'

She smiled. 'No rush. It's a quiet day at the office, so to speak. We're happy to wait as long as it takes.'

I closed the door.

As long as *what* takes?

This was the last thing I needed. The police – and not just the police, but CID – sniffing around. What on earth did they want with Wayne? Had he reneged on our deal and told HQ it was me who took that money? Had they now passed the matter on to the police? Christ.

I needed to buy some time to get my thoughts straight. Work out what to say to them.

As it was, I didn't have a great deal left to do with regards to the patient I was working on, but I dawdled. I pretended there was an area of the rear deltoid that could be contributing to the patient's problem and spent an inordinate amount of time breaking down the tissue, mobilizing the scapula, all quite unnecessary.

When I could delay no more I finished up and told the patient I'd meet her at reception.

The detectives seemed very at home. They had none of the anxiousness apparent in the faces of patients as they waited, knowing they were about to experience some degree of pain. There wasn't a week went by without someone making reference to 'physio-terrorists', and I'd smile as though hearing the term for the first time. The two detectives slouched happily, though, shoulders relaxed, knees dropped slightly apart, as if watching television with a beer.

After I'd scheduled another appointment and bid the patient goodbye, the two detectives approached the desk. I closed the bookings page on the screen and told them I would be with them shortly.

'We'll just loiter here until you're ready,' the man said.

'Loitering without intent,' I answered, and he tried to smile.

Eventually, I told them I was free and asked what I could help them with.

Faces serious, they showed me their warrant cards and I laughed nervously at the formality. It seemed extraneous and silly, like when the waiter pours a little wine for tasting, and you have to go through the rigmarole of saying that it's acceptable. *Very nice, thank you. Please pour the rest.*

'We are trying to ascertain the whereabouts of Wayne Geddes,' DS Aspinall began. 'Any information you can provide us with would be very welcome.'

'I don't know where Wayne is,' I replied.

'Is it normal for him to be absent from work?'

'It's out of character.'

They both nodded thoughtfully and DS Aspinall withdrew a notebook and pencilled something illegible in it.

As she wrote, I turned my face towards DS Quigley. 'Can I ask what this is about?'

'Preliminary inquiries,' he answered.

'Inquiries into what?' I asked.

He made a face as though he wasn't at liberty to say right now.

'So you say it's out of character for Mr Geddes not to be at work for . . . how many days, is it?' DS Aspinall asked.

'If he doesn't come in today this will be the third.'

'He would usually be here by now, would he?' she asked.

I nodded. 'He arrives early.'

'To open up?'

'Yes, but we've all got a set of keys, just in case he's down at HQ, or overseeing another clinic.'

I couldn't believe I'd actually used Wayne's term of 'HQ'.

'And when did you say you last saw him again?' she asked.

I hesitated.

'It would have been Friday afternoon, after work,' I lied.

'How did he seem to you?' she asked.

I thought of Wayne in that moment. Wayne giving me the ultimatum. Wayne threatening to go to the police if I didn't acquiesce, if I didn't give in to his demands.

'I'm not sure what you mean,' I said.

'Did he seem worried? Agitated?'

'Not especially.'

'What did you talk about?'

'I'm not sure I remember. Work. The coming weekend. Our plans.'

'What were Wayne's plans for the weekend?' she asked.

'I don't think he said.'

'So you told him about your plans?'

'I guess I must have. Look,' I said, trying to slow this down before she had me blurting out something I'd regret, not wanting to divulge the real nature of my business at Wayne's house on Saturday, 'I can't really remember. Me and Wayne, we're not what you'd call close. He's my boss. I exchange pleasantries, I keep things neutral. I don't pry into his life, he doesn't pry into mine.'

DS Aspinall smiled. 'I understand.'

She flicked over a page in her notebook and requested I bear with her for a moment as she jotted down a couple of things.

It was one of those awkward silences that I had the tendency to fill with chit-chat. I stayed quiet, rearranging a few items on the desk. I removed the back of the hole punch and tapped it twice, the small white paper discs fluttering into the waste-paper basket.

I looked up and saw she was still writing.

DS Quigley had his hands inside his pockets and was rocking back and forth from his heels to the balls of his feet. His shoes made a soft squelching noise that he seemed to be unaware of. He turned and glanced around the reception area.

'What kinds of things do you get in here?' he asked me.

'You mean what kinds of problems do we treat?'

He nodded.

'Backs and necks mostly.'

He raised his eyebrows, indicating that was not what he expected me to say.

'Since early man decided to stand upright, to go vertical, he has experienced problems with the spine,' I explained.

'I thought it would be knees,' he said, flexing his, and wincing as he did so. I could hear the crepitus, the grating of bone on bone as he straightened up. (Incidentally, the more flirtatious male would ask if we saw a lot of groin strains.)

'We do see quite a few knee problems,' I went on, 'but mostly it's backs and necks . . . then knees, shoulders and feet. Along with a few sporting injuries.'

DS Quigley nodded meditatively.

'What's Mr Geddes's role here?' DS Aspinall asked, her note-taking finished for the time being.

'Practice manager.'

'Is he well liked?'

I widened my eyes involuntarily and laughed a little. 'No comment.'

DS Aspinall smiled in response, then waited to see if I would add anything further.

'Is Wayne in some kind of trouble?' I asked carefully.

'We just need to find him,' she replied.

'Have you checked his house?'

'We're going there next. This was on our way, so it made sense to stop here first. We've been told he has made no contact with work since Friday. Is that correct?'

'As far as I know, but, like I said, I'm not really the one to ask. Gary, who'll be in around eight forty-five, may be able to help you. He's the one who called head office and reported Wayne absent from work.'

She kept her gaze on me and, out of nowhere, it dawned on me how I knew her. She had been a few years below me at school, and since then I'd seen her around from time to time. She'd lost weight, though, or else changed her appearance. There was definitely something different about her. I just couldn't put my finger on it.

After a moment she asked, 'Does Mr Geddes have any family living nearby?'

'His father's dead and his mum is in a home.'

'Any siblings?'

'Not that he's mentioned.'

'Okay, thank you,' she said. 'I think that's all we need for now. We might pop back later, if we need further information.'

I tried to mask my relief that the interrogation was over by doing something I would *never* do – commenting on her posture.

'Do you suffer from neck problems, Detective?'

'Why do you ask?'

'Just in the way you're moving. You seem as though you might have some stiffness at around C5/6 level.'

I refrained from saying she had what we unflatteringly called a pokey-chin posture. Often stiffness in the lower neck and upper thoracic region of the spine causes people to thrust their chins forward. This has the effect of limiting their rotation – when they try to turn their head to the side, they elevate their shoulder at the same time. Think Paula Abdul, robot-like, turning to admonish Simon Cowell in the early days of *American Idol*.

'I had a breast reduction,' DS Aspinall said simply. 'I've been left with stiffness in my upper back from the years of constant—' She stopped mid-sentence. She let me fill in the blanks.

Her partner, DS Quigley, looked to the floor.

'Ah,' I said, unfazed now that we were back on my turf, 'it can be such a cruel condition. Sometimes the upward-facing dog stretch can help. If you lift your head backwards as well, as you do it. Do you know the stretch?'

'I do. I'll try it,' she said.

She closed her notepad and made like she was ready to leave.

Casting around the reception area one last time to make certain nothing had slipped her attention, she thanked me for my time and handed me a card with her details on it, should Wayne get in touch.

She walked a few steps from the desk and, just as I thought I was rid of them, she stopped and turned, frowning as though grappling with a puzzling thought.

'Did Mr Geddes ever mention any missing money?' she asked.

24

'Money?' I repeated.

'Yes,' said DS Aspinall, 'money.'

DS Quigley, who had already exited the clinic, now doubled back, lingering in the passage a few feet behind his partner. His face remained passive, open, and I realized instantly this was a well-practised set piece between the two of them.

Lure the victim with their affable, friendly demeanour before going in for the kill when the victim was off guard.

'I don't think Wayne mentioned anything,' I murmured.

'Try casting your mind back to last week,' encouraged DS Aspinall. 'Did he question you about any irregularities in the accounts?'

Just then, the front door of the clinic opened and Magdalena appeared, carrying a scale model of the spine, complete with all the major nerves, and a prolapsed disc at L5 level. I had been hunting for it yesterday when I couldn't get through to a patient the idea that something pressing on a nerve in his back could give him pain in the front of his shin. He was convinced he had a fracture, even though the X-ray said otherwise.

Magdalena gave a token smile to the two detectives, and said, 'Guten Morgen,' which was what she did when she didn't want to engage in conversation. She disappeared into her treatment room, whereupon she switched on Classic FM, loud enough to be heard through the closed door.

DS Aspinall gestured towards Magdalena's room. 'She works here as well?'

'Yes.'

'German?'

'Austrian.'

'We'll need to interview you all at some point,' she said.

I told her that would be fine and then waited for her to say she was leaving, again.

'You were thinking back to last week?' she prompted, phrasing it as a question.

'Oh yes,' I replied, as though I'd clean forgotten, and made a show of lifting my eyes to the ceiling, pretending to recall the events of the previous few days.

Eventually, I shook my head, saying, 'No. I'm really sorry, but I can't remember Wayne mentioning any irregularities. He tended to keep the accounting stuff to himself. He had a way of making out like it was above our heads. If you know what I mean.'

'Sure,' she said. 'I get it.'

I got the sense the interview was now over, so I moved out from behind the desk, mumbling something about getting ready for the next patient.

DS Aspinall watched me carefully before thanking me again for my time.

'See you later,' she said.

I forced a smile. 'Yes, later then.'

I listened until I heard both car doors bang shut, then I ran to my treatment room and pushed aside the venetian blind. They were in a Ford something or other. I couldn't make out what. But it was a new, black saloon – the type of nondescript, top-of-the-range model the medical reps arrived in.

DS Aspinall was driving. She reversed fast. Recklessly, actually. And then sped off out of the clinic entrance.

I was shaking.

Where *was* Wayne?

If he *had* reported me, why wasn't he here? Something was very wrong with this whole situation.

I needed some air.

I went outside to the car park and sat on the bench. Above me, a buzzard circled, gaining height. I watched as two jackdaws made an assault, dive-bombing the bird, screeching their warnings, until it changed its course away from what must have been their nest.

The clinic door opened behind me.

'What was that about?' Magdalena asked, referring to our two early-morning visitors.

'The police. They're looking for Wayne.'

'Why they look for him when we have many missing children?'

'What missing children?' I asked her.

'I don't know,' she said defensively, 'but there will be some. For sure.'

I didn't pursue it. Conversations with Magdalena often ended with her walking off, oddly wounded, as if you'd made a direct attack on her. I couldn't fathom if things were lost in translation or this was simply how she was.

The patients felt it, too. They'd exit her treatment room wearing befuddled looks of shame, either because they somehow felt they had offended Magdalena, or else because they'd complained she'd hurt them physically . . . which offended Magdalena.

'Did Wayne ever talk to you about the accounts, Magdalena?' I asked.

She shook her head. 'He always talk about his stupid fish.'

'Did he ever ask you about some missing money?'

Her eyes widened.

'He did not,' she said, with a look of *Tell me more.*

I stood up. 'No, me neither,' I said absently, and I headed back indoors.

Trying to keep occupied and not let my thoughts run amok, I put together an invoice to send along to Scott's office. This time I billed them for a lifting-and-handling course.

I billed Scott's firm for the full fifteen hundred. And then I emailed the attachment in the hope I'd get paid soon, rather than printing out a copy and sending it through the post.

Gary arrived, and I told him about the police. He wanted a blow-by-blow account of their questions. When I'd finished he said, 'Sounds like they're investigating a fraud. Do you think he's cleared off with all the takings?'

'Unlikely,' I said quickly. 'Besides, what takings? Most of our transactions are electronic, so the money's in the bank.'

Gary shrugged. 'Remember that guy from the golf club, the secretary, who'd been skimming money off the membership fees?'

'Vaguely.'

'He'd been at it for years. He got away with over sixty thousand before anyone noticed.'

'Whatever happened to him?'

Gary made a spooky action, wiggling his fingers. 'Nobody knows,' he said dramatically. 'But they did find his car near the ferry port at Stranraer. So either he threw himself in the sea, or else he got over to Northern Ireland unseen.'

I looked at Gary, and all at once *I* was filled with the urge to flee.

Was it possible?

I had money in the bank. George wanted to leave. In fact, only that morning, he'd asked once again if we could move to another place. Winston would be gutted not to see his son, but then, he hadn't been thinking about that when he was out screwing other women, had he? I could go today. I could pack up right now, before DS Aspinall and her colleague had the chance to return and question me further. A new start. Where would I go? George and I had up-to-date passports, we could drive south and just keep on driving until we found somewhere we liked. Live by the beach in Aquitaine. Go across the border into Spain and live for cheap in Galicia.

'Roz?'

I could hear Gary's voice, as if from far away.

'Roz!'

'What?'

Gary was regarding me like I'd lost my mind. 'Your patient is here,' he said, pointing to Sue Mitchinson, who was sitting, twisted, on one side of her bottom, a pained expression on her face.

'What've you done to yourself, Sue?' I asked, regaining my lucidity.

'Had a fight with the Hoover,' she said. 'On the stairs.'

She followed me into the treatment room, mumbling, 'Am I glad to see *you*!' whereupon I closed the door, shelving all thoughts of escaping for the time being, telling her I'd have her sorted out as fast as I could.

As it was, the police didn't return that day, and so my rehearsed responses went to waste for the time being. In fact, nothing at all happened, aside from huge speculation from Gary and Magdalena as to Wayne's whereabouts and the amount of money he may have taken with him.

Curiously, I was able to discuss this as though it were real. As though I, too, believed Wayne to be responsible. Terrible, really. But I didn't have a lot of choice. Getting anxious, I tried Wayne's mobile every few hours, but it was always the same. No answer.

*

Thursday evening rolled around before I knew it, and after all the unease, worrying about what exactly Wayne was playing at, it was nice to have something else to think about. I'd texted my address to Nadine's brother after receiving his call, and he was to pick me up at seven. With no clue as to what he had planned, I dressed middle of the road, in a summer skirt, sleeveless shirt and sandals. I didn't bother with any make-up, save for a little gloss on my lips, as my skin had a reasonable colour and, as I think I may have mentioned previously, I'm kind of crap at applying it.

Vince had taken George at five. He'd called, telling me not to bother feeding him. They would pick up fish and chips en route. 'What did I do right to deserve such a great brother-in-law?' I asked him. To which he replied *I* was actually doing *him* a favour. Petra was in a monumental sulk, the likes of which could go on for weeks, and he was pleased to get out of the house.

'What's it about this time?' I asked.

'Ah, the million-dollar question. It's one of those where I have to guess – sorry, where I *should already* know – without her having to tell me.'

'Oh,' I said.

'Yes,' he replied. 'Oh.'

Then he said, 'I'll bring him back around ten? Does that give you enough time?'

'I'm sure that'll be more than enough time. Bring him back at nine if you want. It'll give me an excuse to get rid of my date if he gets boring.'

'As you wish . . . though, Roz?'

'What is it, Vincent?'

'I think this guy might be all right.'

'What makes you say that?'

'Just a feeling I get.'

*

He arrived early. I had the lounge window thrown wide and the back door open to create a wind-tunnel effect through the house. I didn't plan on inviting him inside, on account of the dreary interior and the generally sparse, unloved feel of the place. As Petra mentioned on the phone, I had not yet got around to acquiring new carpets, so we were still managing with the black asphalt flooring. The place looked pitiful and I was embarrassed.

Also, after a full day of sun, the lounge had the tendency to surrender the ingrained odours of tenants past. The room would fill with the pungent smells of scorched coffee, hints of tobacco and worn socks which I could never find the source of.

I was applying a second coat of candy-pink varnish to my toe-nails when I heard Celia's voice through the open window.

'So *you're* the gentleman from work that Roz has been keeping a secret from us!'

My stomach folded in on itself.

Though it was not possible to make out his exact words, I was able to discern from his tone that my date replied with something polite and self-effacing. I just hoped he decided not to quiz me on this mystery man 'from work' later.

As it was, I instantly forgot all about this, because when I opened the door, '*You?*' was out of my mouth before I had the chance to stop it.

He gave an apologetic smile, saying, 'Surprise,' rather flatly.

My face flooded with heat.

It was Henry Peachey. The insurance agent who had pricked my thumb to obtain blood.

Christ, he was attractive. He was attractive and he was Nadine's brother.

Shit.

Shit. Shit. Shit.

This was not something I had anticipated. I had planned to

bow out of this one date gracefully, never to meet again.

I was aware of Celia's perplexed expression as she caught sight of my panicked face. I could almost hear her thinking that it was *no wonder* I was still single if this was how I greeted potential suitors.

'Why didn't you say it was you?' I said in a forced whisper.

'Because I wasn't sure you'd accept the date,' he whispered back.

'I would have,' I replied. 'Anyway, stay there,' I told him, trying to gather myself. 'I'll get my bag. Where are we going?'

And he made a wide, sweeping gesture with his hand. 'Anywhere you like,' he said. 'I thought we'd follow our noses.'

He wore faded jeans and a grey marl T-shirt. He was a little taller than me by a couple of inches and had a neat backside. There was a nice thickness to the musculature of his upper back that was so appealing. And he walked like a boxer. Sure-footed, solid.

What was I doing? I couldn't go. I shouldn't go.

I had to go. I couldn't stop myself.

We headed towards the gate, past Celia, who, in the time it had taken for me to grab my bag and shoes, had managed to apply fresh lipstick and fashion a ridiculously large, wide-brimmed hat on her head. It was held in place with a piece of chiffon tied beneath her chin, and I shot her a bemused look as I passed.

The car was a red Peugeot. It was meticulously clean, around fifteen years old, the kind of sensible vehicle bestowed upon a teenaged boy and in which he would learn to drive.

'Enjoy yourselves!' Celia cried, clapping her hands together happily. She was beaming.

'We will,' replied Henry, opening the passenger door for me.

'Bye, Celia,' I said.

She waved us off and I exhaled, relieved she hadn't pressed Henry for any further details but feeling hugely unsettled and twitchy that I'd been duped by his concealing his identity. I cast my mind back to our first meeting, trying to remember if I'd somehow spoken of Scott Elias. Scott Elias, his brother-in-law.

Had I slept with Scott at that point?

No. That came later. At the hotel, where Henry winked at me. Bloody hell. *Could* he have glimpsed Scott there that night? He must have been moments away from seeing him. Was this some kind of trap?

What a mess. I couldn't think straight. I could feel my composure starting to crack.

We hadn't gone very far, maybe just a few hundred yards, when Henry indicated before pulling over. He lifted the handbrake and turned in his seat to face me. Dread swamped me as I regarded him. He had the look of someone who was about to offload, and I was terrified of what he was going to say.

He thrust out his hand. 'Henry Peachey,' he said, smiling. 'I'm very pleased to meet you.'

'Roz Toovey,' I replied shakily, taking his hand, 'but I think we may have already met.'

'I'm so sorry about that. I should have told you on the phone that I knew who you were. I can see I've alarmed you. You look as though you've seen a ghost. Can we start again?'

I tried to smile. 'Okay,' I said weakly.

There was an awkward silence, during which each of us struggled to find something to fill the void, and then a thought occurred and I started to laugh.

'What is it?' he asked.

'My address.'

'What about your address?'

'You already knew it. I told you I would text you my address when we spoke on the phone, but you already knew where I lived. I gave it to you when you came to the clinic.'

He winced. 'Ah, yes,' he said. 'It was on your records.'

'You know everything about me.'

'Not that much,' he said. 'Anyway, does it bother you?'

I shrugged. 'At least you know I've not got AIDS.'

He shifted in his seat, his face suddenly serious again. 'I'm not really allowed to discuss the results of the blood test. It's confidential. It will be sent out to you in the post.'

I just looked at him.

'Oh, come on,' I said. 'You wouldn't be here if that test was positive.'

I didn't tell him I'd been tested the minute I found out Winston was screwing around. Along with another test six months later, just to be sure.

I told him I could really do with a drink, and he brightened at that. 'Pub?' he suggested eagerly. 'Or the cheapskate option?'

'Explain cheapskate.'

'We call at the Co-op, pick up a selection of beers, and drink them at a beauty spot of your choosing. Crisps optional.'

'Let's do that,' I said.

25

Tarn Hows was as good a place as any. It's a mile or so from Hawkshead and a nice spot to sit and watch the sun go down. People flock here because, basically, you've got all the scenery you're ever going to need packed into one small area.

There is the tarn itself – perfectly placed, pretty cobalt under a blue sky; inky black when beneath cloud. The woodland, with its lone pines at the water's edge, giving the place a romantic feel. And then there's the view to the Langdale Pikes, the fells all the more majestic from this aspect and elevation.

The downside to Tarn Hows is the sheer quantity of people who visit, particularly of late, as the path around the water has been improved to such a degree that you could get around on roller skates if you set your mind to it.

At this time, getting close to seven forty-five, there were only a few stragglers left and a group of Japanese tourists. We stayed in the car as the group exited the minibus, not wanting to get caught up in the general confusion as umbrellas (to be used as parasols) were opened, cameras strung around necks, selfie sticks extended, wedge-heeled trainers adjusted.

We grabbed our beers and sunglasses and headed off. Instead of going towards the path, though, we turned back on ourselves, climbing the small hill which lies due south of the road. The view is immeasurably better, and hardly anyone is anarchic enough to go against the National Trust signposts – so you can more or less bank on having it to yourselves.

Henry also had lived in the area since birth, he said. So, having visited Tarn Hows throughout our youth, we were without the look of loved-up wonder displayed on the faces of many of the folk stumbling upon this beauty spot for the first time, couples whose expressions were so full of hope for the years ahead, as though this one experience would be the benchmark of their entire relationship. *This is how it's going to be,* you would see manifested in the girls' springy gait, the affected cadence of their words, and I'd think, cruelly: *Every day, sweetheart. Every day.*

'Here all right?' Henry asked, gesturing as he reached the summit, the bottles clinking against each other in the bag he carried with him.

There was a patch of grass the size of a double mattress, flattened from an earlier picnic. I told Henry it was fine, and we settled ourselves, Henry taking the opener from his pocket. He offered me a bottle of Miller, giving me another gentle, chiding look of disappointment at my choice. 'All of this,' he'd joked earlier, motioning to the array on offer in the Co-op, 'and you go for bland American beer?'

'Bland American beer *that I happen to like,*' I'd replied.

'What?' I said to him now as he removed the cap from his bottle. 'You'd prefer one of those women who drink pints of Guinness, or Caffrey's, while watching rugby with the boys?'

He cast me an amused smile. 'I've been out with a couple of those, actually.'

'I thought you might have. Ever been married?'

'Just once,' he replied. 'I was married once.'

We went on talking for a time, one of those conversations when you skirt around topics, trying each other out for size, conscious not to offend or try too hard to impress. Our exchanges were frisky and teasing, but the whole time I was more than a little guarded on account of the Scott situation never being far from my mind.

'So,' Henry said, after we'd discussed films, musicians we found irritating, foreign places we'd like to visit. I was relieved he didn't start banging on about his bucket list, as so many of the men I knew did, not realizing their list was exactly the same as everyone else who read *GQ*: scuba dive on the Great Barrier Reef, live in Barcelona for a year, get their pilot's licence. 'So, you're seeing someone from work?' said Henry casually.

This caught me off guard. I'd hoped he'd not really registered Celia's comment of earlier.

As I stumbled on my words, he said, 'I can't think who it might be. Not Wayne, surely?'

'No,' I shot back quickly. 'No, not Wayne.'

He blew out his breath, smiling. 'I couldn't really picture that relationship. If I'm being honest.'

I took a swig and stalled, thinking through the best way to proceed. If I admitted to seeing someone – anyone (they didn't actually have to exist) – I would have an exit strategy.

I could say I was pretty much forced into this date by his sister, Nadine, and was seeing someone secretly that no one knew about.

That's what I should have said.

That would have been the sensible thing to do. To get out now before anyone got hurt.

Except I couldn't bring myself to do it. Henry was too damned beautiful and I was already captivated. I had the sense that, even if I tried to go ahead and tell Henry I was involved with another man, something completely different would shoot out of my mouth.

'I don't mean to pry,' said Henry, cajoling softly, 'but, obviously, it would be nice to know if I'm wasting my time here.'

I drained my bottle.

'There's no one,' I said firmly, and he raised his eyebrows in surprise. 'I was seeing a guy, but it's over. I fobbed my neighbour off with that lie because she's always trying to set me up. I told her I was seeing someone from work just to, you know . . .'

'Oh,' he said, looking relieved and genuinely pleased at the same time. 'Oh, well, that's good then. Didn't want to have to fight over you.'

I smiled weakly.

'Not least because I'm a shitty fighter,' he added, as he passed me another bottle.

'What *are* you good at? Just out of interest,' I asked.

'Me?' he replied, and without missing a beat, said, 'Living.'

'What kind of answer is that?'

'The only answer I have.'

I laughed and began picking at the wet label on the side of the beer bottle. 'That does sound rather big-headed,' I said.

'Does it?' he replied. 'I don't mean it to. I'm not saying, "Hey, isn't my life great, isn't yours rubbish?" Just that I try to spend my days doing as many of the things that I enjoy and hardly any time doing the things I don't.'

'Such as working,' I said.

'Yes,' he said. 'Such as that.'

He tipped the neck of the bottle of his strawberry ale against mine. 'Cheers,' he said happily.

Foxy was yapping in the garden when we returned.

'Be quiet!' yelled Celia, before blowing her whistle.

Not wanting Henry to see the state of the interior of my home, and also not wanting him to be around when George returned, I didn't ask him in for coffee. In fact, I'd said goodbye to him as I'd closed the car door. We didn't kiss. Celia and Dennis were enjoying the last of the evening sun on their newly purchased bench seat, and it would have been supremely awkward.

Nonetheless, Henry took it upon himself to follow me to my front door.

'Nice time?' asked Celia, and I mumbled that it was lovely, thanks. I was aware of her shooting Dennis a look. She now thought I was the type of woman who sabotaged every relationship by being too picky. She didn't have to say it. It was there, plain as day, in the lines of disapproval at the corners of her mouth.

Turning the key in the lock, I said to Henry, 'I'd invite you in, but my son . . .'

I let the words hang, hoping he'd make the leap between George arriving home soon and his presence being inappropriate.

'Then invite me in,' he said.

'George will be back.'

'So, you don't have friends round?' he asked mildly. 'Not ever?'

'Not the male kind.'

'Why not?'

'Because I can't stand that "This is Mummy's new friend" crap. Or, "George, come and meet your Uncle Henry." It's bad for kids.'

He regarded me as if to say I was being over the top, overprotective of George, and so I told him, in a whisper-shouting kind of way, that since he was not a father, he had no real grounds to air his opinion on my parenting decisions.

For a second he appeared angry. It was fleeting, though. The kind of short-lived surge you experience when cut off in traffic, before realizing you actually know the old guy in the car in front.

'Just five minutes,' persisted Henry.

'No,' I said. 'I can't. Sorry.'

'I want to see where you live.'

'And I'd rather you didn't.'

At that moment Celia got up from the bench seat and toddled across the front lawn, hands on hips. 'Would you two love birds care for a glass of Pimm's?'

'Not for me, thanks,' replied Henry quickly. 'I'm driving. And Roz has just offered to treat me to one of her famous coffees.'

Celia's face dropped. 'Perhaps next time,' she said, and Henry threw Celia his most charming smile, saying, 'Definitely. Wouldn't miss it.'

He turned back around, and his eyes were alive with mischief.

So I pushed open the door.

'The lounge,' I said flatly, and gestured for Henry to go on in.

I turned and saw that Celia hadn't moved. She was still in the same spot on the lawn. 'Sorry,' I said quietly, 'do you mind terribly?', feeling bad when I saw how dejected she looked.

'Not at all,' she blustered, recovering herself. 'Go! Enjoy!' And then: 'He's terribly handsome, Roz,' she whispered, her tone now girlish and conspiratorial. 'Is he a keeper?'

Henry had wandered through to the dining room. 'I see you're going for the minimalist look.'

'Listen, if you going to be critical—'

He put his finger to his lips. 'I'm not. But, Roz, you don't have any furniture. What on earth happened?'

'Oh, you know. Stuff.'

'Have you just moved in?' he asked.

'Not exactly. I had a visit from the bailiffs. Anyway, do you still want that coffee?'

He tried to smile sympathetically but wasn't entirely sure if I was pulling his leg. 'Let me,' he said, and he moved towards the kitchen. 'You sit down' – he cast his eyes around the room – 'you sit down there . . . on that box.'

I stayed where I was. My sandals were starting to pinch, so I removed them and stood in my bare feet.

A moment later he reappeared. 'Cups?'

I shook my head. 'Just what's soaking in the sink.'

'It's like my student days all over again,' he said brightly. 'Tea out of a glass, vodka out of a bowl.'

I followed him into the kitchen. The balls of my feet made a soft, thwacking sound on the linoleum as I moved. 'What did you study?' I asked.

'Chemical engineering.'

'Shouldn't you have a job at, like, ICI, or something?'

He nodded. 'You're right. I should.'

'But instead you . . . ?'

'Piss about in insurance two days a week.'

'What do you do when you're not working?'

'Read, mostly,' he said.

'Why?'

He laughed. When he realized I wasn't joking, he considered my question. 'Do you know what,' he said, 'if you'd asked me that a year ago, I'm not sure I could have answered. I certainly don't read to escape, or as some self-improvement exercise, if that's what you were thinking.'

I shrugged. 'I wasn't thinking that.'

'I've always enjoyed reading,' he explained. 'I've always found myself wanting to pick up a book without really questioning the reason. Except last year I read a review of a book by John Malkovich.'

'I didn't know he was a writer,' I said.

'I'm not sure that he is. The *review* was by John Malkovich, not the book.'

'My mistake.'

'Anyway, the book – *May We Be Forgiven* by A. M. Homes.' He paused. 'Do you know it?'

'I don't.'

'No matter. It's not important. It's what Malkovich says in his review that highlights the reason I read. He says everyone is so dull nowadays. Basically, everyone's so frightened of upsetting other people, there are no characters left any more. And when he sat down to read *May We Be Forgiven,* he was at last spending time with someone *interesting.* He found the main character *so* interesting, so compelling, he couldn't wait to get back to the book. In answer to your question, I think that's why I read.'

'Because people are dull?'

'Yes. You have nice teeth, by the way.'

'Thank you.'

He realized at this point that there was not enough water in the kettle, by the sound it was making. Filling it at the sink, he said, casually, 'So, bailiffs. That's kind of a big deal. How did that happen?'

'I spent more money than I had. And I was left in a bit of a mess by my ex-husband. He ran up quite a few debts in my name.'

'Ah, yes. I remember. Shitty thing to do. You don't seem too upset about it, if you don't mind my saying.'

'I was. But what's the point? I picked him, after all. At first I spent a lot of time blaming, back in the beginning, before I realized it wasn't going to get me out of the trouble I was in. No one was going to come along and say, "Do you know what? You are so totally right. It's all Winston's fault." And besides, there are a hell of a lot of people more compromised than me. But I should have handled it better than I did. Anyway,' I said, 'things are easier now. The worst is over. I've managed to climb out of the hole I was in and things are starting to look up.'

'Excellent,' he said. 'I admire you for that.'

I looked away.

'Do you like your job?' he asked.

'I like parts of it. I enjoy offering relief to a person in pain, it's just it takes up—'

'All of your time?'

'Yeah.'

I went on to explain how my own clinic had folded but that I still hankered after working for myself again one day.

'So why don't you?' he asked. 'Why not just go it alone again?'

'There is an opening to do just that, but I'm scared. I made a hash of it last time and ended up working ridiculous hours because I couldn't say no to people. And then I let them down anyway because of my irresponsibility.'

'You're not irresponsible,' he said. 'You bring up a child, alone, whilst working full time, with very little help from anyone, from what I can gather. How is that irresponsible?'

'That's kind of you to say,' I replied. 'But people take rather a different viewpoint when—'

He waved my words away with his hand as if to imply: *What do they know about anything?* He said, 'I read recently that seventy-one per cent of people dislike their jobs. That's a lot of dissatisfied people spending their lives doing something they don't like.'

'Do you like yours?' I asked.

'Not especially, but I only work two days out of seven. I reckon you could do pretty much anything for two days a week. Of course, we were told that, with the advent of all the labour-saving devices, everyone would be on a three-day week by now. That never quite happened, though.'

'Why do you think that is?'

'They need to keep us out of mischief,' he said. 'What would happen if we were suddenly let loose with all that free time? There could be anarchy.' He smiled. 'There will always be some people who want to work all day. Let them, I say, and leave the rest of us in peace. Naturally, there are *some* people who can't seem to understand why I would choose to earn less and work less. Because wealth is the only indicator of success nowadays, and so on.'

Winston, too, went through a protracted anti-commercialism phase. Giving long speeches about autonomy, the misunderstood Luddites, the myth that a rewarding life is to be had through hard work.

The trouble was, he still kept on buying stuff.

I asked Henry who he meant when he said *some* people had a problem with his choices, and he replied, 'Scott Elias.'

I shifted my weight to my other foot.

He said, 'You've met Scott, I assume?'

'Hmm-mm, a couple of times.'

'Total wanker,' he said. 'I can't understand why Nadine stays with him. Well, I suppose I can. The kids, and all that. But still.'

'You don't like him,' I said, my tone neutral, my expression neither one thing nor the other. And he frowned, before saying, 'What's to like?'

'I can see how you might not see eye to eye.'

'I don't see eye to eye with him,' he said, 'because he's a dickhead.'

'Not because he's loaded? You're not jealous of his money?' I asked playfully.

'That's the thing: take away the money and look at the man. What's left? Nothing. Has he ever said one funny or interesting thing in your company?'

I didn't answer.

'I mean, what does he do?' he said. 'What does he actually care about? Scott's got all that wealth, and what does he do with it? Buys objects. That's it.'

'You're suggesting he should save the world?'

'I'm suggesting he could do something useful. The guy shafts everyone he comes into contact with.'

'In what way?' I asked.

'In every way. He has to push everything, he can't let go. He can't stand to lose a penny.'

'Really?' I said doubtfully. 'He seemed pretty generous to me. My sister seems to think so, anyway.'

Henry laughed. 'Oh yeah, Scott the nice guy. Scott'll bring the wine, he'll pay the bill. But, I'm telling you, he doesn't put his hand in his pocket unless it's tax deductible. He doesn't spend one penny of his own money. Everything comes out of his business. Every so-called generous thing he does goes down as a business expense.'

I immediately thought about billing Scott for services rendered. He'd told me he had a hard time scraping the cash together. Which had been hard to believe.

'Hurry up with that coffee,' I said.

'He's got to beat the system,' Henry continued, unabated. 'He's a great example of greed gone nuts . . . never enough, never enough. He takes it all for himself and he puts nothing back. And he has a wicked dark temper.

'Honestly,' said Henry, 'Scott Elias is never happy unless he's screwing someone.'

26

So I was a business expense.

I had no right to be bitter about this – what difference did it make how Scott funded our encounters?

And yet, oddly, I was. What Scott received from me in the way of 'services' was essentially free. By lying, by cooking the books in this way, he was able to fund our encounters with money he would have had to pay in tax to the Inland Revenue. So he could sleep with me as many times as he wished, and, as Henry pointed out, it wouldn't cost him a penny.

Should I have been a little insulted by this? Probably not. But I was. And I couldn't help but wonder how else Scott manipulated his financial statements to his own ends.

I never really bought Scott's excuse of being unable to get enough cash together to pay me. Had he set up this invoicing arrangement so that he could in fact *delay* paying me? I was still waiting to be paid for our last encounter. Was he holding back the payment on purpose, so he had more control of the situation? Had more control of *me*?

It was now the weekend. Saturday morning. We were at George's swimming lesson, which was kindly paid for by Dylis. He was level five, which meant he could swim three strokes, float, dive down for a brick, but not actually swim very far. Not his fault, nor the teacher's actually, it was the result of the municipal pool closing a few years ago when it ran out of money. Now the children of South Lakeland had to learn to swim at various hotel 'spas'. This wasn't ideal, since the pools were generally only ten metres long and, occasionally, a disgruntled guest would object to sharing the space with the kids *when they had paid good money to be here*, and the children would have to get out. Lesson over.

Today there was just one elderly lady doing breaststroke – head out of the water, her body almost vertical, not really going anywhere but smiling all the same. She was enjoying the children as they tried their hardest to stay afloat on their backs: skinny white torsos bobbing, heads colliding.

I sat at the small café bar area with my laptop open. Though it was only ten thirty, there was the smell of chips and cooking oil rather than chlorine hanging heavy in the air. At the table next to me were two mothers. They were regulars whom I saw every other Saturday. One (Gail, I think) had ginger highlights – the hand-painted type applied with a brush; the other changed her hair colour from week to week. They spent the entire lesson hunched over, faces inches apart, eyes narrowed, discussing Gail's divorce. Occasionally, I'd hear the tell-tale words and phrases that surrounded a break-up (Relate, co-parenting...and: 'I made a roast dinner twice a week for that ungrateful bastard. They live on fish fingers when they're with *her*. Lazy bitch.') so I knew to give them a wide berth.

I craned my neck upon hearing spluttering, a child having inhaled too much pool. When I saw it wasn't George, I went back to punching in my bank details, having tapped into the hotel's free Wi-Fi.

My balance was the same.

Scott's last payment had still not arrived.

I chewed on my thumbnail. It wasn't like I could call up the company secretary: 'That invoice I sent you? The fake one? Yes, can you please pay it?'

And I didn't want to call Scott.

I was hoping to avoid him for a few days. Let the dust settle after my date with Henry. Which Scott had been none too happy about, and I sensed he might want to interrogate me over it.

Henry had pressed to see me again and I had agreed. I'd said I would call him but, as yet, I hadn't picked up the phone.

I liked him. I really liked him. But the timing was oh-so-shitty. Why couldn't he have entered my life in a month's time, when I was rid of Scott? When my debts were repaid?

I'd gone a little quiet on Henry towards the end of the date, the enormity of the deception crashing through me as Henry prattled on about Scott, completely oblivious to my state of mind. He'd left, I suspected, somewhat befuddled by my sudden remoteness, perhaps misinterpreting it as an aversion towards him – which couldn't be further from what I was feeling.

I refreshed the page now, somehow hoping to see the money magically appear.

Concentrating on the screen, I didn't notice George approach until he was at the side of me: shoulders hunched over, shivering, hopping from one foot to the other. 'I need to use the bathroom,' he said.

'So go.'

'You said I wasn't to go in there on my own. You said I could only go in there when you're there or there are other kids.'

That's right, I did. I apologized and got up. I'd forgotten that. You can't even let your children use the loo alone any more since being told they can be assaulted in supermarket bathrooms, swimming-pool changing rooms.

Did our parents realize how easy they had it?

'Go out to play and don't come back till tea time,' my mother would say. 'There's fifty pence for chips and gravy. Don't buy sweets.' And that was just about the extent of her parenting.

'You'll have to go in the women's,' I told George, and he scowled.

'I don't want to go in there.'

'Well, I can't go in the men's.'

'Why?'

'Because they'll be naked. Go in the women's, and be quick. You're missing your lesson.'

He scooted off, and I found myself wondering, not for the first time, after all the recent coverage in the press, if the incidence of paedophiles amongst celebrities was higher than in the general population. Or were they simply representative of the population as a whole?

Or, and this was my growing suspicion, was there something present in the psyche of men who were drawn to life in the public eye that also predisposed them to want to have sex with children? Someone should really do a study.

'All done,' said George.

'You wash your hands?'

'Yes.'

'Really?'

'I'm going in the pool,' he argued, and got away from me before I could send him back, doing that half-run, half-step thing you do on wet floor tiles.

I watched him skid a little as he reached the water, eager as he was to get into the warmth again, and my heart juddered. *Stay safe, baby.* My prayer. The thing I said when I felt powerless to protect him.

Two weeks ago, I'd said the same prayer when I'd allowed him to leave the pool with a child I knew little about. Of course George knew everything about him, having spent the whole two days previous playing with him. His grandfather brought him to his swimming lesson, the family were new to the area, and they were keen for the child, Leif, to make friends.

The grandfather was affable, friendly, an earring in his left ear, a semi-circular scar on his chin – an old glassing incident, perhaps? George had hold of my shirt and was pulling at it, begging me to let him go rather than spend a boring afternoon alone with me. I was cornered. I smiled awkwardly at Granddad, trying to think of an excuse and feeling hot with shame at the same time, because I was totally judging this man on his appearance.

What do you do in this situation?

'Okay, you can go,' I eventually said, reluctantly, and spent the afternoon saying the prayer, my mantra, over and over.

Later that night, my fears were realized.

George returned home withdrawn and uncommunicative, he wouldn't eat his meal, and played in his room so as not to be near me. We'd had 'the talk' every so often . . . *If anyone ever tries to touch you in your underpants . . . If anyone ever tells you to keep a secret from me.* But not knowing exactly the seriousness of what I was trying to convey, George always brushed it off fast and said something silly.

I knocked on his door. 'Everything all right?'

He nodded, without looking up.

'Can I get you a drink?' I asked him.

'No, thank you.'

'George? Did something happen today?'

He didn't answer.

'Did Leif's granddad get cross with you?'

'No,' he said quietly.

'Did he . . . did he try to' – I paused, trying to find the right words – 'did he try to touch you at all?'

'No.'

'Was there anyone else at the house?'

'Leif's brother.'

'And how old is he?'

'I don't know.'

'Guess,' I said. 'Younger than you? Older than you?'

'Younger.'

'Any other adults?'

'His nanna.'

'And what was she like?'

'Pretty old.'

'Okay, George, listen. What exactly happened over there, because I can see there was something, and I'm not leaving until you talk to me.'

My voice was shaking. I was trying to remain calm for his sake, but I just couldn't.

He scratched at a scab on his knee, reluctant to talk.

'George!' I pressed. 'Talk.'

And he took a breath.

'Well,' he began, hesitant, not really wanting to. 'Well,' he said, 'you know Pokémon?'

I closed my eyes. Fell back against the wall in relief.

'I do,' I said.

'Well, Leif has got, like, thirty-three figures, Mum . . . and . . . and, well, when I saw them I was *jealous*.'

Jesus Christ.

See this is how it got you. This is how fucked up you became, paranoia plaguing your every thought.

'I'll get you some more Pokémon, love,' I told him, and then I went and downed two shots of brandy.

The children were now jumping in – star jumps for if they ever found themselves in an emergency situation, jumping from a boat perhaps into brackish water, unable to see the bottom. The teacher was explaining the importance of slapping down hard with their arms as they hit the surface, trying to impress the reasons to avoid going deep.

It was pretty much lost on the kids, though, who took it as an opportunity to try to splash each other – legally.

I refreshed the page again. Still no money. And then it dawned on me that since today was Saturday there would be no bank transfer until Monday at the earliest.

Idly, I gazed out of the window to the hotel car park, wondering if there was anything I could feasibly do if that money didn't show up, when my attention was caught by a black Range Rover.

Black Range Rovers were commonplace. At the moment, maybe not so much as white, but they were popular around here all the same. Except this was an enhanced Range Rover, an Overfinch Long Wheelbase. Over two hundred thousand pounds' worth of car. And therefore not so commonplace.

It was Scott's Range Rover.

I slid down a little in my seat so that only my eyes peered over the top of my laptop and watched as the car crawled around the car park, as if searching for something. There were plenty of empty spaces, so he wasn't trying to park.

He began a second circuit. He hadn't yet spotted me observing him. Perhaps I was invisible from out there if the sun was on the glass.

Why was he here? How did he know I was here?

But then if he *was* looking for me, he would have spotted my car immediately. The Jeep was by the entrance. And even if he hadn't memorized my registration, he would know it was mine on account of the dent on the bonnet, caused by a runaway supermarket trolley.

So if he wasn't looking for me, who was he looking for?

My hand hovered over my phone. This was creepy.

Did I have the nerve? Did I allow him to explain himself?

There were five rings before I saw his brake lights illuminate and he answered at the far end of the car park.

'Hey,' I said. 'You free to talk?'

'Sure.'

His voice was lazy. A cover-up, as I'd not heard him speak

slowly unless actually dozing off. My stomach spasmed as I watched him edge the car forward a little.

'There's a bit of a problem,' I said.

'What kind of problem?'

'The invoice I sent. It's not been paid and I'm still waiting for the money.'

'Oh,' he said. 'Oh, that is surprising. Deborah is usually very prompt. She should have sent it on Wednesday. I'll look into it for you as soon as I can and make sure it's sorted out.'

'Wonderful. Sorry to be a nuisance, but, you know.'

'No need to apologize. You want your money, I get that.' There was now a harder edge to his voice. He released the brakes once more and moved the car off to the right. If he continued along that course he would again come right past where I was sitting.

I swallowed.

'So, you're okay, then?' I said.

'Champion.'

'What are you up to? Are you doing anything today?'

The nose of the car came into view.

Through the windscreen I got a clear picture of him, and my breath stuttered in my chest as I feared he may see me.

'Nothing much,' he said casually, while his eyes darted left and right, left and right, scanning the parked cars. 'Just reading the papers, catching up on a few bits and pieces at home.'

His lie sent a shiver right up the length of my spine.

'Sounds good,' I murmured.

'Yeah, relaxing and having a bit of a recharge,' he added.

'A recharge,' I repeated, as he paused now by an old piece-of-shit Peugeot further along. The car was similar to Henry's. Same colour. Same model.

Scott surveyed the car for a full ten seconds before answering.

He thought the car was Henry's. He thought I was at this hotel, with Henry. Scott was checking up on me. But how did he know I was even here at all?

'Listen,' he said, distracted, 'can I call you back? I can hear Nadine on her way through from the kitchen. I need to get off the phone.'

'No problem,' I told him.

And I watched as he hit the accelerator and sped off out of the car park.

27

THAT AFTERNOON SAW the arrival of a new dining table and a new cooker – a free-standing electric oven with a ceramic hob on top. Nothing fancy, but it was clean. And since I tended to subscribe to the late Clarissa Dickson Wright's view that one can make perfectly good food on a two-ring hotplate, I was thrilled to see it replace the grease-covered monstrosity Vince had donated. Even after I'd given it a thorough spray with Mr Muscle, I still couldn't bring myself to use it. The burnt fat gave off an odour of rancidity that lodged in the nasal linings – much like when all those animal carcasses were burned during the foot-and-mouth epidemic of 2001. That smell stayed in the air, and in your nose, for months.

I hadn't expected to miss cooking. Preparing meals for George at the end of a long day had long since lost its appeal. But when faced with the prospect of being unable to cook anything at all, well, I couldn't wait to get back in the kitchen.

Petra and Vince were coming over, as well as Clara, and so I got on with preparing my crowd pleaser: spaghetti carbonara. Vince instructed me to leave the wine to him, and even though I tried to protest, explaining that I wasn't as strapped for cash as I had been of late, he insisted. He had a new Portuguese white – F. P. Branco, which he'd been giddy for me to try since discovering it recently.

I roughly chopped some tomatoes, harvested by Dennis that

morning. I invited both Celia and Dennis, too, since Petra and Celia got along well, even though Petra complained that Celia became terribly boastful about her family after two glasses of wine (Celia would have said the same about Petra, if she weren't my sister). But they had tickets to the Lakeland Book of the Year Awards. One of Celia's book group had self-published a slim biography of William and Dorothy Wordsworth, which Celia said was very well written but not really my kind of thing, so best avoided.

To the tomatoes I added basil (again from Dennis), olive oil, seasoning and a splash of sherry vinegar, before making a plain green salad for the kids. George was positively repulsed by the idea of a raw tomato, not that it stopped him dousing everything in ketchup.

As well as now being in possession of a kitchen full of food for the first time in months, I had wine glasses, cups, two new saucepans and plates that matched. I'd also splurged on new school polo shirts for George, bath towels, tea towels, and bedding for both of our beds.

The school holidays were almost upon us. It would be one of the last quiet evenings before the adjoining holiday cottage became filled with a procession of noisy families. Families shouting at each other after dark when they'd had too much to drink, realizing too late that they didn't actually like spending this amount of time with one another.

'So,' said Petra, as we sat out on the patio.

'So?' I mirrored back.

'So, how was Henry?' she said.

'By which you mean?'

She shot me a look as though to say, *Not how was he in bed, you idiot.*

'I mean, do you like him?' she said.

'He seems nice enough,' I replied, teasing.

'Nice enough for what? A fling? A relationship? Marriage?'

'Oh, marriage definitely,' I replied, deadpan.

'Have you heard that Hollywood now has its own marital version of the 5:2 diet?' said Petra, and I asked her to explain.

'Instead of eating for five days and fasting for two days,' she said, 'you live with your spouse for five days and have two days off.'

Vince looked interested.

'Or is it the other way around?' she said. Petra thought for a moment, working through the logistics of it. 'Yes, it must be the other way around. Five days off, two days on.'

'Like a fireman,' I said.

'Exactly,' she replied. 'Celebrity couples say it makes their marriages work much better, *and* it's more fulfilling.'

'That's because they're essentially dating,' said Vince.

'Where did you read this?' I asked her.

'A magazine in the staff room. Not a trashy one. The head doesn't allow those. It was *Marie Claire*. Or one of those thinking women's magazines where the articles are way too long . . . and depressing.'

Vince said to Petra that they already had their own version of the 5:2. She became cross with him over something he had no idea about, and then proceeded to ignore him for two days. 'Works perfectly well for us, doesn't it, love?'

Petra pretended to swat him away and told him to fetch some more water for the table.

Once Vince was in the kitchen out of earshot, I remarked that they seemed to be on speaking terms again.

'We're fine,' she said.

'What was it about?'

'Honestly?' she asked. 'Dissatisfaction dressed up as something else, I suppose. Do you ever look at your life and think you were meant to have more?'

'More of what?'

'More of everything.'

'Petra, you do have everything.'

'I know. I have all of the important stuff. And I'm not being ungrateful, I'm really not. It's just, sometimes, I look at other people and I think—'

'You're talking about Nadine.'

Sheepishly, she admitted, 'That's wrong, I know,' she said. 'Nadine is a wonderful person and she and Scott are so good together, and they didn't always have all that wealth. Sometimes envy gets the better of me, though, and I get annoyed about everything. I get so bloody angry.'

I stopped eating and held her gaze. 'Vince is a great guy, Petra.'

She nodded. 'I'm a bitch to take it out on him, aren't I?'

'How would you feel if he ignored you for not being good enough? Not being pretty enough? Rich enough?'

She threw me an outraged look as though to say, *He . . . would . . . not . . . dare.*

'Precisely,' I said.

She told me she'd try to be kinder with him. 'You know, Henry might be a great guy for you. Nadine absolutely adores him,' she prattled on, before pausing and glaring at her daughter. 'Clara, that is *way* too much pasta you have on your fork. You really mustn't shovel your food into your mouth like that.'

I caught George's eye as he surreptitiously removed half of the spaghetti loaded on his fork.

A few weeks ago I'd caught him twirling the fork in the centre of the plate to see if it was possible to get his entire serving on to it and, incredibly, he managed it. I didn't reprimand him, as he picked the whole lot up and chewed bits off, much as you would a toffee apple. It took me back to when Petra and I were kids and we'd have competitions to see who could pile the most chips on our forks.

I remember Petra winning on most occasions.

'Nadine is very protective of Henry,' Petra continued now, 'because of what happened.'

I stopped chewing. 'What happened?'

'He didn't tell you?'

'I don't know if he told me or not, because I don't know what you're talking about.'

Petra lowered her eyes to her plate and dropped her voice to all but a whisper. 'His son died.'

'Oh,' I said, utterly floored. 'I didn't know that.'

There was a moment of silence when she let me process what had just been said. Then she went on. 'It was a swimming-pool accident. He got sucked into a faulty filter when diving down for pennies.'

'Oh, God,' I said.

'Terrible thing,' said Petra. 'His wife took her eyes off the boy to help clean up after a party. Their marriage didn't survive after that. Understandable, really.'

Petra put her cutlery at the side of her plate. 'Do you mind if I leave this?' she said, and I shook my head. I'd lost my appetite, too, I told her. 'Nadine said that's why Henry came back here,' Petra explained. 'He couldn't bear to be amongst people who knew. He needed a clean break.'

'Where did it happen?' I asked.

'It was at a friend's house. He and his wife were in London for work. He had a high-powered job to do with chemical some-thing-or-other.'

'Engineering,' I said.

'That's right.' Petra gulped down the remainder of her wine.

'Should I open another?' Vince asked, coming back outside.

His tone was gentle, fatherly. He said it in a way you would ask a person if they needed another ice pack, another painkiller.

'Please,' Petra replied. 'Do you mind driving home?' she asked, and Vince said he didn't.

With her glass refreshed, Petra leaned in towards me. 'Henry didn't mention *any* of this to you?'

'Nothing,' I replied.

'He didn't hint at what had happened to him? You didn't detect the sadness at all?'

'Quite the contrary. He was quite exuberant, pretty forceful in his ideas. For the whole of the evening he was in a jolly mood. Although—' I said and hesitated. Dropped my gaze as I remembered. 'There was one moment when there was something . . .'

I felt the sting of shame as it came back to me fully.

'He wanted to come in – to come into the house – and I didn't want him to.'

'Why not?'

'Various reasons. I didn't want him to meet' – I paused, tilting my head in George's direction – 'so there was that. And of course, the house is a disaster, and I just didn't want him inside – you know, judging me.

'Anyway,' I said, 'he thought I was being over the top about him not meeting George, and I kind of blew my top at him. Saying that, since he wasn't a father, I'd appreciate it if he kept his parenting advice to himself.'

Petra winced.

'I know,' I said. 'I'll apologize.'

Quite unaware of our conversation, Clara and George were talking amongst themselves at the end of the table. 'You two finished with your plates?' I asked, and George said yes, while Clara looked to Petra to check if it was okay to leave what remained of her meal. Petra didn't notice, lost in thought as she was, so I mouthed it was fine. 'Scoot,' I told them quietly. 'Go and play. I'll call you when dessert is ready.'

We sat in silence, each of us watching the kids at the end of the garden. They were pointing to the wild rabbits, and giggling, George making Clara laugh with whatever he was saying.

'Just imagine,' said Petra softly, gesturing to the children, 'just *imagine*. That poor, poor guy,' and her eyes began to fill. Both Vince and I nodded without answering.

The minutes passed.

Eventually, I gave her hand a squeeze. 'I love you, Petra,' I said. 'I don't tell you often enough. You're such a good sister to me and I love you.'

'Oh, honey,' she replied, overwhelmed. She searched for a tissue before blowing her nose. 'I love you, too.'

And then, between the tears, she said, 'Vincent, you tell those children to get back over here right this instant. I need to hold on to them. Tight.'

28

WHEN I ARRIVED at work on Monday morning there was a familiar vehicle in the car park: the black Ford belonging to the two detectives. Wayne hadn't been in work now for a week.

It felt like rain. The air had that thick quality that made it hard to breathe. I closed the sun roof and got out, making my way over to the driver's-side door of the Ford. DS Aspinall lowered the window. 'Morning,' she said. Her partner was finishing a sausage roll, dusting off his moustache with the paper bag. The car smelled of buttery pastry and sage.

'Good morning,' I replied.

'Time for a quick word?' DS Aspinall asked.

'Just let me get opened up. Give me two minutes?'

'Much obliged,' she replied, and raised the window. They remained inside the car, as requested, and by the time they entered the clinic I had the kettle on, had removed the post, opened the window in reception as the air was a little stale, and was more or less ready.

'Any news?' I asked.

'Wayne Geddes is officially missing.'

'He wasn't before?' I said.

'Not exactly. Mr Geddes was accused of theft by his employers. They reported the theft to the police, and we were looking into it for them.'

I got the impression from her tone that the small amount of missing money had not exactly been high priority. That she had not expected theft to turn into a missing-person case.

'So you haven't found the money?' I said shakily.

'No. And we haven't found Wayne Geddes either.'

'There really is no sign of him?' I asked, perplexed, because where the hell was he? Sure, I'd expected Wayne to lie low for a few days. Get over his embarrassment, get his head together and so forth, but now this woman was telling me he was nowhere to be found.

He wouldn't abandon his house and take off. I was almost certain of that. He had a lot of equity in that house. He would be leaving behind everything he had. His security for the future. It didn't make any sense.

'His mobile phone hasn't been used,' DS Aspinall said.

'What about his credit cards?' I asked.

She shook her head. 'Although that's not unusual for a person wanting to disappear. They're aware that most retailers have cameras above the tills, as do most cashpoints. Often there is a period of inactivity on that front for up to a month. Especially if they have a surplus of cash – which we believe Mr Geddes has.'

But he hadn't. That cash was long gone.

'By the way, the stretch you recommended has been working,' she said.

'Sorry?'

'Upward-facing dog?' she said. 'The yoga stretch? My neck's much improved. I felt the benefit straight away. I can reverse the car now without it hurting.'

'Oh – good,' I stammered. 'Good to hear. Listen, did you go to Wayne's house?'

'We did. After speaking to you previously.'

DS Quigley, who had been silent up until now, held his notepad in the arm's-length position of the long-sighted and agreed that's what they had done.

'And, obviously, he wasn't there or else you wouldn't be here,' I said. 'What did you find?'

'As far as we could tell there was no one home and—'

'You didn't go *inside*?' I asked, astonished.

'We were not authorized to do so. There was no warrant at that time, Mrs Toovey. We're not allowed to break in.'

'Was his car there?'

'I believe so.'

Again, a quick glance to her partner, who, after a moment, concurred with her statement.

'So, what we'd like to do, Mrs Toovey, is take a look around here, see if we can't come up with something to point us in the right direction. This was his desk, was it?'

'Yes, this is where Wayne would spend his time.'

'Any other areas you think would be relevant?'

'The kitchen,' I said. 'He did a lot of brewing up. And he was in charge of the stock. To be honest, he had his hands in everything.'

Where had Wayne gone after I hightailed it on Saturday? My memory of leaving the house was sketchy at best. There were pockets of time that were simply missing. Had something happened that I couldn't recall? Had *I* done something to Wayne that I couldn't recall? I remembered waking and there being no sign of Wayne. But what if that wasn't correct? What if I had simply blanked out his presence?

Christ.

'What time do the clients arrive?' DS Aspinall asked.

'Patients. My first arrives in fifteen minutes.'

They started poking around. I suspected they would find little of interest but didn't quibble all the same. They asked a few further questions: did Wayne mention any financial difficulties?

Did he talk about meeting anyone straight from work on the Friday he was last seen, or over the weekend? Did he talk about leaving the area?

No, no and no.

When it seemed as though they had finished, I asked why Wayne was now classed as officially missing, when he wasn't before. What had changed exactly?

'His cousin,' replied DS Aspinall. 'He'd not heard from Mr Geddes and so let himself into the property. Once inside, he became worried. He said it was very out of character for Mr Geddes not to be in touch.'

'So *his cousin* doesn't think Wayne cleared off without telling anyone?' I asked.

'He says not. He says Mr Geddes would never have left without making proper arrangements with him. Arrangements to take care of his fish.'

'Oh,' I said. 'Of course. The fish.'

'Yes,' she replied, without looking my way. 'They're all dead.'

29

Wayne's disappearance had thrown me completely off balance and so, even though I did *want* to call Henry, I kept picking up my mobile, going to contacts, and then bottling out. I was being a coward about it. I just couldn't seem to find the right words.

Henry hadn't been in touch either, since our date of last week. I think after his small speech about Scott Elias, I had clammed up a little and given off an abashed air which may have been mis-interpreted as disinterest.

When I say I *may* have done this, I mean definitely.

Henry must have left with the impression I didn't care for him.

But I couldn't leave it like that. Not now.

He picked up on the tenth ring.

'Henry,' I said.

'Roz,' he replied.

'I didn't think you were going to answer.'

'I didn't think you were going to call.'

'Henry—' I began and stopped.

'What is it, Roz?'

I took a breath. 'Petra told me about your son,' I said, 'and I just wanted to say that I'm really sorry. I was abrupt and insensitive on Thursday, back at the house, and I wanted to apologize. I wouldn't have said what I said about not wanting your parenting advice if I'd known, and—'

'You didn't know,' he cut in, his tone brusque but not unkind. 'No harm done.'

'I feel terrible.'

'I didn't *want* you to know. Not straight away, anyway. And it was six years ago, so you're hardly at fault.'

There was a silence.

I could hear Henry's breath, heavy, as though he was walking.

'What was he like?' I asked quietly, after a moment, and Henry didn't speak. Eventually, he gave a small, humourless laugh and instantly I regretted my question.

'Sorry,' I said. 'Henry, I'm so sorry, I shouldn't have—'

'No,' he replied. Then he sighed. 'No, it's not that. No one ever asks, that's all. No one ever asks me about him. They ask how *I* cope. How I get through the days. "How do you go on," they say, "when the very worst thing in the world has happened?" They make it all about me. No one ever wants to know about Elliot.'

'It's because they're frightened, Henry.'

'I know.'

'Elliot,' I said. 'Tell me about Elliot.'

'I loved him.'

His breathing quietened and I sensed he had stopped walking now. Paused right where he was on the street to think about his son. I didn't talk. I waited.

'Look,' he said, 'do you want to meet up? Because I'd like to tell you about him. Fuck,' he said emphatically, 'I'd *really* like to talk about him. About everything. I don't get to do that any more. And I know it's probably my own doing, but I feel like I need to sometimes . . . I can't talk to Nadine. She cries too much.'

'Sure,' I said softly. 'I'd like that, Henry.'

We got together two days later. I had no babysitter, Winston was in Newquay – his mother pretended not to know *where* he was, until I told her I didn't want any money out of him. Then

230

she admitted he'd taken off with the blonde girl with the dirty, matted hair (dreads) who'd been working at the campsite for the summer. 'He's back Friday,' she assured me. Anyway, it wasn't exactly a date that I'd scheduled with Henry, so he called at the house, and we walked together to the swings with George and his friend Ollie, who had stayed over for tea.

The boys kicked a football around and Henry and I sat on one of the picnic benches. I'd asked Henry if it was okay to bring George along, sensitive to the fact that he was here to talk about his own son, and he'd frowned, answering with, 'Well, what else are you going to do with him?'

We watched the boys for a while. George was no natural and had little control of the ball. A woman in her forties kept sending him black looks each time it went anywhere near her toddler. I pretended not to be aware and turned my attention to Henry.

'Now that I'm here I don't know where to start,' he said.

I told him not to talk at all if he didn't feel like it. I was happy to have someone to sit with. I was happy to be here with him. Usually, I came alone.

'He's a good kid,' Henry said, nodding towards George, who was about to take a corner.

'Yeah . . . did Elliot play?'

'I tried to get him into it, but he had no interest.'

'Same as George,' I said.

'His granddad was devastated,' Henry said, smiling at the memory.

'And George's,' I said. 'My dad's a big Bolton Wanderers fan, and his father before him. He was kind of gutted George couldn't care less. He's over it now, I think.'

'Yeah, my dad was the same, he—'

Somehow, when taking the corner, George had managed to kick the ball *behind* him.

'Excuse me!' came the shrill voice of the nearby mother. She set off, striding towards us, about to give us a piece of her mind. 'I wonder if you would mind telling *those* boys that I'd appreciate it if they kept that ball under—'

'Lads,' I yelled over to George and Ollie, 'play at the other end of the pitch.' They obliged without complaint, and I ignored the woman, turning back to Henry. 'You were saying?'

'Nicely done.'

'I'm well practised. There are a lot of parents who get outraged rather easily around here. They don't seem to think that their offspring will eventually grow up into nine-year-olds as well.'

'I remember the type,' said Henry, 'the full-on parents who behave as though the parks were built especially for them. They used to drive me nuts, going on all the equipment, talking non-stop to their kid, encouraging – Christ, *clapping* – the whole *Aren't I a fantastic parent?* bullshit.'

I nodded in agreement. 'They make you feel crap for reading a newspaper when you should be engaging with your kid.'

'Should you be engaging with your kid at every moment, do you think?' he asked.

'No, do you?'

'It's definitely weird,' he said. 'Anyway, what were we talking about? Football?'

'Your dad,' I said.

'Oh, yeah,' he said, and his expression turned once more reflective.

'How has he coped with the loss of a grandchild?'

'Better than Helena's parents,' he said.

'Helena is your wife?'

He nodded. 'Was.'

'Do you keep in touch with them? Helena's parents?'

'I call every couple of weeks, just to check in. Helena doesn't know. She's pretty heavily medicated, so they look after her. I tried to, but she didn't want me around in the end.'

'She blames you?'

'She blames herself. She wasn't at fault, but it made no difference. She blames herself and, ultimately, I'm not exactly sure what happened to us. I couldn't seem to help her, and she didn't want me near her, so her parents asked me to move away. Reluctantly, though – it was a last resort. I tell people I couldn't bear to be around anyone that knew about the accident, but it wasn't that. My wife couldn't bear to have *me* around any longer. I tried to do what was best for her.'

I nodded.

There wasn't really anything I could say. The worst thing in the world had happened. His marriage had fallen apart as a result. There were no words of consolation.

'Thank you for asking about Elliot,' he said softly.

'We all need to talk about our kids.'

'Most people, even friends, assume I'd hate to talk. That it's the last thing I'd want.'

I hesitated, not exactly sure how to answer. 'I'm no expert,' I said, 'but the people I know who've lost a child do want to talk. Rather than causing pain, it seems to bring some comfort.'

He clasped his hands together and nodded.

I said, 'You should see your face, by the way, when you talk about him. You become a different person. Your whole face shines.'

'It does?'

'Yeah,' I said. 'It does.'

The boys were edging closer to this side of the pitch. I glanced at the woman with the toddler, who was standing, hands on hips, waiting for me to reprimand them, so I didn't.

'I had the feeling I said the wrong thing the other evening,' said Henry. 'I thought I'd annoyed you and, though I really wanted to call, I didn't think you'd want to hear from me again.'

'You didn't annoy me.'

'No?' He looked dubious.

'The last few weeks haven't exactly been plain sailing. And I suppose it was just the fall-out from that.'

'Anything I can help with?' he asked.

'Thanks, but it's over.'

He went to say something further and then changed his mind, sensing, perhaps, that whatever had been troubling me I wasn't willing to share.

'I think that's why I was drawn to you,' he said, after a moment, reaching across and taking my hand. 'You know, when we first met?'

'During the insurance assessment?' I asked, surprised.

He went rueful. 'I like to play my cards close,' he said. 'But I knew almost straight away that you wouldn't try to fix me. You had your own shit going on, so you weren't going to try and make everything better. Or ask stupid fucking questions about how *I* feel . . . I was attracted to that.'

I smiled at him. 'How *do* you feel, Henry?'

'Not so bad, actually.'

We dropped Ollie back at his mother's and walked home, George carrying the football rather than attempting to dribble it along the pavement. Vince had left a bottle of the Portuguese white in the fridge on Saturday, so I opened it, pouring out two glasses, whilst Henry kicked the ball around in the back garden with George.

I watched from the open window.

Henry had an easy way with him. He wasn't out to impress, nor did he try to get George to like him. He was casual. After a minute or so Henry picked up the ball and said to George, 'You want to do something else?' and George nodded. Henry told him he didn't really like football either and I saw George smile coyly in response.

Then the two of them sat on the edge of the patio, shoulder to shoulder, and for a second I got a glimpse of what life could be like.

A glimpse of a future.

30

THE TEXT READ: 'Are you free?'
I replied: 'For?'
Scott wrote: 'The usual???'
Me: 'I've still not been paid for last time . . .'
And of course, then, he called.

It was now Thursday morning and I'd been avoiding Scott partly because of Henry, partly because of my unease at his presence at the swimming pool, but mostly because I knew I needed to end the arrangement and I was too nervous to face him.

I'd sent Scott a couple of innocuous texts, given him a gentle nudge to chase up the remaining money, and he'd replied, telling me he was on to it; and again later, saying they'd had problems with the computing system at work. It was all sorted out now, money on its way, and so on and so forth.

But it hadn't arrived.

'Roz, huge apologies,' Scott said breathlessly when I picked up, 'I had no idea you were still waiting. I'll draw out the cash. I'm terribly embarrassed. I hate owing money.'

'That's okay,' I said evenly. 'Money's not as tight as it once was.'

'No,' he laughed. 'You'll have no further use for me soon. I'll have to come up with some other way to lure you back.'

I laughed along with him, though when I looked at my reflection I wasn't smiling.

'So, how is everything?' he asked. 'You're still busy at work, I presume?'

'Always. You know how it is. I've had an offer, actually, to go back on my own.'

'Oh?'

'Yes, from a patient. A guy I've known for years has offered me premises. Affordable premises. And he doesn't really want any money up front, so there's no great risk involved.'

Scott was silent.

'Scott?'

'Sorry, sorry, I got distracted there for a moment. That's simply wonderful news, Roz. I'm delighted for you.' His words sounded hollow. 'When will you get going on this new venture?'

'A few weeks, I think. There are some renovations that need to be completed, but it shouldn't take too long.'

'Excellent. And what about Henry? How are things working out on that front?'

'Okay,' I said, non-committal.

'Do you see it going anywhere?'

Strange how people think they have a right to know. I wouldn't dream of asking how a person's marriage was going, or their relationship with their mother.

Though I did suspect Scott's enquiry had less to do with concern for my long-term happiness and more to do with finding out if I'd slept with his brother-in-law.

'You didn't think to mention he'd lost his son?' I said carefully.

Scott cleared his throat. 'Must have slipped my mind.'

I was about to reply when he said, 'Why, is he playing the sympathy card again?'

Gut-punched, I nearly dropped the phone.

'I thought he'd stopped with all that,' he said. 'I *thought* that the whole point of him moving back here was to put it all behind him. Anyway, it wasn't like it happened yesterday. And he doesn't like people to talk about it, so . . .'

I wasn't quite sure how to respond.

Eventually, I recovered enough to say, 'So, the money, Scott?'

'Indeed,' he said. 'The money.'

'What do you suggest?'

And he said, 'How about I drop by the clinic with it in an hour?'

I turned on the windscreen wipers. The weather had changed abruptly. A fast-moving storm was sweeping across the area and had everyone scurrying for their homes.

The wiper on the driver's side of the Jeep was damaged. With each stroke it made a soft groan, then juddered, leaving behind a small patch of uncleared glass, obscuring my line of sight. I had to sit tall and slightly forwards in the seat to make out the road ahead.

I was on my way to the Coniston holiday home that Scott had rented for our convenience. I had declined his offer of stopping by the clinic, thinking it prudent to meet where we couldn't be observed. And it occurred to me as we discussed the meet-up that we hadn't fully made use of the place – not as much as perhaps he had first hoped. I wondered if Scott was annoyed by this. If he was, he didn't give the impression of being so. In fact, he brushed away my remark with a comment about how life had the habit of getting in the way of the best-laid plans.

Did I detect a certain brittleness to his tone? I couldn't be sure.

I drove through the hamlet of Hawkshead Hill, past the Baptist chapel – a tiny church slotted right in amongst a row of neat, pretty, white cottages. The road climbed steadily until reaching the crossroads at the summit. Turn right for Tarn Hows, the spot at which I'd watched the sun go down, drinking beer with Henry. Head straight on for Coniston.

I descended slowly, the car buffeted by the crosswinds, and practised the beginnings of my speech.

I planned to tell Scott that we both knew our arrangement must come to a close. That we could not continue, things being as they were. It was too risky. Fate had planted obstacles in our way, in the shape of Henry, amongst other things, and this would be the end of what, for me, had been an enjoyable, not to mention lucrative, few weeks. But it was now over.

That should be all right, I thought. Say that, take the money, and run.

And Scott *had* alluded to the same line of thinking on the phone an hour ago. Just as he bid me goodbye he had laughed, saying that ours had probably been the most successful relationship of his life. He wished they could all be that simple, he said. We both got exactly what we needed out of it.

Ten minutes later, and I turned off the road. A branch had been pulled from a nearby oak and lay strewn across the track. I was upon it before realizing and decided to chance driving over it, rather than get out and hurl the thing over the hedgerow.

There was a hard clunk beneath the chassis, followed by a feeling of dragging a body beneath the car. A few yards further on and it must have released, as I was driving freely again. I didn't get out to check. Always best not to know what damage has been done, I find.

At the end of the track the cottage appeared. Less picturesque than last time, it looked more like what it actually was: secluded, stark and a little shoddy.

There were no lights on inside. I stayed in the car and waited for Scott. The windscreen soon became misted so I got the engine running again, directed some of the heat upwards. Instantly, it was stuffy.

Lowering the window an inch, I heard a bell. It was ringing, faintly, and must have been positioned either on a yacht's mast, or else on a buoy, out on the lake some way from the shore. The way it cried out at irregular intervals was eerie, evoking the image of the lone swimmer taken under the water in the opening scenes of *Jaws*.

I shuddered. And then there were headlights. A full beam hitting my mirror, blinding me for a moment. And the crunch of gravel. A car moving too fast and coming to a stop beside me in a partial skid.

I looked over. Scott lifted his hand and climbed out.

I hoped he might hand over the money and we could be on our way, but no. He strode towards the front door, keys jangling, and when I called his name he ignored me. So I followed.

Once through the door, his mouth was on mine and my weight was pushed against the wall. I had a hook in my back.

'Thank God,' he said breathlessly.

'Scott, wait.'

'I *can't* wait.'

I tried to put some space between us. 'Please,' I said, pushing him away. '*Please*, just give me a minute.'

He took a step back and regarded me. His expression was worried, uncertain. Childlike, in a sense. He was the small boy waiting for the grown-up to explain exactly what he had done wrong.

'I wasn't expecting this,' I began.

'You don't want to?' he said, genuinely astonished.

'I just—' and I paused, trying to clutch at the threads of my speech. I hadn't imagined this scenario. From his manner, from the impression he gave on the phone, I expected Scott and I would have a short conversation – cordial, civilized – in which we would both agree our arrangement was over. We would say goodbye. Perhaps kiss for old times' sake. But it would be a kiss of fondness. A *wish you well* kind of kiss. Not the kiss I'd just had forced upon me. And certainly not followed by the look of utter dejection that was now on Scott's face.

He swallowed.

When I still hadn't answered, he asked, 'Why are we even here then?'

I straightened my spine. 'I came for the money, Scott.'

'Oh,' he said.

'I thought you knew that.'

He gave a sad laugh and shook his head. 'I misinterpreted. When you suggested meeting here, I assumed that you wanted to . . .' He let the words hang.

I moved towards him. 'I didn't want anyone to see us together,' I explained gently. 'I thought if we met here then it could be private.'

He reached out his hand but, before he could touch my face, I took hold of it in mine. 'You're disappointed,' I said.

'Couldn't we just—'

'Sorry, we can't.'

'That sounds rather final,' he said.

I blew out my breath. 'Scott, you're not really suggesting that we go on, are you? This whole thing, it's too risky.'

'Because of Henry,' he said flatly.

'Not because of Henry.'

'Have you fucked him yet?'

'No. But that's not really your business.' There was a flicker in his jaw, a slow, deliberate blink of the eyes. Instinctively, I shrunk back, and in the space of a second he was upon me again. Pushing me hard into the wall.

'I don't want you to,' he hissed into my ear. 'I don't want you ever to fuck Henry.'

His mouth was on mine, and he was grabbing at the hem of my skirt.

'Scott, don't.'

He ignored my words.

His hands were rough, his breathing ragged. He pulled up my skirt and yanked at my knickers, making me yelp.

Then he pulled away to unfasten his jeans.

I stared at him.

'What are you doing?' I said coldly. 'What the hell do you think you're doing?'

And he stopped.

He looked at me with a strange expression. Almost dumb-struck. As though he wasn't quite with it.

'I don't know,' he whispered.

I pulled down my skirt. Straightened myself.

'I don't know what I was doing,' he repeated.

We stood in silence, both of us too shocked to speak.

I longed desperately to get out. To get away from the house. To get away from him. No one knew I was here. Not one person in the world knew where I was right now.

'I'm sorry, that was out of line,' he said eventually.

'You think?'

'It was the idea of you two,' he said. 'The thought of you being together is just too close to home.'

He had a look of hatred in his eyes that contradicted his apology. I swallowed hard, glancing towards the front door.

'Scott, that's exactly why we can't go on,' I said. '*It is* too close to home.'

'And by that what you mean is you don't *want* to go on.'

'*Why* wouldn't I, Scott?' I replied sharply. 'Think about it. Why would I not want to do it? This thing, this arrangement, has almost got me out of debt. I was close to losing my home before this. My son and I would have become *homeless*. And if I were to continue with what we've been doing – Christ, I could have savings. I could get somewhere in life again. But it can't go on.'

'Why?'

I held his gaze, but I didn't answer.

'This is a good arrangement, Roz,' he argued. 'No one is getting hurt. No one will find out.'

'Things have changed. We are no longer two people, practically two strangers, coming together for mutual gain. There are other people involved now, and it's unfair.'

'Who? Why is it unfair?'

'Your wife. My sister. And yes, now there's Henry.'

He flinched again at the sound of Henry's name.

'I don't want to be found out, Scott,' I said. 'I want to end it before we do any damage to the people I care about the most.'

He hung his head.

I went to go on, went to state my case further, but he cut me off. 'It's okay,' he said. 'I understand. When you were buried in debt, you were willing to take the risk. And now that you're not, you're not. I get it.'

He handed me the money he owed me before reaching into his inside pocket and withdrawing a small, midnight-blue Dorothy bag. 'I bought you this.'

When I didn't take it from him, he said, 'Please. It's for you. Please take it.'

I loosened the cord around the neck of the bag. There was a box. Inside, there was a pair of earrings. Small, non-fussy diamonds in a white-gold setting. 'They're really pretty, Scott, thank you, but I really don't—'

'Take them,' he snapped. 'In fact, wear them now.'

Scared, reluctant, I did as he asked, lifting my hair away from my face.

He gazed at me for a time, smiled, and then he shook his head, saying, 'I really thought I'd have you for longer, Roz.'

And I replied, 'I'm so sorry,' as earnestly as I was able.

'I didn't imagine it would end this quickly,' he continued. 'I suppose I expected it would continue as long as I wanted it to.'

'Did you?' I asked carefully.

'Yes,' he said. 'I did.'

I tried to smile. Tried to make light of it. I was conscious of keeping him calm. 'You sound as though you thought you were buying me for life,' I said.

Scott made as if to speak, but he hesitated.

Then he said, 'I would do that for you.'

I dropped my head, embarrassed by his words. 'I don't understand.'

He reached out and took hold of my face. With his grip tight, he lifted my chin.

Squeezing hard, he stepped towards me, until his face was inches from mine. 'I *would* take care of you,' he whispered. 'I'd take care of you for *life*, as you put it, if only you'd allow me to.'

31

THE LATE-AFTERNOON rain splattered against the clinic window. I pushed my thumbs into a hairy gluteus maximus, the flesh unforgiving as the patient tensed in response to my touch. 'Try to let it go loose if you can,' I told him.

'It hurts like hell,' he replied. 'There must be something seriously wrong in there.'

He was a new patient. A fifty-something solicitor who had blustered into the clinic with an authoritative air, answering my questions as though he really didn't have time, and *Couldn't we just get on with this?*

When he undressed I saw he had his underpants on back to front.

I moved across to his other buttock and sunk my thumbs into that side. He flinched and then yelped as though he'd been bitten. 'It's a trigger point, see?' I said. 'It hurts just as much on the left as on the right. Please do relax if you can.'

His silence indicated begrudging acceptance that his arse was not about to fall off any time soon, and he remained uncommunicative for the remainder of the session. Apart from, that is, when I pushed too deep and he would suck the spittle in between his teeth. So I thought about Scott. I thought about what he'd said earlier.

Obviously, we hadn't got as far as the logistics of his absurd proposition because I'd got out of there just as soon as I could.

Now that I had the chance to think about it, though, I was curious as to how he imagined we would maintain such an arrangement – if he was in fact serious about his offer of 'taking care of me for life'.

Would he deposit a monthly sum into my account and pop by whenever he required intercourse? A mistress, then, in the traditional sense?

Or would we remain with the system of my billing him for services rendered?

After his proposition Scott had become aware of the fear in my eyes and had relaxed his grip on my face, once again feeling appalled by his own actions. He apologized profusely, saying he didn't quite know where that behaviour had come from. Following which, I wondered what exactly I'd become saddled with.

Was Scott a psychopath? Was he a lonely, rich guy who couldn't stand any kind of rejection?

Apparently, he was neither.

How did I know this? Because I asked him.

He broke down, expressing mortification at what he'd just done, saying he'd never once hurt a woman, never even come close. He could only conclude that my early termination of our arrangement had hit him harder than he could have anticipated and he'd been taken over by some kind of primitive compulsion. Something he'd never experienced before.

The patient now lifted his head. He said, 'Do you think swimming will help?'

'Do you like to swim?' I asked.

'Not really. I'm not very good.'

I'm not sure why, but all new patients ask about swimming. It may have something to do with taking the weight off the joints, or because they've seen thoroughbreds in the hydrotherapy pool on television and consider their injury to warrant similar treatment.

Truth was, this guy had a bad back because he had a big belly, and swimming would make no difference. It was pulling his weight forward, putting strain on the joints of the lower back, and the pain in his buttock was the result of this.

'I could do with getting a bit of weight off,' he said, more to himself than to me.

I didn't respond. I never did. They didn't come to me to feel bad about their weight, and my thoughts were still stuck on Scott. About how I might avoid encountering him again in the near future. Petra might be a problem. I'd just have to have some good excuses at the ready in case she organized another get-together.

'Do you think I need to lose some?' the patient pressed.

'It can help,' I said vaguely.

Scott's cash was in my handbag. This time, I wasn't going to deposit it in the bank, so I needed to keep it well hidden. Problem was, my landlord had a key to the house, and it didn't exactly have great security. So it wouldn't be wise to leave it in one of my usual hiding places: the bread bin; inside the cheese drawer of the fridge.

And now I would need some of it to fix my car.

Returning to work, after the meeting with Scott, I heard an ominous, metallic clunking coming from beneath that didn't sound good. One of those noises you ignore at your peril. Well, I had ignored it, until Terry the ferry attendant stopped and stared as I'd boarded, tapping my window, saying there was something hanging down from the exhaust. Then I had no alternative but to acknowledge there was a problem and made a note to book the car into the garage. It would be expensive. Driving over that branch would turn out to be an expensive decision. It was like Newton's fourth law or something.

I demonstrated a few back extensions to the solicitor, since the joints of his lumbar spine were locked in forward flexion, and he acted like he was interested, asking how many he should do, what time of day was best.

He wouldn't do the exercises. His wife had most likely made this appointment just to stop him complaining.

'Scott Elias said you were very good,' he remarked as he knotted his tie in front of the mirror, and I did a double take.

'You're friends?' I asked cautiously, trying not to show that he'd unsettled me.

'We go way back.'

He perched on the treatment couch, lifting up alternate knees to tie his shoelaces. When he stood, he said, 'Do you know what, for the last ten years my back's hurt every time I've got up from sitting. And now the pain has gone.'

I smiled at him. 'Glad it's feeling better.'

I was aware of the clock. I needed a quick trip to the loo before the next patient and I wanted to get rid of this one quick.

'The wife reckons a copper bracelet helps with rheumatism. What are your thoughts?'

'You've not got rheumatism.'

'But suppose I did.'

'Then I'd say do anything that helps.'

'You think it's twaddle,' he said.

I made a face like I didn't really want to commit.

'What about magnets, crystals?' he asked. 'She's into all that stuff.'

'Like I said, whatever works.'

'Do I make another appointment?' he asked, and I told him to follow me through to reception, where I'd sort him out with something next week.

When I opened the door, DS Aspinall was waiting. She placed the magazine she'd been reading down on the table in front of her before lifting her hand in a gesture of hello. Her face was blank, unreadable.

I took the solicitor's debit card and asked him to key in his PIN. 'Will I see you at the party?' he asked.

I must have had a look of puzzlement on my face, because he added, 'Scott and Nadine's wedding anniversary?'

I shrugged. 'Must be for close friends and family only,' I said.

He was embarrassed, and apologized, saying he thought from the way Scott spoke of me that we knew each other well.

'Not that well,' I said a little stiffly, and he gathered up his wallet.

Once he'd left the building DS Aspinall approached the desk.

'We've found something,' she said.

32

'A BODY?' I REPEATED.

DS Aspinall nodded.

'A dead body?' I asked.

'We are waiting for a formal identification, but at this stage we are assuming it is the body of Mr Geddes.'

I sat down heavily on the office chair behind me. 'Wayne's dead?' I whispered. 'I can't believe it.'

I stared at my hands. Christ, it didn't seem possible. I looked to DS Aspinall, who at first remained silent, allowing me to process the news. It was only when she asked, 'Can I get you anything? A drink of water? Tea?' that I realized she was staying a while and hadn't come here merely to inform me of the death.

'Does his mother know?' I asked.

'She's been informed. His cousin has agreed to view the body once it's . . .' She paused at this point, stopped herself from speaking further. 'I'll need to ask you and your colleagues a few questions,' DS Aspinall said, 'once you feel ready. I understand this must be difficult for you to make sense of.' But in case I was in any doubt, she added, 'I will need to question each of you now, though, Mrs Toovey. Today.'

I lifted my head. 'Where was he found?'

'At his home.'

I put my hand to my mouth.

'How long has he been dead?' I asked.

'We can't be sure at this stage.'

Wayne, what have you done?

I knew he was depressed when I left him. I knew he was confused – ashamed, even – at what had occurred, but dead? Really?

'How did he do it?' I asked quietly.

'Sorry?'

'How did he kill himself?'

'Oh, Mrs Toovey, I'm so sorry, you misunderstood. Wayne Geddes didn't kill himself.'

I frowned.

'He was found inside the freezer in the outhouse,' she said.

My eyes widened. 'Someone *put* him in there?'

'We believe so, yes.'

A stupid question, I realized. Wayne would hardly climb in himself. If DS Aspinall thought she was speaking to an idiot, she didn't show it. 'Apologies,' I said, 'I can't seem to think straight.'

'At the moment we don't have an exact cause of death, but as you can imagine we're eager to get going on this as quickly as possible. Now that it's a murder inquiry, I have to ask you, Mrs Toovey, were you ever present at the property?'

'At Wayne's house?' I asked shakily.

She nodded.

I swallowed. 'I don't think so.'

She tilted her head. 'I need a definite yes or no.'

'No, then.'

'Okay, good. What we're hoping to do in the first instance, after the initial door-to-door, is to take fingerprints from anyone Mr Geddes was in contact with. Friends, colleagues, and so on. That way we can quickly eliminate them from the case. I wonder if you would be able to supply us with a list of names, Mrs Toovey?'

'Names.'

'Yes,' she said. 'Names of colleagues, patients he may have had a disagreement with, that sort of thing. To be honest, we just need a place to start. There is very little to go on as things stand.'

I could feel the pulse throbbing in my temporal artery. I wondered if it was visible.

My fingerprints were all over that house. All over Wayne.

DS Aspinall went to hand me another card with her details on it, but before releasing it from her grasp she paused. She regarded me for a moment, tilting her head to the side as though looking from a different angle might present an answer.

Then she smiled. 'The sooner the better with that list, Mrs Toovey,' she said, and I told her I would get started on it.

The list:

Roz Toovey.

Roz Toovey.

Roz Toovey.

Later, after she'd gone, I sat with my head in my hands, trying to remember, desperately; trying to recollect anything about that night at Wayne's. Where did I put my prints? My DNA?

'So you never went there, Mrs Toovey?' DS Aspinall would inevitably ask. 'You never once entered Mr Geddes's house? Explain then, if you will, the presence of your pubic hair in the dining room. Explain the line of fingerprints on the windowsill.'

I should hand myself in. I should go after her right now and come clean. I went there to have sex with Wayne, but I didn't murder him. It was consensual sex. Agreed upon beforehand. I went there specifically to have sex with Wayne Geddes, even though it didn't actually happen.

Except this was *Wayne*.

Who in their right mind would believe that? No one would believe that.

So I should tell DS Aspinall that I went there to have sex with Wayne because he was blackmailing me about the stolen money.

Money I'd led DS Aspinall to believe was taken by Wayne.

I would be prosecuted. My name would be in the papers. I could say goodbye to my job, to running my own practice again. No one would trust me.

Fuck.

What if I told her I was being blackmailed by Wayne because I'd been accepting payments for sex from Scott Elias?

Then I would be popped right to the top of their list of suspects because not only was I at the property, I also had a motive for killing him.

Killing him.

Someone had killed Wayne. Poor, poor, pathetic Wayne.

Who would do such a thing? And what if they were at the house when I was there? What if they *saw* what happened between us?

33

NEXT, TWO THINGS happened.

Two phone calls that in themselves were innocuous enough but together would make for a devastating outcome.

I drove home thinking about Wayne's body, thinking about my situation, understanding for the first time what real fear was. By the time I got to the ferry the fear was so strong you could smell it on me. The combination of coffee and adrenalin poured in a rank sweat from my armpits. I sat with my hands gripped tight to the wheel, my face inches from the windscreen.

Terry's shift had finished, so a cocksure kid in his late teens had the job of ticket attendant. He rapped hard on my window, startling me, swathing me in pickled-onion-crisp breath as I lowered the glass. His upper row of teeth was clogged with food.

Reaching into the glove compartment, I retrieved the book of tickets, handing one over, just as my mobile rang.

UNKNOWN NUMBER.

'Roz?'

I sighed out a long, weary breath. 'Winston,' I said.

'Roz, you'll never guess what's happened—'

'You've been stranded in Newquay.'

'How did you know?'

'Lucky guess.'

'Yeah, well, I've lost my lift home, and I can't scrape the money together for the train fare. I won't be back in time to pick George up tomorrow. Any chance you could do this weekend, and I'll do the next two?'

'What happened to the girl?'

'The girl?' he said innocently.

'Your mother said you'd gone to Newquay with the blonde from the campsite.'

'Oh her. Yeah, that didn't really work out. She kind of hooked up with someone else, a slimy bastard who could get really strong skunk. Anyway, listen, if I can't get the money in the next few days, I'll just thumb it back, okay?'

'Okay.'

'Sure you don't mind?'

'I don't mind.'

'You sound weird, Roz. You're not doing that thing when you act all fine about something and then throw it back in my face later on, are you?'

'I'm not doing that.'

'Great. That's a relief. I can never tell. See you when I get home then.'

'Sure, Winston. When you get home.'

We ended the call and I sat back in my seat. Took a breath.

The uncomplicated life of Winston Toovey.

No money to get back to see his son? Hey, things'll work out. And with me and his mother to pick up after him, they usually did.

The ferry docked, groaning more than usual. Tourists scurried back to their cars, engines were started, visors lowered, as we would all be heading west, directly into the sun. The woman in front must have left her car in gear, as it jolted forward when she turned the ignition. She touched her hair repeatedly in embarrassment.

Wayne had been murdered and I was the last person to see him alive. I just couldn't get my head around anyone wanting to kill Wayne and bundle his body into the freezer. House-to-house inquiries, DS Aspinall had said. Would anyone remember a black Jeep creeping towards Wayne's house that night? Leaving again later, tearing up the turf at the edge of the garden, because I was in so much of a hurry to escape?

The farm cottage was on its own at the end of a short stretch of track. But there were one or two houses that had a view of it from across the fields. Someone could have been watching from their bedroom window. Someone could remember *something*.

What if they matched the tyre treads? I could only hope the rain had washed them away by now.

I wound my way over Claife Heights, behind a truck with two collies in the rear, along with a few bales of hay. The days of shepherds tending to one flock were long gone. These guys flitted from place to place, dropping food supplies out the back of their Mitsubishis, more FedEx than farmers.

I am innocent, I repeated as I descended into the valley. The storm of earlier had cleared and the valley was now awash with honey-coloured light. So pretty it made your heart stop. I could not be charged with killing Wayne Geddes, because I didn't do it. I'm innocent, I said again. Hoping something – *anything* – would emerge from DS Aspinall's inquiries that would prove it.

George was sitting on his own when I arrived at after-school club.

He was holding a piece of paper steady with his left hand and looked to be tracing. I was just about to approach when Iona caught my eye.

A word? she mouthed, beckoning me over.

I sensed danger so asked, 'How's the knee?' bright and breezy, as though I wasn't aware of something nasty to come.

Instinctively, Iona lifted her leg, flexing and extending it at the joint. '*So* much better. That tape you put on? It worked a treat. You should patent it.'

'I keep meaning to. All okay?' I asked, with respect to George, and her expression turned at once grave and formal.

'I've been told to give you this.'

She handed me an envelope. 'Mr and Mrs Toovey' was printed across the front. Followed by 'Confidential'.

'Do I read it now?' I asked.

'That's up to you.'

I unfolded it and read. The school requested my attendance at a meeting scheduled for Monday morning to discuss George. A representative from the Local Education Authority would be present.

I looked up at Iona. 'Do you know what this is about?'

She leaned in, lowering her voice. 'Sorry, Roz, it's not really my place, not being his teacher, but I think he's been stealing again.'

I slipped the letter back inside the envelope and pushed it hard into the pocket of my tunic.

'I'm sure it's something and nothing,' Iona said, trying to smile, brushing it off as though it were a minor inconvenience. But it wasn't. If the LEA was involved, it wasn't.

I nodded, thanking Iona for her discretion, and told George to collect his things as quickly as he could. He didn't make eye contact with me the whole time, didn't say a word either. It wasn't until I got him inside the car and was turning the ignition that he said, 'It wasn't me.'

I cut the engine. 'What do you mean, it wasn't you?'

He threw me a look that said *I knew you wouldn't believe me*, and stared hard through the windscreen.

The sun broke through from behind a cloud, blinding us both. 'George, reach into my handbag,' I said to him, 'and get my sunglasses. They might be in the side pocket.'

He lifted the bag on to his lap and pulled at the zip. It was in the habit of jamming and so he tugged hard a couple of times before it flew open, releasing a cloud of twenty-pound notes, which fluttered around us.

George looked at me agog. Shit, the money. I'd forgotten all about it.

'Gather it up!' I cried out. 'Quick, gather it up before somebody sees.'

George did as he was asked, scrabbling around in the footwell. When we'd retrieved the last of the notes, we sat there in silence.

'Are we rich now?' he asked carefully.

'No.'

'Not even with all that money?'

'Not even with all that money,' I said. 'It will only cover three months' rent, sweetheart. So, no, we're not rich. Tell me what happened at school.'

'I don't want to.'

'Unfortunately, there's no choice.'

A look of anger flashed across his face. 'I didn't do it,' he said. 'I told them I didn't do it. I told *you* I didn't do it. But no one will believe me.'

'What was stolen?'

'Pokémon figures.'

My heart sank. 'Which ones exactly?'

'I don't know. Leif says three were taken out of his bag, and the teachers found them in my bag.'

'So how did they get into your bag?'

He glared at me again. 'I *don't know.*'

'Jesus, George, if they found them in your bag – if a teacher found them in your bag – then who else could it be?'

'But I didn't take them.'

'Could you not help it because you really wanted Leif's figures and you didn't think he would notice because he has so many?'

George sighed impatiently, saying, 'You *never* forget which ones you have.'

'So who took them?' I asked.

'I don't know.'

'And why would they put them in your bag?'

'I *don't know.*'

'Have you had an argument? Have you been mean? Would another kid do this to get you into trouble?'

'I don't know.'

'George! For God's sake, I'm trying to help you! Don't you see, once you've stolen stuff, people don't *care* whether it was you who did it the next time or not? You'll be blamed regardless!'

'But I didn't do it. And that's not fair!'

'I know it's not fair, but it's how it is!'

Why did this have to happen today? Why today, of all days?

I looked at George and he was crying. I was too angry to reach out to him. Angry with him. Angry with Winston for not being here again. For leaving me broke. Angry with myself for being such a fuck-up.

I rubbed at my face with my hands. 'Okay,' I said. 'Okay, let's start again. I didn't mean to shout.'

He nodded, tears meandering down his dirty cheeks.

'I'm all you've got right now,' I said softly. 'I'm the *only* person, except for your father, and surprise surprise, he's not here. Do you understand that?'

'Yes,' he whimpered.

'Christ knows I don't need this today, George. I really don't. But I am on your side, and I will back you up because you are my son. And whether you've done it or not, I don't really care, because you're all I have and I love you. But for me to find a way through this you need to stop being *so mad* at me, because I didn't cause this. I didn't make anyone steal anything. Whoever it was.'

I was still breathing hard, and my head was shaking. I worked to stifle a sob that was threatening to build.

'I'm sorry,' said George.

'It's okay. No one likes to be accused. I understand that.'

I turned the ignition and headed out on to the road. We'd gone about twenty yards when I became aware of George gripping his hands together so hard that his knuckles were white.

'Mum,' he said.

'What is it?'

'I didn't take them.'

'I know you didn't, baby. It's okay. Let's go home.'

34

THE SECOND PHONE call came from Nadine.

 I'd barely got inside the house when I could hear her voice echoing through from the dining room. George had seen the answer machine flashing and pressed play, thinking it would be his dad. 'So the upshot of all this is that Henry will be calling around with an invitation this evening. I'm so sorry about this, Roz, but you know what they say: *If you want something doing, ask a busy woman.* I do hope you'll join us. I'm terribly embarrassed. Poor Petra didn't know whether to say anything or not. I've given Scott a real earbashing. He was supposed to give you your invite at his last physio session. Anyway, hopefully no harm done and we'll see you tomorrow.'

I stood looking at the machine. 'No you won't,' I said, and went into the kitchen to find some alcohol.

A garden party, or afternoon tea, whatever you like to call it. This is what Nadine said. It was to celebrate their twenty-fifth wedding anniversary and was being held at a nearby hotel tomorrow. Friday. Nadine played it down on the phone – low key, nothing fancy – but this hotel was not low key. Esthwaite Manor was the place movie stars stayed when visiting the Lakes. No one I knew had eaten there, because it cost an arm and a leg, and non-residents of the hotel were not encouraged.

Anyway, of course I wasn't going. And not that it made any difference to my decision, but Scott didn't want me to be there

– that was made clear by the fact he'd neglected to hand over my invitation. It slipped his mind, apparently. And then he mislaid it. Nadine wanted me there as Henry's guest; *of course* there had always been an invitation for me, she said.

The reason she'd plumped for afternoon tea and not a full evening celebration? They were flying to the Galápagos Islands, via Atlanta, then Ecuador, on Saturday. And Scott knew nothing about it. It was something he'd talked about for years. The giant tortoises, and so on, and Nadine said if they didn't do it now they'd never do it. So a boozy night was out of the question if they were flying long haul a day later.

She'd ended the call by saying, 'Not a word about the trip, Roz.' And then, 'Can't wait to see you!'

She was so bloody nice.

I used to smoke. Right at that moment I missed it like never before. It was the first thing I used to do when faced with a problem, a situation I found difficult. Light up, stand outside the back door, take a few deep inhalations, and the problem didn't seem quite so insurmountable.

If I still smoked, I would smoke one after another now until my lungs were on fire. I needed a vacation from my problems; from my own brain, in fact. The party, I could deal with. I'd make an excuse for not attending and wish them well. The list for DS Aspinall, I couldn't avoid. I had to face it. Along with the meeting with the LEA. And I needed time to think about these things. I needed space to work out what I was going to do. I did not need Henry turning up, wondering what the hell was wrong with me.

I'd get out of the house. That was the answer. Avoid, avoid, avoid.

'George!' I yelled. 'Wash your face, we're going out.'

'Where?' he shouted back from the garden.

'I don't know. Wash your face, change your T-shirt, put on clean socks.'

'I don't want to go out.'

'Do it!'

He ran past, flying up the stairs, treading heavily, making as much noise as possible, in the way kids do when they're unhappy with what's been requested of them. I'd have to tidy myself up as well. I threw the remainder of the wine down the sink and went to change out of my uniform.

Five minutes later, in a white shirt and jeans, I grabbed my bag. The front door was ajar. I could hear Dennis softly murmuring and George chattering away to him. George said once that the reason he liked Dennis so much (aside from him being the owner of a dog) was that he didn't pretend to be interested in him. Unlike other adults.

Dennis either talked or he didn't. He spoke when he wanted to know something but didn't feel the need to fill the silence with words just for the sake of it. Celia did enough of that for both of them.

I'd asked George if he thought *I* pretended to be interested in him and he'd chewed it over for a moment before answering, 'No. You've got to ask me that stuff because you're my mum.'

I went through to close the back door and, when I returned to the lounge, my handbag was lying on the sofa. I couldn't leave with all that money stuffed inside it. I glanced out of the window and saw George squatting on his haunches, minus one shoe, now over on Celia's side of the fence, tickling Foxy's belly. Dennis held George's removed shoe in his hand and appeared to be picking at the sole with a small knife.

No sign of Henry.

I unzipped the sofa cushion and began stuffing the money from my handbag deep inside. George had crumpled many of the notes, but I didn't have time to start smoothing them out so I just hid them the best way I could—

'Anyone home?'

Shit.

'Hey,' Henry said.

I turned slowly. He had pushed the door open and was standing in the gap, smiling warmly.

'Give me a minute?' I said helplessly.

'Sure,' he replied. 'Can I come in?'

'No!' I yelled, and he stood where he was, stock still. 'No,' I said again immediately, milder this time. 'Sorry, just give me a minute and I'll be straight out. There's something I need to do.'

'Ok–ay,' he said slowly, perturbed but trying not to show it. He backed out, saying, 'I'll wait right outside.'

'Shut the door, would you?'

A moment later, money hidden, I came out to find Celia had joined them and was firing questions at Henry.

'I'm not sure what we're having,' Henry was saying, as Celia inquired about the following day's celebration. Her friend Joyce from book club had eaten at Esthwaite Manor when it first opened and raved about the lemon dessert: it 'just *slipped* down', apparently.

Celia was very excited.

'Roz, open your invitation so I can see it. Dennis, go and fetch my reading glasses.'

'It's not from Buckingham Palace, Celia,' I said.

'I know that,' she snapped.

Henry turned to me. 'Are you okay?' he whispered, and I nodded quickly, not meeting his gaze, hoping he wouldn't pursue it.

Before opening the envelope, I said, 'I won't be able to go to this, I'm afraid,' and Celia did a double take, her mouth dropping open.

'What do you mean, you're not going? Of course you're going,' she said.

Henry lifted his eyebrows.

'Winston isn't back,' I explained. 'He's stuck in Cornwall.'

'Bring George along with you,' suggested Henry.

'Thanks, but to be honest I don't really think it's a kids kind of place, especially when—'

'You have *got* to go to this, Roz,' Celia said, as though my life depended on it. 'You cannot pass over this invitation. It's simply too' – she paused, trying to find the right word – 'it's too important,' and she glared at me before flicking her head at Henry. As though he wouldn't notice.

Henry said, 'I'd really like you to come if you can. No pressure, but it's going to be deadly dull. Scott will give one of his *haven't I done well?* speeches, and it would be so much easier to take if you were there.'

'I really wish I could.'

'And he'll have all of his cronies there asking what line of business I'm in, and if I've ever thought of joining Rotary.'

A pause.

'We'll take care of George,' Celia declared loudly. 'Won't we, Dennis?'

Dennis was making his way back across the garden, holding out Celia's glasses. He agreed that it would be no trouble, smiling coyly at George, saying he could help out with walking Foxy.

I was being railroaded.

I protested again, but Celia was having none of it. She told me to stop being ridiculous, that she and Dennis were more than capable, that it was bordering on insulting, in fact, the way I was wavering over this. And then she told me to pass her the invitation.

A peculiar look of melancholy came over Celia then. She mouthed the words as she read. I watched, realizing in that moment that she was coming to terms with the fact that she would probably never be invited to an event at Esthwaite Manor. That ship had sailed. Observing her, you could almost see her letting go of a dream.

She gathered herself. Shook off the moment of sadness and got back to being Celia. She asked Henry if he would like a glass of cava – 'We don't do champagne on a weeknight!' – and how about some of Dennis's strawberries to go with it?

Henry said that he would, as I tried unsuccessfully to appear happy and grateful with the arrangements.

Inside, I was fighting the urge to run away. I wanted to grab hold of George, flee the scene, never to come back.

Which was exactly what I should have done.

35

'WHAT DO YOU buy the couple who has everything?' I asked
Henry.

'I'll get a gift and put your name on it,' he replied.

'I can't turn up empty-handed.'

'You won't *be* empty-handed, you'll be with me.'

'Okay, so what will *you* buy the couple who has everything?'

'I'll think of something.'

As it happened, he didn't think of something, and we did as I'd
feared: turned up without a present. When I became twitchy
about this in the car on the way there, Henry reassured me
that no one would notice, and he wasn't wasting money on that
wanker; he would take Nadine out for a nice lunch when they
returned from the Pacific. 'She'd prefer that,' he said. 'She's always
complaining she doesn't get to spend enough time with me and
never knows what's going on in my life. Honestly, Roz, it's fine.'

I wore my wedding-party staple: the chiffon dress from Coast
with the tea roses on it, and a tense expression. The kind of look
you see on a woman who feels fat in her outfit and no amount of
cajoling can snap her out of it.

I was scared. Scared of the afternoon ahead, scared of seeing
Scott in a public setting. Scared of giving my prints to the
police.

I'd had a rethink with regards to the list that DS Aspinall had
requested and rather than dilly-dally over sending it, I'd gone to

town on it. Put down every Tom, Dick and Harry I could think
of to keep the woman busy. I positioned myself three from the
bottom of a list of around a hundred people, hoping that by
the time she got around to fingerprinting me, something would
have turned up to exonerate me.

A long shot. But it was the best I could do.

Henry told me to remain in the car whilst he jumped out,
appearing on my side, opening the door and offering his arm. He
wore a two-button tailored suit in blue sharkskin and he looked
divine. Before we moved off in the direction of the entrance he
stopped.

Turning to face me, he said, 'Answer me this, were you
reluctant to come here today because you'd rather not be with
me, or because you'd rather not come at all?'

I hesitated.

He said, 'The truth, please, Roz.'

'The latter,' I said, dropping my gaze. 'It's not you, Henry.'

'Okay then,' he said, and he lifted my chin with his finger,
placing a soft kiss above my brow.

His lips barely brushed against my skin but I found myself
gasping at the feel of his touch. Embarrassed, I pulled away.

'Wait,' he said, looking at me intently.

I was aware of a car passing beside us. Aware of the breeze
picking up and my hair coming loose.

With his eyes never leaving mine, Henry reached out and
tucked the few stray strands behind my ear. Then he kissed me.

The smell of him, the soft push of his tongue inside my mouth,
and my legs began to buckle.

'Promise we'll get away from here as soon as we can,' he
whispered as he led me towards the hotel entrance.

He slipped his arm around my waist, and it felt wonderful. I'd
been turning up alone to these things – functions, birthdays,
christenings – for so, so long. Henry pulled me in close like I

belonged to him. And for one short, wonderful moment I felt like I did. I wanted to belong to him. His body was lean and tight beneath his suit. He smelled good. He wasn't a dickhead.

'What time did you tell your neighbours you'd be back to pick up George?' Henry asked.

'Around eight.'

He checked his watch. 'We've got just under three hours. I reckon we show our faces, exchange pleasantries with the happy couple and sneak off the first chance we get.'

At that moment I felt a kind of dopey sensation drawing me towards Henry. And if he told me to follow him anywhere at all, I would do it.

Esthwaite Manor was built entirely from Lakeland Stone. It had a Gothic feel, with its three turrets, the steep pitch of its roof. When we reached the doors Henry said, 'Brace yourself.'

It had been immaculately renovated. It was the type of place where you found yourself walking on the balls of your feet so your heels didn't damage the flooring.

A pretty girl in a good suit who was manning the entrance told us that the Elias party was outside. If we made our way through the drawing room, she said, we'd find them easily enough. Henry took my hand and squeezed it before we continued. 'I'm so glad you came,' he whispered, and we were swept along by a tipsy group in their late fifties; people who populated the society pages of *Cumbria Life* magazine, attending charity events and whatnot. Their laughter was raucous, the accents broad, and I was happy to disappear amongst them as we moved towards the patio.

Outside, beneath a quaint, ivory-painted, wrought-iron gazebo, a string quartet played cover versions of popular songs. Sting's 'Englishman in New York' was just ending as we arrived, and Henry said quietly, 'How long, I wonder, before "Eleanor Rigby"?'

Not long, as it happened. It was next.

There was an uninterrupted view across the lake. Esthwaite Water is a small lake, less than a mile in length, so it's really only popular with fishermen. A rowing boat was visible bobbing over at the western shore, one lone figure inside.

I must have had a wistful look on my face because a voice to my left said, 'Wish you could change places with that guy?'

Scott.

I tried to smile. 'Not at all,' I said. 'And congratulations.'

He kissed my cheek, whispering he was sorry he had neglected to pass on my invitation, and when I intimated that it was sensible not to want me here, that I *shouldn't be here*, he looked surprised.

'Of course I want you here,' he said tersely, though quietly, out of earshot of Henry, who was making conversation with a waiter to his right. 'It slipped my mind on account of you giving me my marching orders when we last met. That's why I didn't mention it,' he said, and then he turned to Henry.

Henry congratulated Scott, shaking his hand, and Scott said, 'Twenty-five years,' his voice booming now, full of good cheer. 'What is it they say again?'

'You get less for murder?' supplied Henry.

'I was going to say the latter years are the best,' replied Scott.

I needed to get away. Having the two of them in such close proximity was too much. Henry was smiling at Scott in a way I'd not seen before; it was a smile that conveyed amused disdain. His eyes danced as he regarded Scott, and the result was chilling.

Not that Scott cared.

He already knew what Henry thought of him. Scott glanced at me and I saw the beginnings of a smile. *Get this guy*, his smirk said. *If only he knew who'd been screwing his nice, new girlfriend.*

'Excuse me,' I said, and slipped away.

My head throbbing, I cut a line across the patio with the vague notion of spending some time in the Ladies. On the way, Petra caught my eye. She was waving madly from over by the musicians. *Back in a sec?* I gestured, and pointed inside. She waved me off and resumed chatting to a woman I didn't know.

The Ladies had a number of chrome art-deco vanity units, each with a lamp and an individual hairdryer. It was like a powder room from the thirties: charming, and totally against the current trend. Two of the seats were occupied by well-dressed women who were chattering about switching to Bulgarian housekeepers, because the initial enthusiasm on the part of the Poles was beginning to wane. 'As lazy as the English now,' one said to the other.

I took a seat and played with my hair a bit, stalling for time. When I emerged from the bathroom I was aware of a pause in the music and headed outside to see what was going on.

The party was gathered in one spot, a kind of rough semi-circle, on the grass just beneath the patio. There were around a hundred people. Nadine was standing on the steps addressing the party, along with Scott, and they had their backs to me. Quickly, I joined the group, mingled in with Petra and Vince. I complimented Petra on her outfit, and she linked my arm. She lifted her chin, hanging on to Nadine's every word.

Nadine was stunning in a beautifully cut, oyster-coloured trouser suit. She looked slim and lovely, her skin radiant. Scott stood beside her, smiling at his wife.

'Of course, what Scott doesn't know about, and what we've all gone to great pains to keep secret,' Nadine was saying, 'is the trip.'

She turned to Scott and took his hands in hers as though renewing her vows. Scott said, 'Trip?', perhaps now a little nervous.

I caught sight of Henry, who was at the far end of the semi-circle. He smiled shyly in my direction.

Nadine said, 'Thank you for a wonderful twenty-five years,

Scott. It's been a wild ride and I wouldn't have missed it for the world. Tomorrow, we leave for the Galápagos.' Scott's eyes widened and, before he could speak, Nadine said, 'And I know what you're thinking. You're thinking you can't take time off work. Well, it's arranged. And you're coming whether you like it or not.'

There was a small cheer, followed by chants of 'Speech! Speech!' before the noise quietened and Scott blustered out a few words. He was overwhelmed to have all his friends in one place, he said, and went on to say how wonderful it was to have his children home. He'd be sorry to have only one night with them, now that they were flying off the following day, but . . . and he paused.

He paused as though the emotion of the occasion was all a bit too much.

Then he looked straight at me.

His silence continued, but everyone was still smiling, unaware. Then it began to get painful and, gradually, faces started to fall. A low murmur spread throughout the gathering.

What was wrong?

'Scott, mate, are you okay?' someone asked, and he didn't have an answer.

Nadine turned to him, the beginnings of panic forming in her eyes.

Scott continued to look my way and I became aware of others, following his gaze, watching me also.

'What's wrong with him?' I could hear from a woman behind me. 'Does he need a doctor?'

And then the worst thing happened.

He closed his eyes, put his hand to his mouth. 'I'm so sorry,' he cried. 'I'm so sorry, but I can't do this.'

'Scott?' Nadine said.

'I can't do this any more,' he said.

My breath caught in my throat.

'Can't do what? You're scaring me, Scott. What is it?' Nadine said.

He rubbed his face with his hands and I was aware of Petra whispering, 'Oh, no,' quietly beside me.

'I'm in love with another person,' he said firmly, and there was a collective gasp of horror. 'I'm in love with another person,' he said again, 'and I believe – no, that's not quite right, I *know for sure* – that this person is in love with me.'

He looked at me and waited.

I couldn't move.

Petra loosened her hold on my elbow and turned around to see who was behind us. There must not have been an obvious candidate for Scott's affections because she turned straight back, saying in my ear, 'What the hell is going on?'

'Roz?' Scott prompted. And when I didn't speak, he said, 'I think it's only right, don't you? We have to tell them. We owe them that much.'

My throat closed. Something like a fist clasped tight around my heart and pulled it down through my belly.

Petra unlinked her arm fully. 'Jesus Christ,' she whispered.

'It wasn't,' I stammered. 'It's not . . .'

Nadine wept.

Scott said, 'I'm so sorry. I didn't want it to happen like this. God, I'm sorry, Nadine,' and all around there was silence. I stood rooted to the spot as a space formed between me and the others. I was vaguely aware of Vince pulling Petra towards him, pulling her away from me.

I looked for Henry. I caught one glimpse of his astonished, stunned expression before the crowd closed around him.

I found my voice. 'I do not love Scott,' I said helplessly. It came out weak and pathetic.

'That's hardly important!' cried Petra now, fighting to get free of Vince. 'Look!' She pointed towards the steps.

Nadine was in a heap. Her body lay crumpled on the patio. People rushed forward to attend to her.

Petra advanced on me, clutching hold of my dress at the neck. Her face was inches from mine.

'It's not what you think,' I said.

'Have you slept with him?' she hissed.

I didn't answer.

'Have you been sleeping with Scott Elias?' she repeated. 'Roz, tell me!'

I nodded.

'Yes,' I said, 'but, Petra, it's not what you think. You *have* to listen—'

But she was already walking away.

There was no music. No music, no voices, no laughter – no sound at all, save for the hushed whispers of the women surrounding Nadine.

I stood alone around twenty feet from Scott. We looked at each other for an extended moment and I mouthed one word.

Why?

I was dazed. Bewildered by what had just occurred. So when he tilted his head, frowned, laughing once to himself, I just didn't get it.

I walked towards him. 'I don't understand,' I said quietly. 'I don't understand what you're doing.' I looked around. Everyone was still staring. 'Why have you done this?'

'You gave me no other choice,' he said simply.

'But look around. You've lost everything.'

'I don't want it,' he replied. 'I don't want any of it.'

'But your wife,' I said. 'Your kids. Look what they think of you.'

He took a step towards me. 'I don't care what they think of me. I don't care what Nadine thinks. I thought I made that quite clear to you the other day.'

'Did you plan this?'

He shrugged.

I was wordless. The look on Nadine's face when he made his announcement was desperate.

'But I don't love you,' I said. 'Why would you chance—'

'You don't love me *yet*,' he said.

I glared at him, appalled. 'I won't *ever* love you.'

He took a breath. 'Maybe you don't need to love me. Maybe I love you enough for the both of—'

'You've lost your mind,' I snapped, and I started to turn away. 'We're humiliating your wife. I'm humiliating myself. Let's not do this here.'

He grabbed my arm. 'Don't you get it?'

'Don't *you* get it?' I said. 'I don't want you. I don't need you, Scott.'

I was aware of some activity over Scott's shoulder. Nadine had been lifted to her feet, and a number of women were pulling her back, restraining her, almost. She forced herself apart from them as they pleaded with her not to do what it was she was about to do.

'How long?' she shouted, directing the question at me.

'Nadine—'

'How fucking long?' she yelled.

'Three weeks,' I answered.

'Do you love him?' she asked.

'No. I don't love him.'

And her face collapsed. 'Then why?' she cried out, her hand to her throat. 'Why would you do such a thing? Marriage may mean nothing to you, but that does not mean you can go around screwing other people's husbands.'

I turned to Scott. 'Perhaps you could explain to your wife what actually happened.'

Scott looked blank. 'I don't know what you mean,' he said.

'Nadine, I—' but then Petra returned. Marching across the patio to tell me to go. 'Just go,' she said.

Nadine shook her head. 'No, Petra, I want to hear this. I want to know how she has been able to come here today. I want to know how she has been able to hold a *conversation* with me, when all along she was doing this.'

I hung my head. What was there to say? There was nothing to say.

Vince was a few feet behind Petra, and I expected, as was his usual way, he would try to calm her. But he spoke up. 'I think Nadine deserves an answer, Roz,' he said reasonably.

I shook my head. 'No,' I whispered.

'No?' Nadine shot back. '*No?* That's it? That's all you've got to say? You wreck my marriage, my life, and you don't even have a reason?'

She was pleading. It was so awful. I said, 'You need to ask Scott.'

'I'm asking you.'

Eventually, my voice barely audible, I said, 'I was paid.'

'He paid you to keep quiet?' asked Petra, confused and stupefied by such a thought.

I looked straight at her. 'No, Petra. He paid me to sleep with him.'

Nobody spoke.

The small group exchanged nervous glances.

What did she just say? She didn't say what I think she said, did she?

'How *much* did he pay you?' asked Nadine, her voice shaking, her eyes now on Scott.

'Enough to make me agree to do it. I'm sorry, Nadine, but I was broke and it seemed like the answer.'

'The answer to what?' interrupted Petra.

'Debt, Petra. I was in debt. It's not like you weren't aware of that.'

And then she slapped me.

'You weren't starving!' Petra shouted. 'You weren't bloody homeless! You weren't so penniless that that was the only option you had! Good God. What sort of woman do you have to be to . . .' She couldn't even say it. 'Do I know you?' she said. 'Do I even know who you are any more?'

I turned to Scott. He watched them attack me, and he did not say one word. Just wore a wry kind of smile as I took the abuse.

Later, in the taxi on the way home, I would wonder why no one attacked *him*. Why not slap Scott? Why not insult him for paying for sex? For cheating on his wife? Humiliating his family in front of everyone they knew? But they didn't. For whatever reason, they chose not to. It may have come later, but I never got to ask.

Scott stood on the sidelines and watched, his manner unmoved and detached as I stammered out my reasoning, my confession. It was almost as if he was enjoying it. And then I realized. I realized in that moment, amidst all the craziness, and all the crying, that yes, Scott *had* planned it. He had wanted it to come out in the way that it did. He had been sincere when he said he didn't care if he lost everything. As long as I did, too.

As far as he was concerned, if he couldn't have me, no one could.

And he stood there smiling. He smiled as though nothing had happened.

36

'NICE AFTERNOON?' THE taxi driver asked. A woman taxi driver. She wore a loose orange vest without a bra and had a battered, well-thumbed Regency romance shoved beneath the handbrake.

'Not exactly,' I replied, climbing into the front seat.

'A wedding? God, I'm sick of weddings.' She rambled on. 'If I have to go to one more bloody wedding—'

'Look, I don't feel like talking. Do you mind if we don't?'

She did. She raised her eyebrows as though to say, *Who the hell do you think you are, lady?*

'Bad afternoon,' I said. 'No offence.'

Henry had taken off. At around the time Nadine had wanted answers. When I finally got away, there was an empty space in the car park where his Peugeot had been. I didn't call him to find out why. He hadn't stuck around to check on his sister, so the message was clear.

I'd gazed at the empty space and been struck by the urge to explain. Henry had gone away thinking I'd had an affair with Scott, and I needed him to know it was a long way off from that. The thing I'd had with Scott was absurd.

'Henry?' I imagined saying to him. 'You see, you've got it all wrong. Scott *paid* me to have sex with him.'

'Oh, well, why didn't you say so? Because that changes *everything.*'

278

No, Roz, Henry would not want to hear your reasons.

Henry hated Scott. He loved his sister. He had been growing to like me, and I had betrayed everyone.

As the taxi wound its way towards Hawkshead, I relived the scene I'd left behind. Each time I ran through it, I would dwell on a different aspect. So many people affected. So many points of view. I would have to leave the area. Petra would never talk to me again, so there was no reason to stay. And even though I could probably handle being the object of ridicule, and gossip, for the duration, I could not bear the thought of George finding out.

'You heard about that body in the freezer?' the taxi driver asked.

'I heard.'

'Poor sod,' she said. 'Looks like he upset the wrong person.'

'It's all very sad.'

'He was pilfering money, you know,' she said, matter-of-fact.

'Is that what people are saying?' I asked, and she nodded grimly.

I told her to pull in a little further along on the right, just in front of my house.

As I waited for my change she gestured to the Jeep, saying, 'That your car?', and I told her it was. 'You've got something hanging down from the chassis,' she said. 'Best get it looked at.'

Around a hundred yards along the road I could make out a small boy with a dog. My small boy. My heart swelled at the sight of him. I waved, but he didn't see me. He was lost in his own thoughts, walking with his eyes firmly on Foxy. Celia was right. Foxy walked particularly well for George. Proud almost. Usually, she would be straining at the lead by this point. Desperate to get back, an awful rasping sound coming from her throat. As they got closer, I could see her lifting her front paws up, high, like a miniature dressage horse. George chattered away to her, oblivious I was there.

Afterwards, I would say it happened so fast.

Afterwards, I would say it was instantaneous, but it wasn't really.

I was aware of something even before I was aware of it, if that makes sense. I was used to the sounds of the village. Used to the flow of cars past the house. And just as when you might hear a distant siren and begin mentally locating your relatives, figuring out if it was at all possible for them to be involved, when I heard the engine gunning from the south-east, and I saw where George was, I knew without doubt it was possible.

And this was when time stopped.

I was too far away to reach him. The sound of the approaching engine told me the car was going too fast, and the distance between us was too great.

Still I ran.

I set off screaming, waving my arms, because I knew what was coming. I knew it before I saw it. The Overfinch. The black Range Rover. Three tons of metal hurtling through the village, its driver demented with grief. The cause of that grief: me.

'Get back!' I screamed helplessly. 'George, get back!'

He was too young, of course. He didn't yet know. He didn't know that pavements were dangerous places. That sometimes cars mounted pavements when the driver was drunk. Or old. Or having a stroke. Or young and stupid and reckless. Or heart-broken and attempting to drive through the tears.

He didn't know that, and so he remained unaware of the Range Rover until it flew past me and I was close enough to see his face just begin to flicker with worry. A small frown appeared as he looked from his mother running to the approaching car.

If I'd been next to him, I would have thrown him out of harm's way. But I wasn't. And as the small Fiat reversed out of the driveway diagonally opposite, its driver blissfully unaware – loud music audible through the sunroof, the jaunty uke of George

Formby – the Range Rover had to swerve to avoid its bumper.

There was the thin sound of brakes, tyres skidding and crunching metal.

And glass. There was so much glass.

Then silence. No sound at all. Just me, alone, in the silence.

37

HERE IS AN odd fact: there are more road deaths in rural areas than on city streets. The reason? The greater distances from the nearest hospital.

It can take over an hour to get to the nearest A&E department from Hawkshead, and that's not including the time it takes for the emergency services to reach the casualty in the first place.

Which is why we rely on the charity-funded air ambulance. And why, at that moment, my son was being transported, along with the driver that hit him, in the Great North Air Ambulance, as I followed in the car.

Later, I would remember nothing of that journey to Furness General Hospital. Which route I took, whether the Friday-afternoon traffic was abysmal, if I bought a ticket at the hospital car park. Later, I would have trouble recollecting anything of that day. Snippets would return in the coming months, fleeting memories that I would try to grasp hold of, but mostly, all I remember thinking was:

If only I'd run faster along the street. If only I'd left the hotel a moment earlier. If only I'd never agreed to Scott Elias's proposal in the first place.

This is what the brain does. It looks for a way out rather than face the appalling truth. It searches out rabbit holes it may have missed. Finds weak spots in reality. It goes back over events as though they are happening for the first time, as though it may actually alter the course of those events.

Your conscious mind tells it to stop. *This is pointless*, it says. But it's unstoppable.

If only I'd transferred money for Winston's train fare, he would have made it back in time. George would have been with him, safely in Outgate, instead of with Celia and Dennis. If only we hadn't split up in the first place, George would still have his own dog and he wouldn't have been walking Foxy. If only I'd married someone more reliable. If only . . .

'Mrs Toovey?'

I stood.

'Come with me,' the nurse said. She was in ICU whites, a tiny-framed woman you could bet could lift twice her own body weight. They're like that in ICU.

'Is he alive?' I asked.

'Come with me, we can talk through here. You're a physio, right?'

'Is he alive?' I repeated, rooted to the spot.

'He's alive.'

'Conscious?'

She dropped her gaze. 'Not yet. He's just being transferred from Emergency through to the unit.'

'What else? What other injuries?' I asked.

I barked my words at her, but she was unoffended. She held my gaze and ticked off George's problems on her fingers.

'Double pneumothorax,' she said. 'Fractured tib and fib on the right – those are compound fractures. Irrigation and debridement already done, and the fractures have been stabilized. Skin loss; he'll probably need a graft. We may need to CT his tummy later, but we had to get the drains into his lungs first. No sign of an abdominal bleed, though. BP's okay for now. Distal pulses all okay below the leg fracture.'

'The loss of consciousness? A head injury?'

'We don't know. No evidence of trauma to the head, but we don't know. You know how it is at this stage. Is there anyone with you? Anyone you'd like to accompany you?'

'My sister's on her way. His father is stuck in Cornwall. I can't get hold of him. My parents are coming, but it will take them a couple of hours to get here.'

She nodded and asked for my sister's name. Said she'd leave word at Admissions that she should be accompanied through to ICU on arrival. Petra was out of her mind. She couldn't speak, let alone drive. And Vince had been drinking, so . . .

The nurse said, 'The lady who was brought in with him in the air ambulance? The driver? Is she—'

'We're not related,' I said coldly.

'Oh.'

'Is she alive?' I asked.

'Yes,' she said. 'She's conscious. I got the impression she knew your son.'

'She drove *over* my son,' I said.

She nodded. 'She's very upset.'

'I suppose she would be,' I said. 'Can I see him now?'

She turned, and I followed her. Her steps were quick across the floor and when we reached ICU she punched in a six-digit code on the keypad. Nothing happened, and she sighed. 'I keep using the old code,' she explained. She tried again and, before we entered, she turned to me. 'Do I need to tell you he won't look like he usually does?'

I shook my head.

'Okay,' she said. 'Let's go.'

There were six beds. Three were occupied. Nadine in one, George in the next one along and another patient opposite. He was a young guy with a tracheotomy tube in his throat, meaning he'd been here a while. I was later told he'd developed Guillain-Barré syndrome, his breathing muscles were paralysed and he had been in the ICU for five weeks. His mother would visit and weep gently for an hour before leaving.

The nurse explained that George may be transferred to a paediatric ICU at another hospital, as long as he was stable enough to move. For now, though, he would stay here. With Nadine.

I didn't look at her. I had to walk past her bed. I was aware of movement, an arm being raised, a gurgling noise. She gave a low, agonizing kind of groan, like an animal trapped in a snare.

I kept my eyes in front and went to George. I knelt by the side of his bed and kissed his hand. He was stripped down to his underpants. His tiny, broken body was smeared with bits of dried blood, and the two chest drains were monstrous, snaking from between his ribs. 'I'm here, baby,' I whispered.

Instinctively, I checked the monitors. His oxygen saturation was a little low. I repositioned the pulse oximeter on his index finger and exhaled as the numbers climbed steadily.

There was a tent over his right leg. A compound fracture is an open fracture, meaning the skin had been torn off. An external fixator was fitted around his leg, but couple that with skin grafts and we were looking at about a year for recovery.

I twisted around to Nadine. Her eyes went wide when she saw my face, and she began shaking her head, trying to convey something important to me. Her expression was urgent and desperate. I turned away.

I got to my feet and drew the curtain across, cutting her off. I was aware of her crying without sound.

She had come looking for me. She had driven through Hawkshead looking for my house. And now we were here.

I kissed George's hand again and whispered that I loved him. Over and over, I told him he was okay, that he would wake up soon and he would be okay. I told him not to be scared. I was here. I wouldn't leave him alone.

He was so beautiful. His skin so smooth. There was a little dried blood around his ear. I asked if I could dab it away, and a nurse brought me a wad of cotton wool and a metal kidney dish half filled with tepid water. George didn't stir. The intubation tube was tied in place with a length of fabric and it pulled downwards on his mouth, making him appear to grimace. I asked if they would adjust it slightly, and they did. The nursing staff tended to him like he was their own child. And it was this, watching the tenderness and care they bestowed upon him, that would cause me to unravel.

I'd held it together okay until then.

38

Nadine remained in intensive care for twenty-four hours before being moved to the high-dependency unit. She had a chest injury. In the time she was in ICU, Scott didn't visit. Her children did, and I heard their hushed voices behind the curtain. By then, word had spread amongst the staff of the unit and they were aware of 'our situation'. They dealt with us in a detached, professional way, granting my request that the barrier be kept between us – which I knew from my time in training on ICU was not strictly allowed. It wasn't until Nadine had moved wards that a gossipy, camp male nurse by the name of Kyle made reference to the curtain, saying, 'I think we can do away with the Wall of Jericho now. Don't you?'

My parents came and went. Winston came and went. He came back with provisions and stayed.

The police arrived, and that was all quite straightforward. There were witnesses to say Nadine had lost control when the old guy opposite reversed into her path. Her blood alcohol level was tested on admission and she was found to be under the limit – although she had been drinking; she admitted that. She also told them she had just found out that her husband had been having an affair, so her responses may have been affected. She told them she was very sorry.

We were all very sorry.

Petra came, and stayed. And cried. And cried some more. She

sat sniffling at George's side for three full days, begging him to wake up, wringing her hands. Occasionally, she would shoot me a look and I would see the muscles on either side of her throat grow taut.

'Say it,' I said eventually, after a few more hours of this.

'Say what?' she asked.

'Say what it is you want to say.'

She went back to smoothing the hair away from George's forehead. 'I have nothing to say.'

'You think I caused this.'

And she turned to me sharply. 'I would *never* say that.'

'You don't have to, Petra.'

She put her hand to her mouth to stifle the beginnings of another sob. Then she screwed her eyes up tight and took one deep inhalation, before grabbing hold of the metal frame of the bed for stability. 'I am not blaming you,' she said. Her words were measured, steady, but like vinegar in her mouth.

'*I'm* blaming me,' I told her, and I looked straight at her. 'I caused this. There. It's said. Now you don't have to.'

'Don't be so flippant,' she flared.

'I'm not being flippant. Of course this is my fault! Of course it is! I know that. But I don't want you here with all that anxiety, all that repressed bloody condemnation inside of you. Not while you're hovering above my unconscious son, anyhow.'

'Your son,' she said tonelessly.

'Yes, my son. For better or worse, Petra, I am his mother. Now you either say all that shit you want to say, or else you let it go. Because I can't stand it like this.'

She stepped away from George. She walked to the end of the bed and gestured with her finger for me to follow.

Her face was hard. 'You are a stupid, reckless woman who I am ashamed to know,' she said. 'Who I am ashamed to be associated with, never mind related to.'

'Go on.'

'Again, you proved that you take the easy way out. Always the easy way out with you. You never think what you do will hurt other people. You never think of the consequences.'

She was holding back somewhat. Her choice of words was almost business like, I suppose out of respect for our surroundings.

She shook her head as she spoke. 'I can't believe you were sleeping with him. I can't believe you had an affair—'

'It wasn't an affair.'

'I can't believe you had *an affair* with my friend's husband. Of all the things.' Her eyes brimmed with tears. She batted the air in front of her as though this might send them back. 'You are a disgrace, Roz, and you have embarrassed me deeply. I don't know that I'll ever be able to—'

George opened his eyes.

He was looking at us with a puzzled expression. He tried to say something, and couldn't understand why the words were not coming out as they should.

Trying to lift his hand to his mouth, he was aware there was something alien there. He frowned when he made contact with the intubation tube.

I rushed to him. 'Don't try to talk, sweetheart,' I said. 'Are you okay?' and he nodded.

He wasn't scared. He just looked pleased to see me, as he would when waking as a baby. He would open his eyes to see me standing next to the cot and give a big, contented, sleepy smile. As though to say, *You've been here the whole time?*

'George, do you know where you are?' Petra demanded, her voice shaking. 'Do you remember anything?' I rolled my eyes at her and told her to give him a minute to get his bearings. Her face fell.

George blinked, and you could see him trying to figure out

what was going on. He glanced down and tilted his head upon seeing the fixator around his leg.

I whispered to Petra, 'Tell the nursing staff he's awake,' and she nodded, before scurrying off.

I crouched by his side. 'George. You're in hospital. That tube in your mouth is to help you breathe. See?' And I followed the tube with my finger, slowly, to where it was attached to the ventilator. 'This thing breathes for you. Can you hear it?' George smiled, and I said, 'I know. Cool, eh?' He watched for a moment and then returned his gaze to me. 'You've hurt your leg pretty bad. That's what all that metal is. It's to hold the break together. Does it hurt?'

He stared at his leg, as though trying to figure out if it was painful or not. Then he looked back at me and communicated it didn't. 'They've given you medicine for that,' I said, 'to take away the soreness.'

I told him I was glad he was awake. Told him I'd been a bit lonely without being able to chat to him. I told him his dad would be along later but had had to nip home to fetch some more bits and pieces I needed. 'He'll be back soon,' I said. George was pretty doped and passive, and I hoped he'd stay that way.

'Well, hello there!' came a voice from my left. Kyle, the nurse, stood at the end of the bed, all smiles, and told George he was way more handsome now that he had his eyes open. George went sheepish.

'Can he come off the ventilator?' I asked, and Kyle said yes, now that he was conscious, though it was likely he'd be on oxygen until the chest drains came out. I tousled George's hair and told him again I was glad he was back, and that's when I saw his face change.

'You okay?' I asked.

He stared at me, wild-eyed and fearful, before making an attempt to move.

'What is it?' I said. 'George, you've got to stay still. What is it? Are you hurting somewhere?'

Petra was trying to pacify him, saying, 'It's okay, it's okay,' over and over but George went rigid in the bed. My first thought was the head injury. His brain was swelling and we were seeing the beginnings of a fit. I turned to the nurse, but he didn't seem unduly worried. 'Are you remembering what happened, George?' he said softly, and George nodded repeatedly, growing more and more afraid by the second.

I moved in closer. 'You had an accident,' I said.

No response.

'George, you were injured by a car.'

And he shook his head as though he couldn't remember that. He seemed in equal parts frustrated and terrified.

Then he tried to speak.

'Foxy.'

39

I HAD SIX MISSED calls from DS Aspinall, along with two text messages asking me to make contact with her as soon as possible. I don't use voicemail. Don't know how. You may as well write your message on a scrap of paper and throw it in the lake.

Winston had returned to the hospital, and I had left him and Petra alone with George, while I stood in the corridor and called Celia to find out the latest on Foxy.

As far as I knew, the dog was fine. I couldn't remember seeing her crushed or injured immediately after the accident, but then, I couldn't remember seeing her at all.

Pacifying George with this was not enough. He couldn't settle, quickly becoming distressed and tearful, to the extent that the registrar pointed out, 'Might it just be easier to call the dog's owner? Check the dog is actually okay?'

The corridor was busy. Two young male medics walked towards me, fresh-faced and full of enthusiasm. There is an unwritten rule inside the hospital whereby medics wear their stethoscopes around their necks, on display, but everyone else who requires a stethoscope – respiratory-care physiotherapists, nurses, and so on – must keep theirs inside their pockets. Just so everyone is clear where they stand in the whole scheme of things. The medics stopped conversing as they passed, smiled gravely, an acknowledgement of my position right next to the ICU. Which was considerate, I thought.

Celia picked up on the third ring.

'Celia?'

'Roz! What are you doing calling? How is he? Is he all right? Please God, let him be all right. How is his leg? Did they manage to save his leg?'

'You were there?' I asked her, a little stunned. I couldn't remember.

'Yes, we were there. How is he? How is George? Good Lord, Roz, *tell* me.'

'He's okay. The leg will be okay, we hope. It's pretty smashed up. He's just come round and . . . Celia? . . . Well, he's asking about Foxy.'

'Oh, she's fine.'

'Is she really?'

'She tore her cruciate ligament in her knee whilst frantically trying to run home faster than she's run in years, but don't tell George that. He'll only worry. She's fine, Roz. Honestly.'

I exhaled.

I brought Celia up to speed and was about to get in touch with the detective and lay it on really thick about George, as it was apparent from her messages that she didn't know about the accident – do the police not *talk* to one another? – when I saw Henry Peachey coming from the other direction. He had a bunch of flowers in one hand and a thick paperback in the other. He must have been on his way to visit Nadine.

At this point he hadn't seen me. His head was down, and I wondered briefly whether I should duck inside the ICU to avoid confrontation. But by the time I had pressed the buzzer and waited for a response, he would see me.

It wasn't that I wanted to avoid him. I was desperate to talk to him, to apologize, to try to begin to make amends. But something in the way he walked made me want to flee. His ordinarily erect posture was absent; the confident, sure-footed way he moved not there. And, for the first time since Nadine had driven her car into my child, I felt an intense rush of guilt over something other than George.

My child was still here, and Henry's was not.

I turned to face him and, when he caught sight of me, he stopped in his tracks. I offered an ineffectual, wan kind of smile and waited for him to come nearer.

For a moment he didn't. He stayed where he was and regarded me in the way you might a rotting creature, blocking your path. Something to be sidestepped, avoided.

A porter pulling a wheelchair backwards along the corridor asked Henry to move over slightly so he could pass. This seemed to startle him, and he resumed walking my way.

'Hey,' I said.

'Hey,' he said back, not meeting my gaze.

'How are you?'

He dodged that question and answered with, 'I heard George was in a bad way. How is he doing?'

'Just come around. He wanted to know how Foxy was so . . .' I let my words hang, holding up the mobile to indicate I'd called Celia to find out.

He nodded, and tried to smile as though to say, *Yes, that sounds like something George would do*, but his face couldn't really work in that way today. He kicked at the floor with the toe of his boot.

'So—' I began, but he cut me off.

'I really need to get on.'

'Henry, wait. There's something I need to tell you.'

He sighed and looked beyond me along the corridor. In a moment of foolishness I reached for him, but he moved away quickly, as though he'd been stung. 'Apologies,' I said. Apologies – that was a mistake.

'It's a bit late for all this, Roz,' he said earnestly. 'I'm really sorry about what happened to George. And I'm so glad he's on the mend. But I'm really not interested in listening to what you have to say. You've wrecked Nadine's life. You made me look a complete fool. I'd rather not be around you, if that's okay.'

'Henry, listen. I appreciate you don't want to see me right now, but I need to tell you this. I was not having an affair with Scott. It simply isn't true. That thing he did at the party? Well, I don't know what that was all about. But we were not in a relationship and we were certainly *not* in love.'

He didn't respond. After a minute of silence he said, 'Is that it? That's what you wanted to say?'

'I really liked being with you, Henry.'

He lifted his eyes to the ceiling.

'No,' I said. 'Really. I wasn't stringing you along—'

'So you're saying you *weren't* sleeping with Scott, is that it?'

I lowered my voice. 'We had an arrangement,' I said.

'An arrangement,' he mirrored, flatly.

'Whereby Scott would pay me. This is not an excuse in any way, but I need you to know that I was not doing what I did willingly.'

'You're saying he forced you?'

'No,' I stammered, misunderstood. 'I was forced through circumstance. You left the party before I had the chance to explain any of this. And, if you recall, I did try to back out of our dates, because I didn't want you to—'

'What? Find out? You were with him that time I saw you at the hotel near Lancaster, weren't you?'

I nodded. 'That was the first time,' I admitted. 'Listen, I didn't want to hurt you. I never expected to feel anything for you. I thought we could go out once, pacify Nadine, and then call an end to it.' I paused. 'I didn't expect you to be *you*, Henry. I didn't expect to like you as I did.'

I thought I saw his jaw relax a little at this, so I gestured to the paperback, saying, 'What's that you're reading?', trying to diffuse the situation a little.

'*Anna Karenina.*'

'Any good?'

'I've read it before. Far less adultery and a lot more farming than I remember.'

I smiled. 'Henry, listen, I know you're hurt. I know you're deeply hurt and humiliated. But I need you to know that the arrangement with Scott started before I met you. And I did it for the money. Pure and simple. You said yourself that one could do practically anything for money if it was only for two days a week. I'm not excusing what I did. But once my money problems started to ease I called a halt to it. And I was desperate. I was being evicted. I wouldn't have done it otherwise.'

There was a tense moment of quiet when Henry seemed to be weighing my words and I thought he may have softened towards me.

Finally he said, 'That's what he said you'd say.'

'What?'

'Scott,' he explained. 'That's what he said you'd say.'

'Henry, I don't understand what you mean.'

'Scott came to see me before he left—'

'Before he left for where?'

Henry shrugged. 'No idea. The Galápagos, for all I care. Nadine certainly doesn't want him around. He took off yesterday.'

'What *did* he say, Henry?'

'He said this story you were peddling, about him paying you for sex, was exactly that. A story. He said you had instigated the affair during the first treatment session for his elbow. He said he'd gone along with it because he found you attractive and couldn't say no.'

My mouth dropped open.

'Scott said you were a gold-digger,' he went on. 'He said you pestered him for gifts – earrings and jewellery and suchlike, and perhaps saw him as a way out of your financial mess. He said you asked him for a loan.'

'And you believed him?'

'Why shouldn't I believe him? It's been lie after lie with you, Roz. And it certainly makes more sense than you being some sort of escort. Sorry, but I just don't buy that.'

I stood there, gaping.

'Look,' he said, 'no hard feelings. But I've had enough shit happen to me in the last few years, and if it's okay with you I'd rather avoid any more.'

'Wait,' I said. 'Please wait, Henry. I know you wish it could have been anyone but Scott, anyone but him that I got involved with—'

And he stopped me.

'No, Roz,' he said softly. 'I don't care what Scott does. Never have. It's you. I didn't want *you* to get involved with another person. Anyone but you. I was falling for you, and now I need to stay away if I'm going to have any chance of getting my head together.'

He took off. And I was left staring at his back as he became smaller and smaller the further he advanced along the corridor, before disappearing from view.

40

THE FOLLOWING DAY George was off the ventilator, his chest drains were removed and he was transferred to the paediatric ward, where he would stay for the remainder of his time at Furness General. He would need a series of operations on the crush injury to his leg, to close the wound, to alter the external fixator, but as things stood right now, he was in better shape than we could have predicted. The fracture site was infection free and his lungs were fully inflated. He was in good spirits. Again, I marvelled at the resilience shown by children. You looked around the ward and you saw fear, worry, exhaustion displayed on the face of every parent. But the kids? They all looked pretty chilled, as though it was their latest adventure. George made a friend called Lucas, who was also rather keen on Pokémon, and I was able to leave him in the hands of Winston for a few hours while I made an appearance at Kendal police station to give prints and a swab. This was voluntary, you understand, but the emphasis was that if I failed to provide samples then I would automatically be considered a suspect.

The results of the post-mortem were back, and it was now known that Wayne had been strangled.

I felt sick at the thought of his last moments, but I no longer felt frightened. Almost losing your child will do that to you. Instead, I felt numb. I relinquished my DNA, my demeanour calm and unruffled, because the worst had already happened. If

I got hauled back to the station when they matched the prints, found evidence of me all over Wayne, so be it.

Does that sound like I was trivializing? I suppose I was, to an extent. Perhaps I was burying my head, but it did feel as though Wayne's death was at the bottom of a very long list of things that needed my attention. So I did as requested, again keeping to my story of never setting foot in his house, and wished them well with their inquiry. Told the detectives I hoped they found his killer and got some justice for Wayne. If they came back with evidence of my lying, I would hit them with the truth. But not before. The hours of interrogation I would have to face were not possible right now, not with George still bedbound and in the condition he was in. He needed me. I needed to be with him. I did not need to be arrested.

Lie after lie, Henry had said.

Yes. That just about covered it. Scott had also commented once that I lied easily.

It's not easy to look at your life and know that you are in every way at fault for the way it turned out. All those untruths were no doubt responsible for what put Nadine behind the wheel, what put George in front of Nadine's car, what made Henry head off before I was able to screw up his life any further.

And, now, no one believed anything I had to say. You could hardly blame them.

Two days later and George was doing well. He was still in a substantial amount of pain but was bravely managing without complaint. On receiving a 'Get Well Soon' card from his classmates, he declared that he no longer wanted to leave his school and relocate. He missed his buddies and so we arranged for a couple of them to visit him in the hospital the following day.

Along with the card from his classmates, there was also a letter of apology from the school, saying that they had mistakenly accused George of taking the Pokémon figures.

Apparently, after George's accident, a distressed boy had come forward and owned up to planting them inside George's rucksack. This was in revenge for George having declared his lunchbox babyish and the matter had now been dropped.

Winston and I decided that George was well enough to be left alone overnight, so we returned to Hawkshead, where I booked my car into the mechanic's. Winston and I would travel to Barrow in his van each day for however long it would take for my car to be fixed. And since HQ had granted me a two-week leave of absence from work, I didn't need a vehicle for anything other than visiting George.

On the second day I received a call. They wanted me to come into the garage to discuss something. 'Sounds expensive,' I said, and there was a stony silence at the other end.

Brian, the owner of the garage, was an old schoolfriend of my dad's. He had four boys, three of whom worked with him. The other had been hit by a drugged-up driver fifteen years ago on the A590 whilst changing a pregnant woman's tyre. Brian now drank surreptitiously throughout the day from an old hip flask he kept inside the pocket of his navy overalls, and though still deemed to be safe enough to tinker with engines, he was never allowed behind the wheel of a car. His sons would be seen ferrying him about, from place to place, dropping him wherever he needed to be.

'How's your dad doing these days?' Brian asked when I walked in. The office was strewn with paperwork, bulldog clips and empty mugs. A Cliff Richard calendar hung on the wall and had been defaced to give Cliff an Amish-style beard, the type without a moustache.

'He's okay,' I answered.

Brian knew about the money I'd lost and the reason my

parents moved away. But if he had an opinion, he didn't air it. 'Not seen him in a good while,' he said.

'I heard you got another grandchild, Brian. A girl this time?'

He went pink with pride, put his hands in his pockets and sat back on his heels. 'Aye,' he said. 'Tiny little thing. Got a good strong grip on her, though.'

'That's good,' I said. 'What did they call her?'

He frowned. 'Summat foreign. I can't bring it to mind right now.'

He shook his head, smiling either at his inability to remember, or else at his daughter-in-law, who was making his life more complicated than it needed to be.

'So what's the damage, Brian?' I asked.

He riffled through some invoices, held up the paper and squinted. 'Two-eighty-seven, including VAT.'

I winced. 'What did I do exactly?'

He shot me an amused look. 'You really want me to explain?'

'Not really.'

'Just damaged the mid-section of the exhaust. But that's not why I hauled you in here.'

'Oh?'

He nodded and was silent for a second whilst gesturing to a mud-splattered thing about the size of a pocket calculator. It was resting on a greasy rag on his desk.

'What is it?' I asked.

'You tell me,' he said.

'I've no idea.'

'How long you had that car now, Roz?' he asked.

'Four or five years, why?'

'When did we last service it?'

'You changed the timing chain around three months ago. And you fitted two new tyres.'

'We'd have spotted it if it was there then,' he said. 'I'm certain of it.'

'Brian, you're worrying me. What's going on?'

'It's a tracker.'

I frowned, confused. 'As in?'

Brian shrugged. 'As in a tracker. Can't think what else to call it. It tells someone who wants to know your whereabouts your whereabouts.'

'Is it *legal*?'

'Do you know what?' he said. 'I don't know the answer to that, but my best guess says not. You had someone following you around?'

'Not that I'm aware of.'

'Well, that thing's working and sending out a signal, so . . .' His words trailed off. He watched my face as I processed what it was he was telling me.

'You might do well to tell the police about this,' he said eventually.

I drove to the lakeshore to consider my options. It was still early, so I could park easily enough. There weren't many people around, save for a few dog walkers and pale-looking mums with toddlers on reins, pushing prams, carrying bags of duck food. Their faces were drawn from lack of sleep and appeared to border on tearfulness at the prospect of filling another whole twelve hours. As I watched, I was transported back to the time in my own life when I would be alone for days on end with George, Winston having disappeared off somewhere.

We had entered a destructive cycle by then that we couldn't seem to get out of. I would nag at the frequency and duration of his absences, which Winston would deal with by not coming home at all, which caused me to nag some more, and then suddenly, almost overnight, I'd been replaced by a woman I never thought I'd be.

But I digress, because I know what you're thinking.

You're thinking: how could she not have known?

Until I saw that tracker, I knew of only one instance of Scott following me: George's swimming lesson at the hotel. Thinking about it now, I realized that Scott tracked me there with the aid of the device.

Of course, I was speculating. But it had to be Scott. Who else would do something like that?

I glanced down at my hands on the wheel and saw they were trembling.

What kind of weirdo follows women around? What kind of weirdo tracks their every move, watching from their home computer?

My stomach folded in on itself.

If what I thought was true *was true*, Scott was capable of far more than I could have imagined. I was in danger, and I needed to do something.

I withdrew my mobile from my pocket. Scrolled through the list of callers, took a steadying breath and pressed the dial key.

When the call connected, I said, 'We really need to talk.'

41

'MRS TOOVEY, WOULD you like to come this way?'
I stood and followed the young man. 'Lovely morning, again,' he said, and I replied, yes, it was. 'We've been so lucky with the weather this year, haven't we?' he said, and again, I agreed.

He stopped a little further along and asked me to wait inside the last office on the right. 'Can I get you anything?' he asked. 'Tea? Some water?'

'Water, thank you.'

'Right you are,' he said, and he did an about-turn on the spot, making me wonder if he was once in the cadets.

I was forced to wait for over an hour. The minutes ticked by and the room became stuffy. My palms grew greasy, my scalp hot and itchy, and my general demeanour became that of a skittish cat. I was just about to exit, leaving my excuses at the front desk, when the door opened and in walked a very collected DS Aspinall. She was accompanied by another plain-clothes officer whom I had not met, who was introduced as Detective Constable Hannah Gidley.

DC Gidley was late twenties, red-haired, milky-skinned but with patches of high colour on her cheeks, earlobes and the tip of her nose. There was a softness to her flesh, a kindness in her eyes. She was more nursery nurse than CID, and when she smiled my way I immediately felt less jumpy.

'You're here to make a statement,' began DS Aspinall.

'That's right,' I replied.

'Mind if I ask, why now?'

'Something came up,' I said. 'Something that . . . it's probably easier if I just give the statement.'

DS Aspinall nodded accordingly. If I had piqued her interest at all, she hid it. She exchanged a few quiet words with the other detective and made like she was ready for me to start. When I hesitated, she said, 'I'm all ears, Mrs Toovey,' in the manner of someone who was jaded, world-weary, and I wondered if they'd had many timewasters in here. Perhaps I was just one in a long line of many.

'I expected you might have been in touch by now,' I said, looking at DS Aspinall.

'Because . . . ?'

'Because of the fingerprints? And DNA swab?'

She looked at me blankly.

'Mrs Toovey,' she said, 'we don't contact a person to say they've been eliminated from an investigation.'

Eliminated?

'Hang on,' I said. 'You're saying you did not find my finger-prints at Wayne's house *at all*?'

'That's right,' she said slowly, extending the words, a look of puzzlement coming over her. 'Should we have, Mrs Toovey?'

I dropped my head.

What the hell was going on? My prints were everywhere in that room. The fish tank. The table. The windowsill.

DS Aspinall waited for me to respond and, when I didn't, she relaxed her shoulders, letting her full weight fall backwards against the chair as though she thought we could be here for quite a while. 'Why don't we start at the beginning?' she said.

So I did. Right at the beginning.

I explained about losing my original practice, about Winston running up debts, about being once again on the brink of financial collapse. I explained about the general state of my affairs in the weeks leading up to Wayne's disappearance.

I told DS Aspinall about my first meeting with Scott Elias and how he'd arrived at my treatment room a few days later with a proposal for me to consider. I outlined the way he expected the arrangement might work and watched as both DS Aspinall and DC Gidley exchanged surreptitious glances, clearly amused at what had happened but at the same time keeping up an air of professionalism. They did not comment on this part other than DC Gidley asking me to spell out Scott's surname.

I told them how much money changed hands and how at first I was paid in cash, but then how that changed as time progressed. And I told them how Wayne wanted in on the deal and was black-mailing me.

At this, they both sat up straighter in their seats.

'Wayne Geddes wanted money from you?' DS Aspinall asked.

I shook my head.

'He wanted sex,' I said.

'For money?' she said.

'For free,' I said. 'Wayne told me if I didn't do as he asked, he would reveal what had been going on between Scott and me and I would lose my job. I didn't have the luxury of calling his bluff, so I agreed to it.'

I didn't tell them about the other part. The part about Wayne saying he would tell the police that I had been ripping the company off.

'Where did this meeting take place?' DS Aspinall asked.

'Wayne's house.'

There was a flicker of distaste evident in her face.

'How many times did this occur?' she asked.

'Once. On the Saturday night. Ultimately, though, Wayne had a bit of a problem and couldn't actually go through with it. And then he panicked and knocked me out, and I ended up staying there for around two hours.'

'Were you injured?' she asked.

'A bad bang to the head. I didn't go to the hospital, though.'

'Okay, but according to your original statement, you said you last saw Wayne on the Friday, after work. Is that correct?'

'I did say that, but I lied. You would have wanted to know why I was with Wayne, and I didn't want to tell you. But remember, I didn't know at that point he was missing. That he was dead. So I didn't think it was terribly important to mislead you by a day.'

She nodded.

'All right,' she said. 'So, to return to my earlier question, why now? What has changed that you felt the need to come forward now?'

'Two things,' I said. 'The secret arrangement I had with Scott Elias is no longer a secret.'

DS Aspinall frowned, unable to see at that point what my sleeping with Scott for money had to do with Wayne.

'And then there's this,' I said.

I removed from my handbag the tracking device, which was wrapped in a plastic bag, and pushed it across the desk.

'It was found stuck beneath my car. Someone has been tracking my movements. Someone knew I was at Wayne's house that night and probably followed me there.'

DS Aspinall turned it over in her hand and read the serial number. 'We should be able to find out where this was purchased easily enough,' she told DC Gidley.

'I think Scott Elias manufactured it,' I said. 'He has an electronics firm. I believe they produce devices like this.'

'You're saying you think it was Scott Elias who placed this tracker and followed you there?'

'That's what I believe, yes.'

'Do we have his prints on file?' she said to her colleague.

'I'd need to check,' replied DS Gidley.

DS Aspinall was silent then, again turning the tracker over in her hands, thinking through, I assumed, possible scenarios. I resisted the urge to tell her I thought Scott could be responsible for Wayne's death, because it was pretty clear from her manner that DS Aspinall dealt only in facts.

'A curious thing,' she said absently, as if to herself. 'I've never actually seen one of these before. Of course, we can't say for sure that it was placed under your car *before* Mr Geddes's death, and I wonder, why would Scott Elias feel the need to track you in particular, Mrs Toovey?'

I shrugged. 'I can only guess as to the answer to that. He did become rather possessive.'

'Violent at all?'

'I believe he came close to it a few times. Grabbing me harder than necessary and suchlike. And he did try to force himself on me sexually once, though he didn't go through with it.'

'Did he make any threats towards you or your family?'

I shook my head. 'Not really. No direct threats.'

'Does he have a history of domestic abuse that you know of?'

'His wife's brother mentioned he had a dark temper.'

'Did his wife ever discuss this with you?'

'No.'

'So when you say "possessiveness", what behaviour are you referring to exactly?' she asked.

My face must have hardened somewhat because she leaned forward a little, saying, 'I'm not doubting you, Mrs Toovey, but I'd just like to know what precisely we're dealing with.'

I exhaled. 'I know how this looks,' I said. 'You think I'm paranoid. You think I've been sleeping with some rich guy who has been monitoring my movements, and now suddenly I've gone unreasonable, crazy, thinking he's responsible for every crime in the area.'

'We don't think that, Mrs Toovey.'

'Yes, well, I would in your situation. I have no evidence at all that Scott Elias is involved in Wayne's death. None. I was at that house and my prints were not found. I can't explain how that can be the case. What I'm here to do is to tell you the truth as I know it. It's up to you to decide whether to follow up on it. I don't want to tell you how to do your job.'

DS Aspinall smiled. 'Appreciate that,' she said.

'When I tried to halt the arrangement with Scott, when I was becoming close to a new man I just met, Scott tried to talk me out of it.'

DS Aspinall waited for me to continue.

'When I refused, he revealed our arrangement to his wife and children, saying he was prepared to lose them so I would stay with him. Still, I refused, and he warned that if he couldn't have me, no else could either.'

'Which now leads you to think that he may have got wind of you and Wayne and put a stop to that as well.'

'Precisely,' I said.

DS Aspinall blew out her breath. 'Certainly an interesting story,' she said.

'You think it's far-fetched.'

'I didn't say that,' she replied evenly. 'But what I will promise you, Mrs Toovey, is that we will certainly follow up on it. And I'll let you know as soon as I hear of any developments.'

'Thank you,' I replied, but I could see I'd lost her.

'There is one more thing,' I said. 'But before I raise this next point, I would just like to say that I have a child in the hospital at the moment and he is—'

'We know about your son's accident,' she replied gently.

'Well, if you could bear that in mind when deciding whether to . . .'

I paused, wondering how best to phrase the next part.

'Arrest you for prostitution?' she offered.

I nodded.

She glanced at her colleague, giving what must have been some kind of imperceptible signal, because DC Hannah Gidley rested her pen down by the side of her notes.

'It's not illegal, Mrs Toovey,' she said.

'It's not?' I asked, astonished.

'Not the kind of prostitution you were engaged in. But, please, remind me again, just how did Scott Elias pay for these encounters?'

'Firstly, I was paid in cash,' I said. 'And on subsequent encounters, I provided an invoice and billed his firm directly.'

'So his business covered the cost of your time together?'

'That's right.'

'Interesting,' she said again.

42

Two weeks passed, and nothing. No phone call from the police. No arrest. Not a whisper that Scott had even been questioned.

I had been so confident, so absolutely certain that something would come of my statement. But no.

And to make matters worse, according to Petra, Scott was back inside the family home after persuading Nadine that what we'd had together was no more than a pointless fling – a fling that he now bitterly regretted. He was deeply ashamed of his behaviour and put it down to a moment of madness in the presence of a predatory female, he said.

It was politician's talk to appease the masses. And the remarkable thing was it seemed to have worked. Scott apologized to all concerned. He'd been a bad boy, he said, and everyone went around with the opinion that *Hell, even the best of us make mistakes sometimes.* Nobody's perfect.

Eventually, when I could take no more waiting, I called DS Aspinall. She was evasive, informing me that she couldn't comment on the ongoing investigation into Wayne Geddes's death, assuring me that, as soon as any arrests were made, I would be told.

'So you found nothing linking Scott Elias to Wayne's death? Nothing?' I cried down the phone to her. Scott had been practically stalking me and she was behaving as though I was being silly and irrational.

'We're still pursuing all lines of inquiry, Mrs Toovey,' she told me.

'You need to actually *do* something!'

'I assure you, we are.'

It was fruitless. It was as though she had disregarded my statement as soon as I'd left the station, possibly not even gone to the trouble of talking to Scott at all.

I should have gone to another detective. I should have given my statement to someone who would take me seriously. I regretted that now.

'Let it go,' Petra advised, when I complained to her that nothing was being done.

'I *can't* let it go.'

By now, I had told Petra the full story about Wayne. Time to stop the cycle of lies, I'd decided. But Petra had the opinion that whatever had led Wayne to end up dead in that freezer was most likely the result of his own deeds. She didn't think for one second it had anything to do with Scott. 'That's laughable,' she said when I told her my theory. 'Scott's not capable of anything like that.'

It was now Wednesday evening. We were in Petra's kitchen, and though she was still frosty towards me, we were at least on speaking terms. Petra was working her way through the stages of grief at the loss of her friendship with Scott and Nadine. She would get to acceptance and, just when I thought she was done with it all, she would quickly double back to denial again. She wanted me to go through the ins and outs of 'the affair', as she insisted on calling it, much as you might when interrogating your spouse about an old flame. You shouldn't want the details, but you just can't help yourself. Like picking at the sides of a scab. Or poking at something dead with a stick.

'And would you say you enjoyed it?' she was asking, as she crimped the pastry edges of a steak-and-kidney pie. 'Would you say that you actually enjoyed it?'

'It was sex, Petra. You know how it goes.'

'He told Nadine you only did it once. And Nadine's telling people that your fanciful story about being his mistress for money was merely the mad claims of a desperate hysteric.'

'Is she?' I said flatly, because I had given up rising to it by now.

She bit her lip. 'Did he shock you, wanting weird things done to him? Did he want you to . . . *you know*.'

'You know . . . ?' I repeated, lifting my eyebrows, because I didn't.

'I can't bring myself to say it,' she said.

And so it went on.

George had been discharged from hospital and was with Winston for the next three days. I'd told Winston to keep an eye out for Scott's Range Rover, just in case, and though Winston clearly thought I was paranoid, he assured me he wouldn't let George out of his sight – which wasn't difficult, because George couldn't get far very fast. He was moving about pretty well with elbow crutches now, and wasn't due back at the hospital until next week, when they planned to adjust the external fixator. I had returned to work, and in my absence a new manager had been employed named Andrea. She was smart, efficient and was already on to Gary, making him demonstrate his efficacy as a clinician and account for the number of treatments it took him to cure a simple injury. 'Patients will not come here if you can't get them better quickly, Gary,' I'd overheard her saying to him, and he'd nodded, replying, 'Absolutely, absolutely.' Later I found him circling NHS job opportunities in the latest copy of *Frontline*, scowling at the text.

Plans to return to running my own clinic had been shelved. After George's accident, it became clear that I'd been delusional in thinking I could ever work for myself again. Self-employment basically means you can never be ill, which, for some reason, your body will agree to. The problem arises when you have children: they cannot be talked out of illness. Or car accidents. Things happen and, with me not having anyone to lean on, the practice would suffer and patients would go elsewhere. Reluctantly, I'd let Keith Hollinghurst know I would be unable to take him up on his offer of the rented premises.

I'd had to let go of my dreams all over again. I felt like I'd failed all over again. And even though I had people around me – Petra, for one, who could witter on happily about anything, nothing, filling up a room with noise and conversation – I felt more acutely alone in the few weeks following the crash than I had done in years.

I thought of poor Wayne being forced into the freezer, no one really bothered by how he'd got in there. And it seemed as though I was the only person half interested in whether his killer was found or not. And yes, this was guilt talking, because if I was right he was put in there on account of me.

I resolved that if there were no new developments within the next twenty-four hours, I would return to the police station and demand an explanation. I would find out exactly what it was they were doing with their time. Wayne deserved that from me at least.

Two nights later I returned home, the twilight turning to darkness. Still, DS Aspinall had remained steadfast at our meeting the previous day, revealing nothing while at the same time notifying me that everything that could be done was being done. And, *For heaven's sake, Mrs Toovey, couldn't I just let them get on with their jobs now?*

The figure at the dining-room table was not visible at first, the house being in semi-darkness.

And so it was only as I went through to the kitchen and flicked on the light that I stopped mid-stride, turning around to stare.

I stood very still. There was a ringing in my ears. An immediate feeling of terror gripped my body.

'Hello, Roz,' he said. 'Long time no see.'

'What are you doing here, Scott?'

'I came to talk. I think it's about time, don't you?'

'Did you break in?'

'The back door was open.'

It wasn't. I knew it wasn't.

I walked into the kitchen to check. There was glass on the floor. I thought about grabbing something from the drawer, a knife, anything, but Scott was already in the doorway behind me. I froze. Scared to breathe. Scared to move.

'I've missed you,' he said tiredly. 'Come and sit down. Let's talk.'

I did as requested, moving back to the dining room, watching him carefully.

We sat opposite one another. 'How is your son?' he asked. 'George, isn't it?' he went on, as if this was all very normal. As if he'd not broken into my house.

'Better,' I said.

'Excellent. Good to hear. Excellent.'

My hands were trembling. Scott glanced down, observed me as I clasped them together tightly, and he cast me a look of wounded bewilderment. As if I was completely overreacting to his presence.

'I saw him in the hospital,' he said. 'He's very like you.'

'You did *what*? *When* did you see him? How did you get in there?'

'It was just for a moment. I wanted to check for myself that he was okay. Don't look so worried, Roz. We had a nice chat. He didn't mention it to you?'

Fine beads of sweat sprung up along my upper lip as I thought about what he had done.

Visiting George. Without my knowledge. Christ.

'Scott,' I whispered. 'Why are you here?'

'You know, Nadine feels terrible about it,' he said, ignoring the question. 'I keep telling her it was an accident. That if she hadn't been in that state of mind then she wouldn't have been driving so recklessly. I keep telling her that she was no more culpable than we were, wouldn't you say?'

I didn't answer, and he frowned, waiting.

'Scott, you're scaring me. Have you come here to hurt me?'

And he gave a half-hearted laugh and shook his head. 'Of course not,' he replied. 'I'd never hurt you. Why would I hurt you?' He seemed genuinely astonished at the suggestion. 'I just want to talk.'

'About?'

His jaw tightened. He hesitated before speaking.

'You've been to the police again,' he said.

'You're watching me? You're still watching me? Why? Why are you following me?'

He shrugged.

'I'm here to ask that you leave it alone,' he continued. 'I'd really rather you didn't pursue whatever it is you think you're pursuing. It won't end well, Roz. And it would be so much better if you stayed out of it.'

'Have the police interviewed you?'

'They have.'

'Oh,' I said.

'You sound surprised.'

'I thought that—'

'You assumed that as soon as you gave them my name and they matched my DNA to the crime scene that there would be an arrest? Won't happen,' he said firmly.

A pause.

'Why did you kill him, Scott?' I asked carefully. 'Was it really—'

He held up his palm to silence me. 'Wayne's death *is*

regrettable,' he said mildly, 'but I didn't intend to do it. I didn't go there to do it. What sort of animal do you think I am?'

'I don't know!' I cried out.

'I did it for you.'

'For me?'

'I *had* to do it.'

'No, you didn't, Scott. And I'd really like you to leave. I need you to leave right now.'

I went to push my chair away from the table to stand, but he reached out and caught hold of my wrist.

'Stay there,' he commanded.

Fear washed through me. I felt sick.

'You're hurting me,' I said, and eventually, reluctantly, he loosened his grip.

'Look,' he said. 'I didn't come here to scare you. I came to ask for your help. I'd like you to drop your investigation, or whatever it is, and let us all get on with our lives. There's nothing to be gained by my admitting to what happened to Wayne.'

I stared at him. I was breathing hard.

'What?' he said defensively. 'What exactly do you want me to do? Say I tracked your car, followed you there, waited until I saw you leave and then killed the guy? That's what you want? What good will that do anybody, Roz?'

Visibly quaking now, I dropped my gaze. I shifted awkwardly in my seat and made like I was readjusting my trousers.

Scott rolled his eyes at me.

'Pass me your phone,' he said wearily.

'My what?'

'Your phone, Roz. You're not recording this. Pass it over.'

I did as requested.

'Let's start again,' he said, once he'd turned it off.

I was trapped. I was alone with this killer and no one knew he was here.

'I will not go to . . . I'll not go to the police,' I told him, stumbling over my words. 'I'll do whatever it is you want me to do. But please, Scott, I just want you to go.'

'No problem. That's all I wanted you to say. As I mentioned, there is absolutely nothing to be gained, and I think we've all suffered enough, don't you?'

I nodded numbly.

'And, honestly, you'd be wasting your time,' he continued. 'There's nothing tying me to that crime scene. I made sure of it.' And then he said, 'It wasn't exactly a messy business. He didn't put up much of a fight. And it wasn't hard to clean up after myself . . . or to clean up after you either, Roz.'

'Me?'

He looked at me, perplexed. 'You didn't think I'd let you take the hit for Wayne's death, did you? Bloody hell, Roz, I *meant* it when I told you I loved you. I'm not playing at this. Wayne explained how he'd panicked and knocked you out with the fire extinguisher. Tell me: what would you have done in my shoes? What would you have done if the person you cared about had gone through that? Any decent man would have done the same. When I heard what he'd done to you I just couldn't bear it.'

'You didn't need to murder him.'

'It was more of an accident really. And there *were* extenuating circumstances. The guy tells me he fucks you—'

'He didn't fuck me.'

'He didn't?'

I shook my head.

'Oh, so he was telling the truth about that, then. Well, disregarding that, he tells me he *hurts* you. And then he tells me he made you go there because he has evidence of you stealing from the company.'

'He told you?' I said.

'Well,' he paused, smiling coldly, 'I may have forced that out of him. I just didn't get why you'd even consider doing what you did with such a lowlife. It was insulting. He didn't want to talk at first. That's why I ended up with my hands around his throat. I just wanted to scare him a little. But then when he told me what he'd made you do, I needed to stop him from ever breathing again. It was necessary.'

I stared at him.

'I removed the fire extinguisher,' he said. 'It's covered in your blood, by the way. It's evidence you were there and that there was a . . . problem. I was hardly going to leave it behind and incriminate you.'

'Do you still have it?'

'I do.'

'Why? Why keep it?'

'I could make it reappear. And I'm more than happy to talk to the police again. Tell them Wayne was blackmailing you about the money. I think they'd be rather interested. It certainly gives you a motive for killing him.'

'I'm not sure my blood on it proves motive for anything.'

'Well, that's a chance you'll have to take,' he said. 'Who knows what the police will make of it? I wouldn't like to guess. I'm sure they'd be interested to know it was you who stole the money from the clinic, in any case. Or maybe I'll just deal with it all another way. It shouldn't be too hard to find out George's where-abouts. And, remember, we already know each other.'

He waited while I digested this piece of news. He had me cornered. If I did as he asked there would be no repercussions. If not—

He reached across the table and took hold of my hands.

'Come back to me,' he whispered.

I stared at him. Tried to mask my horror.

'Why not?' he said, affronted by my response. 'It was good, wasn't it? We were really good together.'

'You were paying me, Scott.'

'Oh yes,' he said, dismissing my reply. 'That's the other thing I forgot to mention about our friend Wayne. He would have made you do it again. And again.'

'I told Wayne I would do it once, and he agreed to that.'

Scott made a gesture with a flick of his head as though what I had said was nonsense. 'With someone like that,' he said, 'you give them an inch and they take a—'

'Did he *tell* you he planned to do it again?' I said.

'He didn't need to.'

I pulled my hands from his. 'Go home, Scott. You've said what you came to say. I'll do as you ask. I'll stay away from the police, because I have no other choice, but it's time for you to go.'

He nodded.

'I miss you,' he said, slipping his arms into his jacket.

I tried to smile. Tried to look as though, *Yes, I miss you, too, psycho*, whilst at the same time edging away from him. He was insane. Completely isane.

'Don't hate me,' he whispered. 'I only did what I did to help. I'm not a violent person. It's just men like Wayne, they never give up. He would have hounded you for ever. He would have made your life a misery, and you don't deserve that, Roz.'

'No,' I said quietly, keeping my head low, pacifying him in the best way I could.

Coat on, he asked, 'What are your plans now?' as though we'd just had a business meeting.

'Carry on as I was.'

'You're not going it alone in the physiotherapy business? That seems a shame.'

'It's not really doable after all.' I was hovering by the kitchen door. A few steps, and I could bolt out the back. 'I thought I could set up independently,' I rambled on, 'but . . . well, you know how it is.'

'Let *me* help.'

'It's okay, Scott.'

'My offer still stands. You don't need to work at all. I can look after you. *Let me* look after you.'

I didn't answer.

'*Why won't* you?' he said, angrily now. 'I don't see the problem. Someone offers you their help, *wants* to make your life a little easier, and you throw it back in their face. Why?'

'Because you can't buy people, Scott,' I said. 'It's not normal. It's not what people do. In fact, it's fucking weird. Why did you choose *me* anyway?'

'I didn't choose you.'

'I feel as if you picked me out as part of some elaborate plan. And now that I won't conform to whatever that plan is, you'd rather destroy me than let me go.'

'Oh, Roz,' he said, spreading his hands wide. 'We don't get to choose who we love. Love chooses us. I have no more control over the way I feel for you than I do over the tides, or the weather. That's what happens. I don't *want* to love you. I don't want to put myself in this compromised position. It is what it is.'

Love? He was out of his mind. Who pays for sex expecting that person to fall in love with them? What kind of deluded sicko do you have to be?

'You made it all seem so random at the beginning,' I said.

'I repeat: I didn't have a choice.'

'Why not just come on to me like a normal person?' I asked. 'Why involve money? Why not just start an affair?'

He gave a short, sarcastic kind of laugh. 'I did come on to you, and you rejected me, remember? You were too highly principled for an affair. So I used what I had. You were desperate for money, and I had plenty. It seemed like the most logical thing to do.'

'You should go.'

He said, 'Yes,' but he didn't move.

'Let's not leave it like this,' he pressed. 'I can't stand to think of you hating me.'

'I don't hate you,' I lied.

'Come here,' he said.

I stayed put.

'Roz, I'm not a monster,' he said.

He advanced my way and I took a step backwards.

'For Christ's sake,' he said. 'What's *wrong* with you? You're acting like . . . Do you *want* me to hurt you? Is that it? Do you need me to put my hands around *your* throat, to justify to yourself that I *am* a monster?'

I stayed silent. Terrified.

He strode across the floor and took hold of my right hand. He squeezed it tight between his. I remained motionless, confused. 'You're sure about this? You're quite sure about this, Roz?' he shouted, levering my thumb back as far as it would go.

'What are you doing?'

Pulling me towards the kitchen, he held my thumb against the door jamb. Then he grabbed hold of the door handle with his other hand, threatening to slam it on my flesh.

'Is this what you want?' he yelled at me.

'Don't,' I whimpered.

'Is this what you want me to do? Put an end to your shitty little career?'

'No,' I said, crying now.

My hands were my instruments. My livelihood. I was next to useless without them.

'I paid you because I loved you,' he shouted. 'I had no other choice. So don't you dare look at me with such disgust! Don't you dare!'

He increased his grip. I could no longer feel my fingers.

He said, 'I could end you right now if I wanted to. I could destroy you right now.'

Suddenly, I flared at him.

'Well, do it then! Fucking do it! I give up. If you're so head-fucked that this is what you need to do, then do it!'

And his breathing became hard and ragged.

He scanned my face for clues, as if he didn't understand.

'You need help, Scott. You're deranged. You are fucking deranged. Don't you see? Don't you see what you've become? You're an animal.'

And he tried to speak but couldn't.

He was a man lost. A man adrift. With no idea how he got here.

Two Months Later

43

IT WAS NOW late October. Almost three months had gone by since George's accident, the crash, and our time was filled with hospital appointments, visits from friends, the general day-to-day things that I once took for granted. That night, the night Scott broke into my home, he didn't smash my thumbs to pieces as I thought he might. As *he* thought he might. And after holding me hostage for what felt like hours, eventually, Scott let go of my hand.

He regarded me with a deep, deep sadness, and I told him it was over.

I told him I did not love him. That I would never love him. And no matter what he decided to throw at me, I would not change my mind. If he wanted to send himself insane by continuing to pursue me, that was his choice. But I could never be persuaded to want him.

So what did I do next?

I kept my head down and got back to normality. Scott still had me over a barrel so there wasn't really a lot of choice. Maybe a better person than me, a stronger, more resourceful person, someone with more grit, more staying power, could have found a way to bring him to justice for killing Wayne. But I'd reached my limit. I made a choice to put it behind me and move forward with my life.

George and I lived simply. After much balancing of the books and realistic examination of the household accounts (and without the old debts hanging over me), I found I was able to cut my hours at work. I told the clinic I could do twenty-six hours maximum and they could take it or leave it.

They took it.

Something of Henry Peachey must have rubbed off on me because I found that, with more time available, I did in fact spend less money. I was better prepared, and instead of life being one frantic whirlwind, meeting myself coming backwards, throwing cash at things just to get through, my days were more manageable. Peaceful. There was happiness to be found in doing the simple stuff.

Winston and I had a talk – *the Talk* – which had been more than a long time coming. I told him his period of playing out was over. That if he couldn't step up to his responsibilities as a parent in the financial sense, then I would move to be near my parents, far enough away that he would see far less of George. Ultimately, I told him I needed help. I couldn't do it alone any more. And Winston, being Winston, said, 'Sure, Roz. No problem.' Like if only I'd asked earlier, he would have happily obliged.

And finally, after a great deal of procrastination, I also wrote an email.

It's amazing the self-deception that comes when you need to get something written down. Suddenly, it was very important that the pile of ironing, which had been sitting in the corner of the bedroom for months, be dealt with.

I sorted through my kitchen cupboards, under the pretence of being organized for the approaching Harvest Festival, so that George didn't have to turn up at school with some out-of-date English mustard, and a packet of cornflour.

I made dental appointments for half-term.

And then, when I couldn't find another thing to put in the way of my bottom being in the chair and staying there until it was finished, I did it. I looked up his address and I wrote the thing.

From: RToovey@hotmail.co.uk
To: henry.peachey@live.com
Subject: Us

Dear Henry

I'll try to keep this short and to the point, though there is much I want to say.

I'm not sure if I ever said sorry, so I'll begin with that. Sorry. It's not enough, I know, and I can picture you reading this, rolling your eyes, deeply offended, with a strong urge not to read any further.

The truth is, I miss you. And I can't help wondering whether if we'd met at another time, under another set of circumstances, things could have turned out differently for us.

George gets better every day and is very close to losing his crutches.

And if you think I've mentioned George to try to make you soften a little towards me, then you would be right.

Thanks to you, I seem to be getting my life in some kind of order. I've been reading books on how to stay debt free, how to work less and spend less, how to enjoy life without being a slave to commerce. And if you think I mention this to flatter you, you would be right about that, too.

As soon as I met you I tried to bring the arrangement with Scott to an end. Desperation led me to accept that offer, but meeting you helped me see what an absurd arrangement it really was, and that there had to be an alternative way of doing things.

I say again, I miss you. I am trying not to write nonsense like *There are so few people we feel a connection with.*

But that *is* what I want to say. And if I could find a better way of saying it, I would.

If you ever find yourself thinking along the same lines (even for a moment, even with the spectacular mess I made of everything), then know that I'm here, waiting for you.

Yours
Roz.

And while I waited for a response from Henry, slowly, bit by bit, George and I were rebuilding ourselves. That night, the night of Scott's visit, had marked a strange kind of turning point.

Sometimes, I found myself wondering about Scott; about what made him tick, why he did what he did, and whether it was possible that he really was motivated by love.

What exactly pushed Scott over into that other realm – murder – the realm where so few of us go?

Perhaps winning was the same as love to Scott. Perhaps the two things evoked the same emotion in him and he couldn't tell them apart.

Or perhaps he simply had no fear and felt free to do as he pleased.

And *he was* free.

That was the tragedy. Scott had not been held accountable for Wayne's death because he'd been steadfast in his belief that he could get away with it. He had no remorse, because, in his mind, he had no alternative but to kill Wayne. Wayne, a disposable human being. Someone who was just going to get in the way of what Scott wanted. And I could do nothing about it because, if I did, Scott was fully prepared to try and fit me up for the murder and tell the police about the money I'd taken – or, worse, he would harm George.

My word against his.

If I went to the police and told them he had confessed to killing Wayne, he would simply tell them I had confessed a similar crime to him. Wayne was blackmailing me, he would say.

So that's where we were. And that's how I thought things would remain.

Until I got the call, anyway.

George and I gazed through the windscreen of the Jeep at the barrier in front. We were the first on the ferry this morning; out particularly early on account of the appointment which George was trying to get out of. I had the window lowered in an attempt to rouse us. The days had now shortened. The dense, thick air of summer had been replaced by a fresher, rarefied, autumnal band from the north.

High in the sky, and following the line of the lake, a flock of geese headed south. They were noisy, jostling for position, and I pointed them out to George, gesturing for him to take a look.

He sighed out long and hard.

'I wish I could fly south,' he said, all melancholy. I ignored his comment. He sighed again. 'She's just so mean,' he added.

'She has to be mean to do her job,' I replied.

'You're not mean.'

'I'm not trying to get you to walk correctly.'

George had lost over an inch in leg length. The consultant orthopaedist was confident the discrepancy could be improved with time but, for now, George had been ordered to wear a raised shoe to avoid problems with his pelvis later. It was not going down well. And he didn't like his physiotherapist one bit.

She was a severe, humourless woman, with neat, short hair, ugly shoes and a big bottom that dimpled when she walked. She made it quite clear that she had no time for physiotherapists who'd moved over to the private sector. They'd 'sold out', as she phrased it, on our first meeting. And I didn't challenge her because there's just no winning with a woman like that.

George couldn't understand why I wasn't his clinician, since I'd always managed to tidy up his aches and pains in the past. But gait analysis was not my strong point. And the treatment had been ordered by his consultant and had to be undertaken at Kendal Hospital. So that's where we found ourselves, two mornings a week.

I delivered George to the department and saw his physio's face turn sour as he swung his bad leg out to the side rather than bending it at the knee, as she had instructed. He was in for a tough session, and it broke my heart to watch. He was still so full of apprehension, frightened to weight-bear through his injured leg, scared to let go of his crutch. But there was no other option. It had to be done, or he'd limp for life. And, as much as I disliked his clinician, there was no doubt she knew what she was doing. And a certain amount of austerity *was* necessary when endeavouring to mobilize patients. The affable physiotherapist who is everybody's friend is not particularly useful in this instance.

I told George I needed a coffee and would be back with him in five minutes. Not strictly true: I didn't need coffee; it was a ploy I used to get the session underway. If I remained in the department, as I had at the beginning, George would sense in me my own suffering at watching him in pain and would lose all confidence. So I would slip away. And so far it had worked. By the time I returned, he would be focused on what was being asked of him, his fear dissipating with each new step taken.

As the door closed behind me, my phone vibrated in my pocket. I answered, and on hearing the voice at the other end, I stopped in my tracks.

'Roz Toovey?'

'Yes,' I said.

'DS Aspinall. Can we meet? There's something I need to discuss.'

I told the detective where I was, which turned out to be quite fortuitous, since she was based in Kendal, and she said she would meet me in the outpatients' department in ten minutes' time.

I grabbed two coffees, found a quiet corner and waited.

She was there in five.

As she entered and spotted me, DS Joanne Aspinall smiled. She was alone and, unlike the previous occasions we'd met, she seemed harried. Her face was tired and drawn. Her skin had the lacklustre appearance of a person needing a holiday. Or a good night's sleep.

'Got you a coffee,' I said as she sat beside me, and she thanked me, saying it was just what she needed. She removed the lid and gulped down half of it in three mouthfuls, not bothering to ask if it contained sugar.

'Are you okay?' I asked, and she nodded fast, fervently, to indicate, I presumed, she was short of time.

'I can't get to him,' she began.

I must have frowned, because she added, 'Scott Elias. With regards to the murder of Wayne Geddes,' she said. 'It appears he's untouchable.'

I told her I hadn't thought she was still working on that case and she gave a small laugh. 'I work on nothing else,' she answered.

I looked at DS Aspinall for a sign of where she was going with this, but she appeared to be waiting for me to speak, so I said, 'I'm not sure what it is you want me to say.'

'You think he did it,' she replied bluntly. And then: 'Let me rephrase that . . . *I know* he did it, but I can't prove it. Not enough to secure a conviction anyway.'

'I'm curious,' I said. 'How do you know he did it?'

'His story doesn't add up. Then there was his general self-assurance and confidence when questioned. Along with your statement. And the tracker. Experience, I suppose you could call it. I know he did it, but I have nothing at all to place him at the scene – and no real motive – and so I've come to ask for your help. Will you help?'

I hesitated.

'He visited George when he was in hospital. I think he meant it as some sort of warning. And then he threatened me,' I said.

'Threatened you with?'

'He has evidence that I was there that night with Wayne and that he assaulted me. Remember I told you that Wayne knocked me out? Well, it was with a fire extinguisher, and it has my blood on it. Scott threatened to—'

'I don't suppose you know where he keeps this fire extinguisher?'

I shook my head. 'I imagine it's well hidden. He's meticulous. I can't see him leaving it around for the likes of you to stumble upon.'

'Okay, never mind,' she said quickly, letting it go. 'What if I were to ask you to become part of a new inquiry?'

'An inquiry into what?'

'His business affairs,' she said. 'Something you once said about invoicing his firm lodged at the back of my brain. For the past couple of months it's been nagging away at me. The upshot is that we're now investigating his tax evasion, and we've reached the stage of interviewing witnesses.'

'Has he been hiding money?'

She nodded.

'How much?' I asked.

'More than I thought possible,' she said.

'And how likely is he to serve time for this . . . deception?'

'Very likely,' she said. 'I can't go into the list of the tax-evasion offences with you, naturally, but there are lots.'

'What sort of prison sentence would he get?'

'For these types of offences, they're usually looking at a term of between four and five years. But there is the possibility of a longer sentence in this case, as there's so much money involved.'

'Doesn't really seem enough,' I said. 'Not when you consider what he did to Wayne.'

'No,' she admitted. 'But he would lose everything. All his assets would be seized. And I don't know about you, but I think there's a certain poetic justice to that. I met him only briefly, but from what I saw I'd say he's not the kind of man who would cope too well with losing his fortune.'

44

SCOTT PARKER ELIAS
PART ONE OF RECORDED INTERVIEW
Date: 14/11/2014
Location: Kendal Police Station, Busher Walk, Kendal,
LA9 4RJ
Conducted by officers from Cumbria Police: DS Joanne
Aspinall, DS Ronald Quigley. Also present: defence legal
adviser, Mr Jeremy Inglis, and HM Revenue and Customs
Investigator, Ms Jennifer McCauley

DS Joanne Aspinall: The purpose of this interview is to
collect information to further the investigation and/or
evidence of the alleged fraud. You understand, Mr Elias,
why you've been detained here today?

Scott Elias: I understand perfectly.

DS JA: Good. Just before we proceed, I'll read out the caution
to you . . . You do not have to say anything. But it may harm
your defence if you do not mention when questioned about
something which you later rely on in court. And anything
you do say may be given in evidence. What that means,
basically, is you do not have to answer my questions, not if
you don't want to.

SE: I know what it means. And I have nothing to hide, so I'm happy to answer your questions, Detective.

DS JA: Excellent. I'd like to start then, if I may, with your relationship with Mrs Rosalind Toovey—

SE: I have nothing to say on that matter. As stated, I have done nothing wrong, so I am prepared to answer questions about my *business affairs*. But not about my private life.

DS JA: The two are linked, Mr Elias. I'm afraid these questions form part of the investigation into the alleged fraud.

SE: No comment, then.

DS JA: How would you describe your relationship with Mrs Toovey?

SE: No comment.

DS JA: Was there a relationship?

SE: (*Inaudible*)

DS JA: Mr Elias?

SE: There was a relationship, yes. A short one.

DS JA: A sexual relationship?

SE: We did have sex. That's correct.

DS JA: And was money exchanged at any time?

SE: No comment.

DS JA: Okay, we can come back to that. Let's move on to your wife. Nadine Elias.

SE: None of this has anything to do with my wife.

DS JA: A preliminary examination of the accounts for your firm, SPE Electronics, revealed that Mrs Elias is listed as an employee of the company. Can you tell me in what capacity your wife is employed?

SE: She is an adviser.

DS JA: An adviser on what exactly?

SE: A business adviser.

DS JA: And she's paid handsomely for this job, is she not? How much per year does Mrs Elias receive as an adviser for your company?

SE: That's a question for the accounts department.

DS JA: I'll help you out. She receives an annual wage of one hundred and seventy thousand pounds. Quite a lot.

SE: You get what you pay for.

DS JA: How many hours a week would you say Mrs Elias spends at SPE Electronics? Ten? Fifty?

SE: I can't be sure. You would have to ask her.

DS JA: When questioned, your secretary, Debbie Harris, claims never to have seen Mrs Elias in the offices. Not once.

SE: Nadine does most of her work from home, I suppose.

DS JA: I see. Could it be that you invented this role for Mrs Elias? Could it be that she does not actually do any work for your company? That you are drawing a wage for Mrs Elias rather than pay tax on the company's profits?

SE: No.

DS JA: How about these employees then? Graham Fisher, listed as an electrical engineer; Robert Wood, listed as a management consultant; Eileen Young, a financial adviser? We have not been able to trace these people, Mr Elias.

SE: (*Interviewee does not answer*)

DS JA: Could it be that these people don't exist *at all*? That they were invented by you, Mr Elias, and you pocketed their wages as extra income for yourself?

SE: That's out of the question!

DS JA: Is it?

SE: If that were the case, there would be evidence of that money in my bank account.

DS JA: Perhaps. Perhaps not. There are a further eighteen employees without recognizable national insurance numbers. Including a gardener paid to the tune of twenty-one thousand a year, when, as far as I'm aware, the SPE site is surrounded by concrete.

SE: No comment.

DS JA: Why do you suppose your accountant has disappeared, Mr Elias?

SE: I really couldn't say.

DS JA: Perhaps you'd like to try and offer an explanation. Because, as of 2 November, we've been unable to locate him.

SE: He was having marital difficulties. He was seeing another woman. Maybe he's gone off with her.

DS JA: How long had Mr Bennett been your accountant?

SE: Around twenty years.

DS JA: Odd that he left without telling you, don't you think?

SE: People do the strangest things for love, Detective.

DS JA: Don't they just? . . . I'd like you to take a look at this invoice now, Mr Elias, and tell me if that is your company's VAT number at the top right of the page. The invoice is for – forgive my ignorance – a large order for some kind of electrical component. It's made out for the sum of seventeen thousand four hundred pounds. Inclusive of VAT.

SE: I wouldn't know the VAT number off the top of my head. Who would?

DS JA: Okay, well, I can tell you that it's not SPE's VAT number. I can tell you that, so far, we have uncovered a substantial number of invoices such as this, all with an alternative VAT number.

SE: Again, that would be something you would need to talk over with the accounts department.

DS JA: Not really. Because the VAT charged never reached the Revenue. In fact, it was redirected to an account we believe to be in Nigeria.

SE: I know nothing of such an account.

DS JA: Even though it's in your wife's name, Mr Elias?

SE: (*Interviewee does not respond*)

DS JA: Let's move on to your holiday home. The one in Antibes. According to the website, it's been booked fairly consistently, generating an income of around one hundred and forty thousand. Now, I appreciate these earnings will not be taxable until next year, but I'm curious to take a look at the booking schedule for previous years. HMRC have informed us that no earnings on this property have ever been declared.

SE: No comment.

DS JA: Perhaps you'd like to comment on this, then. It's a copy of your bank statement from July. There's an amount here . . . Three hundred thousand pounds, which was sent to a bank in Sierra Leone.

SE: No comment.

DS JA: That's okay, Mr Elias, I think we have more than enough to pass on to the Director of Criminal Investigations at Her Majesty's Revenue and Customs. I'm sure they'll want to conduct full searches of your home and business premises. And, who knows, they might even stumble upon that fire extinguisher. The one which has Roz Toovey's blood on it.

SE: They'll never find that.

DS JA: No, Mr Elias? How odd that you even know what I'm referring to.

45

THE DAYS CAME shorter, colder and brighter as the gloom of November passed, and the end of the year was almost upon us. Sadly, there was no word from Henry, and though I tried to put him from my thoughts I would find myself checking my emails each day with a sense of anticipation. This would soon be quashed, however, when, again, there was nothing from him.

Petra had mostly thawed and we were back to being sisters. I can't say if Scott Elias's arrest and ultimate fall from grace had any bearing on how she felt about things, but she certainly was a lot friendlier to me than she'd been of late. I heard that after Nadine was questioned by HMRC officers she left the Lake District. Went south, though I didn't know where. The official version was that she found it unbearable to stay in the area after her husband was detained on remand in Cheshire, awaiting trial. But the word in the village was that she couldn't *afford* to stay. With no money of her own, and with all their assets seized, she'd had to flee. We didn't yet know if she was to be charged for her involvement or not.

Wayne's death still wouldn't leave me alone but, thanks to the tenacity and thoroughness of DS Aspinall, I did feel we got something close to justice for him in the end. Since Scott had confessed to me I'd felt terribly guilty and struggled with the feelings of responsibility for Wayne's death. I aired these feelings to DS Aspinall, who looked at me with a puzzled expression, before replying, 'Wayne was a big boy, Roz. And he was blackmailing you. There are often unexpected repercussions when you dabble in a world you're unfamiliar with.'

Which didn't really make me feel a whole lot better.

So each morning I would say a small prayer to Wayne Geddes. Well, maybe more of a general chit-chat about things, rather than a prayer, which was an odd way to start the day, granted. And I made a few visits to his mother.

Glenda was in sheltered accommodation in Ulverston, and she seemed to enjoy the time I spent with her. Largely, I suppose, because I had nothing but kind words to say about Wayne – he was an excellent boss, generous with his staff, always willing to listen if I had a problem. Lies, I know, but I didn't see the harm in them. Last week I turned up with a Christmas card, a feeble-looking poinsettia and a box of mince pies, and I thought she might burst into tears.

Which brings me to George and the Christmas problem – as we'd been referring to it. Santa, being unusually strapped for cash this year, was unable to fulfil George's request for a games console. Even though, yes, George had been a good boy. And yes, Santa had taken into account how hard he'd been trying when learning to walk without his crutches. Sometimes, though, regrettably, even Santa must be careful not to overextend himself and spend money his business just can't afford.

George was stoic, though disappointed, revising his list to a mere three items, which I assured him Santa would most certainly be able to provide.

And then something happened.

I opened the door one evening to find a very worried-looking Dennis on my step. My immediate thought was: Celia.

'Dennis,' I said. 'Has something happened? Is Celia okay?'

'Not really,' he said.

'Is she injured?'

At this he laughed softly and shook his head.

'Is George here?' he asked, and I told him he was. 'I got him something,' he said. 'An early present, so to speak.'

On hearing his name, George rose from the floor, where he'd been writing his Christmas cards, and came to the door. Dennis didn't say anything, just gestured to his left, and George stuck his head out to take a look.

There, trembling, was a tiny, sorry-looking animal, tied to the drainpipe. 'She's called Tess,' Dennis said, 'and she's yours if you want her.'

I was about to speak when Celia's voice rang out. 'He's lost his mind, Roz! I told him, "Dennis, *you have lost your mind,*"' and she strutted down her path, out of her gate and up towards us.

By this time George was outside, trying to crouch (unable to on account of the limited flexion in his knee), and Tess, the puppy, was urinating with excitement. She was up on her hind legs, trying to scrabble into George's arms.

'I thought he'd done so well with his walking and all,' Dennis whispered. 'Thought this might push him that extra bit.'

'Oh, Dennis,' I said, overcome. 'That's so lovely of you, but I don't think we can take her. My landlord—'

'This is his idiotic plan, Roz,' snapped Celia, silencing me. 'You take the dog. It's George's dog on paper. But we look after it when you're at work. And if your landlord says anything, then you tell him she's ours.'

Dennis squinted, saying, 'Foxy's getting on a bit now, so it'd be nice to have a pup about the place.'

'Foxy won't thank you for it,' I told him.

'Aw, she'll come around.'

'I don't know what to say,' I said.

George now had the pup in his arms. She was the size of a guinea pig, with café-au-lait-coloured fur, and a pair of black dots for eyebrows. She wore a tentative look as though she, too, was waiting for me to decide her fate.

'Thank you, Dennis,' I said firmly, and he nodded just once.

'You all right to take her now?' he asked, and I told him, glancing at George's rapturous expression, that I doubted I would have any choice in the matter.

'Right you are,' he said, smiling, not meeting my eye. 'I'll go and fetch her bowl and blankets.'

George stood rooted to the spot. He held on to the tiny pup as if his life depended on it. 'You coming in?' I asked, and he nodded. I reached out and cupped the puppy's chin gently in my hand. 'Welcome,' I said to her. 'Welcome, Tess.'

And we all went inside to get ourselves acquainted.

46

From: henry.peachey@live.com
To: RToovey@hotmail.co.uk
Subject: RE: Us

Dear Roz

Just got your email. I'm doing the Santiago de Compostela pilgrimage in an attempt to 'find myself'.
  No sign of me yet, so I'm heading home.
  I realize running away was not the answer. I've been unable to stop thinking about you. Let's pick up where we left off.
  Will call in as soon as I'm back.

Love, Henry.

Acknowledgements

I would like to thank:

James Long, Debbie Leatherbarrow and Zoe Lea.

And also: Jane Gregory, Stephanie Glencross, Claire Morris and everyone at Gregory & Company. Frankie Gray, Sarah Adams, Alison Barrow, Rachel Rayner, Claire Ward and everyone at Transworld. Corinna Barsan at Grove Atlantic. Thanks, too, to Cathy Rentzenbrink.

Whilst writing, I found the book *How to be Idle* by Tom Hodgkinson very useful.

Paula Daly lives in Cumbria with her husband, three children and whippet Skippy. Before becoming a writer she was a freelance physiotherapist.